T. HANDS

WE'RE

GIVEN

ACES HIGH

JOKERS
WILD

ACES HIGH, JOKERS WILD BOOK 1

O. E. TEARMANN

Originally published in 2018 by Spine Press and Post

Amphibian Press
P. O. Box 190
West Peterborough NH
03468

www. amphibianpressbooks. com
www. aceshighjokerswild. com

Printed in the United States of America

ISBN: 978-1-949693-83-6

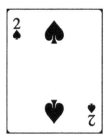

For my partner in this wild ride. Remember you rock. Always.

Event File 01
File Tag: Orientation
Timestamp: 0900-4-1-2155

The ancient Humvee rattled as it hit another pothole. On the other side of the vehicle's window clouds of grit obscured the view, kicked up as they rumbled through the dry soil of the Dust. Tumbleweeds and rabbit-brush crunched like bird bones beneath the tires.

Aidan flipped through his new personnel roster on the holographic screen projected from the tablet in his lap. The nails of his free hand scratched out erratic rhythms against the fabric of his pants.

His eyes skittered over the flickering images for the third time, trying to memorize names and faces. He'd only needed one read-through of the attached disciplinary files. Those he wasn't going to forget in a hurry.

Sarah Flesher. Skinny white woman with black hair and a smirk. Munitions specialist. Jim Crawford. Skinny black guy with a tired face. Hell, everybody was skinny and tired out here. Operations specialist. Yvonne Flesher. Muscly blonde woman. Runner, maybe? Requisitions specialist. Blake Frachette. The only pudgy guy Aidan had seen in a year. Finance officer. Figured, he would be the only one sitting still. Kevin McIllian. Red-headed guy, smiling just a bit. Logistics officer.

Cute. Logistics officer.

Shit, he was never going to learn all this before he arrived.

The big man across from Aidan laughed, pulling Aidan's attention away from his compulsive study. It was an honest sound, rare out here in the Dust. Hell, real laughter was probably rare all across America nowadays, on-Grid and off.

"It's good you're nervous, Headly," Front Range Sector Commander Magnum observed. "Nerves mean you'll care about these people. That's what they need."

"I'm not nervous, sir." It was a lie and they both knew it. Aidan switched his tablet to sleep mode, and its shivering screen slid back into the flat black pane. The truck's movement and the tightness in his gut was making reading impossible anyway. He might as well humor the sector commander. "I just want to make sure I know what you're dropping me into. The Wildcards have an insane reputation."

Sector Commander Magnum laughed again. The dry leather creaked under his bulk. "Which is why we want to see how you do with them. They've been through two seasoned commanders in two months since Commander Taylor died. Figured it was time to see how they manage with one fresh out of training. We're hoping they don't chew you up and spit you out, too."

Aidan swallowed hard. That comment wasn't exactly helping his roiling stomach. He had only finished Command training a week ago. This morning he'd been told that he'd been assigned. Only when he'd climbed into the transport for the three-hour drive had he been told which base he'd been assigned to.

"Relax, Headly. I'm not asking you to turn these guys into a normally functioning base," Magnum added with quiet exasperation. "Fact is, I don't want them functioning like all our other bases. I want them functioning like the Wildcards on top of their game. Standard operation procedure isn't the objective here. Do what you need to do. Run them the way you want. The objective's to get them back on mission."

"Yes, sir," Aidan agreed. He tried to breathe normally, but it wasn't easy.

The loosely-organized insurgent bases collectively glorified by the name of Democratic State Force couldn't have offered a new commander anything more terrifying. He wasn't ready to take on the most famous—well, infamous—base and their mess. How had he been crazy enough to accept this assignment? He should have opened the door and run for the hills, gone Fringe, anything but say yes.

At least the base was a long way from the one he'd grown up on. He repeated the thought, trying to calm himself. A long way from anyone he'd known before. The odds of anyone recognizing him from his pre-transition life were slim.

The vehicle pulled to a stop and the driver cut the engine.

Aidan leaned forward to look out of the tinted windshield. The low, tan shape of the base complex sat baking in the sun beyond the window. Covered by its heat-shielding, sensor-disrupting slick tarp, it could be mistaken for angular rock formations at a distance.

As he watched, a corner of the tarp peeled away to reveal a rusting garage door. A woman stepped out. He squinted at her, trying to place her face with one of the names from the base manifest, but she was too far away to make out her features.

"Liza Carlan, if I had to guess," the sector commander said, jerking his cleft chin toward the woman. "Your personnel officer and second-in-command."

Aidan nodded thoughtfully. Liza Carlan's record was peppered with disciplinary write-ups, though most of this base's personnel had checkered pasts. It was part of the reputation the Wildcards had created for themselves. Part of the reason Aidan really didn't want to get out of the Humvee.

The sector commander elbowed his newest command officer. "Go on, Headly. You have your orders. You have your base. Go meet 'em."

"Yes, sir." Aidan was relatively convinced he was going to vomit the instant his feet touched the dusty ground. But he popped open the door, grabbed his duffle from the floorboard, and climbed out into the hot, dry air.

Behind him, the window rolled down.

"And, Headly?" the big man called from the cool interior.

Aidan glanced back into Magnum's dark eyes. "Sir?"

"Remember what I said. We need this base back on mission. Make it happen."

Aidan's stomach clenched. He threw a clumsy salute. "Sir. Orders received."

The sector commander smiled grimly, his driver rolled up the window, and the vehicle's tires kicked up grit in its wake.

Aidan swallowed hard and turned to the base. As he approached the lone woman outside the slick tarp, she gave him a crisp salute. She was as tall as he was—not much of an achievement—and it looked like her dun-colored uniform was two sizes too big for her, held on with a tight belt cinched around her waist. All muscle and no fat, Aidan thought. A classic Duster. In classrooms and press reports, they might be the Democratic State Force, but on the ground, everybody knew they were Dusters.

"Commander Headly?"

He hoisted his duffle higher on his shoulder and nodded politely. "That's me."

"Welcome to Base 1407."

She held her salute. Her slightly oversized brown eyes studied him, cold and curious.

Aidan sighed. He hated standing on formality. It had gotten him several lectures during his training. Technically, he knew all the arguments for the command structure. He'd gotten them shouted down his ear often enough. The only thing that had gotten him more tellings off was saying 'um' when speaking. But it still seemed like the strict military setup so many commanders used was against the essence of the

Dusters' mission. They were fighting to break the rigid social structures the United Corporations of America had put in and return the country to freedom and equality, weren't they? So why did they try to force their own people to act like toy soldiers?

But Personnel Officer Liza Carlan seemed insistent on holding that salute until he returned it, so he lifted his free hand to his brow for a moment and dropped it again.

Liza held hers a breath longer before letting her hand fall. She nodded and turned toward the slick tarp. "If you'll follow me, sir, we'll get you situated in your quarters."

Aidan cleared his throat.

"If it's all the same, I'd rather meet the rest of the unit first."

Liza's step faltered. She wobbled a moment before regaining her balance and glancing over her shoulder, brows pinched above her hawk-like nose. "Sir?"

"I'd like to give you all my condolences on Commander Taylor." Aidan nodded toward the black armband over Liza's uniform sleeve. When she stiffened, he realized he might have completely misread things and back-pedaled. "Unless you're mourning someone else. Um. I'm sorry. I assumed you hadn't lost anyone else lately, based on the reports, but I realize they might be—"

"Why do you care?" Liza's voice was quiet as she began walking again.

Aidan scrambled to keep up. They ducked under the corner of the slick tarp and into the motor pool garage. The smell of oil and engine exhaust nearly made Aidan gag. He forced back the impulse and tried to answer Liza's question while he took quick stock of three tired vehicles and a motley herd of all-terrain bikes lined up side-by-side, tools and spare parts used to maintain them covering every inch of wall space. "I'm not here to shove you around, Liza. I'm here to help try and get this base back on track. Far as I'm concerned, that starts with respecting my team and their past."

They were out of the garage and halfway down a narrow corridor walled in pockmarked pre-fab plastic before Liza spoke again. "Let's get you settled first, sir. Then you can listen to our sob stories if you have to."

Aidan considered calling her on that and decided against it. No sense being the bad guy in his first five minutes. He could put his foot down when the issue mattered. Besides, he could use a second to breathe.

This base was a lot smaller than the sector hub he had trained on. After all, down here large bases with large footprints wouldn't last a day. Only the sector hub and the R&R bases hidden up in the mountains had the luxury of getting bigger without being picked up by search-and-destroy drones. Aidan wished he could go up to a Rest and Retirement base right now. The days he'd spent up there recovering from injuries were the only times he could remember being relaxed.

The halls were laid out roughly the same way as the base he'd trained on: common area with the canteen and the rec room in the center, barracks down the left hand hall, work rooms and offices down the right, garage up front. The pre-fab buildings were easy to assemble and organize any way you wanted, but most Duster units used the same general base plan. It made it easy for transfers to find their way around. Poles jutting from the roof at crazy angles secured the slick tarp overhead, holding the nanomesh fiber so that it broke up the outline of the base as it masked the building's EM signatures and showed a rock outcropping or more desert to visual scans.

As a bonus, the paper-thin protective tarp kept the base cool and somewhat shaded.

It felt odd to be led to the commander's quarters at the back of the dormitory wing instead of to a smaller personal barracks room. "Commander" had been written on the door in black marker, and someone had tried to rub away the name "Taylor" underneath. It hadn't really worked.

Liza shoved the door open and stepped back. "Sir."

Reluctantly, Aidan moved into the room. It was still small—barely big enough for the thin mattress in one corner and a tiny chest for his clothes—and one pre-fab wall didn't quite meet the ceiling. For the first time in a long time, Aidan was glad he wasn't in a relationship. He didn't want to worry about making noise and waking up his neighbors in the middle of the night. But it had been years since he'd had a boyfriend. No worries there. He didn't let anyone get close enough for even a casual fling these days. He dropped his duffel on top of the small dresser and turned back, but Liza was already gone. Without asking if she was dismissed. Passive-aggressive insubordination already. Great.

With a sigh, he unzipped his bag and moved his small collection of clothing into the top drawer of the chest. Might as well unpack while he waited for Liza to decide he could meet the rest of the unit. Not that there was much to unpack: his clothes, data tab, a small collection of metalworking and engraving tools, several vials of testosterone with a micro-injector and a printout of a sketch a friend had made of his sister ages ago. He settled the tools and med gear in the drawer beside his clothing, set the data tab on top of the dresser, and tacked the sketch to the wall opposite the thin mattress. It wasn't much, but it helped make the room feel slightly more like home.

He glanced at the room's cracked mirror, nervously adjusting his jacket. He'd gotten lucky, actually finding the coloring agents for the official uniform colors: khaki coolant-lined jacket, grey shirt for his new rank underneath, khaki pants, American star pin on his lapel.

Considering most people scrounged any camouflage-worthy pigment their base's 3D printer would use on cloth, it wasn't really a uniform anymore. Their Force was barely surviving against the Corps. Details like strict uniform regulations had gotten dropped a long time ago.

But making the effort felt right.

Glancing in the mirror, he ran his fingers through his dark blond hair. As far as a first test of his leadership went, this was about as difficult as they could get. And he had to get it right. The Force needed the Wildcards up and running again. Magnum had been clear on that.

By the time Liza returned, Aidan had taken to pacing the room in tiny steps, measuring it from wall to wall. He looked up at the sound of footsteps in the hallway and greeted her at the door.

"Base's ready, sir," she said shortly. She looked at a place over his shoulder instead of meeting his gaze, her hands clasped behind her back. She was every bit the military woman, from the tilt of her chin to her severe bun. That stance made Aidan tense, but he swallowed it as best he could. This was his base now. He could deal with the attitude once they all got more comfortable with each other.

"Well, let's get going."

She nodded curtly and turned on her heel. Aidan sucked in a breath and followed.

Sixteen people were gathered in the small base canteen, making it feel crowded. It should have been noisy with this many people in one place—including four children ranging from a baby to two pre-teens—but none of them made a sound. Every single one of the adults had their eyes fixed on him. Every single one of them wore a black armband over their uniform sleeve.

"Wildcards, attention!" Liza barked, her voice startling in the tense silence.

Twelve adults snapped to attention, their faces in various emotional states from curious to irritated. Even the kids gave straightening up and staring forward a try.

With the eyes of the unit on him, Aidan wished fervently that he looked more like a commander and less like an awkward teenager playing soldier. He wished he could grow a decent beard and mustache to hide the softness of his chin. Even after six years on a regular testosterone dose, he still thought his face looked too feminine. He'd never managed to grow decent facial hair either, another genetic failure.

He wished he looked tougher and less scruffy, wished that he'd had the time and energy to bulk up a little more before taking this assignment. Looking underfed didn't help.

Mostly, he wished he wasn't standing here with all these eyes on him.

He forced himself to step forward and sweep his gaze down the line, smiling at the toddler in a woman's arms. His eyes slid from face to face, caught for a moment on something odd: the red-headed man from the files standing near the center of the line, grey eyes watchful behind a pair of old wire-rimmed glasses. Where the hell had he found those ancient things, and why bother to wear them?

Corrective eye surgery only took about five minutes, even out in the Dust.

Aidan drew a breath, realizing he was distracting himself. He needed to focus. He couldn't afford to look like his new base wasn't his top priority. "At ease, all of you."

The crew shuffled into more comfortable positions.

Liza walked Aidan down the line, introducing the base personnel in a clipped, professional tone. Most of them looked like their ID photos in the Duster network, which helped Aidan put names—and discipline write-ups—to faces.

The woman with the baby, Andrea the cook, gave him a weak smile. Her ten-year-old son, Tommy, stood pressed against her leg, watching him with something like reproach. Jim Crawford stood close to the woman holding his daughter, giving Aidan a professional smile as he passed.

Damian Coson, the tall black medical officer, looked at him with whirring cybernetic eyes that reflected Aidan's stare from glossy black surfaces. His twelve-year-old brother and sister, twins, watched Aidan with the terrifyingly solemn eyes of children. Somebody had named the poor things Dilly and Donny. Aidan looked away. Kids' lives were his responsibility on this base, too. As if he wasn't scared enough.

The senior transport specialist, a guy named Dozer Short, did not live down to his name. He looked like a walking armored crew car. But at least he was smiling. He'd been the one to get written up for taking the bolts out of a truck seat, so Commander Adams went over backwards the day he left. Great sense of humor around here.

The redhead was introduced as Kevin McIllian, the logistics officer. He'd been written up three times this month for insubordination, once for punching a superior officer. He was even more attractive close up. Of course, Aidan couldn't let himself think like that. The guy was in mourning, probably not attracted to men, and there was Aidan's mess of a body and this new rank to consider.

Don't go there, he told himself.

The hydroelectrics specialist, a wiry Latina woman named Janice Danvers, shouldered a wrench longer than his arm and watched him with a deadpan expression. There had been something about physical assault in her discipline details. Hadn't she threatened to hit somebody with a wrench?

He quickly broke eye contact with her and continued down the line, until he had met the entire group of Duster delinquents now under his command. He stepped back to take them all in, hands folded behind his back. He smiled as best he could and took a moment to organize his thoughts. Don't pause and don't say um. Just talk.

"Okay. As I'm sure you've all heard by now, I'm Commander Aidan Headly. First things first, I want to give you all my condolences. Commander Taylor's death was a blow to all of us, and I can't imagine what you're going through in losing him. I've had a briefing on how he ran this base, but I'm sure that doesn't cover half of what he actually did for you while he was here. If I can do anything to help you get through this, let me know."

His new crew glanced at each other, surprise running between them like electricity.

Aidan cleared his throat, slightly unnerved by the fact that none of them said anything. "Not to be a burden right out of the gate, but any

chance I could get a cup of the shit we pass off as coffee?" The joke
he'd been trying for didn't get a single smile.

Yvonne Flesher gave a small cough. Aidan glanced at the
athletic blonde woman, remembering her title as the physical
requisitions specialist, and some of the stunts she'd been written up for.
Sending an inflatable sheep sex toy to another base was the one that
stuck in his mind. He hoped desperately that his expression didn't
change as she spoke.

"We drank the last of it at the funeral and the wake for
Commander Taylor. Sir."

Her superior, McIllian, cleared his throat.

"Sorry, sir. I'll have more by the end of the week. I haven't done
a luxury run since…"

Aidan realized with a shock that the guy was blushing.

The logistics officer hesitated, then began again, his voice
sounding more like a high-level newscaster for a Corporation than
anyone Aidan had met in real life. "We're a bit at loose ends after the
loss."

Aidan swallowed the desire to wince, trying to keep his face as
neutral as possible. He shouldn't have asked. He should have known
better. Definitely not the first impression he wanted to make. "Right.
Sorry. Don't worry about it."

Silence.

Someone coughed quietly. Feet shuffled.

Tension ran like a wire along Aidan's spine. He should say
something else. Clear the air. Try to give them a better impression. He
rubbed at the back of his neck, trying to put words into coherent
sentences.

"Look. I-I'm not here to try to be Commander Taylor. And I'm
not here to try to break your backs like the other two commanders that
Sector Personnel sent down for you. My goal here is… well, to make
this base the best it can be and maybe give the Corps a bit of hell in the
meantime. So, give me a few weeks to learn the ropes and how you've

done things around here, and we'll figure out how to get through this. Okay?"

Around the room, eyes blinked. Aidan thought he saw surprise, maybe even a little bit of hope. A precious few faces even smiled at him.

Then the hydroelectrics officer folded her arms. "How 'bout you get through the month here 'fore we start talkin' 'bout doin' anything together?"

No one else said a word.

Event File 2
File Tag: Situation Assessment
Timestamp: 19:30-4-1-2155

It was well after sunset when Aidan finally finished filling out the hours' worth of base assignment paperwork and command invoicing to send to the Regional Hub, escaped back to his room, shut the door and tried to catch his breath.

He never should have accepted this. Him? A base commander? He could barely handle himself. He'd been an absolute mess right before Magnum had dragged him into Command training. Hell, he was still a mess. Training had just made him better at hiding it. Raking his fingers through his hair, he paced his bedroom.

It was too small to provide much room to move, but the floor didn't creak and he didn't have a roommate. Better than the room he'd had at the Sector hub. Better than it used to be. He had to focus on that.

How the hell could Sector think he could do this? Him, take the freaking Wildcards and bring them back into line? As a brand-new commander?

On the wall, the sketch of his sister fluttered in the weak AC breeze coming through the grating. He watched it blankly for a moment, then turned to grab the data tab off the top of the dresser.

He needed someone to talk to before he exploded, before he asked for a transfer on his first day. No one on his new crew was safe to expose his weakness to, and he didn't want Sector to ship him off somewhere for another filing job or a Grid assignment because he wasn't fit for command. That only left one person he could discuss all this with. Well, not exactly a person, but close enough.

His fingers flew across the tab's surface as he dropped onto the hard mattress, typing in his password, swiping his thumbprint over the reader and letting the tab scan his retina to access the hidden AI program a friend had built for him the last time his depression had really gone off the rails. As the load bar moved, he flicked his fingertip across the surface, activating the holographic projector.

The green light flashed, forming into a shuddering ball. Red and yellow ran through the sphere as the program continued to load. A moment later it was replaced by the holographic image of a young woman with ice-tinted eyes and long, blond hair.

Sometimes, Aidan wondered how much Naomi had changed since she'd posed for the pic Jackson had used to model this psychological health coaching program. He wished he could really talk to his sister. But it was better if they didn't communicate, the way things were now. The program was better than nothing.

"Hello, Aidan," the AI program said, her head tilting slightly. "What can I do for you?"

"What the hell am I doing, Omi?" Aidan asked, hearing the hopelessness in his own voice.

"I require more information to analyze the request," Omi said, her voice flat and digitized. It was a good octave higher than Naomi's had ever been.

Aidan sighed and ground the heels of his palms against his eyelids. If the program was really his sister, he wouldn't have to spell it out. But Omi only had the limited processing capacity inherent in the program on his tab. She couldn't know information he hadn't entered or events that happened while she was off. He had to spell it out. God that was annoying.

"The future of this whole base is on my head," he muttered. "If I can't get them back on track and off the disciplinary rosters every week by the end of the year, Sector's going to disband them. Destroy what used to be the most successful base we had."

Omi's head cocked to the other side. Data flashed across the tablet's screen too fast for Aidan to read. After a moment, she said, "Location: Base 1407. Nickname: The Wildcards. Disciplinary actions in the last year: one hundred forty-two. Most frequent offenders: Kevin McIllian, logistics and requisitions officer; Janice Danvers, hydroelectrics specialist; Yvonne Flesher, physical requisitions specialist; Lazarus Smith, munitions officer. Between the four of them, eighty-four of the total disciplinary actions. Number of successful missions in the last two years: one hundred ninety-eight. Average number of successful missions per base in this time frame: seventy-five. Number of fully completed successful missions in the past eight months: five. Decrease in success rate of Base 1407 in the past year: eighty five percent. Increase of disciplinary issues: one hundred ten percent. Odds of successfully rehabilitating the base—"

"I really don't need to hear that one," Aidan interrupted. He sighed and ran his fingers through his hair. The odds were slim, and he knew it. But he couldn't face the idea of being the commander who let the Wildcards get disbanded.

According to the records, Base 1407 had been started twenty-five years ago as a reconnaissance and research outpost. They'd had the same commander since the base began. Aidan still couldn't get over that. In this sixty-year old war, he'd never heard of a base commander surviving that long.

According to rumor, the Wildcards had been unstoppable. The stories about missions they'd pulled off, executives they'd disgraced by outing information to the Net, and things they'd invented were legendary. The base had been insane in their success record until the commander who had led them had developed bone cancer. No one had been able to supply the base with the right treatments. In the six months before the man's death, everything in the unit's record had gone to shit.

Aidan sighed. If he couldn't pull this off, Base 1407 would go down in the rule books with one last procedure before they got disbanded. He scrolled over the addendum tacked to the bottom of the file, and Naomi read it aloud.

"Base 1407 is remanded for a six month period of review. It is suggested by this Sector that, should it prove impossible to bring Base 1407 back to full function, this base be used as a case study. Long term bonds formed between personnel and a single commander can, should the commander be incapacitated, become detrimental to morale. In the case of base failure, it is suggested by this Sector that the Regional and-or National Command Council put in place a cap on the number of years a commander may serve on any base."

"Shit. I didn't need to hear that either," Aidan grumbled. "Please rephrase for clarity," the program stated. Aidan sighed. "Don't give me any more statistics okay?"

"Okay. Would you like me to continue with an observation?"

"Sure."

"Your body heat is elevated, and your speech patterns indicate anxiety. You would do well to take several deep breaths and consider the situation. You are not the only one upon whom the fate of this base rests, Aidan," Omi said, her voice oddly gentle. She reached out to place a holographic hand on his shoulder. "You cannot be responsible for the fates of others. That is their choice."

Aidan shook his head. "As commander, it's my job to look after the people beneath me. If I can't make this work, they don't have any other options. Neither do I. I'll end up filing papers fora jackass again when I screw this up. If I'm lucky."

"As commander you can only do so much. It is not psychologically healthy for you to blame yourself for the failings of your crew."

Aidan groaned and stood to begin pacing the small room again. "I should be able to make them all succeed again. Pull them together. Something. They did incredible work until Taylor got diagnosed. Then they all turned into rebellious shitheads."

Omi's digital laughter was soft. "Your own file is not without signs of rebellion."

"And how did you get access to my original file?" Aidan spun to face the psychological health coach hologram, folding his arms over his chest.

Magnum had promised he'd sealed the file containing Aidan's own disciplinary write-ups and the depression diagnosis from before he transitioned, which meant it was off the secured web of decentralized networks the Dusters used. If it was off the GreyNet and off his personal tab, Omi shouldn't have access to it.

The holographic girl smiled. "Jackson coded your history into my data banks, in anticipation that you would require a companion who fully understood your circumstances."

"Of course he did." Aidan groaned and took up his three-step pacing once more. He shouldn't have expected any different from his former roommate and favorite coder. For the first time in months, he wished the guy had been buried in a grave that he could visit to leave flowers or something instead of being scattered to the winds. Fucking Viper-drone bombings.

He shoved the thought aside. This wasn't the time to dwell on the past. He was here, with the Wildcards, facing his first command. He couldn't spend time moping.

"My point," Omi said after a moment, "is that you have a relatively effortless way of bonding with your new command."

Aidan threw her a dry look. "Tell them I was assigned female at birth and got written up for self-harm when I realized I couldn't get help at my home base? That seems like a brilliant idea. Yes, let's tell them my deep, dark secret and hope they don't do the same thing everyone else did."

Silence held the room for a moment, broken only by Aidan's breathing and the thump of his boots on the prefab floor.

"Perhaps begin by telling them how you disobeyed direct orders to save your friends on Base 1446," Omi suggested quietly. "That may be a better first impression."

Aidan almost thought he heard his sister's rampant sarcasm in the voice. But the AI hadn't been programmed with cynicism.

"I already shot my first impression," Aidan grumbled. He paused in his pacing and braced himself against the wobbly little chest of drawers. "I asked for coffee."

The miniature cooling fan in the tab whirred as the holographic projector taxed the system and Omi tipped her head. "I'm sorry, I do not seem to have a protocol against this action recorded. It is a reasonable request. Does Base 1407 have differing protocol that has not been recorded?"

Aidan sighed as he pushed himself away from the dresser and began to unbutton his shirt. The chest binder digging into the skin under his arms was only making everything about this situation worse. At least that was something he could change. Omi was the one person—well, semi-person, he supposed—that he had felt comfortable undressing around since he had begun the hormone treatment.

"Not that I know of. They're just out of coffee, and I sounded like a selfish jackass asking for it."

"You had no knowledge of their supply depletion," Omi said. "You cannot be held accountable for reasonable actions taken in ignorance."

Aidan resisted the urge to roll his eyes as he shrugged out of his shirt and tossed it on top of the little dresser. "You'd understand if you weren't just a program."

He could feel the holographic eyes on his back as he grabbed the hem of the old black binder and worked the coarse mesh up through a practiced series of squirms and wiggles. The fabric scraped across his skin in the usual places, but at least he didn't get stuck this time. That was embarrassing, even when he was alone.

If this command had worked out, he might have gotten a chance at a real fix for the way his body was. But the chances of that already looked like they were going down the toilet.

"Aidan," Omi said after a long moment. "You are being foolish."

Despite himself Aidan chuckled. He rubbed the tender spots around his diminishing breast tissue a moment, then dug in the top drawer for his patched pajamas. "When am I ever not foolish, Omi? That's why I asked Jackson to build you for me. To smack me around when I need it."

"I do not have the physical form necessary to accomplish such a task."

"It's just an expression." He slipped into his pajamas and retreated to the bed, flopping down with a sigh. He still wasn't entirely certain how he was going to deal with his new base, but at least the bad binder seam wasn't rubbing his armpit anymore. "If I'm being so foolish, what do you suggest I do here?"

Omi's head tilted, the green light that formed her holographic shape flickering. Data flashed across the tab beneath her image. "According to the Democratic State Force Command Handbook, section three, subsection A, 'a commander's duty, first and foremost, is to unite their base for a common goal, and to ensure the survival of their unit to the best of their ability.' I suggest you attempt to do that."

Aidan ran a hand over his face. "That was already the plan. It's the smaller steps that are tripping me up. How can I unite them for a common cause if they don't trust me? How can I make them a functioning base again if they think I'm some dumbass who asks for coffee when there is none? How can I follow Magnum's orders when I've got a crew of people who actively disobey command and threaten people with wrenches? I'm not going to act like Dad and slap people down, I won't. But I don't know how to get these people to listen."

"You must make them trust you." More words and numbers sped across the tab's screen as Omi accessed the GreyNet again. The cooling fan whirred louder. "There is a limited amount of data available about the personnel on this base, beyond their disciplinary actions. Perhaps gathering more information would be wise."

Aidan dropped his hands from his face to give the hologram a mock-horrified look. "You mean actually talk to them? I can't do that. Commanders aren't supposed to fraternize with their subordinates, you know that."

Omi blinked. "Sarcasm is not advised at this time, Aidan." Aidan smirked. "Yeah, I know. You keep telling me."

Closing his eyes, he considered the idea. Talk to his crew and get to know them, huh? Aidan could have kicked himself for not thinking of that earlier. It was the easy solution. Figure out the people under his command, what they wanted from a leader, how they needed him to support them. Be there to hold them up, not to smack them down. That was what Magnum had said in training, wasn't it?

"I'll schedule some debriefs in the morning. Try to talk to all my officers, at least, and get a better sense of what's happening here," Aidan promised as he leaned further back against the cool prefab wall. The thin pillow barely cushioned the small of his back. "Thanks, Omi. That'll be all tonight."

The AI smiled just a little. "Good night, Aidan."

He tapped the screen of the tab to shut off the holographic projector. The tab clicked quietly and the lines of code that had been flashing over the screen disappeared, leaving him back at his cluttered menu screen. He made a quick note to schedule meetings with his various officers—Officer McIllian in Logistics and Requisitions, Officer Carlan in Command, Officer Frachette in Finance, and Dr. Coson in Medical at least. Ideally, he'd have a quick debrief with everyone and get to know them a little before taking charge in more than name, but he wasn't certain he'd have the luxury of that much time.

The officers would have to do for now.

Note made, he flipped the tab off completely and lay back, staring blankly at the ceiling. The lights faded into the soft orange of night cycle and he sighed.

One month. He'd agreed to try this crazy idea of Magnum's for one month. Was he going to last that long? Would the crew actually take to him? Would he be able to pull them together enough to avoid disbanding?

He couldn't focus on the fear. He couldn't let himself fall into that dangerous spiral. Then he'd certainly fail. And he owed it to the Wildcards, to the rest of the Dusters, to at least try.

Event File 3
File Tag: Raising Morale
Timestamp: 06:30-4-2-2155

In the morning, Kevin's tab pinged a message alert half an hour before he was officially on duty. Of course, the official duty schedule rarely matched the hours people worked on the Wildcards' base. They had been working incredible amounts of overtime for months, everyone running ragged during Commander Taylor's long illness. Kevin himself had been working a good ninety hours a week, running on modafinil patches and StayWake pills until Damian had threatened to tie him down and sedate him. What was half an hour early?

He paused in pulling on his shirt to glance at the base-wide memo that had popped up. The new commander was requesting private meetings, mandatory for the officers and optional for everyone else. How quixotic of him.

Brushing his hair, Kevin smiled to himself. Quixotic. That really was such a wonderful word. Quixotic. Derived from a novel written in 1605, meaning overly idealistic and hopeful. A beautiful word.

And he was letting himself wander off into his ivory tower again, wasn't he? Kevin shook his head and mentally filed "Quixotic" back with the other antiquated words and ideas from history he collected. "Quixotic" and words like it had bewildered his peers at the Citizen Excellent Standing prep school he'd attended since the age of two. Words like that had only earned him more blank looks once he made it out to the Dust. But someone had to keep the words in general usage, or their language and culture would become ever more impoverished. Besides, he loved the sounds.

A smile still quirking the corners of his lips, Kevin tapped out a response to the memo.

> **Available this morning at ten, sir. Will ensure my division has time.**
>
> **-Kevin**

"Hey, Suckup!" Yvonne's voice shouted through the wall dividing Kevin's room from hers and Sarah's. "You didn't have to reply to the whole damn base. We already know you never stop working!"

"And I'm the only one keeping this rabble together, you ungrateful plebe," Kevin called back, affecting the cultured pre-Dissolution accent he always used when teasing his base mates. He set the tab aside again and checked himself in the mirror, pulling on his cooling jacket as he called through the wall. "I'm off on a short-distance req run later today. Do keep Dilly and Don from raiding my office while I'm occupied this time, will you?"

A muffled snicker was his only reply.

He slid his tab into the side pocket of his cargo pants and manhandled his door open. Though he'd never admit it aloud, he did miss the slick glide of the automatic doors on the city Grid. But little conveniences never made up for the hell the Corps had created for most people in this country.

The next door down opened a breath later and Yvonne stepped out, standing conspicuously to one side to give Kevin an uninterrupted view of her wife, Sarah, toying with the bra she had yet to put on and grinning.

Kevin caught an unfortunate eyeful of Sarah's naked torso and her leer before wrenching his gaze back to Yvonne's face in one gut-churning, mortifying second. He could feel the rush of blood reddening his cheeks as he yanked off his glasses and squeezed his eyes shut in protest.

"Ladies. We talked about this. Third time this week," he groaned. The sound of raucous laughter bounced off the paneling.

"Third time this week, and you're still blushing!" Sarah's voice drew out every syllable in a sing-song.

"Yes, Sarah, I'm blushing," Kevin sighed, refusing to open his eyes. "You knew I would blush. You've known me nine years. You know I always blush. You know for a fact that, while you ladies had the good fortune to be raised in the Dust, I had my upbringing courtesy of Cavanaugh and, furthermore, you know perfectly well how that Corporation indoctrinates their children on the subjects of modesty, shame, the Perfection Mandate, and the sanctity of intimate relations. I can't help how I was taught," he finished in a weary monotone. "And I can't help that I blush. So have some pity and put a damn shirt on."

That set them off into new fits of the giggles. It was Yvonne who managed to speak first. "Aw, Kev, baby, we can't help it. You look ridiculous when you get all flustered…"

"I'm working on it," Kevin replied tartly. "And you aren't helping."

"We need to do something for entertainment around here," Sarah added, pulling on her shirt. "Besides, for all you know, the new commander could secretly be a nudist."

Kevin slid his glasses back onto his nose, giving them his patent glare over the rims. "I highly doubt that."

Instead of the subdued reaction he had been hoping for, Yvonne snickered. "Buzzkill."

"Yes, well, someone has to be responsible on this base. And it certainly isn't either of you." Kevin sighed as his tab pinged again. He dug it out of his pocket and glanced at the private memo. Liza was asking to see him. Wonderful.

"Apparently I'm not the only one starting early. Yvonne, I need you prepped for the run with Ed by the afternoon."

The taller of the two women nodded curtly, the humor draining from her as if he had popped a balloon. "Sure, Kev. I'm on it."

He shot Yvonne a smile, nodded in reply and hurried down the narrow corridor.

It was one of the things Kevin loved about his crew. As ridiculous as they could be, when it came down to the wire, they worked their posteriors off. Especially his requisitions team. They knew it was their work that ensured the base had the 3D printing blueprints, food, and materials to keep them all alive.

Liza was already in his cramped office, sitting in the spare chair beside his cluttered desk. She looked as pristine as she had the day before, her hair pulled back so tightly Kevin wondered if it might actually deform her face, were she to leave it up too long.

Her smile was uncertain. "Morning."

"Everything all right?" Kevin asked as he closed the door behind him and carefully rounded the desk.

Liza didn't request meetings often. She had a tendency to simply show up when she needed something or send a long list of things she needed added to the requisitions lists. Add to that the unusual attention she had paid to her uniform and appearance, and Kevin knew her anxiety must be going through the roof.

Liza took a breath, held it a moment, and let it out in a long sigh.

"It's the new commander. Well, not really. I mean, it's the crew. You got the same briefing I did from Sector, right?"

Kevin blinked at her and adjusted the glasses on his nose.

She must be really nervous if she wasn't completing a thought.

"The briefing about Commander Headly?" he asked, shoving his red hair back from his eyes with an absent swipe of the hand.

"About this being our last chance," Liza elaborated quietly. She glanced up. "I'll give you a haircut later. Your hair's too long."

"Yes nanny," Kevin replied dryly. Watching Liza's face fall, he sighed, slid his tab onto the desktop and sat back in his chair. The old plastic creaked beneath him. "Sorry, Liza. Please, try to relax. I can't imagine they'd truly be insane enough to disband us."

Liza gave him a long, hard look. "Kev, we're a base of fuck-ups and clowns without Taylor, and they know it." She looked down, nervously plucking at one of the calibrators on his desk. "But I can't lose this. I can't lose my family."

Kevin chewed his lip a moment, trying to find the right words. What was there to say when his friend and superior was suffering an emotional crisis across the desk from him?

"They're my family, too, Liza," he stated quietly. "And we're not going to get disbanded."

"Laz is already talking about planting snappers under the commander's mattress," Liza sighed, dropping her head into her hands. "And Janice was grumbling about dumb-ass kids all night. They're going to run this one off too, unless I can get them under control."

Kevin leaned forward and reached across the desk to touch her arm. "Liza, listen. You're not the only officer on this base. It isn't your responsibility alone to get our riotous ducklings to behave."

She snorted behind her fingers. "Riotous ducklings?"

"It seemed appropriate." At least he had gotten a reaction out of her that wasn't despair. Gently, he reached to pull one of her hands away from her face. "But the point is, if you're that worried they're going to misbehave, you have resources. Me. Damian. Blake. I imagine Janice would help keep everyone else in line, if you bribed her well, and even Lazarus won't risk circumventing her. We'll make it through this, Liza. We've faced more catastrophic circumstances together, haven't we?"

"You really think we can get them in line?" After a moment, Liza looked up, her dark brows pulled together. "They decimated Commander Quinn last week."

Kevin wrinkled his nose at the name and swallowed the urge to correct her improper usage of 'decimated'. Unfortunately, Quinn was alive and well, and still in possession of one hundred percent of his body mass.

"Commander Quinn was an autocratic, homophobic jackass. Headly seems like he has a much better understanding of basic human decency."

She studied him for a moment before a slow smirk crawled across her face. "You're not just saying that because you think he's cute, are you?"

Heat crawled up the back of Kevin's neck and pooled in his cheeks. He slipped his glasses off and focused on polishing them with a cloth pulled from his breast pocket to hide the flash of instinctive panic. Liza didn't need to see how the teasing affected him.

It was easy for Liza to tease about this kind of thing, he reminded himself. That was no reason to get snappish with her. She was Duster born, like Yvonne and Sarah and Laz. She hadn't been raised under the constant threat of the Cavanaugh Perfection Mandate and the EagleCorp Morality Laws that half the major Corporations ascribed to. She hadn't been taught to live with fear of her own body lodged in her gut. He had, and talking casually about wanting to do things with a man which carried mandatory jail time and a likely death sentence in half the nation's cities would probably never come easy to him.

He'd never be able to tell Liza how closely he'd been scrutinized as a child, the things his parents had taught him to hide. That would involve admitting just how high up the Cavanaugh totem pole his family had been. No one was watched for signs of deviation as closely as the next generation of CEOs, CFOs and executives. If the base ever found out what he'd been on the Grid…

The two fears wound around each other, a Gordian knot in the pit of his stomach. And, to add insult to injury, his emotional reaction to the teasing made him blush. His damnably fair skin made it obvious.

He cleared his throat. "Of course not. He's a commander. But he's the first they've sent that gave us condolences for Taylor's death. And he seemed quite earnest about his desire to learn our rather...unorthodox methods."

"And the insta-crush is just a bonus, right?" Liza smirked a little more widely. "Ask him out, if he lasts more than week."

Kevin gave her the best withering glare he could manage without his glasses on. It was sweet that she still went out of her way to encourage him to have a personal life. It was also intensely aggravating.

"Stay out of my romantic life, Liza. It's really not something sister-figures ought to be meddling in, don't you think? Especially not when we have much bigger fish to fry."

"What I wouldn't give for a real fish fry," she groaned, sinking into her chair as if she'd lost the entirety of her spine. "Anything better than protein patties and rehydrated spinach."

Kevin remembered entirely too late that mentions of real food tended to derail any and all conversations with Liza. He had only himself to blame, too. When he'd first taken over the responsibilities of Logistics Officer five years ago, he'd attempted to get better food for the base. Real produce grown on the American AgCo farms that covered the Eastern plains, fresh meat shipped in from slaughterhouses at the other end of the CO-WY Grid. They'd had an entire month of fresh produce before he'd nearly gotten both himself and Yvonne killed on a run and he'd put the idea aside. But that month had spoiled the culinary-leaning members of the Wildcards quite thoroughly.

"I'll put 'food we can't afford or grow' on the requisitions list," he replied dryly. He replaced his glasses and studied his friend across the desk for a long moment. "In all seriousness, though, let me know if I need to talk sense into anyone, will you? And don't let Laz take the snappers out of munitions."

Liza gave a brittle little laugh. "Like I can make that prank-happy asshat do anything."

"Try?"

She let out a sigh, her sour expression shifting into something softer. "Why aren't you personnel officer, again?"

"Because I prefer puzzles to people," Kevin replied. The tension in his shoulders relaxed a little as he sat back once more. "And because you've been on this base far longer than I have."

Liza huffed a weak chuckle. "Can't argue with that. Think you can get your team together for a meeting before they run the Commander off?"

"I'll try," Kevin agreed. "I can help whip munitions into shape, too. If you need it."

Liza took a breath and let it out slowly. Her smile looked a little more genuine this time. "Thanks, Kev."

"Any time." He waited until his office door closed behind her before allowing himself to drop bonelessly into his chair.

Putting on an act of calm was one of his specialties, he reflected, and it had its perks. Especially now, when his base mates needed someone to lean on. But damn it was getting exhausting.

Maybe this was why the Regional Hub didn't recommend keeping units cohesive for more than a few years at a time. Granted, with the number of casualties the Dusters suffered, it was usually a moot point. People cycled through bases. They were assigned where their specialties were needed on a regular basis, and were killed on a regular basis, too.

But Commander Taylor had kept his people together. He and the older members had trained half the base personnel. Every one of the younger members had been mentored in their assignments by an older specialist before they took the positions as their teachers died or retired from strenuous field duty. Kevin himself had inherited Logistics from Blake when the older man had gotten slow. He still asked for advice on occasion.

Commander Taylor had encouraged relationships like that. He'd wanted a team that bonded to one another. He'd taught them all to act like a family, not like a military unit. Kevin knew personnel higher up the command chain hadn't liked it. He'd overheard a few of the arguments. But that tight bond had been their greatest strength before Commander Taylor died.

The problem, Kevin thought wryly, was that they acted like a family at its worst these days. Everyone knew one another's vulnerabilities too well.

Pulling his glasses off, he toyed with them, the world gone out of focus around him. He knew it wasn't logical to keep them instead of simply having his eyes repaired. But he liked the glasses for a host of reasons. They were occupation for his nervous hands. They represented his parents' defiance of Cavanaugh Corporation's Perfection Mandate. They were a mark of his defiance, too. A mark of his humanity. And they helped him make a point when needed to. All he had to do was look over the rims and people got the message.

Well, occasionally, at least.

After a long moment to catch his breath, he sat back up and plugged his tab into the desktop console. The tab had barely connected when Kevin's door opened again. He looked up and blinked. "What can I do for you, Janice?"

"Got some shit I need to get on the req list," the hydroelectrics specialist said. She slipped inside and kicked the door shut, but didn't sit. Instead, she set her wide-gauge pipe wrench carefully on the edge of Kevin's desk and sighed.

"Hope to fuckin' God I won't have to use this on the new asshole."

"I'm sure Liza would appreciate not having to explain to Sector why our new commander was in the medical bay with a concussion," Kevin agreed as lightly as he could.

Of all the people on this base, he hadn't expected Janice to be one of those coming to him for reassurance. The req list request was a pretty poor smokescreen too. Janice prided herself on her strength, on her ability to protect the base that was their family, and to squeeze water out of the hidden aquifers left in the Dust. She hid any worries she did have behind her cursing and her work. But here she was, in Kevin's office with the door closed, as close to vulnerable as he had ever seen her.

Janice snorted, folded her arms, and looked down her nose at him. "Sector can suck it. They keep sending us fucking idiots with sticks so far up their tight asses they—"

"I get the picture," Kevin interrupted gently. It was best to keep Janice from one of her curse-filled tirades if one wanted to get anything done without losing body parts. "But, like it or not, we're rather at their mercy at the moment."

Janice grumbled under her breath in Spanish. After a long moment, she looked up from the wrench and met Kevin's gaze, her dark eyes full of unsettling worry. "What the fuck're we gonna do if this one's as bad as the others?"

Kevin forced a small smile and tried for a joke. "Knowing you, you'll hospitalize him and demand another replacement. Life and lemons and all that."

"The hell do lemons have to do with shit?" Janice asked, bewildered.

"Old saying. Forget it." He shrugged, shoulders slumping wearily. "We all have reservations about Commander Headly. But what choice do we have except giving him a chance? He's already leaps and bounds better than Quinn, right?"

"Anyone'd be better than that asswipe," Janice grumbled, frowning down at her wrench on the table instead of meeting his gaze. After a long moment, she snatched the tool back up. "I'll give him a week. If'n he doesn't fuck up too bad, maybe longer."

Kevin found himself hoping fervently that Commander Headly could cut it with Janice's standards. Otherwise, he wasn't entirely certain he could keep that promise to Liza. "A week will have to do. Now, what did you need to put on the list?"

Event File 4
File Tag: Situational Awareness
Timestamp: 10:30-4-2-2155

By the time the gaggle of basemates had left his office, Kevin was hours behind where he'd wanted to be. He left the door open but pulled up his most archaic playlist in self-defense, cranking the volume as high as it went on his tab. A blaring wall of Guns N' Roses might as well have 'keep out' written on it in caps. This morning, that was exactly the way Kevin liked it.

Spinning easily in his chair, he flipped between three different holographic screens, analyzing the hacks of Corps shipment schedules and routes. His eyes brightened, and he leaned in to highlight an entry on one of ZonCom's shipping rosters. Shipment of synthesized coffee and dehydrated foodstuffs leaving the Foothills Metro Sector for the New England Regional Hub in two days.

That wasn't enough time to send someone on-Grid to fetch it, but plenty of time to reach out to their contacts and organize a drop point. He'd take Yvonne with him. Quick and dirty. Perfect.

His fingers tapped on the touch screen of his console, an underscore to the song. A bitter smile quirked his lips as he sang along under his breath.

"Welcome to the jungle, it gets worse here every day…"

That done, he had time to run through the new access codes he'd just acquired through his on-Grid supplier. Reading them over, his brows rose. Jazz had always sold them good work, but this was something special. If they wrote these codes into a manual access card, the places they could gain entry might expand by a factor of ten.

Might. If he was right. If the codes were as legitimate as they looked. They'd wager an awful lot on that 'if'.

He ran a finger over the coder's signature in the header, studying the odd little glyph.

<(-_-)>^^^^^/

"Hello. You're new," he whispered, studying the screen.

The loud knock on his door frame made him jump. He glanced up from his work and felt the blood drain from his face.

Commander Headly stood in the doorway, looking bemused.

Kevin closed all his projected windows with a single sharp motion and looked at the clock in the top corner of his tab screen. Ten-thirty. He was half an hour late for his debrief with the commander. *Idiot!* Mentally kicking himself, Kevin flicked his music off. The sudden silence made his head spin.

"Commander! Sorry, I didn't notice you there."

"I guess not," Commander Headly said into the quiet.

Kevin couldn't place the man's tone. Was he amused or irritated? Probably irritated, Kevin thought, scolding himself internally. He had good reason.

The commander cleared his throat. "I can come back, if this is a bad time."

Kevin realized he was still sitting and rocketed to his feet, saluting as crisply as if he had been doing it his entire life. "No, sir. This is fine, sir. I just got caught up in work, and I apologize."

Something akin to frustration crossed Commander Headly's face, the moment so brief Kevin wasn't sure if he'd imagined it.

The commander coughed again. "At ease. I'm not exactly a fan of saluting."

Kevin let the salute drop but remained standing, the two of them stiff on either side of the small room. *We must look like two junkyard dogs with a bone*, he thought distantly. *Two feral dogs sizing each other up for potential threats. One of us is going to make a move, display weakness or strength, and hope the other accepts the signal.*

As soon as the thought crossed his mind, he realized how crazy it was. They were people, not dogs, and they certainly weren't fighting for the same scrap of food. If anything, he was here to help the commander keep the base alive. Assuming the new commander was as hot—intelligent, he berated himself, intelligent—under the uniform as he seemed.

In the awkward moment that followed, Kevin took stock of the man in front of him. Slightly shorter than himself, around the same age, with the typical Duster stance that screamed "ready to run at a moment's notice." This man looked like he had accepted the fact that the world was dangerous long ago. Kevin had read the commander's file of course, and knew he was Dust-born, but it was always fascinating to see who stood like a born and bred Duster when they weren't fighting.

The new commander had rich, dark blond hair in the kind of quasi-pageboy cut you ended up with when you had straight hair and didn't pay attention to getting it cut in a timely manner. His eyes were a deep blue, set in a soulful face tanned by Colorado's sun. It had been what struck Kevin so emphatically the day before: those eyes, and that expression. The man reminded Kevin oddly of the portrait of Saint Jude that his mother had kept on her bedside table.

He had the vague urge to bring out a smile on that poignant countenance. It would be dazzling.

Damn, he was getting hard up these days. Focus.

"You wanted to speak to me, sir?" Kevin finally asked. At the same moment the commander apparently nerved himself to ask, "What music were you playing?"

The warmth of a self-conscious blush kindled in Kevin's cheeks. He gave a sheepish smile and a half-shrug.

"'Welcome to the Jungle.' It's pre-Incorporation music. I've got rather a penchant for it. Well, pre-Dissolution music, actually. It's a bit over a hundred and fifty years old, quite a bit more melodically and stylistically creative than what's produced on the Grid nowadays and—"

He cut himself off at the blank look on the commander's face.

Straightening his shoulders, he cleared his throat and reminded himself that this was his superior officer, not his friend.

"Excuse me, sir. Didn't mean to waste your time. What was it you wanted to speak with me about, sir?"

Commander Headly bit his lip. It was obviously a nervous gesture, but one that Kevin wasn't entirely certain he could interpret. After a moment, the commander inhaled sharply and smiled. "I wanted to talk to you about your division. See how things are going and if there was anything you needed."

Kevin nodded. "I can have a report sent to your tab by morning, if you give me your current GreyNet handle."

He kept his face carefully blank and his tone professional. Behind the facade, his mind raced. Had he shot himself in the foot by attempting to begin an over-eager discussion of old music? Was the commander going to tell him to quit listening to music while he worked?

"No, I don't need a report." Commander Headly cleared his throat and shifted his weight from one foot to the other. "I just wanted to talk about how things are working for you. Um. Informally. One officer to another."

Kevin blinked. It was a little uncomfortable how easily he'd expected some form of discipline for doing absolutely nothing against the rules. Maybe those last few temporary commanders had left more of an impression than he'd realized. Okay. Fresh start.

He reached to roll a second chair out from its place between plastic supply cabinets against the wall. "Please. Take a seat."

Gingerly, Commander Headly lowered himself into the chair and folded his hands in his lap.

Kevin had to wonder if the man was trying not to fidget.

Rather than letting himself appear to be staring, he turned to pull up a handful of holographic windows: a detailed map of the CO-WY Grid dotted with symbols, the requisitions list, his notes for the run he had just begun to organize, and the half-finished code for a game he was working on. He quickly flicked the last one away and hoped the commander hadn't noticed.

"We've been having rather a rough time," he said as he worked. "But I think we're pulling through. My crew's been staying pretty well supplied in all the staples, and we seem to be staying well under the radar at this location. We haven't had to move in four months. I've been working on several new physical routes onto the Grid using an algorithm that should help to ensure that they're both feasible and randomized enough to get lost in the crowd. We have four go-to entrances, but it doesn't do to overuse them. Especially not with EagleCorp cracking down on anything they see as a deviation from the norm."

"I see." The commander nodded, his startling eyes scanning over the information on the screens. After a moment, he took a breath and looked back to Kevin. "Can I ask you something?"

Kevin tried not to tense. What could Headly possibly have to ask that required that kind of preface? If it was a question pertaining to his duties, the commander had every right to ask it, whether or not Kevin actually wanted to answer. And if it was a personal question? Well, Kevin was well-versed in delicately skirting situations as needed. "Of course, sir."

Commander Headly twisted his hands together, then pried his fingers apart and set them carefully on the armrests of his chair. He took a deep breath and met Kevin's gaze. "What are your long-term goals for your division? I mean the ones you really want, not what's logged with Sector."

"Sir?" Kevin nervously adjusted his glasses on his nose.

Long-term goals? Had Headly been told about Commander Taylor's Ten Year Plan? It had been the entire base's shared daydream, but it had seemed like such an impossible fantasy that they'd kept it amongst themselves. It had only drifted even further out of reach once Taylor had gotten sick and their family had started falling apart. It had been months since Kevin had so much as thought about the Plan. He was fairly certain the new commander would laugh if he told the truth.

"Well, sir, we want to keep the base well-supplied in the necessities, and I'd sleep easier if we could get some higher-grade slick tarp patches."

"That's all? Tafa—oh, crap. I thought I'd had it. Tafar—"

"Tafarah," Kevin put in easily, the Lebanese name rolling off his tongue. "He prefers Topher, though."

Commander Headly nodded, his face creasing with frustration. "Right. This morning, he was telling me he'd love to work on a modern Go System enabled truck one day, instead of the ancient hand-me-down manuals we get. Likely to happen any time soon? Not really. But it gives me a chance to know him and what he wants to do here, and how I can help him work toward that. I'd like to know the same thing about everyone, especially division officers. Don't worry about achievability. I know we're talking long-term here, and Sector or Regional might not approve. But if I can get that intel, we can organize the run."

Kevin blinked. This soft-spoken, humble man was their new Commander? It was almost unbelievable, and the polar opposite of what Sector had been sending them since Taylor passed away.

Was this some elaborate prank Lazarus and Yvonne had cooked up to screw with him? If it turned out those two were behind this, he'd strangle them bare-handed.

The commander shifted uncomfortably, and Kevin realized he'd been staring in silence for quite some time. He really needed to stop doing that. Unfortunately, soulful and scruffy men had always been his weakness. He cleared his throat and pulled his glasses off, polishing them as a convenient excuse to avoid Commander Headly's gaze. "Well, Commander, it's not exactly possible, but—"

"Two things," Headly interrupted quietly. "One, my name is Aidan. Please use it instead of 'Sir' or 'Commander.' Rigid command structures don't exactly sit well with me. Two, what did I just say about dealing with achievability together?"

The heat in Kevin's cheeks spread to the tips of his ears, and he applied himself even more studiously to polishing his glasses. He added another tally to the "Times Commander Headly has Surprised Me Today" column in his brain and took a breath. "Well. In an ideal world, we—I would love to make the base self-sufficient. Find a decent water source, some arable land, get our hands on unpatented seed and livestock embryos, and be able to properly look after ourselves without relying on Grid supply runs every few weeks."

The silence that greeted that statement made Kevin look up, squinting at his new commander. Damian had been right about the new lens prescription. His eyesight was getting worse.

He couldn't be certain, but it looked like Headly—Aidan, he corrected himself—was seriously considering the idea.

After an impossibly long moment, Aidan nodded. "If we're not constantly scrounging for supplies, we might actually be able to make some headway in the fight. That's an incredible idea—Um. Do you prefer Kevin or McIllian?"

"Kevin's fine, sir. Aidan. Sorry." Another question Kevin had never expected to hear out of a commander's mouth. He slipped his glasses back on and smiled as best he could.

Aidan acknowledged the attempt with a smile and a quick nod. "Well, let's see what we can do to work toward that goal of yours. In the meantime, is there anything I can do for you or your division?"

Kevin considered the question a moment. Anything the new commander could do? Well, he couldn't exactly be Taylor, so that was out. And asking for a date was incredibly inappropriate. That left only the hard answer.

"A list of expectations might be nice, if you don't mind." He glanced at the slowly moving readouts of drone flight patterns in the Sector, studying the screen as he spoke. "And remembering that we're human and have limits. I can't make a miracle happen, no matter how long you want me to run my crew without rest."

Much to Kevin's surprise, the commander chuckled. Kevin stiffened. Logically, he knew the commander was probably attempting to sympathize. But logic didn't stop the anger that cut through Kevin like a hot knife. This man had laughed at the idea of his friends, his *family* being run ragged.

Commander Quinn had laughed in his face too. Commander Adams had shown this kind of disregard for his family's lives. Kevin didn't have the patience to deal with a man who could turn out to be just as much of an asshole. So Headly had only been playing nice. Now the gloves came off.

Kevin gave the commander an icy stare over the rims of his glasses.

"It's not funny. *Sir,"* he stated, making sure to emphasize the title. "The last two commanders Sector sent us didn't acknowledge the conspicuous little fact that we're mortal, and tried to work us to death. We were given four on-Grid shipment runs in seven days, and told to lay out personnel transport routes for the next six months to boot, with the logic—if you can call it that—that we'd done it once before. Yes, we had done it once before, in dire straits. Once. And those runs failed and landed most of the logistics division and part of munitions in surgery. I swore I'd never push my division like that again."

Kevin clenched his hands into fists in his lap to keep from surging upright. "Even if we'd all worked around the clock for a full week—which, by the way, our med team would slaughter us all over—we still wouldn't have been able to finish the work 'to satisfaction.' And that's not counting how sloppy we would have gotten with the on-Grid requisitions runs. Sir."

Commander Aidan Headly's eyes had widened, his back stiffening.

"I didn't realize it was that bad. I mean, I'd read the reports, but—"

Kevin continued to pierce him with the coldest stare he could manage, the fury burning in his gut. "What, you thought we were simply a collection of delinquents? Committing insubordination just for the hell of it? I hate to disrupt your cozy little bubble of illusion, sir, but, for as much vexation as we've caused over the last few months, we weren't the irritant. We're not spoiled children, so spare the rod. We've had enough attempts at 'whipping into shape' lately, the operative word being whipping."

The confusion that crossed the commander's face made Kevin wince internally. He'd done it again, let his anger elevate his vocabulary. It had been a mannerism he'd used habitually while he was still living on the Grid. If you sounded haughty enough almost anyone would back down. It was a hard habit to break. Apparently, he still hadn't. And he'd lost his temper again. At the worst possible time. Hadn't he sworn he was going to keep himself under control? He took a deep breath and let it out slowly. "I'm sorry, sir. I spoke out of frustration. What I'm trying to say is that we're not always like this. We don't take kindly to orders without reason, and even less so to unreasonable expectations. We've had nothing but unreasonable since we lost Commander Taylor, and we all know the stakes for your post here. So, if you don't mind, please, try to remember that we're humans, not bots."

"I… don't think that will be a problem," Aidan said after a long moment. He searched Kevin's face, his own unreadable. Slowly, he nodded. "I'll send a list of what I'd like to see to your tab by tonight. Queen of Hearts is your current handle, right?"

Kevin rolled his eyes. "Oh, not again. It's King. King of Hearts."

"Your file said Queen." Aidan's brow furrowed as he glanced at the tab in his hand.

Kevin sighed and gave a helpless shrug. "We're really not insubordinate by nature, but… well, some of us relieve stress with humor. And getting into the personnel files to make jokes is a favorite pastime."

Aidan gave him a very small smile. "Yeah. I guess that explains a lot. And, keep in mind everything I'll give you is flexible. If anything seems unreasonable or like it might cause issues, just let me know and we'll talk it through. Okay?"

For a long moment, Kevin studied the commander's face.

It really was handsome with that faintly wistful look, just a touch of peach fuzz stubble and a worry line between his brows far too deep for someone his age.

He'd just balled the man out. His Commanding officer. And in return he was getting… understanding?

Eventually, Kevin found himself returning Aidan's smile. He stuck his hand out. "I think you have a deal, Com—Aidan."

The commander's smile strengthened as he shook Kevin's hand. "I look forward to working with you."

For the first time since Commander Taylor died, Kevin felt like those words might be true.

Event File 5
File Tag: Medical Assessment
Timestamp: 11:00-4-2-2155

The sound of Kevin's office door clicking shut behind him cut the strings that had been holding Aidan's calm in place. Alone in the hall, he leaned against the wall, feeling his heart hammering against his ribs. Great. He had already pissed off the base logistics officer in their first debrief, and Kevin apparently wasn't one to pull his punches.

Aidan forced himself to take a few deep breaths, trying to calm his racing pulse. At least he'd been able to salvage it a little. That was something, right?

He swallowed a sigh and ran his hands over his face. Why the hell had he accepted this position in the first place? There were emotional minefields on any base, but the Wildcards seemed to have more than he'd expected. And he still had to see the base doctor for his transfer physical. Ugh.

A muffled ping sounded from his pocket and he pulled the tablet out, absently tapping to bring up the message.

Message Handle: JOKER

> In response to base-wide memo from CommandAH
>
> Message: You're seriously asking for us to take time out of our duties for a tea party? Guess I'll ask Kev to get you a pretty pink dress on the next req run. Don't you think he'd look nice in pink, guys?

Every muscle in Aidan's body stiffened. A dress? Had someone found out about him? His brain ground to a halt. Who used the handle JOKER?

A door slammed open further down the hall. Aidan flattened himself against the wall, adrenaline spiking through his body as if he'd heard the drone proximity alert.

"Laz, you gamma dipshit!" The shout followed the bang, and Liza barreled out into the hall, almost unrecognizable as the stiff soldier she had been yesterday. Her uniform jacket hung as if she'd slung it over her shoulders in a hurry and her eyes were wide and feral. She ran a few steps, caught sight of Aidan and skidded to a stop, throwing up a salute that was an abbreviated sketch of her previous crisp gesture. "Commander! I'm so sorry. I was just on my way to rip Laz a—to discipline him for that message. That was way out of line, even for him."

The sound of a second door, much quieter, made Aidan's breath hitch.

"Tell me Lazarus didn't just—" Kevin's voice groaned behind him, but it cut off with an "Oh."

Though Liza addressed him, Aidan noted that her eyes were fixed on a point down the hall. He didn't want to turn and see Kevin's expression. He'd already embarrassed himself in front of the logistics officer enough for one morning.

Aidan swallowed hard, caught between Liza, the wall, and Kevin. He fixed his eyes on the slight trembling of Liza's saluting hand. He didn't want to deal with this right now. He wanted to go back to his quarters and curl up with the pillow over his head for a few hours. But

Liza was standing right in front of him, waiting for a response, and he was commander here. Falling apart simply wasn't an option.

He could feel Kevin's eyes on his back like a pair of lead weights, pinning him to the spot as his mind spun. What the hell could he say? Don't worry about it? Please give him the harshest punishment you can think of? What the hell was the happy medium between sounding like a complete ass and a total pushover?

Luckily, Liza kept talking instead of making him decide. "He's always had a problem with authority, sir, and it's especially bad after… I never expected him to pull something like this. I take full responsibility."

"Commander?" Kevin asked from Aidan's other side, voice cautiously polite.

Aidan realized he'd been staring at Liza's shaking hand. He forced his eyes back to her face, squared his shoulders, and attempted to pull himself together. It wasn't easy, with his brain fritzing. "Sorry. Just… thinking it through."

Liza dropped her hand like a child caught doing something she shouldn't, and Aidan's mind jolted as the pieces clicked. This was what she hid behind her military facade. She was scared. He didn't know what was frightening her, but that was definitely fear in her eyes.

She drew herself up in a visible attempt to replace the shield she hid behind.

"I'll take care of it, sir. Don't worry, sir. He's just trying to make trouble. Nothing that you need to add to your plate, sir."

"Thank you." Aidan did his best to sound calm and collected.

Liza nodded. She swallowed hard. "I really am sorry, sir."

"It won't happen again," Kevin promised over the soft shuffle of his boots.

Aidan sucked in a deep breath, trying not to feel like they were closing some sort of trap in on him. They were doing their jobs, being his officers, just trying to reassure him. Not their fault he felt surrounded and out of his depth. *Don't snap at them*, he reminded himself. *Don't let them see that you're falling apart. Don't freeze up. Breathe. Say something. Don't say um.*

He forced a smile. "I'll trust you two to look after it. I'd rather not get involved if I don't have to."

Liza nodded, looking a little more like she had the situation under control. "Of course, sir."

Aidan returned the nod, though his chest still felt tight with panic. Were they just pretending not to know or care? He swallowed the questions that would only give him away and slipped past Liza to continue his walk toward the med bay, carefully keeping his back to Kevin.

Behind him, the two officers whispered. The sound of their voices made his stomach clench. He ducked his head and walked faster, telling himself they weren't talking about him. There was no reason to gossip about their new commander.

Right. No reason. No reason but the little fact that he'd just been freaking out about a stupid memo. No reason but the fact that he'd wound up sounding like a complete idiot during both their debriefings. No reason but the fact that he still didn't look like a commander. Like a leader. Like a man.

Aidan shook his head as he rounded the corner, trying to shake off the mess of anxious thoughts circling in his head. They weren't talking about him. They didn't know. There was no reason to panic. Everything was alright. He had to pull himself together before he reached the med bay. He had to calm the hell down. He had obligations. There was no time for this shit.

Even if the unit did find out, they weren't on the Grid. The EagleCorp Morality Laws would sentence him to a messy, public death for being what he was if he was caught on any land where they applied. Who he was, he corrected himself. Out here in the Dust, there was a lot more leeway. On the Grid, everything depended on who owned the patch of land you stood on and what they thought 'moral' was.

At least, there was leeway out here if your base mates were tolerant. There were still stories of folks getting beaten or worse because someone on-base decided they didn't like living with a person who didn't fit their idea of 'normal.'

If he was honest with himself, that was what really had Aidan on edge. If Lazarus had found out his secret, what would the man do? Was he the kind of guy to give him a hard time and let it go, or the kind who might take a piece of rebar to Aidan's head?

His thoughts chased themselves in circles as his feet moved.

If Lazarus knew, did the rest of the base? Magnum had promised to scrub and rewrite his records if he accepted Command training. He'd been promised there would be no problem on the base he'd be assigned to.

No problems? He'd already made an ass of himself, and now someone was talking about putting him in a dress. Someone knew. Magnum must have dropped the ball on rewriting his records.

"Commander?"

The voice snapped Aidan back to reality. He froze mid-step, blinked, and turned toward the speaker.

Damian Coson leaned against a doorframe, his arms crossed. The gesture pulled his splotched lab coat tight across his shoulders, accenting what little muscle he had. One black brow rose over his unreadable, cybernetic eyes.

"If you're coming for our appointment, you missed the turn."

Aidan had to take a breath and remind himself not to freak out. The chief medical officer was trying to be helpful, not trying to jump on him. His own frayed nerves were no reason to snap at the guy. He forced a self-conscious smile and rubbed at the back of his neck. "Sorry. Still getting the layout. Bit smaller than Sector. Um. Damian, right?"

Damn, he was saying um again. He had to calm himself down.

The other eyebrow rose to join the first, and the man replied with a voice nearly as flat as the mechanical eyes. "If you want a first name basis, yes."

Aidan cleared his throat uncomfortably. The unnatural-looking implants combined with the unreadable tone of the voice and everything else that had happened today just made him want to run and hide. But he was commander here.

"Would you prefer Doctor Coson?"

"Protocol's at the discretion of the base commander. I just check the medical records." The man shrugged, his white coat wrinkling with the motion. After a moment, he tipped his head toward the room behind him. "Speaking of that, we should get started on your intake exam."

Aidan sucked in a deep breath instead of letting himself wince. Of course, the doctor would jump right to it. Not even a moment to relax before getting poked and prodded and asked questions he didn't particularly want to answer. That fit the pattern of this day all right.

At least he knew Magnum had told Damian about his biological issues, so that was one thing he didn't have to worry about. How the doctor was going to react to that? Well, that was still up in the air.

He nodded weakly and slipped past Damian into the med bay. The air smelled painfully antiseptic, but at least the room was empty. It could be worse, Aidan told himself. It could smell like blood. Some clinics did. And at least this one was clean.

Make that painfully clean. Even the man's tab had been squared with the corner of a table when he set it down.

"If you don't mind multitasking, we can get that debrief you wanted out of the way while I look you over," the lanky doctor said as he pulled a pair of nitrile gloves from a dispenser on the wall under a wall cabinet marked with block letters: Don't Even Think About Getting In Here. The thin, white rubber contrasted almost hypnotically with his skin.

Aidan considered that as he reluctantly pulled himself up onto one of the three cool ceramic examination tables. He tugged uncomfortably on the hem of his shirt and binder, a bad habit that had helped develop a hole near the hem of the compression mesh.

"Yeah, sounds good. But I have to ask. How do you handle patient confidentiality? I know not every base runs it the same way. And you know I've got a kind of... sensitive issue here."

The doctor gave him a long, slow look. "That's putting it mildly. But you can believe me when I tell you that the encryption on our medical files is as good as the encryption on our mission files." The spare man glanced down as he pulled a precisely organized examination tray over on its small rolling table, his lips quirked up ever so slightly at the corners. He slipped a fingertip pulse monitor onto Aidan's index finger.

"As far as how I handle it personally? Extremely seriously. What happens in my med bay stays in here unless circumstances demand a different approach. Like when idiots try to run on stimulants for six days in a row."

Aidan shifted uncomfortably, tugging on his binder again. He'd barely moved, so why did it feel like it had ridden up?

Damian ran his finger over the mandatory implant in Aidan's arm. The light in the slow-release STD prevention blinked blue under Aidan's skin, projecting a date to be replaced in a weak LED display. The doctor nodded, made a note. He glanced over the image of Aidan's genome the monitor had recorded from skin cells, checked the pulse reading, made a note on his battered tab and removed the monitor.

"That's a high pulse rate. Feeling stressed? Or is that a stupid question?"

Aidan snorted a little despite himself and forced his hands back into his lap. The medic's assurance that confidentiality was a high priority made him feel a bit better, but even mission files got hacked. If medical files used the same sort of encryptions, who knew whether or not they would get hacked as well, especially with the kind of crew on this base? But he knew better than to say that aloud. He wasn't going to let Damian see how afraid he was if he could help it.

"I just got assigned to the base with a sector record for the most disciplinary write-ups as my first command. Yeah, I'm a bit stressed."

The doctor looked away from him, studying the picture-perfect examination tray for a moment. "Well, we always were good at standing out. Now, are you alright with removing your shirt and undershirt so I can take a look at your lymph nodes and lung function?"

Aidan swallowed hard. Take his shirt off. Right. He knew the odds of anyone else seeing him undressed in the med bay were slim, but that didn't stop his stomach flipping over. The doctor lifted two needles longer than his hand out of a drawer, eying them. The things were huge, long and metallic.

"What do you use those for?" Aidan asked, not sure he wanted to know. The doctor sighed, setting the needles down.

"I don't use them. Alice knits on her down time. These are knitting needles. Why she leaves them in a medical drawer is something I'll ask her later."

"I-is Alice likely to come in while we're doing this?" Aidan asked, tripping over the words in an effort to get them out.

"I have my assistant doing other work today. She won't see you. Relax." the doctor stated.

Aidan's discomfort must have shown on his face, because Damian folded his arms and said, "What I just told you about medical confidentiality, Commander? I meant that. And you're wasting time. Either you take the shirts off or we stare at each other all day. Your choice."

"The last time I got promised confidentiality, I got my ass beat because the secret got out," Aidan muttered, carefully looking away from the doctor's creepy cybernetic gaze.

Damian's brow rose, making his ocular implants whir as the skin and muscles moved around them.

Aidan repressed the urge to wince at that expression. Great, now the guy was pissed. Or disgusted. Or something. He'd been on this base less than twenty-four hours and he had already pissed off the logistics officer, the personnel officer and the munitions officer. His heart hammered in his chest. Add the doctor to the list now.

If Damian was pissed, would he keep his secret, use it as leverage, or just let someone with more violent tendencies take care of the problem, like the trainee at his base before Sector? Should he just jump the gun and ask Magnum for a transfer? It was stupid to think he could do this, anyway. But he could feel the doctor's gaze on him and words forced themselves out of his throat, small and strangled. "Sorry. Just… stressed."

"First of all, I'll repeat myself," Damain stated. "Secrets don't get out with me. Nobody hacks me on this base. They know better. Secondly, this crew is ten levels of stupid and I've treated them for more prank-related injuries than I like to think about, but nobody here is that kind of an asshole. And thirdly, if you think you're the only one here with problems they're trying to work through, wake the hell up. With respect."

Aidan passed a hand over his face, carefully counting out his breaths to try and calm himself down. Most of the Dusters had issues, but issues like this? Was Damian certain no one on this base would turn him in for a Corps bounty or blow his brains out? What was the easiest way out of this?

"Look. I'm sorry. I'm just new here. And with everything, I-Trust doesn't come easy."

The doctor stared at him for a long, long moment. The silence added weight to his words when he broke it. "You're right. It doesn't come easy. But you need to be aware that it doesn't come easy to the people on this base, either. Check the enlistment and duty dates. Most of us never had a commander aside from Taylor. Now Sector Personnel has sent us two bastards in two months. And you haven't given us any reason to trust you yet."

He placed an oddly gentle hand on Aidan's shoulder in response to the unconscious jerk of Aidan's back. "Now, I'm not saying you won't. But this is the situation you've got. I think you should know that, before you give yourself a panic attack or something. You've got sixteen people in various stages of the grieving process, and that's been aggravated with the interim commanders. This is not about you. This is bigger than you. I know Magnum. I know he wouldn't have overridden the Sector personnel officer and assigned you here if he didn't think you had a fighting chance. Understand?"

Aidan slowly looked up. The thump of his heart in his ears sounded deafening in the quiet of the med bay. But, beyond the unnerving implants, Damian seemed genuine, and concerned. In fact, the doctor seemed to be saying that he wanted to be on Aidan's side. Aidan licked his lips.

"I guess you'd know better than I would."

"Yeah. I would," Damian agreed, his voice flat, but the hint of a smile on his lips. "The question is, are you going to listen to me?"

"It's the least I can do if you're going to keep my secret." Aidan smiled, a little wobbly, and pinned his hands between his knees to hide their shaking. "How are you going to get the testosterone on the req lists without raising eyebrows?"

The doctor shrugged dismissively. "Hypogonadism is written into your official records. And our requisitions division has only failed to get me what I needed twice in five years. You can relax. You'll get what you need. So, are you going to take off your shirt, or are we going to waste the rest of the day memorizing each other's faces?"

Aidan closed his eyes and took a deep breath. He wanted to get this exam over with, and he had to trust someone on this base if he was going to survive. Might as well be Damian. He yanked his shirt off in one smooth movement, then grabbed the hem of the compression mesh and carefully worked it up over his head.

It was a physical relief to be out of the binder, for a moment. The seams were really beginning to dig in too much. He'd have to find some way to get a new one. All the same, it took all his self-control not to fold his arms over his chest to hide his breasts.

The medical officer's gloved fingers ran quick and professional over Aidan's throat, under his armpits, down his spine. Then he grabbed a stethoscope and pressed the cold circle of metal against Aidan's back.

"Deep breath. If you have any other medical needs, now's the time to ask questions. And get to that debrief you were supposed to be giving me, maybe."

Aidan waited until the stethoscope had left his skin to clear his throat. Medical needs? Yeah, he needed a new body. But considering what the conservative Corps did to people who performed transition surgeries outside Zoncom and TechoCo territory and the short leash the permissive Corporations kept their specialists on, the people who did that kind of work were almost impossible to find. He hadn't found anyone, anyway, not even someone who could get rid of these damn breasts. Damian wouldn't be able to help.

But according to Commander Magnum there were people who could do the work on his body that he needed. It had been the promise that had gotten him into Command training: serve as a commander, try it for at least a month, and you'll get the procedures.

It had been a hell of a carrot. He'd had to bite, to find out if it was true.

One month. He just had to get through one month.

The only thing Damian could give him, he didn't want. He had convinced Magnum he didn't need psych treatment on top of the transition meds. He wasn't going to blow that by making Damian think he was too anxious to do his job. He could handle this. He just had to calm the hell down. Focus on the debrief. Right. "Yeah. I was just looking for a rundown of your department. Things you need, anything I can do to help. That sort of thing."

This time, Damian looked up, surprise wrinkling his brow. Again, the barest hint of a smile twitched his lips upward. "You can get dressed now. How closely did you read that record-breaking disciplinary list?"

Aidan shrugged a little and reached for his binder, eager to get covered again. "I started skimming halfway through."

"Well, read a little more closely. A lot of those write-ups are for stimulant abuse. A few more are for concealing medical injuries and conditions that degraded performance. I wrote most of those disciplinary actions." Standing, Damian stripped off his gloves. "I hate writing those things. What I need is help cutting down the number of write-ups I need to fill out. That's where you come in."

Aidan pulled the binder back on and adjusted his breasts under the rough mesh, ensuring they flattened down as much as possible. "How can I help?"

"You can help me watch out for people doing their best to work themselves to death," Damian replied wearily, "because they will. Watch for twenty-four-hour work days. Watch for the martyr act when our supplies get low. More than one of the crew will decide to save rations by eating and drinking less. And more than that, you need an understanding of what you're seeing.

"You need to understand that the people here are trying to cope with psych trauma, and they don't do it well." Damian tossed his gloves in a bin without looking. "Lazarus and his cousin, Yvonne, handle it by pulling pranks. Janice and Kevin handle it by working nights and biting off heads. I can keep listing symptoms, but you get the idea. You're not seeing insubordination. Well, you are. But it's a symptom. What you're seeing is psych trauma in action. You'll help everyone if you remember it."

Aidan pulled his shirt on over his binder and spent a few moments fussing with the fabric to give himself time to consider that. Psych trauma? Was that what that memo had been? Just acting out because that was how Lazarus dealt with things? "And you think... He doesn't know, does he? About me?"

"Lazarus?" Damian gave a small snort of a laugh. "That's what raised your pulse rate? Laz's memo? Commander, if you take Lazarus seriously you'll give yourself ulcers in a week."

Aidan let his shoulders slump in relief. So, it had just been a joke in poor taste. Lazarus hadn't meant anything. He was still safe. He had still screwed up with Kevin, and the situation was still far from ideal, but at least he didn't have to worry about getting cornered and beat up or worse. That was something. "Thanks."

"Just doing my job, sir." The ocular implants whirred again as Damian studied him. "Going back to your earlier question.

Taylor hated his first name, but he always called us by ours unless somebody was in the shit. Then they got their full names read over the loudspeaker. I like keeping that up, if you're comfortable with it. And what title do you prefer? Commander? Headly?"

"Aidan's fine," he assured with a weak smile. It was a name he'd chosen for himself. Might as well put it to good use. And maybe not being the commander all the time would help the base feel more comfortable with him. After all, the interim commanders had all been rigid with their chain of command. It looked like the Wildcards needed something a little different.

Damian nodded, giving Aidan the first honest smile he'd seen on the man as he reorganized his tools, which had been pretty well organized to begin with. "Aidan it is, then. And I meant what I said about the sense of humor around here. Don't take it seriously, and don't take it personally. I've gotten glued to my chair and somebody left a plastic toupé and a pair of eyeball sunglasses they printed outside my door last week. Basically, welcome back to middle school."

Aidan relaxed a little more and let his smile grow more genuine. Damian really was in his corner. Maybe he could make this work after all, with at least one ally. "I appreciate the advice."

The man shrugged, closing his tools in a cabinet. "No problem. And, in fact, the toupé doesn't look that bad either. Of course, I'm still going to make Yvonne regret the day she was born for that one." The medical officer nodded in the direction of his door. "I think we covered everything. I'm done if you are."

Aidan almost grinned. He'd made it through the exam without issue, and he seemed to have actually won over the medical officer. That was one part of the day that had gone better than expected. He slid off the table and held his hand out. "Damian? Thank you."

For a moment, the bony man studied him. Then he took the offered hand and shook. "Thank you for exceeding my expectations. Do me a favor and keep doing it."

"I'll try." Aidan wasn't sure how he was exceeding expectations when the day had been one big clusterfuck so far, but, if Damian thought he was doing alright... Well, maybe this post was still salvageable. He just had to hope he kept from putting his foot in his mouth for the rest of the day.

"By the way, who're you meeting with later?" Damian asked as he switched off his tab.

Aidan glanced at his own device. "Looks like the hydroelectrics specialist."

The lean man snorted, deliberately not looking at his new commander. "Good luck with that one."

The tone of his voice made Aidan's stomach lurch. Maybe he'd started the celebration a bit too soon.

Damian's words echoed in Aidan's mind as he shuffled down the hallway, hands in his pockets and head down. "Good luck with that one." What was that supposed to mean?

He knew Janice Danvers, the hydroelectric specialist, was the worst of the worst as far as disciplinary write-ups on the base, but she hadn't actually hit one of the interim commanders with a wrench, had she?

Aidan groaned. For a moment, he dug his fingers into his forehead, using the pressure to remind himself to keep breathing. He was a commander now, damn it. He could handle this.

Footsteps sounded down the hall and Aidan straightened with a jerk. The last thing he wanted was one of his new subordinates seeing him freak out like this.

The people who turned the corner were worse than he'd expected: Damian's younger siblings, Dilly and Donny, twelve years old and the only non-combatants who had gotten themselves on the official disciplinary rosters.

The two pre-teens were chattering happily over something in Donny's hands. For a moment, Aidan was certain they'd just walk right past him and he could slip by unnoticed.

Then Dilly looked up, and her dark brown eyes went wide. She elbowed her twin brother hard and they both stopped walking, staring at Aidan as if he'd just threatened to eat them.

Aidan did his best to smile. He was only thirteen years older than them. This shouldn't be that difficult, right? It wasn't like anyone had asked him to babysit.

He still couldn't believe there were kids here. Most bases as involved in Grid runs as the Wildcards had some sort of policy in place to send kids up to R&R bases until they hit sixteen. No kid should have to grow up on the front lines of a sixty-year war that wasn't stopping any time soon. But leave it to the Wildcards to break the rules.

"Uh, hey," he managed.

Donny quickly shoved whatever he held in his pocket and saluted with his free hand. The motion was crisp and quick, as if someone had been giving him lessons and he was eager to show off. "Commander Headly, sir!"

Aidan almost winced at the military emphasis in the kid's voice. God, it was as bad as the base his dad used to command, where you had to salute by the age of five. Donny was non-com. No kid his age should sound like a seasoned soldier.

All the same, Aidan forced a smile and a return salute. "At ease. Um. Don't let me keep you."

Dilly studied him for a long moment, then lifted her chin defiantly. "We're not going to be bullied by you."

"What?" Aidan blinked at her.

"You heard her," Donny said just as emphatically. He gave Aidan a look reminiscent of one Damian had given him just moments before, mild irritation and disbelief. "Laz said you were stupid, but not deaf."

Aidan raked his fingers through his hair. What the hell was going on? Lazarus, the same guy who'd make a crack about putting him in a dress, had told the twins that he was stupid, too? He really had to have a talk with this bastard, whether or not these pranks were the coping mechanism the doctor had them down as.

But he had a more immediate problem: two kids who looked dead-set on causing trouble. Of course, he had to run into another crisis on his way to the most intimidating debrief on his list. Why had he hoped the universe would give him a few minutes to decompress beforehand? Maybe he really was stupid.

"Look. Dilly. Donny. I have no idea who's told you what, but I have no intention of bullying anyone. Okay?" Aidan took a breath and let it out slowly. He squared his shoulders, trying to look more in charge than he felt. "My job here is to make sure everyone can do their jobs to the best of their abilities. That includes the two of you."

Dilly rolled her eyes. "We don't have jobs."

Aidan opened his mouth to remind her that they had the Duster educational programming and optional vocational training on their tabs, but the squirming in Donny's pocket distracted him. He closed his eyes and ran one hand over his face. "What's in your pocket, Donny?"

"Nothing!" he said, even as he clamped his free hand over the moving fabric. After a moment he tacked on, "Sir!"

"I can see it moving." Aidan gave the twins what he hoped was a stern look and folded his arms. "What is it?"

"We're not going to be bullied by you!" Dilly repeated, half-shouting it this time. She grabbed her brother's arm and ran, yanking him around Aidan and down the hall.

Aidan whipped around to try and stop them, but they were around the corner before he got their names out. He closed his eyes and leaned against the wall. On top of everything, now he'd have to keep his eyes out for some sort of small animal, assuming the twins didn't accidentally squash it or run some sort of experiment on it.

Didn't Dilly's file say she was learning to help Damian in the med lab?

God, he hoped whatever they'd caught didn't have rabies or something. Making a mental note to ask Damian to reprimand his siblings for him, Aidan hauled himself back on track, tugged his uniform shirt straight, and continued the long walk to the hydroelectric specialist's office.

The door was cracked open when he arrived, allowing a long string of muttered curses in an oddly affectionate tone to slip out into the corridor. It almost sounded like the woman was talking to a pet. Crap, not another prohibited animal he'd have to deal with. Please, let it not be another animal.

Aidan sucked in a breath and cautiously tapped on the doorframe. "Specialist Danvers?"

Janice Danvers' voice yelped the most creative curse Aidan had ever heard and metal clanged. A moment later, the wiry woman ripped the door open and demanded, "D'you got any goat-fucking clue what'd happen if I slipped with the soldering gun on the photoelectric plate? We'd be fucked to high heaven! Those things ain't handed out like fucking candy, and what the hell does a closed door mean to..." She paused, pushing up the heavy welding visor she wore. Her spine straightened and she cleared her throat. "Oh. Commander. Uh. Need somethin'?"

Aidan cleared his throat and tried not to feel too proud of himself for standing his ground. The hydroelectrics officer was tall, muscled, and the streak of oil on her cheek looked like a well-defined bruise. He could believe she had actually hit someone with a wrench. Hell, he'd believe it if someone told him she fought in the Dissolution Riots. She looked like she could have held her own way back then.

He cleared his throat. "Got time for your debrief? I know I'm running a little late."

"Got work t'do." Janice folded her arms. "Make it quick."

"Mind if I come in?" Aidan glanced meaningfully at the room behind her. He didn't particularly want to hold a debrief meeting in the hallway, but he wasn't about to trespass in her space without permission. Not with her record.

Her eyes narrowed just a little. For a long moment, she glowered at him as if that could scare him off. Finally, she nodded once and stepped back to allow him entry.

"Don't touch nothin'," she added in a thick American AgCo accent that turned her words into a drawl. "All this shit's fragile, 'specially if you don't know what the fuck you're doin'."

"I'll keep that in mind," Aidan promised, shoving his hands pointedly in his pockets. He stepped inside and nearly choked on the thick air smelling of rain, hot metal and sweat. How the hell could she work in here? It had to be the hottest room on the base. Clearing his throat again, he awkwardly lowered himself into the one empty chair he could see. "Right. So. Let's get to the point. What can I do for you?"

Janice remained near the door, leaning against the wall. The same emotion Aidan had seen so often today flickered over her face for a brief moment—pleasant surprise mixed with wariness—but was quickly replaced by what seemed to be a baseline scowl. "You cannot tell me how to do my fuckin' job, for starters."

Aidan nodded and, after a moment of hesitation, decided to risk a joke. Maybe that would keep her from pulling out any makeshift weaponry. "That's what you're here for, isn't it? To do your job so I don't have to."

"Try tellin' that to the other asswipes they sent us." Janice snorted, giving her head a shake. She studied him for a long moment, then tipped her chin toward the door. "If there's nothin' else, I got to get back to work."

Aidan chewed the inside of his cheek as his mind kicked into gear. He couldn't let those be the only words he had with her. Sure, there was time to get to know her on a personal level later, but he needed to make sure he had her trust as a commander if he was going to make this work. Which meant he had to spend more time with her, figure out what was happening, and keep his desire to get out of this room from overcoming him.

He glanced around the hot room, taking in the cracked solar panel on one of the workbenches, the tangle of piping that covered one wall to the ceiling and the array of tools arranged neatly on every flat surface. In the back of the room, the hydraulic pumps that pushed water through the base's plumbing, the water purifiers, central air filter and all the mechanisms that kept their recycled water drinkable and their base's atmosphere livable rumbled and clanked to themselves.

"Actually, would you mind walking me through some of your work? I'd like to understand the challenges we have here, see if I can do anything to help."

The older woman tipped her head, thick black ponytail falling over her shoulder as she studied him. After a long, tense silence, she snorted.

"You serious, boy? I ain't never seen a commanding officer give a shit 'bout plumbing before. 'Sides shoutin' at me to do better."

"Way I see it, it's suicide not to care about the plumbing." Aidan smiled weakly. Work was a safe topic. After a day full of screw-ups, he'd finally started to realize that the way to make a good impression was to show interest in the way this crew worked together. Best way to avoid getting hit with a massive wrench.

Hopefully. "If we're not paying attention to drilling groundwater and storing electricity, we're dead anyway, one way or another. I'd like to give this base a fighting chance, and that means making sure you have everything you need to do your job well."

Another long silence enveloped the room. Janice's eyes narrowed a little, sharpening the webs of lines in the corners. Finally, she nodded slightly. "Let's see what you got, I guess."

Aidan didn't even have time to respond before Janice was inundating him with information about the groundwater drilling and water reclamation, the bots and valve sensors that monitored water quality and cleaned out pipe blockages, the solar panels, storage batteries, and all the other bits and pieces that provided their base with consistent plumbing and power wherever they moved. According to Janice, it was all quick to disassemble and move when the crew trekked to a new base site every few months, but that only made the systems more complicated to Aidan's eye. He only understood a quarter of what she told him, but he got the important parts.

The Wildcards were constantly under threat of two things: detection and water shortage. Aidan had thought the water restrictions were bad on his former base, but it was worse here.

They were too close to the Denver Metro Grid to drill wells for any length of time. Their water reclamation was pretty amazing when it was properly supplied, but when it wasn't, you could only recycle the same water so many times through failing filters. According to Janice, the system was usually out of something.

Aidan took notes on his tab about equipment she wanted in an ideal world, processes she needed Sector approval for, and all the little irritations she listed off.

Janice paced as she talked, stroking piping and tools as if they were prize cats. Every now and then, Aidan caught her staring at him as if she were sizing him up and his shoulders would hunch a little before he forced them to straighten. He was commander, he reminded himself. He was just trying to get a feel for his base. He was doing the right thing.

When Janice finally trailed off half an hour later, the file of notes sat at six pages long and Aidan's head spun. Everyone else he'd debriefed with had given him maybe one or two simple, hesitant requests, but Janice had apparently thrown everything she had at him.

He glanced up from his notes at the sudden silence and the feeling of eyes on him. "Is that all?"

For the first time, she gave him a smile. Or a smirk. It was hard to tell. "Shit, your eyes only glazed over twice. Gotta say, I'm impressed, boy." She coughed theatrically. "'Scuse me. Commander."

Aidan switched his tab into sleep mode and slipped it into his pocket in a weak attempt to cover his surprise. He'd impressed her? By listening and taking notes? What kinds of assholes had Sector Personnel sent this base before? No wonder the Wildcards were so suspicious. He still wasn't sure he could actually bring them back to fully functional, but if just listening to his crew was going to impress them, he had a bit more hope.

He cleared his throat awkwardly as he stood. "Aidan's fine. I'm not so big on titles."

That earned him another long, appraising look. Janice folded her arms and leaned against the wall beside the door frame. Her smile faded into a stern expression that made Aidan wonder if he'd said something wrong.

"Before you get cocky, let me tell you how this is gonna go. You seem to got more brains than the other chicken-fuckers they sent us, so maybe you'll get it. I'm an engineer, see? I talk straight. I come to you once a month and tell you how we're doin' on water and power. If it's shitty, I tell you how much we got to use for how long, what parts I need, an' why. You don't tell me to look harder for water or get higher efficiency rates outta the shit we use for photoelectric cells. You understand that if it's bad enough that I'm comin' to you, I done every damn thing I know how, and trust me, Aidan, that's everything you can do.

"You don't tell me to do a better job. You don't act like I sit in my chair diddlin' myself 'til it's quittin' time, 'cause I ain't even got a quittin' time on this job. I'm working 24-7 to take care of this base.

"In return, I don't lie to you." Janice held his gaze as if daring him to look away. "I don't tell you we're doin' fine when I know we're in shit up to our eyeballs, just 'cause I don't wanna deal with your whiny ass screamin' in my ear like a two-year-old. You're straight with me. I'm straight with you. You understand that, we're gonna get along just fine. That gonna work or do we got a problem?"

Aidan blinked as the tirade ended. A slow, awkward smile spread across his lips. "Janice, honestly, that's exactly how I want this base to run. I trust you to do your job to the best of your abilities, and you trust me to help you however I can. You tell me there's a problem, and we work to find a solution."

She studied him one more time before jerking her chin toward the door. "C'mon. Reckon it's about lunchtime. Let's get you somethin' to eat."

"Sure." Aidan stood and smoothed his uniform jacket, making sure it lay as flat as possible. Something about the way she looked at him made him feel exposed. Easier to focus on that than wonder about the sudden change of topic. "Anything else you want to talk about before we go?"

"Figure I talked your ear off enough for one day," Janice said with a throaty chuckle. She pushed off the wall and motioned for him to go first. "Go on. I got somethin' to grab from my room first."

Aidan realized she was trying to get rid of him and smiled weakly. At least she hadn't threatened him. He'd take it. "Yeah. Right. Thanks for your time, Janice."

The older woman gave him a dry look. "You were doin' good," she remarked over her shoulder as she followed him out of her office, shut the door and turned away. "Don't start sounding like a condescendin' pissant now."

Aidan's stomach dropped. Condescending? He had meant it to be polite! Had he just ruined any progress he'd made? He swallowed a mouthful of anxious bile and forced himself not to watch Janice's retreating back. Running his hands over his hair, he turned toward the canteen and hoped he could make it through lunch without too many problems.

Event File 7
File Tag: Comestibles
Timestamp: 12:45-4-2-2155

In the canteen, Kevin took his customary seat on the bench between Yvonne and Topher and listlessly considered his lunch.

The protein patties and reconstituted vegetables looked slightly less soggy than usual, but Kevin still wasn't certain what sort of veg it was supposed to be. He amused himself by considering the question. The mash of green and orange could have been broccoli and carrots, or sweet potato and asparagus. Not that it mattered. It would taste like sour cardboard regardless.

After nine years out in the Dust, one would think he would have adjusted to the awful food, but he still unconsciously compared it to the fresh produce his parents had always had on the table. And good God did it fall short.

He really had to requisition something better than this.

Anything better. But how? Only the CPS Standard Ration Allotment shipments were monitored so loosely by American AgCo and its subsidiaries that they were easy to recode out of existence and steal.

He'd tried for fresh produce before, and it had been a massive mistake that landed him and Yvonne both in the med bay. So how—?

Yvonne elbowed him in the ribs just as he managed to get his first bite situated on his plastic fork. "We supposed to salute or something?" Kevin glanced up as he was yanked out of his train of thought.

Commander Headly—no, Aidan—stood awkwardly in the doorway, looking like a child uncertain if he should intrude on his parents' conversation.

The analogy made the corners of Kevin's lips twitch up. If the commander was that uncomfortable with the idea of intruding on his subordinates' time, maybe their debrief hadn't been a fluke. Maybe Aidan really was a decent human being.

"We're off-duty," Kevin replied quietly, shrugging. He shoved the forkful of mushy vegetables into his mouth. They barely required chewing. "If he wants us to salute, he'll say something. Unless he does, enjoy dinner."

Yvonne snorted.

"Yeah, right," Topher grumbled, stabbing his protein patty disinterestedly with his fork.

Kevin gave a long-suffering sigh and adjusted his glasses. "I know, I know. It was the best I could land this month. Have some pity. I'm eating it, too, aren't I?" He did his best not to watch Aidan skirt the edges of the room toward the long table that operated as a serving area between the dining table and the kitchen.

"Hey, Sarah," Yvonne said in a voice just loud enough for Kevin to hear. "We should start the betting pool up. Five to one odds on Kev jumping the commander's bones next week."

"Yvonne! Must you?" Kevin groaned, knowing the conversation would keep going no matter what. Yvonne, her cousin Lazarus, and her wife Sarah had been playing this game with him since he'd arrived a decade ago, teasing and encouraging him about what passed for his romantic life by turns.

The game never really changed, much to his chagrin.

Sometimes he wondered if he was the only one of their quartet who'd really grown up. The Three Stooges had just gotten older and better at their pranks.

Sarah giggled and slung her arm over her wife's shoulders. "Nah, three to one. Did you see that blush last night?"

"There's betting?" Lazarus asked as he slid into his seat on the opposite side of the table, an extra protein patty on his tray in place of the reconstituted veg. "Who're we looking at?"

"Kev and the commander," Topher snickered.

Lazarus turned a huge grin on his base mate. "Awesome! If he's busy with your ass, maybe he won't try to bust mine every—"

"Will you lot shut up?!" Kevin hissed, glaring at the three of them. "The new commander does not, in fact, need to know I'm unconventional on his second day, thanks."

Sarah rolled her eyes. "Oh, drop the Morality Laws crap Kev. The term's 'gay as hell.' You can say it. Besides, he's seen me and Yve already. He's not Corporation."

"Yeah, he's a human being, with, like, normal reactions," Yvonne added. "You can tell Corps kids, they've got faces like plastic dolls and a sign that says 'your ad here' behind their eyes. This guy won't care that you're—"

"Commander Quinn did care, if you recall," Kevin interjected, words pointedly clipped.

Yvonne grinned wickedly. "Yeah, well, we got rid of him for a reason. And this guy's nice. Besides, when was the last time you got your system debugged? That technical specialist eight months ago? You're overdue."

Kevin gave her a look over the rims of his glasses at the euphemism. Since his last boyfriend had decommissioned from the Force and gone Fringe, he'd made a habit of finding some cute guy for a night among the visiting specialists or the bases he occasionally helped out on, once every six months or so. It did help take the edge off.

Unfortunately, once they'd realized that he had a timetable of sorts, the Three Stooges had started calling it 'debugging his system' and the damned phrase had stuck.

"I hate you sometimes," he muttered.

Sarah draped herself over her wife and blew him a kiss. "Love you, too."

Kevin slipped his glasses off and turned his eyes to the ceiling in exasperation as the conversation continued around him. He could feel the blush creeping up the back of his neck.

Damn his pale skin. If he could tan, he wouldn't have such an issue with these warning-beacon blushes. But Cavanaugh Corporation had always liked its top people and their families to have a certain look, and, thanks to skin cells that produced their own zinc oxide sunblock, he was stuck with skin the color of cream. Lowered chances of melanoma weren't much use if he died of mortification one of these days.

Or, for that matter, if his base family ever caught on to the reason he was so damn pale. His life would basically be over at that point as well. They wouldn't take well to learning he was a Cavanaugh executive's son. Let alone which executive.

Heaving a sigh, he shoved the old fear back down where it belonged in order to focus on the present disaster. At least he didn't fit Yvonne's description of a Corporation kid. "In all seriousness, everyone, do me a favor and don't start meddling. I'm not idiotic enough to make a pass at a superior—"

"Hey, Joker!" Janice's voice cut through the chatter in the canteen like a gunshot.

Lazarus's shoulders hunched automatically, his face twisting in an expectant wince. Kevin replaced his glasses and resigned himself as best he could to a shouting match.

If Liza was the elder sister in Kevin's base family analogy, Janice was the crotchety base aunt. A member of the Wildcards since she was a teen, the older woman encouraged shenanigans if they suited her agenda, but she steamrolled anyone whose behavior wasn't good for the team.

Kevin had been scolded by her vitriol-laden tongue more than once for being reckless, finicky, sullen, or a nuisance. He'd arrived at sixteen, and, since being sixteen mainly consisted of being reckless, finicky, sullen, and a nuisance, he'd gotten more than one lecture peppered with curses. But at least she had always pulled him aside and berated him privately. If Janice was yelling at someone in public, she wanted the entire base to know what they'd done, and she had a point to make.

The wiry hydroelectrics specialist stalked forward and slammed a dark bottle on the table beside Lazarus hard enough to make everyone jump. She leaned down, one calloused hand on Laz's shoulder, and spoke loud enough for the entire canteen to hear. "Saw your message this morning. Nice move, asshat."

"What'd I do? I just—" Lazarus began, but Janice cut him off. "You just *nothin'*. Since when was it cool to prank people who didn't do nothin' to you? Talkin' about stickin' the commander in some goddamn dress 'fore you even know if this one's good or not. Cut that shit out!"

Considering he'd grown up with Janice, Laz ought to know better, Kevin reflected. But he always did try for the self-defense clause. Which, generally, only made things worse for the spectators. The munitions man's voice sounded thin and downtrodden after Janice's. "C'mon, Janice, it was just a joke. Commander won't make it here if he can't take a joke."

"He's not gonna make it if you keep fuckin' with him, neither." Janice smacked the back of Laz's head, and Kevin winced in sympathy. "This one's got some brains where all you got is balls, so quit bein' a fuckwad. You get me?"

Kevin blinked, shoving his glasses up his nose with one finger. So, Janice was defending the new commander? That was a change. She'd practically led the rebellions against the last two idiots Sector had sent them. What had Aidan done to earn her trust?

He glanced at the commander, who was frozen wide-eyed beside the serving table, questionable vegetables dripping from the spoon. Kevin blinked. The man looked... frightened.

"What'd he do, eat you out?" Lazarus asked bitterly, which earned him another smack to the back of his head.

"What'd I just say about not bein' a fuckwad? He listened, dumbass. Which's better'n you bunch of fucking kindergarteners." Janice straightened, taking her bottle with her. "All I'm sayin' is give him a chance, for fuck's sake. Lay off unless he deserves a goddamn wakeup call an' then I'll give it, got it?"

"But Janice—"

"And another thing. This rum bottle had a hell of a lot more in it last time I checked. Did you—"

Kevin shook his head as the tirade rambled on. Shoving one more forkful of so-called food into his mouth, he slipped off the bench while everyone else's attention was on Janice and Laz.

Someone had to tell the commander to close his mouth before one of the more mischievous members of the crew noticed. Carrying his tray so he looked like he might be grabbing seconds—God forbid—he slipped to the long table and cleared his throat delicately.

"Excuse me, sir."

Aidan visibly stiffened, and nearly dropped the serving spoon.

He turned, blinked. "Oh. Um. Kevin. Hi." "Hi." Kevin gave him a small smile.

Now that he was over here, he realized he should have figured out what he was going to say beforehand. One simply did not approach a superior officer to tell him to stop gawping. Of course, Yvonne's teasing didn't help either. The heat of embarrassment was still burning the back of his neck, threatening to spread across his cheeks. Damn it, he was a logistics officer. He bluffed his way past ZonCom personnel and EagleCorp security contractors three times a week. So why did this have to be so unnerving?

"Can I help you with something?" Aidan asked. He seemed to realize then that he was still holding the serving spoon and returned it to the bowl as if it might be explosive.

Kevin adjusted his glasses in a weak attempt to hide his nerves. How did he get himself in these kinds of situations again?

An indignant squawk from Laz drew his attention to the table for a moment before he looked back to his commander with a nervous smile. "Ah, no. I just thought I'd... well, congratulate you, I suppose. Janice doesn't start shouting for just anyone. Her opinion carries a great deal of weight in this neighborhood."

"Thank you?" Commander Headly looked uncertain if this was a good thing or not. He shifted his weight, rubbed the back of his neck, and very pointedly looked away from the table full of Wildcards behind him as he managed to finally get a spoonful of vegetables on his plate. "I'm just grabbing dinner, then I'll be out of everyone's hair."

"You could join us, sir," Kevin suggested. Maybe that would help solidify the foundation Janice's lecture had put in place. Taylor had always eaten with the crew until he'd gotten too sick. Then they'd all cram into his quarters to eat together more often than not.

The other commanders had all ordered someone to bring them meals in their office, refusing to even fetch their own food for fear of fraternizing too much with the troublemakers. But Aidan was here, looking like a lost dog begging for scraps, and Kevin couldn't help but offer for both their sakes. Spending time with the gang off-duty might help start building bridges. Start working toward saving his family.

Aidan lifted his head and studied Kevin's face.

Kevin's breath caught and he fought down the urge to blush again. Why did the most gorgeous man he'd met in a year have to be a commander? He cleared his throat and pushed that thought very firmly away. "If you'd like, sir. There's plenty of room."

"Aidan," the commander corrected quietly, turning back to arranging food on his plate. "If you don't mind."

Kevin could have kicked himself. First name, damn it. He'd forgotten again. Habit would trip him up. He'd always called Taylor "sir," and before that, he'd called every man older than him in the Corporation 'sir' except his dad. Forgetting that training was not going to be easy.

He pushed his glasses up again to hide the momentary pause. "Sorry. Habit. But you're still welcome to eat with us. With Janice on your side, no one's going to bother you. Tonight, at least."

"I'll pass," Aidan said without looking up. "Maybe later in the week. I've got too much transfer paperwork to finish up."

"I see." Kevin swallowed a sigh. He hadn't realized how much he'd wanted to see the man eat with them. The refusal felt like a punch to the gut. But why?

Socratic method, he told himself. *There is a reason for every reaction.*

Why was he reacting like this? Because he'd been imagining what Aidan might look and act like when he finally relaxed. And because the man looked lovely and lost.

Kevin would have rolled his eyes if he'd been alone. He really needed to focus on the fact that the man was the new commander, a superior officer. Unobtainable. Verboten. Taboo. *Trouble.*

He opened his mouth to apologize, but three short beeps over the intercom beat him to the punch. A chorus of tab alerts shrilled around the room, underlined with a digitized shout of "Oh, shit, it's the fuzz!" from Laz's device.

Kevin's heart leapt into his throat. The drone proximity alarm.

Above them, a search-and-destroy ViperDrone was within firing range. If they had been detected, the bombs would start falling any minute now.

Event File 8
File Tag: ViperDrone
Timestamp: 13:10-4-2-2155

In one instinctive motion, Kevin grabbed Aidan's arm, pulled him around the corner into the makeshift kitchen and shoved him under the stainless steel counter. He wedged himself into the remaining space, hunched over his drawn-up knees. The counter wouldn't do a damn thing to protect them if the EagleCorp drone over their heads did drop a bomb, but it was standard procedure to take cover during a proximity alarm unless you were of any use on the base's defenses.

Janice cursed long and hard over the sound of thumping boots and chairs scraping on the prefab floor. Her voice trailed away as she ran out of the canteen to make sure the white noise filters and slick tarps that defended them against the drone's sensors were up and working.

Kevin made a mental note to brush up on his slick tarp coding. At least then he wouldn't feel helpless every time the alarms went off.

It took him a moment to realize the ragged breathing under the counter wasn't his own. He looked over at Aidan. They sat with their shins pressed together, Kevin's feet awkwardly placed between the commander's.

He swallowed. He'd grabbed Aidan and yanked him around as if he was some fresh-off-the-Grid recruit. Some kid too clueless to know to run for cover when the drone proximity alarms went off. A kid like Kevin himself had been once. How idiotic could he get?

Wincing, he whispered, "Apologies for the manhandling, sir. I get a bit over-enthusiastic about the proximity alarms."

"Better than ignoring them," Aidan whispered back. He shifted, kicking Kevin in the process, and muttered his own apology. Kevin waved it away.

The exchange circuit on the power storage unit clunked as the base went into defensive shutdown, cutting all non-vital systems in order to bring the base's footprint to a bare minimum across the electromagnetic spectrum. The canteen lights flickered and went out, plunging the room into complete darkness. Baby Henrietta started wailing. Someone shushed her gently.

Kevin carefully pulled his tab out of his pocket and flipped it on. The soft blue light of the screen display was blended into a wash of light by the smears on his glasses. Swallowing a curse, he balanced the tab on his knees and squirmed until he could pull the cleaning cloth he carried out of his breast pocket. He wiped the lenses and squinted at the tab screen through them, trying to see if he'd actually cleaned the blemishes. No luck. Another round of wiping cloth against plastic.

At least it was something to focus on beside the proximity to Aidan and the distant thwap of the drone's rotor blades. He smiled distractedly in Aidan's general direction. "Damn things never stay clean…"

"Is the eye injury too new for surgery?" Aidan asked, his voice barely a whisper in the tense quiet. "How long do you have to wait?"

Kevin didn't look up from polishing the lenses. The question was an old one. The surgery argument had been going on since his eyes had started acting up. Damian had tried to wheedle him into it more times than he could count. But his nearsightedness was one of the few truly human flaws he had after the genome sculpting Cavanaugh Corporation had done before he was born.

A man in a Cavanaugh Corporation board room had presented a standard for human perfection, other men had voted on it, and Kevin and three generations of children before him had been shaped by those hands. His parents had managed to get away with the minimum of genome optimization in his case. They'd gone so far as to falsify some of his medical paperwork to make sure his brain chemistry wasn't part of what the Corporation altered. The imperfection of his eyes and the imperfection of his sexual preferences were side effects of an unaltered brain. Proof that he was more than a set of someone else's specs made to order.

He wasn't giving that up.

He supposed he ought to be thankful that his gene sculpting had been the result of decades of practice, unlike the offspring of the first test subjects. He'd read the history. In susceptible areas of the world, Cavanaugh had made deals with governments to set up The Beta Project. That first generation of genetically modified Beta Babies had been brilliant. But their children, the Gammas, had more often than not inherited the chaotic results of poor gene-splicing in their germline.

He forced himself to replace his glasses on his nose. No use dwelling on the irritating nature of his DNA. His commander had asked him a question, and he had a long-practiced response. Best to give it before the silence drew on too long.

"It's less of an injury than a personal quirk, sir. I'm a nostalgic aesthete, as the base is terribly fond of reminding me. I enjoy the pre-Dissolution look." He cleared his throat. "It doesn't impair my job performance, sir. Damian has contacts for me when I go on-Grid. Wearing those, I'm just another face in the crowd."

"I see." But Aidan's tone sounded like he didn't.

Kevin sighed and awkwardly tucked the cleaning cloth back in his pocket.

"Shut up, Kev!" Liza hissed from the other side of the counter. "You don't know if they've got sound monitoring on this one!"

"EagleCorp haven't used sound monitoring since they hit their own guys couple months back," Yvonne whispered down the wall.

"Could've started again," Liza protested.

"Shut up! I hear it!" Topher's voice had sharpened in the way Kevin recognized as the sound of the junior transport specialist trying not to panic.

A deeper hush fell over the canteen, broken only by the muffled wails of the toddler. The distant whir of rotary blades filtered down to Kevin's ears, growing closer. He fought the urge to hold his breath. It could be up to two hours before the drone was out of range again. He'd been through hundreds of these. But the knowledge didn't ease the tension between his shoulders or the pounding of his heart. This one could always be his last.

He shoved the thought pointedly aside. No use getting too worked up. Janice was watching the layers of defense tech, ensuring the base was hidden from the drone's sensors. They were going to be fine. They were always fine. They'd get through. If only telling himself that would allow him to breathe easier. If only he could stop the urge to move closer to the man beside him, just for the comfort.

Kevin drew a breath. Under the whir of the rotors above him, he could hear his base family breathing all around him. He knew that Yvonne, Lazarus and Sarah would be huddled together against a wall somewhere. Jim and Andrea would be hunched over Henrietta and Tommy. Damian would be curled up with his siblings, Donny in Alice's lap more often than not. Dozer would be sitting with Topher, pretending he wasn't comforting his young assistant and distracting him with car talk. Liza would be sitting with Blake's arms around her, the one time she allowed anyone to support her.

The way everyone paired off during raids had sent a pang of longing through him for years, only barely hidden by the fear. And now, for the first time in years, he was hiding with someone else. An attractive someone else. Who was his superior officer, damn it.

"Mom?" Tommy's tremulous voice quavered.

"Tommy, I heard you doing the Corporation Callout earlier. You did such a good job," Andrea's voice whispered in the dark. Kevin could hear the frantic cheer in her tone as she tried to distract her son. "Can you do it for me again?"

Slowly, Tommy's thin whisper chanted out the doggerel. The words shivered into the dark.

"NatBank buys us and ZonCom sells.
ArgusCo tells us where we dwell.
TechCo owns what we read and play.
AgCo decides what we eat today.
EagleCorp tells us to obey.
Cavanaugh drugs us to make us well.
But one day we'll ring the Liberty Bell.
And then all the Corps will go to Hell."

The buzz of the drone's rotors grew louder, until Kevin was certain it was flying right above them. The metal counter tapped against the wall. He did hold his breath then, his bottom lip between his teeth.

Aidan placed a hand over his own mouth, eyes squeezed shut. His knees tensed together, squeezing Kevin's. Kevin bit down harder on his lip. Hiding with this man had been a terrible idea. He should have known better than to put himself in such close quarters with a man who—an explosion neatly distracted him from those thoughts. The prefab walls rattled. Plastic dishes jumped off the tables. Henrietta's wailing redoubled, joined by quiet curses from several of the older base members.

Kevin worked his jaw to try to stop the ringing in his ears. Had the bomb hit the base? It certainly had felt close enough. But they were still alive. Must have been a lucky pot-shot. All the same, he pulled up the message app on his tab and sent a line to Janice, asking simply

Report?

While he waited for an answer, he glanced up at Aidan. The commander still sat with his eyes closed, hand over his mouth. He'd started to tremble. Drone flyovers were stressful for everyone, but did such a routine part of their lives really freak him out that much?

Carefully, Kevin shifted his tab on his thighs and reached to gently tap Aidan's knee and get the commander's attention. When those blue eyes met his, he smirked as best he could and made a show of extending his middle finger toward the ceiling and the drone still buzzing overhead. He rolled his eyes theatrically.

Aidan blinked, then slowly returned the smile with a weak one of his own as he nodded.

Kevin hesitated a moment, then pulled up the memo app, tapped out,

> Seriously hope this doesn't last as long as the last one—two hours of boredom almost killed me

and turned it so the commander could see.

Aidan's brow wrinkled in the flickering blue light. Then his smile strengthened just a little. He dug out his own tab and wrote a memo back.

> Longest I ever had was six hours. Bits of the tarp kept going out.

> Six hours? It's a wonder you survived.

Aidan shrugged with one shoulder as he wrote.

> I did. The base didn't. Buddy got me through. Having company helped.

> Good thing I'm here, then.

Kevin finished the message off with a winking emoji before turning the tab back around.

Aidan started chuckling softly, then clapped a hand over his mouth again to muffle the sound. He had to finish giggling before tapping out his next words.

Good thing I'm here, then. Yeah, weirdly lucky today, I guess.

The drone rotors grew deafening again and Kevin froze halfway through his response, glancing up at the bottom of the countertop as if he could see through it and pinpoint the location of the machine. He forced his gaze back down, carefully counting his breaths until his heartbeat slowed. He watched the minutes slide by in the top corner of his tab. Five. Ten. Twenty. Thirty.

The whir of the drone shifted erratically, louder and softer by turns, never steadying into a pattern. Finally, his tab vibrated and a base-wide message from Janice popped up on the screen.

It's fine. Bastard's heading out. Get off my ass, you paranoid gamma-brained turkey-fuckers.

Kevin let out a long breath and sank back against the wall. Of course, this had the unfortunate side effect of pressing his legs more firmly into Aidan's. He instinctively straightened up. That move slammed his head on the bottom of the counter. Bewildered, he rolled gracelessly out into the kitchen.

"All clear," Liza called into the quiet, relief palpable in her voice as the sounds of the drone faded into the distance.

Kevin reached down to help Aidan out from under the counter, his head throbbing from connecting with the metal. As the commander found his feet, something dropped from the ceiling to land on his shoulder. Kevin hadn't anticipated hearing his commander scream on the man's second day of duty. But life with the Wildcards was full of surprises.

Aidan hadn't meant to scream. He wished he could go back in time and clap his hand over his mouth before the sound had escaped. But the thing had landed on his shoulder without warning. It had claws, and his body had been pumping adrenaline since he'd gotten under that table. So now he'd screamed in front of his unit. Idiot!

"Sir?" Kevin's face looked washed out in the soft light of the tab screen, eyes dark and watchful. In the blue light, his red hair had a purple tinge.

Aidan had to bite his lip to keep from yelping as whatever was on his shoulder dug sharp claws into his skin, crawling down his back. He wanted to scrabble for it, but whatever was on him might have teeth as well. Plenty of things out here were poisonous.

"Something's landed on me. Um, you got a light?"

The power storage unit outside buzzed back to the life, followed by the canteen lights flickering on one at a time. By the time all the lights were on, Aidan could feel the gazes of the entire team on him. Just what he didn't need, looking like a panicking coward just when he'd started making positive impressions. Damn it!

"You okay, sir?" Liza asked as she inched around the kitchen counter. Her hand darted out and grabbed the thing from his back, yanking it off.

Aidan took a deep breath and glanced at what she'd grabbed. A lizard. It was a goddamn lizard. He could have kicked himself. "Yeah. Sorry. Just startled. Is everyone else all right?"

"For now," Liza muttered, glowering at the squirming lizard in her hand. Without another word, she spun around to face the rest of the base, holding the offending reptile high. "Okay, guys. I know Janice has kept the tarps up to date, and we haven't had animal issues in years. So, who brought a lizard in?"

Stiff silence filled the room, suffocating Aidan with unspoken words as people glanced at one another, glanced away, shifted. Kevin cleared his throat behind him. Yvonne uncomfortably glanced down at her tab. Then her eyes shot wide.

"Kev! Fuck, Ed's asking where we are!"

Aidan glanced between the specialist and the logistics officer as the man groaned.

"Shit! The timing! I should have thought!" Then the redhead was moving, jogging across the room, grabbing Yvonne and Sarah by their elbows as he passed. "Get geared up, we've got an ETA under twenty at seventy, if we can get away with it. I want us out together, that flyover was too close for comfort, make sure that—"

Aidan blinked as his logistics team moved and talked, completely ignoring him. What was this, and who was Ed? He didn't have any Ed on the rosters, and there hadn't been anything scheduled on his tab. What kind of commander didn't know what was going on with his own base?

"I'm coming," Lazarus added sharply, swinging around and loping after the trio. "If Ed got tracked again—"

"God forbid," Kevin shot back in clipped tones. "But not a bad idea. Let's get geared and—"

They were almost out of the room before Aidan managed to clear his throat. "Um, logistics?" He hated the squeak that came out. The logistics team kept moving. Aidan drew a deep breath, forced his voice to strengthen. "Logistics?"

The four people froze in the doorway. Aidan hurried across the room to join them as the rest of the base filed past, getting back to their days.

"So, who's Ed?" Aidan asked, and Kevin blinked as if he'd just woken up.

"Er, sorry, sir. Contact, sir. He's a Go Systems on-call serviceman. When the delivery rigs break down on the road, he's the one the local ZonCom outpost sends out to do diagnostics, but we contract with him to arrange breakdowns nearby. He provides us with his employee codes for opening the main door on the rigs, and we crack the shipping containers and share the takings with him. The missing goods from the trucks are blamed on Fringers crazy enough to live out here, scavenging the stranded rigs. We make sure to leave burn holes and tampered wiring behind us. He's arranged something great for us this afternoon, two trucks at once, but Ed will start to look suspicious if—"

"We waste all his time standing around talking, let's go!" Lazarus put in impatiently.

Kevin fixed him with an icy stare. "We have ample time to brief the commander," he stated, every word perfectly annunciated. Then he glanced at Aidan and gave a quick, tight smile. "Sorry sir. I'll go on this run, apologize to our contact and be back before sunset. With your approval."

Aidan stared blankly at the other man as his mind buzzed. He was supposed to command around here, and he didn't know the first thing about what his men were doing. Maybe this was a chance to fix that.

"No, I think I'll go," he suggested, wishing he sounded surer of that. "I'll meet with our contact and make the apology in person. He should get to know me anyway."

Kevin blinked several times. When he spoke, each word came out as if it was being carefully chosen from a shelf. "Ah, sir, that really isn't necessary. Commander Taylor's been leaving contact liaison to me for the last four years—"

Aidan wondered how long it'd be before he'd stop being compared to a dead man. He covered the thought with his best professional smile. "I understand that, and I'm happy to leave it in your hands, but I'd like to meet our Grid contacts in person and see how our logistics team works in the field." He kept his eyes fixed on Kevin, though he could feel the eyes of the other three people on him. *Don't look away*, he told himself. *Don't look away, don't blink, don't chicken out.* "Does that sound okay?"

Kevin was the one who looked away, glancing from the two women on his left to the man on his right with an expression that reminded Aidan of the lady who'd helped out with childcare on his home base wondering if it was safe to leave the kids to someone in training.

Then the man gave him a polite smile and a nod. "Of course, sir." He glanced down, touched his tab. "I just sent the requisitions list and the passphrase we use with Ed to your handle. I'll be ready for a debrief when you return if you'd like one, sir. You've got a three-hour window before the next low-level drone flyover, and the satellites are out of range right now."

Aidan felt his heart pulse in his throat, but he smiled back.

"One last thing. First names?"

Kevin closed his eyes for a beat too long to be a blink. "Right," he said with a quick smile. "I'll keep it in mind. Safe run, everyone. Better use the chill vests, it's a hundred and fourteen in the shade today." With a quick salute, he walked briskly away down the hall.

Aidan glanced at the three base members still watching him, blank faced. He smiled. "Well, I guess we better go."

He walked down the hall asking himself if he'd made the right decision as he read over the information he'd been given, but an odd sense of calm came over him once he was in the seat of the all-terrain bike. His layers of chill vest, slick poncho, gloves and helmet cocooned him, making it easier to breathe. Behind a helmet he didn't have to look anyone in the eye.

The microtube mesh flexed around him as he shifted on his seat. "Go," he murmured into his helmet mic, and the electric motors on the bikes sizzled to life, humming as Dozer hit the button to open the garage door.

The heat hit like a wall as they rode out, but Aidan didn't have a lot of time to think about that. Yvonne revved her bike and shot off, the other two right behind her, and he had to scramble to keep up.

The wide wheels of their all-terrains moved easily over the wiry grasses, sending up plumes of dust whenever they hit patches of dirt between the scrubby plants.

Aidan still couldn't believe how close they were to the Grid down here. They were still in the protection of the foothills, but there were hints of the city all around. They passed the ruins of pre-Incorporation houses. Their tires bumped over the crumbling remains of an old concrete walking path at one point, hints that maybe Denver Metro had been even wider in the days when this part of the country had been more forgiving.

Aidan had heard once that this place used to be called Golden. He could see why. The land rolled hot and yellow all the way to the smudge of the Denver Metro Grid on the horizon.

Finally, the grey band of I-70 came into sight, sizzling in the heat.

"Covering." Lazarus's voice crackled in Aidan's ear, and he watched the man and Sarah peel off in opposite directions above the road. Good. They'd set a perimeter watch and make sure the drop-off happened seamlessly. He and Yvonne continued down toward the shining white rig stuck on the side of the road, the baggage trailers attached to their bikes rattling.

A Go Systems delivery rig was a featureless white bullet of a thing on eighteen wheels, gaudy advertisements scrolling along its sides. But this one's advert panels were dead black, and a man was standing beside panels opened up in the side, toolboxes open at his feet.

"Spotting," Yvonne added in Aidan's ear. He nodded, then realized she wouldn't see the gesture.

"Right," he agreed. "Thanks Yvonne."

She stopped just uphill of the trucks, acting as a lookout for the interaction. So far, the team was really working well in the field, Aidan thought, feeling a little of the tension in his chest ease. Maybe what Damian had said was right. Maybe they really were a good crew dealing with personal problems.

He pulled up with careful deliberation and killed the engine, not wanting to freak the man beside the truck. Pulling off his helmet and setting it over the handlebars, he tugged the bike's little slick tarp over it and walked down the embankment to the road.

"Hi," he called when he was ten feet away. The man in the yellow jumpsuit looked up with a frown as Aidan came up.

"Okay, what—" He got a look at Aidan below the hood of his slick poncho, and stiffened.

"Man, I don't know you." The comment came out as a complaint.

"Aidan Headly, Commander. Just assigned." Aidan had been ready for this. Carefully, he held out his American star pin in one gloved hand.

The man gave him a disgusted glance. "Yeah? How far is it to Neverland?"

"Second star to the right and straight on 'til morning," Aidan parroted, repeating the phrase he'd read.

The repairman eyed him. "And which way's the wind blowing?"

Aidan blinked. "What?"

The man's shoulders stiffened, his weight shifting. "I said which way's the wind blowing?"

"East?" Aidan asked weakly. "I mean, look I've got the requisitions sheet from my logistics division, but there isn't anything about wind on it. Here, I'll show you—" He dug under his poncho for his pad, but glanced up at the sound of the man taking a step back.

"Fuck that noise, I'm out." Aidan's stomach clenched as the man bent and started packing up his tools. Fingers fumbling in his haste, he yanked out his tab. "No, look, here's the req, we're getting coffee, milk concentrate, fortified granola, protein powder and—"

"Man, do you think I'm going to buy an emailed req list and some stupid pin anybody can print?" the older man snarled, glaring at him. "I didn't do nothing you can pin on me, and I just got these rigs fixed. So, you can go back to your boss at HQ and tell him that I'm straight. And then go fuck yourself." Slamming his tools into his bags, he slung them over his shoulders, his old fashioned water-cooled vest whirring as his body heat rose with exertion.

Aidan stood frozen, mind racing. The guy thought he was a ZonCom investigator posing as a Duster to test him out for fraud. The guy must know there was a chance he was under watch, and he was paranoid. There was some kind of second pass phrase nobody had written down, nobody had told the new guy, and they were going to lose this gigantic shipment because of it.

Ed stomped to the side of the first rig and typed in the code that directed the vehicle to rev up and return to its pre-planned path, slamming and locking the panel with his employee pass card. The autonomous vehicle lumbered off the shoulder of the road and back onto the highway, already picking up speed.

Aidan felt his heart start to race. He had to do something. He had to do something now. They were going to lose all this food because he'd fucked up. He was going to fuck everything up.

Glaring at Aidan, Ed turned to the open diagnostic panel and started typing in the code that would turn the second Go rig back on and send it back down into Denver Metro, out of reach for the Wildcards.

Event File 10
File Tag: Reorganization
Timestamp: 14:20-4-2-2155

Aidan felt his chest constricting with panic. The first chance he had to prove himself in the field, he was going to screw up. Maybe nobody would die if they missed this shipment, but he was going to lose this chance to show that he was a decent commander, lose their respect and lose any chance he had to hit the ground running in his new command. Damn his luck!

He jumped at the sound of running feet and the yell behind him. "Ed! Ed, DON'T!"

Ed and Aidan both looked up as Yvonne came barreling down the rise, racing to stand beside them, her chill vest whirring as it cooled her down. She glared at the repairman. "Ed, you shithead."

The man blinked at her. "Yve, what the… How do you get to Neverland?

"Second star to the right and straight on till morning."

"And which way's the wind blowing?"

"To the place where the sidewalks end, asshole. This is my new commander, what the hell? Why'd you send half our shipment away?!"

Ed snorted. "You were late and he wasn't legit. Tell your new commander to get with it, because he doesn't know shit. I don't care how legit he looks, if I don't hear both pass codes I'm out of here. You know the deal."

Under her hood, Yvonne's eyes went wide. "Yeah, I know the deal," she managed distantly. "Sorry Ed."

The heavy-set man gave her another one of his disgusted looks. "Yeah, well, let's get this show on the road. I want out of the heat. Move your asses."

When he turned away, Yvonne glanced at Aidan. "Commander, I'm really sorry. We—"

Aidan swallowed down his panic. "We'll talk later. Let's get moving on the shipment."

They drilled holes with a handheld electric drill for the look of the thing, opening the rig, and Aidan and Yvonne loaded up their bikes with the boxes. Lazarus and Sarah took turns coming down to load their bikes as well, keeping one person on guard at all times.

Nobody said a word, but by their body language Aidan knew how his crew were reacting. Yvonne was contrite, but the other two were pissed. One more thing he'd have to deal with later.

Finally, they were loaded up, and Ed's share had been neatly loaded into his personal Go Car. He shot them all a glare as he closed the rig up. "Next time, get your shit together," he muttered, brushing past Aidan to enter the code and slam the rig's panels closed, locking it with his employee pass card. The Go Rig rumbled to life, moving off like a gigantic animal waking from sleep.

Finally, Aidan turned to Yvonne and Lazarus, meeting one glare and one contrite stare. He could feel a yell trying to claw its way up his throat. He fought it down.

"I should have been told that there was a second pass code," he stated finally, quietly.

Lazarus dropped his eyes, his expression still sullen. Yvonne wet her lips. "Sir, I'm just used to running these with Kevin. I didn't think about it."

Aidan drew a few deep breaths. "We lost half of that shipment," he stated, keeping his voice even with every bit of self control he had.

Yvonne dropped her eyes. Lazarus held Aidan's gaze with narrowed eyes. "She forgot, okay? Big deal."

Big deal? Aidan almost lost it right then. Yeah, it was a big deal. It was a big deal that they were leaving him hanging, that they had lost resources, that everything could have gone so wrong. What if the guy had really freaked and pulled a weapon? What if they'd lost him as a contact because they freaked him out?

But he forced that shout down too. He refused to be the kind of man who screamed at people.

"We'll talk about it at base. Let's get back," he stated quietly.

Yvonne nodded. Lazarus turned away without a word. Feeling the hollowness as adrenaline drained out of his blood, Aidan climbed back onto his bike.

"-complete shit show," he heard Lazarus's voice mutter in his mic as he pulled on his helmet. Followed by Sarah's sharp voice snapping, "Shut the hell up, Laz. We all screwed up okay? Drop it." Her blank UV-reflective helmet visor turned in his direction, and he heard her voice again. "Commander..."

"Let's focus on getting back to base," Aidan muttered into his mic. "We'll talk there, okay?"

"Yessir," the two women agreed in his ears.

"Yeah," Lazarus's voice grumbled. Aidan gritted his teeth and revved his bike.

Despite the heat, his hands were shaking when he pulled in, and he had to force himself to breathe steadily. "I'd like to see everybody in my office," he managed as the others pulled their helmets off, focusing on hanging up his gear in order to avoid looking at them.

Sitting behind his desk, he hid his hands as the two women took the available chairs. Lazarus opted for slouching against the wall. Aidan swallowed hard. How was he going to handle this? What would work?

Everyone was staring at him. He had to say something.

"Look," he managed finally, "I'm not happy about the screw-up with the unwritten pass code, but I'm not worried about that. What worries me is how we handled it after that. We're not helping each other by copping attitudes, getting pissed or blaming one another. So, how do we stop this from happening again?"

Silence blanketed the room for too long. Aidan realized that he was holding his breath only when his chest began to ache. It was Lazarus who finally broke the quiet.

"You can send the right people out to do their jobs," he muttered, loping out of the room and down the hall.

Aidan considered stepping out and demanding that the man come back, but he couldn't face it. Instead, he turned his eyes to the two women, noticing that Sarah had reached over and taken

Yvonne's hand. Damn, they were lucky to have somebody they could do that with.

"Do you guys think that's the best fix? For me to let everybody do what they're used to and stay out of it?" he asked, surprised by the gentleness of his own voice.

Yvonne looked away. "I'm the logistics specialist, sir. Not the officer. I'm just…" She fell silent, staring at her hand in her wife's.

Sarah glanced up at Aidan and managed a small smile. "We'll be more on top of it in future sir. Sorry."

Aidan sighed. "Okay. In future, we need to get this right. Dismissed."

Slowly, the two women stood and stepped out, moving as if they might break something on the floor if they trod too heavily.

For a moment, Aidan hid his face in his hands. But he didn't have time to indulge himself, not yet. Forcing himself upright, he wearily pulled out his tab and messaged the cook. Not long later the prefab floor creaked as Andrea stepped inside. "Um, Aidan? You messaged me?"

Aidan smiled up at the sweet faced woman. Finally, somebody who had listened when he asked not to be called 'sir' all the time. The little girl in her arms smiled at him, and he managed a weak smile of his own and a wave. "Hey, yeah. Sorry to call you up when you're busy."

"It's okay," Andrea replied with a smile, adjusting Henrietta as she spoke, "Jim's just working on something he needs to focus with, so I'm taking Hen. Can I help?"

"Yeah," Aidan pulled up their food supply report on his main console. "I was hoping you and I could talk about how to stretch our food supply. The requisitions you were expecting got cut in half." He tried and failed to keep the frustration out of his voice as he said the words.

To his shock, Andrea didn't so much as use a curse word. Instead, she sat down beside him and studied the readouts, handing Henrietta a teething ring to keep her amused.

"Okay, yeah. If we do the menu like this..." With one hand, she tapped the hologram, moving and reorganizing food prep plans with Aidan for half an hour. Soon they had a menu that was almost as full as it had been, and Aidan's chest expanded. They were okay. They were going to be okay.

He glanced at Andrea with a grateful grin, and she managed only a small smile in return. "They screwed up again, didn't they?"

Aidan felt his smile fade. "Um, yeah. Kind of. Yeah..." He glanced back at the screen, considering. Again. This had become what this crew did. Screwed up. Mistrusted one another. Blamed others for their mistakes. And Sector expected him to fix that? Where would he even begin?

The touch on his shoulder almost made him jump out of his chair. He turned wide eyes on Andrea, and found a wider smile this time.

"Things will work out better next time, Commander."

Aidan felt his stomach drop. Even the cook was trying to tell him it was going to be okay. He must really look hopeless. But he pasted on a smile. "Yeah. Thanks, Andrea. Feel free to get back to your day, and thanks."

"Sure," Andrea agreed with a nod.

For a few minutes after she left, Aidan stared blankly at his console. Finally, he shut it down and stood, turning away. It was already past seven, and he'd had enough. He couldn't handle any more.

Escaping to his room, he leaned against the door and let out a long, slow breath. Day Two: official disaster.

"Good evening, Aidan," Omi's automated voice remarked quietly in the room. "You have arrived later than I had been instructed to expect."

"Trouble came up," Aidan muttered. Turning, he glanced at the image of the girl keeping a pretense of sitting on the edge of the bed. Finally, he flopped onto the bed, grabbed a pillow and covered his face.

"I don't know if I can do this."

"My auditory equipment is not able to parse that comment," the AI's quiet voice replied.

Aidan had to chuckle at that. Shoving the pillow under his head, he closed his eyes. "I don't know if I can do this. Today was a complete clusterfuck."

The image of his sister leaned in, a smile on her digital lips. "Then we will analyze the issues and find solutions to improve tomorrow."

Aidan shook his head, sighing. "I wish it was that easy." There was a modulated chuckle. "It is only your second day. There is a saying. Third time, lucky."

Smiling weakly, Aidan forced his eyes open. "Third time, lucky. Yeah. Maybe."

Event File 11
File Tag: Failure To Report
Timestamp: 19:45-4-2-2155

"Guys?" Kevin almost ducked back out of the rec room as the blasts of noise slammed into his ear drums. On screen, holographic cars rammed one another off the track.

"Aw, you gamma bastard!" Sarah wailed in her seat between the two cousins, waving her joystick so her car barreled into Lazarus's racer and pushed it off the other side of the simulated road.

"Guys?" Kevin repeated, raising his voice, "Can you turn it down? Logistical question!"

"Ever heard of off-duty?" Lazarus called as his car sideswiped Yvonne's into a tailspin.

"Yes, actually," Kevin shot back lightly. "But I can't achieve the blissful state until I finish my mission report and turn it into Sector. Five minutes guys, have pity."

Finally, Yvonne glanced back at him, smiled weakly and waved her joystick down. The game froze on screen, and three blank faces turned his way. Kevin's eyebrows rose.

"Something wrong? It really won't take that long. I'll be out of your hair in a jiffy."

"It's all good!" Sarah replied, but her voice was too high, too false.

Kevin eyed her cautiously. "Right. Well then, why did half of Ed's delivery get removed from our requisition tally? I never got a report from anyone, hence my gracing you with my presence."

Stepping inside, he dropped into a cross-legged seat on the floor, hands on his tab and eyes on his friends. "Did Ed get spooked by our tardiness and send a rig off before you arrived?" he asked solicitously, mind already lining up comforting words. *It isn't your fault. Drone flyovers happen. I understand. We'll be fine.*

But Yvonne, who usually looked him in the eye when she was eager for absolution, picked at her fingernails. Kevin's heart fell. That was not a good sign. "We... kind of screwed up," Yvonne admitted quietly, leaving her nails alone and beginning to poke the escaping stuffing back into the ancient blue couch cushion.

On the other side of the couch, Lazarus snorted. "We did fine. He screwed up."

"Which he?" Kevin asked patiently, though he was afraid he already knew the answer.

Lazarus stared fixedly at the screen. "The guy tells you to stay home. He drags us out there, fucks over the pass codes, loses us half a shipment, and now he's blaming us. I'm telling you, man, he's an asshole."

"Care to explain that a little more thoroughly?" Kevin tried to hold Lazarus's gaze, but the older man wouldn't look at him.

"Like I said, he fucked over the pass codes."

"How exactly?" Kevin asked. He glanced from Yvonne, back to picking at her cuticles, to Sarah, staring at Lazarus. He wasn't looking at anyone.

A leaden fear crept up Kevin's spine and curled around his brainstem. "You didn't tell him the secondary pass code. Did you?" he stated woodenly.

It had seemed like such a good way to reassure Ed, promising him a second pass code that no one would write down. If it wasn't written, it couldn't be hacked. But it could be forgotten.

Silence. Kevin pulled off his glasses and massaged the bridge of his nose between finger and thumb. "You morons," he added wearily.

The couch creaked as Lazarus jumped to his feet. "Hey, Kev, don't land this on us! You're the officer. You're the one who always does these contacts! Yve forgot was all. Lay off!"

Kevin raised his head, giving the other man a squinting look composed of one part nearsightedness and two parts annoyance. "And no one reminded her?"

"Who made that my job? If he doesn't know what he's doing, how's that my problem?" Lazarus demanded, opening his mouth to say more until his cousin touched his hand.

"Laz, chill." Yvonne glanced at her officer, smiling weakly. "Sorry, Kev. Really."

Kevin sighed. Slipping his glasses back into place, he ran a hand through his hair. "Tell me someone explained the situation to the commander and apologized."

"For what?" Lazarus demanded, self-righteous to the last. "We didn't order the guy who knows what the hell is going on to stay home, and we weren't the ones who thought we knew everything about everything! He's the one who fucked up. He can live with it."

Turning away, the munitions officer flumped back into his seat and turned the game back on, viciously racing his car down a holographic open road.

Kevin's gray eyes narrowed. Slowly, he stood and stepped to the couch. With the precision of a machine, he took the controller out of Lazarus's hand and shut the game down.

"Hey!" Lazarus glared up at him in bewildered anger, "I didn't hit a save point!" Then he met Kevin's eyes. Whatever else he'd been about to say died on his lips.

"You may want to fuck over our last chance to stay together as a unit," Kevin stated into the quiet, "and that's your prerogative. If you want out, apply for a transfer. But, if you want us to stay together, do everyone the courtesy of borrowing a crowbar and getting your head out of your ass, because the longer you act like a petulant plebeian neophyte, the greater chance we run of being disbanded. Examine your priorities."

Lazarus sneered. "Cut the school principal shit, Kev, I'm older'n you. You want somebody to kiss up to the guy, you do it." Grabbing the controller back, he turned the game back on and resolutely fixed his eyes on it.

Anger burned up Kevin's throat. He turned away stiffly before it escaped him and stalked out of the room. "Idiots," he hissed under his breath. "Immature jackasses. All of them."

Disgusted, he slammed open the door of his room, kicked it shut and almost slammed his tab down before common sense overrode the instinct. He dropped with a sigh onto the bed as the rage began to ebb. Overhead, his scrounged ropes of soft-light LED swung with the force of the door's slamming, making the lighting flicker. Even the painting displayed on his wall screen juddered fractionally.

Kevin drew a long, slow breath. He had to get himself under control. Pulling off his glasses, he set them on the packing crate he'd rigged as a nightstand and covered his face with both hands. He'd almost punched Lazarus. The boy who'd taught him how to handle a manual truck after he'd spent a lifetime with Go vehicles. The eighteen-year-old who'd comforted a sixteen-year-old he'd found sobbing in a closet on the younger boy's third day in the Dust and never breathed a word. The man who'd helped to keep Kevin from running himself into the ground when he'd failed everyone and Commander Taylor had died.

One of his best and oldest friends. He'd nearly punched one of his oldest friends.

How had they gotten to this point?

"This is not going well," he muttered to his empty room.

There was a tentative tap on his door. He forced himself to straighten. "Yes?"

The door opened on Topher's nervously smiling face. "Uh, hey, man. Heard you going down the hall…"

Kevin gave a quiet bark of laughter. "My, I'm getting indiscreet in my old age." He glanced up, nodding in the boy's direction. "Come in if you want to. Shut the door."

Carefully, Topher took a seat on the edge of Kevin's bed, staring at the screen on the opposite wall rather than the older man's face. The simulated painting's colors reflected gold in Topher's black hair.

"Laz and the girls being dickwads again?"

Kevin sighed. "That obvious?"

Topher watched as the screen changed paintings. "Where's that?" He asked idly.

Kevin glanced up, and smiled at the painting full of color and light. "A hundred or so years ago, that was a café on the Colfax Expressway. It used to be Colfax Avenue, did you know?"

Topher gave an incredulous laugh. "The Shit Strip? People used to hang out there?"

"Before Incorporation, sure. Before they turned it into a four-lane highway. Suppose they had to, with all the migrants from the Coasts coming inland." Kevin glanced at his base mate with a tired smile. "Granted, it had a bit of a reputation, even then."

It was so easy to see the fourteen-year-old boy who'd arrived on their base clutching his small duffel bag when he looked at the twenty-year-old. Kevin still remembered how much he'd felt for the younger boy. He'd arrived in exactly the same way. Parents dead, still shivering with the shock, barely holding it together. Trying to be brave.

And here they both were, both still trying to be brave. About to lose another family. The thought was a little sliver of glass in the guts. Wearily, Kevin gestured at the screen. "You know, we're supposed to be out here fighting to bring that back. But, some days, I wonder if that's achievable. Especially when we're so preoccupied with ripping into one another." Glancing at his hands, he sighed. "I almost punched Lazarus tonight."

"Good!" the junior transport specialist exclaimed. "He could use it. He's been a dick since Taylor…"

For a moment, the room was quiet. Then Kevin shook his head. "Toph, Laz and the ladies are the closest thing I've got to siblings. They kept an eye on me when I was placed on Base. They're essentially the reason I survived when I got out here. But lately it feels as if…" He sighed, shook his head once more, then reached over to lift Topher's favorite fedora hat off his head and meet his eyes. "Are you doing okay? If I'm this frazzled, I can only imagine how you're feeling."

Topher gave him a dour look. "Kev, don't do that."

"Fair enough." The older man replaced the hat, which made the younger roll his eyes.

"I mean don't try to take care of everybody else so you don't have to think about you."

"Was that what I was doing?" Kevin asked, blinking theatrically. "I never would have guessed."

Topher did an encore performance of his eye roll. The screen flicked to a new scene.

"Where's that one?" Topher asked quietly.

Kevin studied it. "Old Union Station. Used to stand at the end of Sixteenth Street downtown."

"Where all the fancy CES level trains come in and all the EagleCorp Security buildings are?" Topher asked, wide eyed. "Damn. They sure wrecked that place. Freaks most people out just looking down Sixteenth, with EagleCorp sitting there." He gave a quick twitch of a shudder.

And no wonder, Kevin thought. After all, that was where Topher's parents had died in custody. Where Cavanaugh Corporation had made Kevin's parents' deaths look natural, EagleCorp had splashed the news of Topher's family's capture and killing all across the news feeds, branding them as terrorists. Kevin still wasn't sure which was worse. "It was people who wrecked the place, though," Kevin amended quietly. "Not the Corps. The station got burned down in the Dissolution. Eagle just stepped in and used what was left when things fell apart."

Topher kept his eyes on the painting. "Wish it was that pretty now."

"Me, too," Kevin agreed quietly.

For a few heartbeats, man and boy sat in silence. Topher drew a breath. "So, what's going to happen?"

Kevin shook his head. Raising his eyes, he studied the painting as he spoke rather than looking at Topher's face.

"Right now, I don't know. But just in case, Toph, keep an eye out for a base you like."

Topher shifted beside him. "Yeah, but. . . I like it here."

Kevin closed his eyes. "Yeah," he agreed quietly. "Me, too."

Event File 12
File Tag: Goods Acquired
Timestamp: 2-4-2155/ 4-3-2155

For a long time after Topher left, Kevin sat on his bed, watching his wall screen cycle through its images. Around him, the base settled into sleep. His base. His family. People he loved, for all their vices.

People he'd failed. Again.

People who were going to be hungry because he hadn't stood up to the new commander and insisted on his place in the field. He should have explained his contact with Ed and its precarious nature. He should have demanded his field position. But then the commander had turned and looked at him and…

And he'd caved. And they'd lost half a rations shipment. His fault.

Silence slowly crept in to fill the rooms. And then the clock read midnight, and the base was still. Moving with care, Kevin reached under his bed and lifted out a black bottle. The white pill fizzed as he slipped it under his tongue.

His fault. His responsibility.

As the StayWake began to tingle through his blood, Kevin stood at the tiny sanitation station in his room and put in his contacts, glad the prescription Damian had worked up for him was still printing well out of their 3D rig.

He turned and silently slipped out into the hall. He could feel the focus coming into play as the drug went to work. The movement of his muscles smoothed out until he moved like a precisely tuned machine, his reaction time halved. The painless tightness settled in behind his eyes as the cocktail of modafinil, dopamine and norepinephrine precursors kicked in.

Sliding the door of his office open as soundlessly as he could, he brought up his screens, entered his password and his biometrics, and sat down to type.

By one in the morning the first half of Kevin's work was done.

Pocketing the data card his console extruded, he shut it down and headed out.

Exiting the garage was the noisiest part of the whole affair, but Kevin had learned how to get around that little issue. Opening the maintenance door for the building's air filtration system, he slid himself and his bike carefully past the humming air filtration unit, wary of snagging his slick poncho on the whirring machinery behind the unit's casing. Then he was out into the warm night air, closing the door softly behind him. Walking his bike a thousand feet away, he glanced over his shoulder, the world made green with the night vision built into his helmet visor.

No movement. Clear.

The bike's electric motor sizzled into life.

Kevin rode for an hour and a half, his wide all-terrain tires eating up the uneven ground. He heard his destination before he saw it: a low buzz as the harmless yellow-and-white delivery drones of the Sunshine Company, one of American AgCo's subsidiary brands, buzzed their way out to make their deliveries and buzzed their way back for restocking and recharging.

It had always reminded Kevin of ancient pictures of beehives.

Conveniently located in what looked like the middle of nowhere by American AgCo to ensure delivery drones had less distance to go when crossing the Rockies, it was fairly convenient for Dusters too, providing that the Duster in question was clever and extremely careful.

Kevin met those specs. After all, Cavanaugh had put good money into training him. He'd started learning the basics of management for automated distributions centers in preschool. Who was he to let a good education go to waste? The thought turned his lips up in a sour smile.

Finally, the long shape of the delivery drone distribution center came into sight. Kevin drew a calming breath. Parking his bike outside the short range sensors' perimeter, he got it covered, flicked the night vision off on his HUD. He pulled out his tab, bringing up his tracker.

On screen, blue and red dots traced ellipses and circles within circles. Kevin studied the patterns. Good. He'd timed it well. The long-range security drones that trawled the Dust weren't due in this area for another four hours if they kept to schedule, and the Sunshine Food Delivery Center's own short-range guard drones were busy patrolling the warehouses.

Carefully, Kevin pulled the small black square of a signal box from his pocket. Calibrating it, he hit the button. He imagined he could feel the soundless blast as the signaller sent its code out across every frequency, exploiting a flaw in the warehouse compound security's diagnostic system. It would trick the compound into assuming it was in diagnostic mode for routine repairs and should ignore any human being crossing its sensor field or any breaches of electrical flow for the next two hours.

Kevin smiled thinly. Now for the interesting part.

Walking fast, he slipped to the smallest of the prefab block buildings, the windowless cube grey in the blue starlight. The door's key code pad gleamed black.

Kevin carefully pulled a grey disc the size of his palm out of the inner lining of his slick poncho, activated the handheld EMP, and pressed it to the key code pad. His skin tingled with the electric blast, and the tightness behind his eyes intensified.

The door clicked.

Stepping inside, Kevin wrinkled his nose at the blended scents of stale beer, unwashed clothes, unwashed man and hopelessness. He supposed he ought to be grateful that the security foreman left out here alone was happy to drink himself to sleep every night, but it was never easy to see the big man sprawled snoring in his chair in this tiny, single-roomed prison of a living space, so obviously giving up on life and on himself.

Kevin felt for the poor bastard. But that didn't stop him from stepping to the table and picking up his employee passkey card. He left the door slightly ajar. The man wouldn't wake enough to notice. He never did.

Speeding his steps, he jogged to the warehouse he needed, using the employee passkey card to snik the door open. He entered a clicking, whirring world of cold machines.

Overhead drones followed their programming, flying in through the entry dock and dropping into their allotted recharging stations in long shelves of cubicles. Slow-crawling StockBots moved on their treads, their automated shelving arms lifting the programmed boxes from the stacks on their carrier baskets and slotting them into the carrying nets hanging open beneath each drone.

On the far end, the conveyor belt from the Distributions Room delivered more packages. Kevin's breath puffed white clouds into the refrigerated air. He grinned. He hadn't dared to try this in months, not since he'd gotten Yvonne hurt, and himself for that matter.

But this would make up for his error in judgment then, and his cowardice today. A really amazing shipment would bring a smile to everyone's face. It'd be worth it.

Using the borrowed passkey, he slid into the Distributions Room. This time he'd planned ahead. This time, he was ready.

Boxes sat open in their carefully labeled grids all across the floor of the huge warehouse, the aisles around them trawled by StockBots fitted with manipulators that allowed them to fetch single apples or bananas without bruising them. One by one, the boxes were packed and sent to those who could afford them. Each grid section was labeled in orange letters four feet tall: CES Level. CSS Level. CAS Level. CPS Level.

Kevin's jaw clenched. Even here, even in a room no one was meant to see, people were segregated by their Citizen Standing Level according to the judgment of the Corporations who owned them. He knew without looking in the boxes that the quality in the Citizen Excellent Standing Level boxes would be exquisite. Those boxes of fruit and vegetables were being delivered to the homes of executives, the restaurants they frequented, perhaps for a snack in their air conditioned offices.

The squashed fruit, the diseased, the undersized or rotting would go down the row to the Citizen Poor Standing level boxes. In other buildings across this area, across this country, the same judgment call was being made on bread, meat, medicine, housing. Life.

American AgCo and every other Corporation checked and aggregated people's credit score and the Citizen Rating their corporation assigned them based on how closely they conformed to the standards for good citizenship in the Corporate Citizen contract their parents had signed the day they were born. Together, the aggregate numbers gave every citizen a Citizen Standing Score and assigned them a priority level for every possible amenity. Every corporation's standards for what constituted 'a good citizen' was different, but they had all agreed on the Citizen Standing System and what it would be used to do.

The bastards.

A slow, cold smile turned up Kevin's lips as he stepped to the wall panel. Well. Tonight, he could throw at least a small wrench into the system that ground people down. Only a small wrench, but enough small injuries could bring anything down. He could do his part.

He slid the foreman's card into the reader. The screen's holographic display fizzed into life, highlighting his hands in blue.

Welcome, Douglas Deaver.

The name sent its familiar pang through Kevin. A rare name, Douglas. His father's name. But this wasn't the time to think about that. Once he was in, he brought up the delivery schedule, clicked 'Make Correction Manually: Card Insert' and slid the carefully-tailored data card the new codes had been written on into the reader.

Kevin held his breath. This had been when it all went to hell last time. God, they needed a decent hacker on base to double-check his work. Since Peter had abandoned the fight to live a low-tech, nonviolent life on the Fringe they'd been barely getting by between his own middling coding and Janice's.

Not a time to think about Peter, either. If the screen turned red...

The blue screen flickered green.

Changes Made.

Kevin breathed out a long sigh of relief. "Thank you, Lord," he whispered into the privacy of his helmet. Twenty minutes later, the passkey card was replaced and the guard's house door closed, locking itself. Kevin was already driving.

It was nearly four in the morning when Kevin arrived at the drop point he'd entered. Killing the bike's engine and uncovering the bike trailer he'd hidden in a stand of rabbit brush, he lay down, crossed his arms behind his head and watched the sky.

The wind was blessedly cool. The night sky had taken on the clear blue that hinted at the possibility of dawn, stars pinpricks of cold fire. Feeling the world turn beneath him and hearing his blood coursing in his ears, Kevin waited.

The buzz began far off. Kevin's blood was loud in his own ears. He'd checked. He'd double-checked. But that could always be the sound of an armed ViperDrone.

Then he saw the shape, bright white against the stars. The delivery drone swooped gracefully low on its six whirring rotors, carrying net unfolding like a flower to drop a shining white box. And then there was another, and another, and Kevin threw his head back to the stars and laughed in delight as the boxes stacked themselves up at his feet.

It was close to six in the morning by the time Kevin carefully maneuvered his laden bike under the slick tarp and entered his base pass code. The temperature was already beginning to rise, and he breathed a sigh of relief as he brought the first stack of boxes down the stairs into the base cool. The thrill of what he'd just pulled off and the giddiness of the StayWake made him feel hyper-alive. "Bounce, bounce, nothing's gonna bring me down!" he sang quietly under his breath, rounding a corner with his bounty in his arms.

He almost ran into Liza, who was glaring at him.

Kevin grinned, hefting the boxes onto one arm and using his free hand to shove his flattened red hair out of his eyes. "Top of the morning! Fancy strawberries for your breakfast?"

Liza stepped close enough to Kevin that they were nearly nose to nose. When she spoke, her voice shook. "Where. The hell. Were you?" Her eyes narrowed. "Are you on StayWake? Your pupils are tiny."

"Ah, but my success was enormous," Kevin quipped, tipping his chin down towards his burden with a bright grin.

Liza stared at him for a long, long moment. Then she sighed and turned away. "I'm writing you up," she muttered wearily. "God damnit, Kev."

"Liza!" Setting down the boxes in the hall, Kevin took a few steps and touched his friend's shoulder gently. "Liza, I just—"

Liza whirled on him, her dark eyes gleaming with tears. "No, you didn't 'just', Kevin. *You fucked up!* You went on a run without informing anyone. You could've fucking *died* out there, and we never would've *known*. And you're hopping yourself up again. You're going to destroy your kidneys if you don't quit, and you don't give a shit at all. All you care about is getting something that'll make everybody grin and proving that you can do anything! Well, you know what? *You can't!* And when you fuck up, people *die*, remember? Last time you took a stupid fucking risk, you ended up in surgery and Taylor ended up *dead*, and...and..."

Kevin felt as if his muscles had frozen. Liza stared at him, her expression dropping from anger to horror in the blink of an eye.

"Kev," she murmured. "Kev, I didn't—I didn't mean..." When Kevin spoke, his words were unusually perfect in their pronunciation and totally uninflected. Even he thought he sounded robotic. "I know quite well what happens when I fail. But thank you for the reminder."

The tears brimmed over in Liza's eyes. "Damn it, Kev. Don't you pull this bullshit on me! You said you were going to be there to help me get everybody straightened out. I can't do this alone, but if you're going off pulling stupid shit, too...You said you'd—"

"I said I'd be here. I said I'd help hold us together. That's what I'm doing," Kevin stated with quiet precision. "And I'm standing right here."

In the breathless silence, someone cleared their throat. Kevin and Liza both turned sharply. The new commander was standing there, looking tousled, looking bewildered, and most definitely looking annoyed.

"Okay," the man began eventually, eyes moving from one face to the other. "Is somebody going to tell me what's going on?"

Kevin swallowed. Of all the times. And of course the man had to look as if he'd just rolled out of bed, still soft and gentle around the eyes with sleep, his blonde hair still mussed and catching the day-cycle lights in a faint halo. If ever Kevin didn't need to be distracted it was now, and the very man that he needed to impress was the distraction.

Kevin forced himself to straighten and cleared his throat.

"Sorry sir. Just a difference of opinion." Liza snorted.

Aidan studied Kevin's face. Kevin realized that his body was shivering subtly with the tail end of his dose. Terrible timing.

"Are you okay?" Aidan asked eventually. "You look kind of—"

"Just fine," Kevin interrupted brightly. "Just a little—"

"No, sir, he's not," Liza interrupted him, glaring at Kevin. "He's sleep deprived and high on StayWake. Again. With your permission, sir, I'm writing him up for abuse of stimulants and failure to follow procedure."

Aidan blinked. "Wait. Failure to follow—Did I miss something?" Liza poked Kevin hard in the chest. "This thrill seeking idiot just went on an unsanctioned run and got us a bunch of CES level supplies from somewhere."

"The words 'thank you' could have been inserted so easily," Kevin added dryly in Liza's direction, then glanced at Aidan and decided to shut up.

The other man was staring at him in a wide-eyed emotion he couldn't quite read. Then, to his surprise, his new commander covered his face with one hand. He stood like that for a long, long moment. Then Aidan sucked in a deep breath and raised his head.

"You want to explain this?"

Kevin swallowed hard. "It was my mistake that lost us half a supply shipment yesterday. I felt it was my place to rectify the situation."

Aidan's blue eyes held his for what felt like an eternity. Then the commander turned away. "I'll write the reprimand, Liza. Thanks. Kevin, get stuff put away. I understand that you thought you needed to do this, but going on a mission without approval was a totally unacceptable move."

"I understand, sir," Kevin murmured. He wasn't sure if the man heard him or not.

Feeling the thrill draining out through his boots, Kevin turned to do his duty. No, this was not going well at all.

"Okay, you're good!" Dozer shouted over the sound of the garage door rattling up. The jeep's electric motor whirred into life, sizzling under Aidan as he flicked on the vehicle's holographic HUD and pressed the go pedal. He heard the old jeep's AC rev up as he drove out of the break in the slick tarp and hard sunlight slanted across the machine's roof.

Aidan took a breath. Okay. Two hours out, meet with Commander Magnum for a first-week in person debrief and report, two hours back. Five hours. In five hours, it'd all be over and he could relax.

Five hours. He could do that. He could do that.

Couldn't he?

The jeep's all-terrain tires rattled over scrub grass and pebbly soil, sending a plume of dust out behind him that made Aidan glad Dozer had checked the surveillance drone patterns and planned a route for him. That dust looked like a banner in his rearview mirror. What if a random EagleCorp patrol saw? What if some Fringer desperate for cash bounties called him in?

"Stop it," he whispered to himself as the jeep topped a rise. "Just stop."

He hated this. He hated the paranoid scenarios his mind threw up when he was anxious, making difficult situations that much more terrifying.

"You're fine," he whispered. "Stop freaking."

And, yet, the idea of what he'd say in his report still made his pulse race. How was he supposed to make everything that had happened this week and everything he'd screwed up sound good? He'd completely screwed over a simple requisition run. He'd screamed because of a lizard, for godsakes. He was screwed.

His heart missed a beat at the sight of a rock he hadn't noticed and he skewed the jeep sideways, fishtailing on the loose soil. For a handful of frantic heartbeats, the world spun.

When the landscape steadied down, Aidan took a whooping lungful of air. Resting his head on the steering wheel, he listened to his frantic heartbeat. "Fuck."

Raising his head, he pulled out his tab. He had to get himself calmed down. Had to make this meeting in time and in a state to make sense. Had to make a good impression. If he was going to pull that off, he needed to get his head on straight.

Fingers fumbling, he typed fast as the holographic screen shuddered, trying to compensate for his jerky movements. The cooling fan began to whine in the tab's case as the holographic generator got to work.

"Hello, Aidan," Omi's digitized voice murmured gently. "How are things?"

Aidan felt the hysterical laugh claw its way up his throat. "How are things? My logistics officer is hot as hell and he's getting high, taking crazy risks and skipping out on procedure. My munitions officer is batshit crazy. My hydroelectrics officer and my medical officer both scare the crap out of me. I screwed up a req run that a first-year specialist should've been able to handle because nobody told me what the hell was going on, and my personnel officer broke down crying and screaming yesterday in front of me in the hallway and I think I'm going to do the same thing any time now. That's how things are. I'm screwed!" He dropped his head onto the steering wheel again. "I'm totally screwed."

The holographic generator eased into a lower pitch as the psychological health coach program worked. "Let's work through the points one by one," Omi's voice murmured gently. "You are worried because you don't think you did well on a requisitions pickup?"

Aidan sucked in three long breaths the way he'd been coached, forehead resting against the cool plastic. He unbuttoned the top button of the dress-uniform shirt he'd put on to see Magnum in.

"They had a second pass code with the contact as a safety measure. Nobody remembered to tell me about it. The guy sent the semi with half the shipment we were expecting away before Yvonne talked him around," he whispered. "Nobody told me. I didn't ask. And I lost us half a shipment. We needed that. I mean Kevin replaced it the next day, but if I hadn't screwed up... and the way he replaced them is a whole other problem."

Slowly, he raised his head, eyes closed. "Omi, they don't trust me. And all I did was make sure they keep thinking I'm useless."

"On the contrary, Aidan," Omi's soft voice stated, "I believe you displayed an important point. When they fail to confide in you, there is difficulty. When they cooperate, there is success. They will not forget. I believe you've increased their respect."

Aidan laughed softly. "I wish."

"Did you notice a change in their behavior after you spoke with them on the subject? Did you notice a change in behavior when you spoke with your medical and hydroelectric officers?" the modulated voice asked gently.

Aidan shrugged. "Yeah, I guess. Janice started smiling at me. And..." He considered his next words. "And she stood up for me in front of everybody in the canteen. I know she's supposed to be my subordinate, that it's not a big deal. But Kevin says she runs the show and, if she likes me, everybody else will listen."

That had felt good, hadn't it? Seeing Janice grin at him, watching her cuss out Lazarus and then turn to him and smile.

Smiles. The way Kevin had smiled at him yesterday... and the way that smile had faded.

"Aidan?"

"Yeah?" he asked into the whir of the air conditioning. "You should begin driving if you want to arrive on time. We can speak during the trip."

"Oh. Yeah." Blinking his eyes clear, Aidan brought the engine back to life and carefully maneuvered out of the long skid divots he'd left in the soil.

"Based on my information, I think your logistics and requisitions officer is right," Omi's modulated voice stated, "And, speaking of Kevin, would you be alright speaking about him?"

Aidan nodded slowly. "Yeah." "You are attracted to him."

Aidan nodded weakly. "Yeah, but it's my job to reprimand him when he disobeys."

"As you should, Aidan. You are protecting his life by deterring him from taking unsafe actions." The cooling fan kicked up to a higher pitch in the tab. "Don't think of it as yelling at someone you like. Think of it as protecting him from his bad decisions. That is what you're doing. You're protecting someone who hasn't realized that he needs assistance. Yet."

"Yeah, but if he ends up hating me for it..." Aidan sighed.

"Aidan, based on the man's records he is highly intelligent and socially aware. He does not appear to suffer from misplaced animosity. Running a behavioral algorithm of his previous actions, I believe he will take the admonition as constructive." The hologram's face flickered in a smile. "He may not obey, but he will understand your motivations. I have also run behavioral algorithms on the other three crew members you are concerned over. I believe you are succeeding."

Aidan shook his head. "That's just code."

"It is code that produces very accurate analyses," the hologram stated quietly.

Outside, the yellow grasses rolled away endlessly under the bowl of the hot sky. Aidan thought the words over for a breath.

Jackson had been an amazing coder, working with kickass programs he'd tried for a month to pirate out from under TechoCo. He knew he could trust this analysis. But his emotions just didn't want to hear it.

"You are doing well, Aidan," Omi's voice repeated. Aidan glanced at the representation of his sister, and felt himself smile. It might not be his sister, but it looked like her. Sounded like her.

Jackson had been right to use her image. He'd always trusted Naomi.

God, he missed her. Slowly, he breathed out. "Yeah. Yeah, I guess."

Aidan maneuvered down into a protected culvert between hills, the jeep's AC whirring in counterpoint with the tab. At this rate he'd sweat through the damn dress uniform.

"Aidan?"

"Yeah, Omi?"

"May I bring up another issue with you?"

"Yeah?" he asked, slowly easing the jeep between rock outcroppings.

"You must address your attraction to your logistical officer."

Aidan rolled his eyes. "Omi, I've got about a million bigger issues to take care of before I get to that. And I seriously don't need my jaw broke again."

"On the contrary, your repressed romantic feelings toward the man will constantly affect your interactions with him adversely. It will reduce your efficiency. Based on my algorithms, I doubt he will react unfavorably to your condition, but I understand how frightening this is."

Aidan snorted. The psych-coach AI program might be good, but it really needed more natural speech patterns.

The hologram cocked its head, the way his sister really had when she was making a point. "I suggest discussing the issue with him, or resolving it internally. My algorithm shows that the next month is the optimum time period in which to address this issue for the best psychological and morale-related results."

Aidan sighed. "Omi?"

"Yes, Aidan?"

"That'll be all. Switch off."

"Are you sure you intend your request? Was that sarcasm?"

"No, Omi. Switch off." Then Aidan was alone in the jeep. Whether it was an improvement or not, he wasn't sure.

Event File 14
File Tag: Debriefing
Timestamp: 13:00-4-8-2155

"So, how's it going with the base?"

Sitting in front of his Sector Commander, Aidan swallowed. "It's still a little... iffy, sir, but I think we're getting somewhere." Commander Mangum eyed him. Aidan kept his face neutral.

He'd gotten backhanded often enough for disrespectful behavior on his father's base to make it second nature to keep his face a bland mask under the eyes of a superior.

"Unh-hunh," the big man stated eventually. Bringing up the screen of his tab, he studied the readouts.

"Says here that you wrote up your logistics officer for abuse of stimulants and failure of protocol?"

"He took StayWake and headed out on a requisitions run without notification, sir," Aidan replied woodenly, staring straight ahead.

Commander Magnum sighed, his wide shoulders slumping. "I thought he was done with that. McIllian's too smart to be keeping up that crap."

Aidan shrugged. When the silence got too deep, he cleared his throat. "He said it was to make up for messing up with the earlier run—"

"And what'd you say to that?" Magnum asked, voice neutral. "I told him it wasn't acceptable?" He wished the statement hadn't sounded so much like a question.

Magnum raised graying brows. "And?"

Aidan could feel his chest grow tight with the words. And? And what?

"I felt a written reprimand covered the situation," he tried, his mouth dry.

Magnum stared at him for a long, long time. Then he glanced back to his screen and Aidan breathed again.

Slowly, the older man scrolled through the paperwork. "So, Peter Sayers never got replaced after his decommission. You're still missing a Technical Officer to take over your coding needs."

"Kevin and Janice divvied up the duties between them. They say they're stretched, but they've got it for now," Aidan supplied, watching the Sector Commander. What was the man thinking about all this? Had he screwed all this up already? "Do you think I need one?" he added carefully.

Commander Magnum cocked one dark eye at him. "Do you? It's your base."

Aidan froze for a moment, caught in the commander's gaze. Did the guy want the truth or a good soldier saying everything was fine? Would the truth help the base?

Finally, he opted for honesty and shrugged. "We're doing okay, sir, but it's not great. If you find somebody, let me know."

The heavier man nodded thoughtfully, scrolling to the bottom of Aidan's report. Shutting the screen off, he steepled his fingers and studied Aidan closely. "Does that answer go for all aspects of your assignment?"

"Sir?" Aidan asked, stiffening. Now what was the commander looking for from him?

"How are you feeling about your position so far?" Magnum clarified patiently. "I want you to level with me Headly. How's it feeling?"

Aidan tried to calm himself, but his breathing was already growing faster. How did the position feel? Terrifying, exasperating, bewildering, and so much more than he could really handle.

But there'd been those smiles too. There'd been Janice standing up for him. Kevin under the tables during the flyover. That had felt... good.

Aidan swallowed. "I'm still not sure, sir. I feel like... I guess I still feel like for every one thing I do right, I screw two other things up. And I don't think I'm doing the base members a lot of good. A lot of them just... aren't into having me around." "But you haven't asked for a transfer," Magnum pressed, his fleshy face pensive.

Aidan shook his head. "No, sir."

Magnum smiled slightly. "I'm taking that as a good sign. Besides, right now I've got a trained commander on my hands who doesn't want to be in command, and I've got an unorthodox base that doesn't want to take orders. Perfect combination."

"Sir," Aidan replied, not sure what else to say. Unorthodox. Magnum didn't have to remind him. These people were nothing like any base he'd been on in his life.

And what did Magnum mean, good sign? Of what, that he wasn't completely screwing up? Or that he hadn't broken yet? Or that he might actually pull this off?

Magnum leaned back in his chair, his smile a little wider. "Headly, I'm looking forward to the day when you realize you're actually good at this."

"Sir?" Aidan blinked. The man across the desk held his gaze. "We've had this talk before. I knew you were right for this the day I heard about what you did for your crew on Base 1446. I don't need people who want to be in command, Headly. I need people who do the right things and make the right decisions when the world's burning down around them. Because that's what's happening most of the time." One square brown finger pointed across the desk at Aidan. "And that's why you're a commander now."

Aidan did his best imitation of a polite smile, wishing his Sector Commander would quit repeating the same damn story like it was something amazing. Their water pumping unit had blown up. It had killed their hydroelectric officer and their commander and practically taken off the roof, shredding their slick tarp. And then everyone else had acted like a bunch of kids. The personnel officer who should have taken charge had gotten hysterical and insisted that everyone go to their rooms and stay there until he received instructions from Sector on how to proceed.

Aidan might have been only a Command Division adjunct who mostly did filing, but he had known, without a doubt, that the guy had lost touch with reality at that point. Sitting in their rooms with a downed slick tarp leaking their heat and electrical signatures out into the desert night was suicidal.

So, he'd done what he had to do. He'd called the guy out on his bullshit and told everyone to get into the vehicles and evacuate the fifty miles to the nearest viable base. And they'd done it, because it made sense. It hadn't been anything special. By rights, he could have been brought up on charges of insubordination, even mutiny. Yet somehow, it had landed him in this seat in front of the

Sector Commander, giving a report on the base he was responsible for. Maybe a quick drone blast would have been the easy way out.

"Thank you, sir," he managed eventually.

Sector Commander Magnum watched him steadily. Then his wide lips turned up in a smile. "You've still got a deal with me, right?"

"Right. Three more weeks," Aidan agreed wearily. He'd promised he'd give this crazy experiment a month, which meant he still had three more weeks, and he wasn't going to break his end of the deal that might—might—get him the surgeries he needed. It'd be worth it to look the way he felt. It'd be worth it to stop being afraid every single day. Wouldn't it?

The Sector Commander nodded slowly. "Okay. As long as our deal's still on. Seriously, Headly. Don't look at me like I killed your dog."

Aidan blinked. "Uh, sorry, sir. Didn't realize I looked that way." Magnum snorted, standing. "I'll see you again in two weeks, Headly. It'll be a better report next time, I assume. And I don't expect my commanders to wear dress uniform every time they sit down with me."

Aidan had to fight down the urge to laugh helplessly. How exactly was it supposed to be better? "Yes, sir," he managed to mutter, saluting weakly.

It was a long two hour drive back to Base 1407, too long. The empty land gave him no relief from his own thoughts. By the time he was back inside the base garage, he was almost glad, especially when Dozer pulled his head out of a half-assembled engine and smiled at him. "Heya, Commander."

"Um, hi." Aidan dredged up the energy to give the man a quick smile as he stepped out of the jeep and walked inside. Over his head, something gave a long, shuddering clank. Aidan jumped, glad that he was able to bite down the yelp he'd almost made when he heard the cursing overhead. Noticing the ladder further down the hall, he let out a long breath.

Okay. Just Janice. Nothing wrong. Then he had to smile at his own thought. It was probably the only time the woman had been thought of as 'just' anything.

"Hah! Gotcha!" the triumphant words echoed hollowly over his head, and he could hear her crawling down the overhead repair area. Then she was climbing down the ladder, wiping her hands on a rag. "Fucking dust storms, guys who designed this system oughta go suck tail pipe, fuckin'—" Then she glanced up from her hands and caught sight of Aidan. The older woman gave a wry smile. "'Lo. You look like somebody just run your dog over."

Aidan blinked. Then he chuckled, rubbing the back of his neck uncomfortably. "Commander Magnum said about the same thing. But I'm still standing, I guess. Do you want a hand with anything?"

Janice looked him up and down in his dress uniform, a smirk turning her lips up. "Not when you're dressed up so fine." Throwing the folded ladder easily over one shoulder, she turned away. "What I really want is somebody to take care of the fucking code work when Kev's busy, I got enough shit to do around here without fighting a computer for three an' four fuckin' hours a day on top of it."

"I'll keep it in mind," Aidan called after her, not sure if it was a good idea to follow her. She waved her free hand in response, but didn't try to continue the conversation.

That was a relief. Aidan didn't think he could take many more conversations. What he really needed was a way to turn his brain off for a few hours. He needed to stop thinking. Glancing down the hall, he turned his steps toward the rec room.

There wasn't much in there: a battered blue couch with stuffing leaking out of one arm, a vid screen, six games controllers in various states of repair and a dart board peppered with holes hanging on a wall that had a few more. Aidan flopped down onto the couch. For a moment, he let himself close his eyes.

What a week.

"Um, hi."

Aidan's eyes snapped open at the sound of the voice. His logistics officer was standing right beside the couch, staring down at him.

The redhead smiled. "This seat taken?"

Event File 15
File Tag: Disclosure
Timestamp: 18:00-4-8-2155

Kevin stared down at his commanding officer, his mouth going dry. The man blinked blankly at him. Kevin hoped he didn't look like a complete ass. He adjusted his glasses on the bridge of his nose, looking for a way to salvage this attempt at making a friendly overture. Why had he tried this? The man had already reprimanded him once this week.

"Er. If you were looking to relax, I can leave. Sorry, sir."

The commander blinked again. Then a smile slid into place as the man snapped out of whatever thoughts had been occupying him and spoke. "Wha—oh! No. I mean, it's the rec room. It's everybody's couch. Go for it." Sliding further down, the commander nodded at the space he'd left with a smile. "And it's Aidan, please. Especially when we're off duty." He tilted his head deprecatingly, making him look more approachable. "Every time you call me 'sir' I feel like looking over my shoulder to make sure somebody important isn't standing there."

Kevin smiled in relief and rueful amusement as he took the seat he'd been offered. "I felt the same way during my first commissioned year. Every time I received a message for the Logistics Officer I had to resist the urge to forward it to Blake's handle." Lifting his tab, he keyed up the TV screen with it. "Got a preference?"

The other man shrugged. "Anything that doesn't drop my IQ?"

Kevin chuckled at the small joke, flicking through the choices of available vid files. His expression faded into dismay. "Speaking of requisitions duties, I have got to get us some new material. Sector hasn't sent us anything new in months." Flicking past the pics for a handful of action vids, he grimaced. "If I have to see King Cobra or Death In Tulsa one more time I'll go play tag with a ViperDrone."

"Yeah, don't do that," Aidan added quietly, and Kevin turned his head at the tone.

The other man was curled into the corner of the couch, arms folded over his chest as if he was cold, watching him with thoughtful eyes. Kevin glanced away quickly.

"I'll have a talk with Sector and see what we can come up with," Aidan suggested into the quiet.

"Maybe I can pick something up when I'm requisitioning our new hardware," Kevin added for the sake of conversation, eyes on the screen.

"Yeah, I saw you were headed on Grid tomorrow." Aidan's voice had the forced cheerfulness Kevin remembered as part of his family's cocktail hours and house parties, the tone of people trying to classify one another through conversation. "I've got you signed off. Good luck?"

"Thanks," Kevin replied offhandedly, "I'm not worried about it. It's a simple enough pickup. All we're falsifying are the Citizen Cards we're buying with and the registration of the car we're using. I've done this kind of thing in my sleep."

Aidan nodded slowly. "Or without sleep, from what I hear," he added eventually as Kevin flipped through pics. "Kind of a lot."

Kevin repressed the urge to wince. He really had upset the commander—Aidan—with that unsanctioned run, hadn't he? Eventually, he cleared his throat. "I'm more aware of my physical limitations than Liza believes, but I did mean to apologize to you properly. I've gotten used to doing things with a certain amount of operational sovereignty in my division, and I realize that it can become an issue if unchecked."

The silence was absolute. Then Aidan wet his lips. "Um, I don't know what 'sovereignty' means."

Kevin did wince this time, smiling weakly. "Sorry, Comman— Aidan. I read old books and collect outmoded words. It's a bad habit. I meant, I didn't mean to circumvent—to go around you." He glanced at Aidan out of the corner of his eye, giving a quick smile. "I hope it won't be an issue going forward."

The man gave a wry twist of the lips. "If I don't have to write you up for unsanctioned runs again, it won't."

Kevin flicked his eyes back to the screen. Lovely. He was still on the commander's shit list. Just great.

Sighing, he put in his personal code and brought his own vid collection up on the screen. His collection slid by, many of the images flat and muted by comparison to what had been in the general collection.

The couch springs creaked beside him. "How old is that stuff?"

"Most of the fic vids are between a century and two centuries old. Mostly research, retro-technologies that we can use. The doc vids are current," Kevin lied absently, hunting the file he'd just finished pirating. He didn't watch vids from the days before the American Dissolution purely for research and everyone on base knew it. But the commander didn't have to find out what a sap he was just yet.

"In fact, this one on the history of medicine just came out on a British station last week. Looks interesting too," he continued thoughtfully.

The couch springs creaked a little more emphatically at that, and Kevin knew without looking that Aidan had turned to stare at him.

"How'd you get around the net blockages to get stuff from other countries?" Aidan asked, eyes wide.

Kevin shot him a sly grin. "Logistics. It's my forte as well as my vocation. Meaning that I know people who know people. There's a fairly informative section in here on the first vaccines."

With the commander's eyes on him, he scrambled to explain. "My mother was a British contractor working over here. I stayed in touch with a few people who used to get us vids on the sly after I Dusted. Damian and I have been trying to produce our own supply of several vaccines and a basic immunopotentiator, you see, and I'm really hoping for an insight in this vid that will help us improve our setup. If we could produce it ourselves, it could cut our dependence on Grid sources by twenty percent, at least, which could save somebody's life one day."

He smiled half heartedly, knowing he was babbling, but knowing just as surely that he couldn't stop now. "In ancient history, you know, it was discovered by trial and error. Someone got pus from a diseased pox lesion on themselves, and, presto, they were inoculated. Makes us take our medical bay a little less for granted, even as limited as it is."

The commander—Aidan. He really had to start respecting the man's wishes and using his name already—Aidan was looking at him as if he really wasn't sure what was going on at this point, the blue of his eyes intensified in the screen's glow. Kevin wished heartily that he didn't have that effect on so many people. Just once, it'd be nice to get more than an uncomprehending stare.

Awkwardly, Kevin set down his tab, feeling his rush of enthusiasm drain away. "I understand it's not everyone's interest, the hist vids. Really, I just came in for some downtime. Put on any old thing." Uncomfortably, he pulled off his glasses, cleaning them with the kerchief from his breast pocket. To his utter disgust, he could feel a blush staining his high cheekbones. Of all times.

Aidan's voice was quiet when he spoke. "Actually, I think the hist vid would be interesting. Uh, if you don't mind."

Kevin glanced up, blinked nearsightedly, and slipped his glasses back on with a half-smile.

"Um, sure."

Lifting his tab, he keyed in the vid. The blue flag and its yellow circle of stars came up on the screen, followed by the three bold letters inside their boxes.

"Health. It has been the preoccupation of humanity since our inception."

Kevin felt his body relax as the British-accented voice washed over him. A British accent had always relaxed him. His mother had been a British citizen, and the one thing she'd absolutely refused to give up was the BBC.

Their family had paid premium fees to keep her dual citizenship and get an international media subscription when he'd been small, and his father had splurged on a hacker's services to unlock the programs that Cavanaugh Corporation had blocked. It had been worth every penny. Watching these programs after school with his parents had been how Kevin had gotten his real historical education.

The beginning of the vid ran through ancient history, through the archaic medical techniques of the World Wars, the appalling medicine and the advances discovered in the Middle Eastern Conflicts and into the discovery of CRISPR that kindled the era of personalized medicine. Kevin's face set as images of old America flicked on the screen.

"The issue of genetically-tailored medicine caused the final collapse of the former United States' democratic bodies known as the House and Senate. Periodically gridlocked for decades on issues as varied as the funding of education, the management of civil defense and the laws governing immigration, the United States Senate and House had suffered from inaction and an increasing rate of assassinations on members throughout the twenty-first century. Research today suggests that shootings early in the twenty first century were committed by unstable and disgruntled members of the public. But as the act became normalized, some American corporations began to disguise politically-motivated killings as the actions of the populace."

Kevin's fists clenched in his lap as the vid went on.

"During this time there had been numerous failures to pass national budgets due to partisan in-fighting between the two major parties in existence, often concerned with the funding of medical aid and the lawfulness of many health services in the country. These led to government shutdowns of ever-increasing duration. In 2065, the government failed to agree on a budget for over eleven months. By the time a weak bill was passed, the country had descended into the chaos known as the Dissolution."

On the screen, images of the Dissolution flicked by in a bloody montage of destruction and hopelessness.

"In a widely-publicized attempt to restore order, the company then known as Eagle Security Services erected fences around several suburbs in Illinois and began to police them in exchange for direct taxation. Other large firms and corporations did the same for their employees. In exchange for safety, employees and residents of a patrolled area were asked to sign contracts with these new entities. Privately-owned businesses following the philosophies of each founder and board of trustees soon bought up most resources," the host continued implacably over images of gated communities and EagleCorp office buildings.

"...Until America became, over the course of the next ten years, the country we know today. Seven main Corporations eventually monopolized every facet of American life and now run them according to seven separate sets of guiding principles. Far from its egalitarian roots, America has become one of the world's strongest warnings against the abuses of human rights. Asylum seekers regularly arrive today in Canada, travelling overland, or on the shores of Europe and Japan in stolen boats and hidden in the cargo bays of planes. They embark on harrowing journeys, fleeing the corporations who seek to punish those with genetic 'flaws' and lifestyles deemed unacceptable by the specific Corporation they are indentured to. In the year 2100, the United Nations revoked the right of the United Corporations of America to sit on the Council. The CEO of Cavanaugh Corporation had publicly allocated funds to find the genes responsible for homosexuality, in order to add the gene cluster to the list of undesirable traits to be edited out of the genomes of future children. In recent years, there were signs that Cavanaugh might be taking a more humanitarian route, but in the wake of the deaths of Mr. Craydon, the progressively-leaning hereditary CEO of Cavanaugh Corporation, and his family, Cavanaugh has strengthened its adherence to their stated eugenic goals. The deaths of the Craydon family are believed by reputable sources to have been an internal Corporate assassination. Many international bodies do not condone their actions, but Cavanaugh Corporation holds the patents on most major breakthroughs in medicine including—"

The screen flicked out of existence. Standing sharply, Kevin set aside his tab and crossed the room, grabbed up the darts and began to throw them with mechanical precision.

Thunk.

Bad enough Cavanaugh Corporation had incentivized people to decide what human perfection looked like, discard what didn't fit their picture and shape their children's bodies accordingly. Shape him accordingly. Decided for him how tall he was. How much collagen was in his joints. Bad enough they'd shaped his bone structure. Bad enough they'd decided what his skin color should be and adjusted him to suit their standards.

Thunk.

Bad enough that they'd decided they knew what 'perfect' looked like and shaped him to match. Bad enough they discarded anyone who didn't match their goddamn standards like defective parts off an assembly line.

Bad enough that they'd planned his life out for him while he was still in the womb.

Thunk.

But, if his parents had let them, they would have done even more. They had decided what human perfection behaved like as well. They would have reached inside his mind and shaped who and what he was, decided for him who and what he would want.

His parents were the reason he had his own mind. His parents had held onto what they believed. They'd stood up for those beliefs. They'd tried to change the Corporation for the better.

Thunk.

Which was why they were dead.

Thunk.

Behind him, the couch groaned as Aidan stood. "Um…"

Kevin kept his eyes trained on the board. The center of the bull's-eye was full. He aimed the next four at the inner circle.

Thunk.

"Are you okay?"

"Fine, sir," Kevin replied shortly. Stepping forward in three strides, he yanked the darts out of the board.

"Because you look pissed as hell…"

"Sorry, sir," Kevin replied, wishing with every fiber of his being that the man would leave him alone to get himself under control. "Just had enough for one night. Only so much I can take."

"Of the Corps?" Aidan's soft voice asked behind him. Kevin stepped back, took aim.

"Among other things, sir."

Thunk. Thunk.

"Kevin? My name's Aidan. And I need to know what's going on with you."

Kevin dropped his eyes, staring at the darts clutched in his hand. "It isn't easy hearing yourself described as an undesirable element in need of editing out of existence." The words came out with clipped precision. "I wasn't expecting it tonight. Wasn't prepared. Apologies." For a moment, he closed his eyes. Even telling this much of the truth might have unpleasant consequences, but he had to say something at this point. The whole truth most certainly wasn't an option.

"I'm of the Grecian persuasion, if we're being polite," he stated. The soft intake of breath seemed amplified in the room's quiet. He glanced up with a storm in his grey eyes, ready to face his new commander's reaction.

"It's not something that affects my duties," he added, hearing the sharp note in his own voice.

"No," Aidan replied, his voice unexpectedly gentle. "I don't expect it would."

Kevin held his eyes. "Is this going to be a problem, sir?" he asked, wearing his polite mask like armor. He could feel his body tensing. If this man took issue as Commander Quinn had... Well. They'd dealt with Quinn. But if they rejected another commander then Sector would—

Aidan gave a startled laugh, making Kevin blink as a baffled half-grin enlivened the man's face. "Wait, you thought I was going to... Look, Kevin, I seriously don't give a damn who my crew sleeps with as long as it doesn't cause issues. I don't want domestic disputes in the field, that's all."

Kevin felt every muscle in his body relax, his knees weakening for a moment. Swallowing hard, he forced himself to smile. "Thank you, sir—Aidan. Thanks. And sorry about that. Just now."

Aidan shrugged, shifting his weight from foot to foot, looking at the dart board. "'Grecian persuasion,'" he muttered, awkwardly rubbing the back of his neck. "I like that. Might use it sometime, if I can."

This time, Kevin was the one who sucked in a breath, his brain stalling. Realization and mortification hit him like a tidal wave. Of all the people to lose it on, he had to take his anger out on someone who was dealing with the same problem. *Idiot!*

He pulled his glasses off, polishing them industriously rather than look the other man in the eye. "It's rather a nicer phrase than what I... than what we usually have to contend with," he managed, holding his glasses up to the light once, twice, checking for blemishes on the glass.

"I've heard a few," Aidan agreed. "Not in a while, though. And it's not... I don't want it to be an issue here. We've got enough going on."

Kevin nodded. "It won't be a problem among the Wildcards. You know about Yvonne and Sarah, and there's me, and there's Blake. The rest of the base has always been very genial about it. Live and let live's our motto around here." Eyes on the blurry outline of his glasses, he smirked. "Well. It's actually phrased as 'it's my life, not yours, so butt out.'"

For a moment, the room was so quiet that Kevin could hear the sound of cloth squeaking on plastic. Then his new commander sucked in a breath. "Good. Great. Thanks."

Slipping his glasses back on, Kevin forced a smile. "Look. I owe you for the way I acted just now. Let me introduce you to something more congenial. Ever watched this classic movie Shrek?"

Event File 16
File Tag: Expertise
Timestamp: 05:00-4-9-2155

It was well before dawn when Kevin checked his coding work and put in his contacts. He pulled on his Grid quality outfit, tucked his tab and his ID cards into his back pocket and slid on his riding gear over it all. Stepping down the hall, he knocked quietly on a door. "Yve? Time."

Yvonne stepped out on silent feet, dressed for the ride and pale-faced in the dim orange night-cycle lights. "We good?" she asked, closing the door on her sleeping wife.

Kevin nodded once, gave her a quick thumbs up and a smile. Wary of waking their base mates, the two members of the logistics division walked silent down the hall, pulling on their slick ponchos, helmets and gloves in the engine-lubricant scented gloom of the garage. They kicked their engines to life once they were outside and took off.

They raced dawn down the long plateau, paralleling the I-70 Corridor as the highway grew from four-lane to six-lane, then eight. Stopping at a long-term storage garage on the outskirts of the Central Grid, they entered their forged Citizen Cards at the gate. The gate system dinged, displaying the readout: 'Now cleared for access to Storage Space 41B.'

They rode up the ramp to the fourth floor, stowed their bikes and riding gear in the storage space that had opened for them, checked each other over and extricated the little Go car that Sector had given them the access info to.

"Welcome, Jim!" the car chirped blithely as Kevin inserted his Citizen Card and let the car scan what it thought was his retina. He shot Yvonne a quick grin as she took the seat across from him in the upholstered bubble on wheels, pressing a grey box into the center of the console. The sound wave modulator plugged into the car's sound system, its codes finding every sound detection apparatus in the car and feeding them the sounds of music, pop-ups and occasional sounds of breathing, coughing or a sneeze. The devices were illegal, of course, but what wasn't.

"A pair of contacts and a little code does the trick," Kevin remarked once the blue light flicked on in the grey casing of the sound box. "Perhaps you'll stop insulting my eyewear now?"

Yvonne rolled her eyes at the old joke as the car slid smoothly out of its storage cubby and hissed down the exit ramp.

"Anybody can wear contacts, show-off," she muttered, running her eyes around the space with the beginnings of a grin. "Hey, we got lucky. Look at this baby! Gotta be CSS Level at least!"

"Nice enough," Kevin agreed offhandedly. "Check and see if there's a wet bar. We can celebrate on the way back home if so."

Yvonne brought up the amenities tab on the car's HUD and grinned. "Rum, bourbon and something called... cog-nak?"

"Cognac," Kevin corrected with relish, his eyes lighting up. "Now, that I'm looking forward to. You'll love it. If we didn't need to leave this car as we found it, I'd take the bottle home with us."

"If we're supposed to do that, we kinda shouldn't drink it," Yvonne suggested with a smirk.

Catching her eyes, Kevin leaned back in his seat with an elaborate shrug. "I'm not above adding a little water to the bottle. I doubt our friend 'Jim' will notice."

Yvonne grinned as the Go car joined the main traffic into Denver Central. "So, where're we headed?" Yvonne asked as she eased back into the comfort of someone else's cushioned seat for the ride.

Kevin tipped his head at the Go car's windshield, where the virtual map of their progress was playing out in real-time. "Down onto Sixteenth for the hardware, and then up into Commerce City."

Yvonne pulled a face. "Again?"

"I want to check in with Jazz about any new codes she might have on hand. That last one gave us an editing card solid enough to get me into the Sunshine system we've been banging our heads against for more than two years." Kevin smiled dryly. "At this rate, perhaps we should simply subcontract our coding out to her organization. She's getting surprisingly good."

Yvonne gave him a level stare. "Subcontract. You're joking, right?"

Kevin returned the expression with interest, one brow raised, and Yvonne waved a dismissive hand.

"Okay, okay, I just hate that area, I—"

"Jim, while you are on your way, would you like to stop for a macchiato? They have a sale today. Macchiatos for only $17. 95."

"Gah!" Yvonne yelped as their HUD flashed with the advertisement for the coffee chain and the voice filled the car.

Kevin grinned. "You'll never adjust to pop-ups will you?"

Yvonne sighed, glaring at the hologram as Kevin reached over and swiped left to decline, then hit the inevitable 'are you sure' prompt.

"I don't care about the ones on the street," Yvonne defended in a mutter. "It's the ones that go off when it's quiet that get to me. Can you at least hit the mute?"

Kevin checked the vehicle settings as the car drove placidly along its lane, bracketed by other cars doing the same. "No, unfortunately. I can turn down the sound, but it looks like Jim preferred his drinks to his peace. It's one of the cheaper systems. Can't block the ads."

"Crap." Yvonne sighed, leaning back in her seat. Kevin glanced at their readouts. "We've only got six miles to go, only half an hour."

Yvonne shrugged, then winced as another pop-up flashed on the screen. Kevin dismissed it. In the momentary quiet, Yvonne glanced at him, worry in her rain-colored eyes.

"Did Laz ever apologize to you?"

"I doubt he feels it's his duty to apologize to me on any subject," Kevin demurred, looking out the window at the buildings crawling past. He listened to Yvonne sigh.

"Kev."

For a moment, the silence stretched out. Kevin considered his options. At this point nothing he said would really help. He knew she worried about him and her cousin both, and nothing he said was going to repair that. Better to get her mind off it.

"This'll help block out the pop-ups," he announced eventually, digging in his pocket for his tab. He didn't dare plug his secured and unregistered device into the car in order to use the speakers, but he set it on the dash and brought up his music program. Poppy synthesizer filled the car as Men At Work's 'Snakes And Ladders' started, and Kevin smiled thinly. Fitting, given their surroundings.

His smile grew genuine at Yvonne's groan.

"Oh, I am seriously not spending half an hour listening to your weird oldies!"

"You've got no taste!" he retorted in mock affront, grinning at his friend's dismay. Problem solved. The rest of the ride would be spent bickering over music. Given the options, not a bad outcome.

"You have arrived," the car chirped, and the doors popped open in the frosted glass cubicle of their parking spot. Stepping out, Kevin braced himself.

"Hi there, Jim and Caroline!" the painfully cheerful voice of the hologram set his teeth on edge as it flowed out of its inlaid generators in the glass, spraying color across the adjacent panels and displaying a cheerful blonde in a business suit in front of them. "Welcome to the historic Sixteenth Street Outdoor Esplanade. We're happy to have you today!"

"I hate these things," Yvonne muttered, and Kevin shot her a warning look. They might have the registrations and Citizen Standing clearances to turn off the cubicle cameras on entry, but there could easily be audio bugs in the cubicle. Chattering right now was a bad idea.

"Your Citizen Standing chips have been read, and we've generated a list of stores to suit your personal needs," the hologram continued in her quiver of enthusiasm. "Would you like to see it now?"

"No," Kevin stated loudly and clearly.

The hologram gave her false smile. "Have a wonderful day! Your parking fee has been deducted."

"Thanks ever so much," Kevin replied dryly as the glass walls faded into innocent white again. He shot Yvonne a tight smile and sketched a bow. "Once more into the breach. Ladies first."

Yvonne smirked and flipped him off as she stepped out of the parking space, which made him smile all the wider. He'd always been able to defuse her nerves with the old-world gentleman act he'd copied off vids. At least one thing still worked in their team.

And then they were in the elevator down to Sixteenth Street, and the Grid really hit them. A wash of advert jingle blared out of a directional loudspeaker as they passed, following them until they were out of range and into the scope of a holographic pop-up that wrapped them in a wash of dazzling color.

Kevin resisted the urge to shade his eyes with one hand. That kind of sensitivity to stimuli was as good as a sign reading 'Unaccustomed To Grid' hung around his neck. An oddity like that would be picked up by general security cams in a nanosecond.

"Buy LaDouc today. You're worth it," a sensuous female voice whispered in Kevin's ear as if he was the only man on the planet. That was rather impressive directional mic work, he judged distantly, stepping through the hologram and out of the mic's reach. They'd even played with harmonics to make him feel an instant of pleasure. Very slick.

He glanced at the little eagle decal discreetly tucked beneath the store's logo, reading the three letters on the glass. CSS. Of course. Anybody with tech that good could afford to bar anyone below CSS level from entering their stores.

On the ground, arrows and dancing ice cream cones projected themselves on the concrete in blinking colors. 'This Way To The Best Ice Cream In Town! CAS Welcome!'

Around him, people walked with their eyes on their feet, ears covered with 'buds. Those who could afford it covered their eyes with Eazee glasses running blocking programs. Others followed their social feeds on their glasses or projected a wrap-around augmented reality holo from their tabs to mask what they didn't want to see with something they did.

But nothing could completely block out the advertising bombardment. That was the point.

At least he was having a better experience these days than he'd had when he was a teen. He'd still had the Wellness Chip shining blue in the skin of his wrist then, showing his place in society for anyone to see. The things might conveniently act as a Citizen Card and monitor your body chemistry to help you stay optimum in health and appearance, but they also sent Cavanaugh's corporate affiliates a constant stream of information on the stimuli that caused surges of cortisol or dopamine in your bloodstream. The Corporation had known exactly what attracted and repelled him as a teenager, and the pop-ups on the street had targeted him accordingly. It had been a nuisance.

At least, they'd thought they'd known exactly what attracted him. He'd been lucky that his parents could afford hackers who could quietly check his Wellness feed and overwrite anything dangerous in his emotional data. So many people weren't so lucky. There were so many things to hide when you were a Cavanaugh Citizen. It had almost been worth the pain to be rid of that damn chip. The Fringe chopper who'd cut it out for him on that day from hell hadn't used nearly enough anesthetic. Kevin had been a mess that day. He'd been sixteen. He'd screamed.

Kevin's feet fell into a brisk quickstep, moving him fast and easy through the crowds, using the trick he'd learned from his dad of remembering poems he'd memorized while he walked to keep his mind off the sensory overload. Ahead, a barker for a t-shirt and souvenir store was actually outside in-person, plucking at the sleeves and patting the shoulders of passers-by. "In here, best stuff in town, come on in!"

Kevin took an easy step out of range, but Yvonne wasn't as fast. The man had her upper arm in his hand and was already into his sales spiel, but he dropped his grip the moment he got a look at Kevin and the expression on his face.

Kevin had been taught in kindergarten how to talk to the lower standings. You were expected to be able to cow plebes by the time you were ten. He'd been good at faking the stance, the expressions and the body language he'd been trained to use as a member of CES society. He'd had to be. The lessons and his looks came in handy at times like this.

The man swallowed and dropped his gaze. He'd picked up on the signals, and Kevin could practically read the thought that had flickered in his eyes: pissing off High Standing wasn't worth the grief.

"Uh, sorry," the salesman grunted.

Kevin nodded coldly and shepherd Yvonne away.

"Wish I could pull that act off," Yvonne grumbled, rubbing irritably at her arm.

Kevin shrugged, shoving his hands in his pockets as he let his body language relax. "It's all in the stance. Come on, stay close."

They ran the gauntlet of Sixteenth street and into the blessed peace of the largest electronics store on the strip. At the clean white concierge desk, a clean white woman with white-dyed hair smiled. "Hello! What can we do for you today?"

Yvonne smiled her peppy Grid smile, stepping forward. "Hi! Got a list to fill, we were hoping you could help us out." Pulling out her tab, she displayed her list. The store concierge studied it, typed. "Yes, I think we have everything, would you like it delivered?"

"No, thanks. We're picking up today."

"Of course," the store concierge agreed with another plastic grin, "Would you like a secured purchasing container coded to your personal Citizen Cards?"

"No, thanks," Yvonne chirped, "We're not all that worried."

The woman smiled her acknowledging smile. "One moment please, I—" then she paused, glaring at the rattle of the doors.

Kevin resisted the urge to glance back at whoever had tried to enter and found themselves locked out. He wondered momentarily how long it had been since their Citizen Standing had dropped and the stores they'd always gone to had begun to read the information on their Citizen Card that labeled them an unfit consumer and locking them out. Was this the first moment they'd realized?

He didn't look back. It'd be cruel to add to their humiliation.

The concierge smiled another fake grin. Holding that expression had to hurt by the end of the day. "Excuse me. I'll have everything right up."

Two minutes later, a shelf-stocking employee came hurrying up with their boxes. Kevin took two and tucked them under his arm. "Thanks very much."

He handed over his Citizen Card, his pulse jumping. He knew he'd done the code properly. He'd disconnected the CSS couple's actual bank account, borrowed their credentials while they were staying in the Vail Resort Complex and re-connected them to a false bank account that fooled computer systems into believing they'd received money. But there was always a chance the hack had been detected.

He forced himself to breathe normally. If the store's monitoring systems picked up an overly fast heart rate and respiration, they'd be more carefully scrutinized by security.

Nothing to see here, he willed silently, just another consumer.

The card binged, sliding back out of its slot.

"Have a nice day," the store concierge added sweetly.

And they were out on the street, back in the noise, carrying all the hardware they'd need to update their slick tarp and their computer system against EagleCorp's newest detection work.

At the thought, he turned his eyes up Sixteenth, away from the looming bulk of the EagleCorp building squatting a mile down the Esplanade.

"One more stop," Kevin remarked, raising his voice over a sneaker hologram's loud music as they walked through it.

In the car, Kevin watched his base mate carefully. "Ears bothering you?" he asked quietly when Yvonne dropped her head back against the headrest. She closed her eyes. "Yeah. Bit. Least it was short."

Kevin nodded. "If you do start feeling the 'buzz, let me know, will you?"

Yvonne smirked, eyes closed. "Yes, Dad."

Kevin smiled despite himself. Pulling out his tab, he put on Yvonne's favorite band by way of apology as they rolled through traffic.

Idly, he watched out the windows as the cityscape crawled by.

Moving south on Broadway, they left the fashionable areas around the Capitol and the gated employee communities of Cavanaugh Creek, The Village and Eagle's Nest. Used car places, CAS and CPS grocery chains and restaurants, strip joints and lower-standing housing areas spread out ahead, segregated into Corporate-affiliated neighborhoods. By the time the Go car turned onto Quebec, the neighborhood had really gone downhill.

They parked their Go car inside a garage. As an added protection Kevin set the vehicle's Hands-Off feature and stepped away, his skin prickling as the machine electrified its metal surfaces.

"Let's see how Jazz is feeling."

The contrast between the store they'd been in and the one they now entered couldn't have been more marked. Jazz saved money by keeping the lights low. Shadows hugged the walls, shades drawn to block out the hot sun. An old AC unit fought to keep the reconditioned tech cool enough to function.

Kevin idly glanced through the wares. All of them had the required 'TechoCo Certified Pre-Owned' sticker on them, but he was fairly sure that Jazz was finding ways to register her revamped machines without paying the royalties to TechoCo. Good for her.

At the desk, a woman raised her dreadlocked head lazily, eyes studying them. "Hot day," she remarked.

Kevin nodded. "Looks like there's a storm coming in, by the way."

"Best to get inside," the woman behind the counter remarked blankly.

Kevin held her eyes. "Mind if we come in out of the dust?"

Jazz's black eyes twinkled. "Hey man. Way you act, I always half think you're a fucking mimic faking me out, you know that?"

Kevin put a hand over his heart theatrically. "You wound, madam! I'm emotionally crushed!"

Laughing, the techie stepped out from behind her desk and gave him and Yvonne quick, one armed hugs. "How you guys been? How's the new program working?"

"Well it got us into a Sunshine Distributions Center, so I'd say pretty awesome!" Yvonne replied with a grin.

Jazz blinked, her face blank. "You're shitting me."

"Did the run this week," Kevin replied with a flourishing half bow.

Jazz glanced between the two Wildcards. "You people are fucking nuts. Seriously. Fucking nuts."

Kevin shrugged, his grin boyish. "Business as usual. You get us code and we'll put it through its paces. Speaking of which, I'd heard you might have a new buying reroute program in the works?"

Jazz eyed him for a moment that stretched just a little too long for comfort. "Got something," she admitted finally. "Gonna cost you though."

"Fair enough," Kevin agreed with a nod of acknowledgement. "Let's take a look."

Jazz glanced at the door. Then she turned her head. "Hey, Billie!"

In the back room there was a small noise, and a gawky black girl stepped out. "Yeah?"

The fear in her voice made Kevin glance back at his contact, but everything about Jazz was as relaxed as it had ever been over the last three years. "Watch the front okay?"

"Sure," the girl agreed, scuttling to take the older woman's seat.

"New hire?" Yvonne asked as Jazz led them down a short hall to her personal quarters.

"Sorta," Jazz agreed, sliding into a car seat that had been retrofitted into a coding rig and bringing up her system. The screen flickered into life, bathing her face in green light. She put in two layers of passwords, bent her head to let her system scan her retina, then spat into an attached tube. The machine beeped its affirmation.

This was why Kevin liked working with Jazz: she took the precautions too many people on the GreyNet skipped. Getting sloppy with the details was what got people killed.

"Okay. Take a look," Jazz murmured eventually, and Kevin stepped in, reading through the code with narrowed eyes. Scrolling down, he blinked as he studied the algorithms and the subsystems.

"Jesus, Mary and Joseph. Jazz, who do you have doing your code these days?" he asked in awe.

"Who says this isn't mine?" Jazz demanded.

Kevin countered the edge in her voice with a dry look. "Jazz, you're an amazing mech'n'tech, but I know your code. This is the work of a true artist. This is... Well, frankly some of it is miles beyond me. It's genius."

"You saying I'm not that smart?" Jazz retorted.

Kevin caught her eye with a level stare of his own. "Jazz, I'm saying I'm not this smart, and you know how I value my seat in the ivory tower. And I'm also saying that we'll most definitely buy. What's the coder's rate?"

Jazz snorted. "Too low. Stupid kid sold me this work for a thousand."

"Shit," Yvonne whispered.

Kevin nodded. "We'd be willing to offer six thousand, on two conditions."

"Yeah?" Jazz asked, shoulders subtly tensing.

Kevin forced his body to relax. He wanted this, but he knew the game. Too much eagerness would only raise the price, and they needed that money. Blake was going to have his hide for six thousand as it was. "That two thousand of the fee goes to the original coder. And I get introduced to them."

Jazz stared at him for a long time, chewing the inside of her cheek. "I can do the first. The second? Nope."

"Why?" Kevin watched Jazz's face as he asked the question, reading her reactions. What was this hesitation over? That wasn't like Jazz.

Then he got it. "You don't want the coder getting involved with us. You said the kid. How old are they?"

Jazz looked away. "Too young for this shit," she muttered quietly. "So, back off." Standing, she shut down her system. "Get your card out and let's trade."

Kevin's heart quickened. "Jazz, this kind of work is valuable. If the kid's selling their work in CPS areas, maybe we can subcontract with them and help—"

Jazz's head whipped around fast enough to make her beaded dreads clack together as she turned a glare on him. Kevin almost took a step back.

"Help the girl get labeled terrorist?" Jazz demanded. "Get a bullet or a cell? Shut that noise down."

Kevin sighed. "I didn't say she had to join the Force to work with us Jazz. You didn't."

"Yeah, well." Jazz turned away from him, refusing to meet his eyes. "You want this thing or not? Get out your card."

Repressing a sigh, Kevin dug out his actual credit card, the one leading back to the Bengali accounts where the Force kept each base's funds through several dummy accounts and two other countries.

"Some things are worth fighting for, Jazz," he added, holding it out. "And people have the right to decide what they're going to do in this world. Will you tell her we'd like to set up a meeting at least?"

The techie took the card and swiped it across the reader in her tab, typing furiously as she stared at the screen rather than looking the Duster in the eye.

"Don't get all motivational poster on me, Kevin," Jazz stated eventually as the money transferred on the screen. "I like what you guys do. Don't get me wrong. You win someday and I'll be out in the streets dancing. But people around you get fucked up. This kid's fucked enough as it is. Not everybody's built like you people."

"I'll bear it in mind," Kevin stated quietly. Pocketing his card, he gave the GreyNet techie a half salute. "We'll be off. Keep your head down in the storm."

"Yeah," Jazz muttered as they left the room. "You, too."

In the hall, Kevin snapped his fingers. "Yve, wait a moment." Turning, he stuck his head back into Jazz's code room, flashing his best grin. "Before we head out, Jazz, got any vids?"

Event File 17
File Tag: Operational Planning
Timestamp: 19:15-4-10-2155

"Er, could you spare some of your time after duty hours?"

Aidan raised his head from his operational planning brief, brow furrowed. "Hunh?"

In the doorway, his logistics officer gave him a half smile. "It's a quarter of seven. If you're able to sign off anytime soon, I've got a lead I'd like to go over with you."

Aidan ran a hand over his face, trying to clear his eyes. "Um, yeah. Sorry. What time is it again?" And what did a quarter of seven mean? Wouldn't that be some weird fraction?

"Six forty-five," Kevin replied quietly.

Aidan blinked. "Give me a second." He glanced at his screen. Kevin was right. Past six-thirty. How had he been working on this plan so long?

"Problems?" the diffident voice in the doorway asked. Aidan gave a hollow laugh. "Yeah. Problems. We got word from the guys embedded in American AgCo—"

"The Grapevine?" Kevin asked.

Aidan nodded. "Yeah. We're supposed to get a group of eight off the Grid next month—a bunch of farm labor activists loud enough that American AgCo and ZonCom are putting them under house arrest—and get them started on their way out of the country. Anyway. Yeah. Signing off."

He typed in his password.

Behind him, Kevin cleared his throat. "I could take a look, if you're worried..."

Turning in his chair, Aidan blinked at his officer. Did the man really think he looked that freaked? Maybe he did. He drew in a breath. "Yeah. Here, I've got the basics together." Bringing up the mission spec outline, he brightened his screen as the other man drew up a chair, peering at the words.

"CAS level civilians?" Kevin asked, adjusting his glasses as he studied the information. "Oh. CPS too. And from the housing divisions of two different Corporations. Two children in the group, too. Tricky."

"No shit," Aidan agreed dryly. "That's why it's taking so long. Personal vehicles are too easy to track, but we can't ask a family with kids to walk across the Grid. If we get them falsified Citizen Cards, they can use the midtown busses to bring the group out of AgCo areas of town and down into ZonCom, but that part of the bus system doesn't run out far enough to be any good to us. We need them out somewhere on I-70 or the back roads before it's safe for us to pick them up in manual rigs, but public transit doesn't go out that far and any shuttle service would log a weird trip to nowhere."

Kevin read through the outline, nodding to himself. "Okay. Could any of them request legitimate Vacation Visas to leave the city limits for a camping trip?"

Aidan shook his head. "Three of them had their Citizen Standing numbers drop. They're too low for travel privileges now. The rest don't want to risk asking. I agree with them."

"Mm, it would look suspicious," Kevin agreed. "But if they could all get closer to the edge of the Grid... Have you considered going with the AgCo train system? Usually lower security around passenger trains in the stations, and there's a station within walking distance of everyone's residences. It's not unusual for people to take a weekend jaunt out to see the test breeding gardens at Sunnyvale. Plenty of crowds to confuse the cameras as well."

Aidan leaned in. "Where's there a station near...?"

Kevin ran his finger over the hologram, and the icon lit up. "Oh, right," Aidan muttered. "But then they'll just hit the fences around Sunnyvale."

Kevin glanced up with a thin smile. "We have a few tricks to use there. All we need to do is time it according to the drone patterns. If I act as their liaison and guide them in...here, try this." Step by step, they worked through the plan they would use to get the people off the Grid. It surprised Aidan how much he calmed as they talked the ideas through. He'd been sure a group who screwed up something as simple as picking up food couldn't handle a mission like this. He'd been debating sending Sector a notice of mission non-functionality and sitting this one out.

But, as they tossed ideas back and forth, something that actually looked like a working plan emerged.

The clock read eight forty-two when Aidan sat back. "So, I guess we'll go with that," he stated, still surprised. He glanced at his logistics officer with a smile.

"You had something you wanted to go over when you first came in, right?"

Kevin held up his tab. "Can I show you a bit of code?"

Aidan shrugged. "Sure."

Kevin nodded. A few clicks later, they were watching code slide by.

"So, what am I looking at here?" Aidan asked, watching the lines of characters flicker.

Kevin glanced at him with a light in his eyes. "What you're looking at is sheer artistry in action, si—" He cut himself off with a quick smile, "Sorry. Aidan. This code is amazing, as good as, or possibly better than, most of the Corporation code work that's available. It's designed to seamlessly hijack the electronic funds transfer process from vendors using National Banking's systems and send the transaction through a proxy mirror that will make it appear that funds have been exchanged.

"There's a subroutine that allows us to entered drop points by address, or longitude and latitude, and overwrite them with addresses the system delivers to on a regular basis in the ISP records. We'll look like legitimate buyers to every Corporate system in existence."

Aidan watched as the enter and overwrite windows popped up and disappeared while his logistics officer explained, "These codes are going to make our lives incredibly easy on the supply requisitions front, and they won't lose potency unless the base code for National Banking's underlying credit exchange systems is given an overhaul. And whoever wrote this, my contacts tell me they're selling their work for a thousand."

Aidan's brows shot up, and he raised his head to look the other man in the eye. A jolt ran through him as he realized just how close they'd gotten leaning over the tab, nearly nose to nose. He leaned back.

"Do you think it's some kind of scam? Maybe it's got a virus? Or is it supposed to get us interested and catch us in the open when we try to go back for more code like this?"

"Mm." Kevin considered the words for a long moment, fingers fiddling absently with the cloth he used to clean his glasses. Then he shook his head. "I really don't think so. I've sent it to Sector, they popped it up the line to Regional, and it's been thoroughly vetted for any virus or subprograms. There aren't any. And the Corps would be making an incredibly asinine assumption handing us software this powerful as bait and thinking they could snag us before we could disseminate it. Sowing that kind of whirlwind wouldn't be worthwhile to capture a Sector hub, much less an individual base like ours. Besides, I trust the source of these codes."

"Whirlwind?" Aidan asked, bewildered again. Was this guy always going to talk a mile over his head? And what did 'asinine' mean? He was starting to feel like an idiot around his logistics officer.

He blinked as Kevin lowered his eyes, that bright blush of his staining his high cheekbones again. Aidan wished that look didn't make the back of his neck tingle.

"Sorry," Kevin demurred with another quick smile, "Cavanaugh Corporation kid originally, you know. They have high educational standards for their future workers. Mother from Britain to boot. I'm afraid it's left me with a bit of an elevated lexicon."

"Unh-hunh," Aidan managed, watching the other man. He had no idea what lexicon meant, but if he pretended long enough maybe something would make sense.

Kevin glanced up, and Aidan flicked his eyes to the tab. *Way to go*, Aidan thought, *just keep staring at the guy until he realizes how much of a freak you are.* He scraped the bottom of his brain for something to fill the silence with.

"I thought Cavanaugh paid for medtech on all their people. You've got scars." The statement came out flat, too blunt, and Aidan immediately wished that he could grab the words out of the air. Could he *sound* any more like an ass? "Sorry, I just noticed that square scar on your wrist," he added lamely.

Kevin gave a small, dismissive snort, one hand covering the scarred wrist. "I imagine we all have scars in this vicinity. Our skin reconstruction tech isn't the height of fashion, though I'm working on that as and when I can. One more reason to get these codes in play and improve our supply chain." He pushed red hair out of his face, a weary gesture.

Aidan glanced away. Great. Now not only was he noticing everything about how the guy looked, he'd made it obvious by talking about where he had scars. He cleared his throat.

"So, did you want written approval to start using this for your division?"

"It's a little more than that actually. I was hoping to get your approval to set up a meeting with the creator." Kevin poked the code, making the hologram judder. "If we can contract or recruit this coder, the edge we would get would be... Well, phenomenal. My code equates to crayon drawings, for the sake of analogy, and the hub coders at Sector paint in watercolors. Regional can pull off oils on a good day, but... Whoever this is has painted the Mona Lisa, and then done it a few more times. What we couldn't do with someone like that on our crew."

Aidan stared at the tab, running the idea through his head, turning it over. If his logistics officer was wrong, the code could be a weapon against their base when it was installed in their systems. But Kevin had checked it with Sector, who had checked it with Regional. If they marked it clean, the code itself was clean. He could relax about that.

But what about the coder?

If he gave his approval to set up a meet and it was a trap, the worst outcome was Kevin got killed. Then he backtracked his thinking with a shake of the head. No, the worst outcome was that his logistics officer was caught and everything he knew wrung out of him, which would give the Corporation who caught the man information to sell to other Corporations or a chance to take out a Duster base. Either way, it could get the Wildcards killed. But if it was legit...

"Sir?"

Aidan drew a sharp breath. "Sorry. Sorry, just thinking about it." He hadn't noticed how tight his chest had gotten until he'd tried to speak. He was going to need to get out of his binder soon. His binders were too cheap to wear for more than eight or nine hours without problems.

He took another breath. "So, I've got a lot of concerns here. Have you activated the code yet?"

"I was waiting on your approval," Kevin returned quietly. "But I've got a stolen Grid-attached tab with the GPS access removed ready to test it on as a safety measure. If it acts normally there, Sector has given their approval for us to use it on our own systems."

Aidan nodded slowly. "Okay, yeah, run the test for a week, see how it goes. And if it's really that great—" He glanced up from the screen. Dammit, they were almost nose to nose again. How had that happened?

Aidan swallowed, but he forced himself to sit still and study Kevin's face. "Explain to me why this doesn't feel like a trap to you."

Kevin smiled thinly, poking the hologram with one finger. "Several reasons. First, Jazz supplied the intel, and I trust her. Secondly, this code is just too good to be cooked up for the purpose of baiting a line. See this little glyph? That coder's signature was also on some amazing access software that we've used recently. Working on the supposition that the first batch being effective and safe lends some validation to the next, I've got confidence. I've also got an eye for dissimulation, and Jazz got cagey with me at several points.

She's set up similar meetings with GreyNet coders for me in the past without blinking. Adding that to some of the comments she made, I'm ninety-nine percent sure that she feels some kind of loyalty or protective instinct towards this coder. If Jazz has taken enough of a liking to them to feel protective, I've got high hopes." The taller man shrugged. "In fact, it's part of my reason to feel confident. I don't see a teenager selling cut-price code in the CPS districts as a very credible Corporation plant. Any Corporation. So, what do you think?"

Aidan's binder seemed to get tighter around his chest. His throat felt tense. What did he think? What did he think? He thought it could go wrong in so many awful ways. But if it went right…

"Okay," he began, not sure how the sentence would end. "Provisionally, I want to give my approval. But I need some time to think about it, and I've still got some concerns. For one, I know you know this contact, but if that 'cagey' thing was her hiding a Corps payoff instead of a friend who codes or something, we're toast. If we go ahead, I'm going to have to ask you to run this one solo. If it goes bad, I want as few lives on the line as possible. And you know it's a risk, if it does go bad. I mean if you got caught—"

Kevin cut him off quietly. "Sir... Aidan, I've got an implanted neurotoxin emitter set to lethal levels around my brainstem. It's code-word locked. Damian did it for me. Trust me, I won't be taken alive. You don't need to worry about that."

For some weird reason, the suggestion that his logistics officer had a coded implant he could use to kill himself at will did make Aidan relax. Either that, or the way the guy said it did.

"So, I'll wait on your approval to go ahead?" Kevin asked.

Aidan nodded. "Yeah. I understand you need time to plana

run for this. I just..." He shrugged. "You know, can't be too careful."

"Care and caution, watchwords to live by," Kevin replied with a quick smile.

Aidan couldn't help but return the expression.

Kevin blinked, snapped his fingers. "Oh! By the way, I was able to fulfill the last requisitions request we discussed."

"Which one?" Aidan asked, his mind scrambling for that conversation. All he could remember was Kevin looking like he wanted to kill the dart board. What had they talked about?

"New vids," Kevin explained with a smile.

"Oh!" In Aidan's ears the syllable came out like a gunshot. He wished it hadn't come out so loudly. "Um, great. What'd you get?"

"I can show you, if you'd like?" The redhead turned the statement into a question halfway through, a brow quirking behind those weird glasses.

Five minutes later, the vid screen in the rec room lit up. The movie was ancient. It was weird. But it was surprisingly fun. Kevin sighed as the movie ended, and glanced at Aidan, grey eyes dancing. "So, what did you think?"

Aidan grinned. "Honestly, I think you better not show that to anybody else. They'll give you shit."

Kevin rolled his eyes. "This is nothing new by any stretch of the imagination. They always give me shit," he agreed with theatrical weariness. "They believe sticking pins in my ego is good for me."

For a moment, they sat and watched the credits roll on opposite sides of the couch.

"I actually have a lot of vids in my collection nobody else can stand," Kevin remarked eventually. "Any time you'd like to see something new and unusual, check in with me, will you?"

Aidan's eyes widened. One heartbeat passed in silence. Two. *What do I say?* Aidan's brain asked itself frantically. *What do I say that won't sound weird, creepy as hell or totally idiotic? What do I say to keep this from getting weird? All right, weirder?* He swallowed. "They aren't all this bad, are they?"

Kevin shot him an acknowledging smirk. "Ouch."

Aidan grinned as his muscles relaxed. Joking. He could do joking. He could do this.

"Anyway," Kevin added with a gesture at the screen. "The rec room is usually fairly free on Tuesdays. Maybe we can institute a Movies That Don't Rot Your Brain night for base members with taste."

Aidan sat frozen, staring straight ahead. Check in with Kevin. Regular vid nights. For the whole base, he scolded himself. A regular vid night for the base. Not for the two of you. He's not asking you out. He has no reason to ask you out. Get your head on straight.

"Yeah. That sounds good," he managed eventually. It took all his energy to turn and give his logistics officer a smile, but he managed it. "I don't know a lot about old vids, so maybe I can learn."

The smile he got from Kevin made the effort worth it. "I'd be happy to provide a bit of an education," the officer replied quietly.

Event File 18
File Tag: Operational Maneuvers
Timestamp: 13:00-5-1-2155

This heat could drive you crazy. Lying in the rabbit brush, Aidan could feel the sun pounding through his slick poncho, making his chill vest hum into overdrive. This heat could drive you out of your mind.

Breathing in, he caught a nose full of dust, coughed, and cursed himself for an idiot as he lowered the visor of his riding helmet. It wasn't fun breathing recirculated air, but it was even less fun trying to breathe hot dust.

"Anything?" he asked into his mic.

"Fifteen minute ETA," Kevin's voice murmured in his ear.

Lazarus shifted in the brush on his left, adjusting the small slick tarp that hid his rifle's barrel. His slick poncho rippled as its nanowire fabric adjusted, making Aidan blink reflexively as his eyes tried to focus on something barely visible. The munitions officer said nothing, all his focus on the tab recording drone signatures in the area and the view in front of him.

The disused maintenance shed behind the warehouse sat and baked on its concrete slab. The nanomesh of the fence between them and it glinted in the hard sunlight, shifting on its struts as thin breezes moved its fabric. The nanomesh was enough to keep Fringers from trying to raid the little suburb full of American AgCo botanists, plant breeders, crop-drone programmers and information analysts. As a side benefit, it made sure no one started thinking about leaving their area of the Grid without a visa. If the warning signs posted eight feet from the fence didn't deter them, the scattering of small bird and animal corpses were a reminder that touching the fence was a really bad move.

"Just finished the garden tour. We're on our free exploration time, now." Kevin's voice whispered in Aidan's ear. "Ten minute ETA."

"Roger," Lazarus's voice agreed quietly. Shifting, the other man slid like an eel out of the brush and jogged up to the nearest electrified strut. Keeping his position, Aidan checked his tab.

"Reading?" Aidan asked quietly. In the pause between question and answer, he could hear his own blood pumping in his ears. He counted his breaths. *Relax.*

They'd planned every detail of this for a week. Kevin had spent two days on Grid making arrangements. *Nothing was going to go wrong. Relax.*

Lazarus read slowly, flickers outlining where he stood scanning the strut with a repurposed digital multimeter. "Looks like two hundred milliamps, and the mesh is on network. Yeah, there it is. Network's at five GHz. Fragmentation threshold for the mesh's at twenty-three six, beacon interval's at ten."

Aidan put the information into the algorithm on his tab. "Right. Set the EMP for alpha setting. And... go."

He held his breath. If they didn't get the EMP charge right, or if American AgCo had upgraded the nanobots forming the mesh, the microscopic machines would recover from the signal interruption and send up an alert far too soon.

There was a soft thunk. The hairs on the back of Aidan's neck stood up.

"Out," Lazarus stated in his ear.

Aidan breathed again. "Okay. We've got thirty minutes starting now. Kevin?"

The answer came hesitantly. "ETA five minutes. Sir, we have a potential issue. Health related."

Aidan's gut clenched. "Mission impacting?"

"Possibly."

Aidan drew three slow breaths. In. Out. In. Out. Stay calm. "Okay. Just get them to the fence. We'll assess from here."

"Roger. ETA three minutes."

Aidan focused on keeping his breathing slow. And there they were. Nine people scuttling behind the prefab shed, Kevin bringing up the rear. They huddled behind the building as Kevin held the nanomesh fabric taut and Lazarus began to slice. It didn't take long to cut a hole large enough for a person to duck through.

Kevin ushered the refugees through one by one. Aidan could hear him in his mic as he coached four men, two women and two girls with quick, cheerful words. "Right this way, folks. Mind the edges. The mesh can cut. Ladies, quickly now, thanks. And—"

One of the girls yipped in terror as a man swayed. Aidan watched as Kevin turned and caught him under the arms, holding the man up until he steadied.

Health-related issues, Aidan thought. Not good.

"You're doing fine, girls," Kevin's voice was encouraging in Aidan's mic. "Let's just keep moving, shall we? A mile's walk to the vehicle we've got for you, a nice drive down to Pueblo, and you're on your way. Nothing to worry about as long as we keep moving."

Aidan wished they could have pulled the vehicle in closer, but within a mile of a Corporate installation they ran too high a risk of something as large as a truck being spotted as they drove in.

He flipped up his visor, checked his tab. Twenty-eight minutes before the fence came back online. Thirty-five minutes before the next ViperDrone flyover. Fifty minutes before the next satellite pass.

Lazarus helped Kevin get the weak member of the party through the mesh. The logistics officer smiled wryly as he herded the group to his commander. The man he supported gave a weak travesty of a smile as well, reaching out to shake Aidan's hand with fingers that trembled. "Saul. Thanks for taking care of us."

"Part of what we're here for," Aidan replied with a grim smile.

"You okay?"

Saul's jaw tightened. "I guess I've gotta be."

Aidan didn't exactly love the sound of that answer, but he gave the man a nod. "Okay, everybody stick close and follow us. We'll get you out of here."

They made a ragged line, the civilians tripping over rabbit brush and kochia, coughing as they breathed gritty dust kicked up in the wind. Aidan glanced over his shoulder and winced. Lazarus had dropped back to support Saul, who was barely on his feet.

Discreetly, Aidan dropped back. "What's up?"

Lazarus shot him a dark look. "Guy's having some trouble, is all. He'll get there," he snapped.

Aidan held Lazarus's eyes until Saul gave a dry bark of a chuckle. "Hope so. Been stuck in a safe house for two weeks. Go-between got spooked. Didn't get food for a week. Kinda hard to walk."

Aidan's mouth grew dry, but he managed a smile. "Keep leaning on us. We'll get you through."

Saul's death's-head smile flickered again. "Thanks."

Aidan gave both men a smile. Lazarus returned only a glower. Okay, not helpful. Stepping away, Aidan helped one of the little girls step around a patch of nasty cholla. From behind, he heard a bottle rattle softly.

"Glucose tabs," Kevin murmured. "See if they help."

"Thanks," Saul muttered.

Aidan shot his logistics officer a quick, grateful grin over his shoulder. The logistics officer returned a discreet thumbs' up and a small smile.

A quarter of a mile later, Aidan turned at the sound of a yelp behind him. His gut turned over on itself. Saul was on the ground, hands and knees braced against the gritty soil. He could barely raise his head when Aidan knelt beside him.

"Saul? I need you to try to lean on Lazarus. I need you to try to get up." He put as much calm as he could into his voice, wishing he sounded more sure himself.

Saul shook his head. "Can't." As if to prove his point, the man tried to push himself up, slipped, and would have fallen face first into the dirt if the two men on either side hadn't caught him.

Aidan could hear the rest of the group slowing, hear their anxious murmurs as they clustered around.

Saul drew a ragged breath. "Look. I know your guys' protocol. Mills Clause. Just get the kids out of hearing range first."

Aidan's heart skipped a beat. He raised his head. His munitions officer stared at him blankly, thoughts shuttered behind his eyes. Page fifteen of the Civilian Evacuation Procedure. The Mills Clause.

Behind him, Kevin spoke quietly. "Try a few more of the glucose—"

Saul hacked a parody of a laugh. "Man, grow up. I'm out. Get moving. No time for this."

Aidan felt as if he'd been riveted to the ground. The Mills Clause. It was procedure, and as ranking officer, his job included its execution. If a civilian was incapacitated but still coherent, they would become a goldmine of information if they fell into Corporate hands.

That couldn't happen. And leaving a man behind to slowly die in the desert was probably worse than a bullet. A bullet. He could hear his breathing, ragged in the confines of his helmet. The Mills Clause. His throat felt tight. Procedure.

A bullet.

Aidan shook his head so fast he felt as if he'd wrenched his neck. "Yeah. No time. Lazarus?"

The man stared at him with empty eyes. Aidan swallowed, feeling the ache in his tight throat. "You've got the tripods for two guns right?"

The taller man nodded, watching Aidan like a bird of prey. Aidan glanced at Saul. "Get them out."

They were fifteen minutes late to the truck, and eighteen minutes late arriving in Pueblo. Their dark-eyed go-between already had his mouth open when Aidan got out of the truck inside the old warehouse, already complaining.

"--the hell were you? I thought you'd got nabbed. Another five minutes, and I was *gone*, man! What the fuck?"

"Ran into a problem," Aidan stated shortly. "We're here now." The darker man sneered. "Yeah? You were supposed to be here half an hour ago, *mama guevo*. I want to get out of here and now I have to wait another fucking hour while the satellite finishes its pass and--*Hijo de la gran puta.*"

Aidan followed the man's shocked gaze to where Saul was being manhandled out of the back of the jeep. The makeshift stretcher couldn't have been comfortable, but Saul had fallen asleep on it. The belts of the three Dusters and everyone else in the party wrapped around the struts that had been Lazarus's gun tripods had made carrying him possible. Four of his fellow activists laid the sleeping man gently on the floor.

The border runner turned hot eyes on Aidan. Stepping in, he glared down at the shorter man. His voice was a hiss. "You're supposed to leave the ones who can't make it in the desert with a bullet in them, you *amemao*. That's the procedure."

Aidan had expected to feel his body tense as the man tried to loom over him. He hadn't expected the cold anger that came instead, but it ran into his gut and up his backbone. One more person who wanted to throw away anybody who wasn't up to their standards. One more asshole.

But this asshole had to listen to him.

"He can make it fine," Aidan stated, absently thrilled that anger dropped his voice so low. "He needs sleep and a couple meals. But he's going to make it. You do your job and you'll get your money."

"We'll help," one of the activists added, defiance and fear in his voice. Aidan glanced at the man kneeling beside his friend, met his eyes and gave a quick nod. The man smiled anxiously, nodded in reply.

Behind Aidan, the border runner snorted. "Here. I need a thumbprint saying you dropped them off. I'm reporting this to your people, I hope you know that. It's your fucking procedure."

Aidan shrugged, holding the man's eyes as he placed his thumb on the surface of the tab the man held out. "Then it's not your problem. It's mine."

Before the machine beeped, the border runner had looked away.

Aidan glanced at his men, nodded in the direction of their truck. "Let's go."

It was quiet inside the vehicle for a long, long time. Aidan stared out the window as Lazarus drove, trying to control the shaking of his hands.

He'd just done that. He'd really just done that. He'd just figured out a situation that could have killed them all and stared down a Dominican border runner. He'd have to explain breaking procedure to Magnum. But that shit-show could wait for another day. He drew a slow breath. "Kevin?"

"Yes?" the man in the back seat asked.

"Add new tripods for Munitions to the 3D-print list for the base. Check and see if we need any special materials for it."

"Of course."

Silence.

Half an hour later, Lazarus shifted in his driving seat. "I thought you were supposed to be the one who made us follow procedure from now on."

"Depends on the procedure," Aidan replied quietly. "Always thought the Mills Clause was stupid."

Silence.

Lazarus cleared his throat. "I got a bottle of black rum the other day. Told Sarah it was rifle-barrel cleaner, so maybe she hasn't drunk it. You guys want a drink when we get back?"

Aidan had to force himself not to whip around and stare at the man. Swallowing hard, he managed a smile. "Yeah. That'd be great."

Lazarus nodded once. "Okay, then."

The rum was awful, but the drinking felt good. For the first time since he'd arrived, Aidan found himself smiling as he walked into his quarters and shut the door that night.

In his pocket, his tab pinged.

Pulling it out, he read the words. Then he read them again.

Message Handle: Sector40COM

Message: Congratulations Headly. One month today. You kept the deal.

Meeting with me day after tomorrow. Going to do two months?

Aidan stared at the message for a long, long time. When his hand was steady enough, he typed six letters.

Message Handle: AceOfSpades

Message: Yes sir.

Event File 19
File Tag: Talent Search
Timestamp: 13:00-7-4-2155

"And in further news, the woman charged with copyright infringement by the Cavanaugh Corporation when her daughter's genome was found to contain proprietary information was—"

"Can't you turn that thing down?"

"Hmm?" Kevin asked, pulling out one ear bud. The strains of The Doobie Brothers' 'Drift Away' floated out into the room.

Yvonne rolled her eyes. "I said, can't you turn the room's wall screen down? It's driving me nuts."

Absently, Kevin tossed her a set of 'buds in their baggie, eyes on his screen and tab in his lap. "It's a cheap room and they'll notice tampering or signal interference. Stiff upper lip, my dear girl."

He saw Yvonne give him her patent 'older sister is not amused' expression out of the corner of his eye.

"You put four white noise and sound box filters on the room and you're worried about messing up the wall screen?"

Kevin shrugged. "White noise filters aren't interrupting any other signals. We've only got one more day to go. Now do be quiet.

You wouldn't want to let the neighbors hear a married couple fight would you? It'd set a terrible example."

He smiled thinly as he heard Yvonne sigh and flop onto the bed. Of course, the question of 'the neighbors' hearing anything was moot with four sound boxes sitting discreetly under and inside furniture, sending out a subsonic white-noise buzz that blocked anyone more than twenty feet away from discerning actual sounds. This model created electrical signals that would be read by any listening devices as the normal sounds of a couple chatting about nothing and moving in a room.

The question of the two of them being a married couple was laughable too, though they could pass for either husband and wife or brother and sister easily on undercover runs. That was always useful. This sort of teasing served him well for dispelling the tension in the room, but he wished Yvonne would hush and let him really concentrate.

Yvonne glanced up with mild interest from her spot.

"What are you working so hard on anyway? We got the contact, the new ID and intel they needed."

"Trying to track that coder we heard about a while ago," Kevin replied distractedly, studying the screen. "Several of the best session prediction algorithm software sets recently put up for sale on the GreyNet have the same signature in their headers. It was on the software Jazz sold us too." He hit the directional button on his tab, and the hologram of the screen dissolved and reformed facing Yvonne. "See this?" he added, underlining the little glyph with a finger as Yvonne leaned in.

<(-_-)>^^^^^/

"It may be entirely coincidence, but the work's very much of the caliber that Jazz's new friend produces. I'm interested in seeing what else this kid's getting up to. I got the contact approval, so I'm hoping to find somewhere in the Social Feeds or the Greynet where she's active and I can discuss terms with her, but so far no dice."

Yvonne snorted a laugh. "What the hell is that? Is it supposed to be some kind of bug?"

"A bogeyman of some sort, I was thinking," Kevin replied thoughtfully, squinting. He reached up, then dropped his hand with an annoyed sigh yet again. The contacts did a fine job, but they didn't give the tactile satisfaction his glasses did. "Or maybe a dragon?"

Yvonne glanced up slowly, an entirely different sort of giggle escaping her.

Kevin raised a brow. "What?"

"I was just thinking about the way Aidan looked when you showed him the vid with the dragon in it." Yvonne held her barely controlled grin a moment longer before losing control and bursting out in a fit of giggles. "Oh god, his face. I think that level of gamma broke his brains."

"I object!" Kevin exclaimed, shoving the woman in mock affront as she rolled helplessly giggling into his lap, "*Dragonheart's* a cult classic!"

"That bullshit is so gamma it's got three heads," Yvonne refuted, shaking her head with a grin.

Kevin rolled his eyes, a sheepish smile stealing across his face. "All right, it isn't the best thing ever made, but you're supposed to watch it for the conceptual message. I mean, valor! Chivalry! The world needs rather more of that."

"Yeah, well," Yvonne shrugged, sitting up. "Your all valor-y knight was a total scammer." Brushing her hair out of her eyes, she rested her chin on her fists, watching her basemate.

"You and Aidan have been doing a lot of movie nights. Nobody is even bothering with the rec room on Tuesdays anymore."

"He's interested in the history of film, so we've been doing an informal tour of film eras," Kevin demurred, turning his screen back to its forward position. "I'm enjoying discussing the subject with someone who evinces a modicum of taste." In fact, he'd been enjoying discussing everything with Aidan on Tuesday nights these past months. It had been a long time since he'd been around someone who listened and actually considered ideas you tossed out before speaking.

Most people were only waiting until their conversational companion shut up and let them talk, but not Aidan. The man was possibly the most relaxing conversation partner Kevin had known. He was the kind of man you could say anything to without fear.

Almost anything, Kevin reminded himself. He'd been getting dangerously sloppy lately around Aidan. He'd said things he shouldn't about his own childhood, and he knew it. Aidan was all too easy to talk to sometimes. But he really was interested in the movies and the ideas that came out of them. Finding films that would make his blue eyes light up had become something of a hobby in itself for Kevin.

But Yvonne didn't need to know that. The wall screen's inane chatter didn't fill the silence in the room. Kevin kept his eyes on his screen as Yvonne watched him. "It's been three whole months of vid nights. You started into this century yet?"

Kevin smirked, shook his head. "Not even close. We started with 'Who's On First'."

"Hunh?"

"Black and white vid. Don't worry about it."

"Okay then."

Kevin found another code sample, glanced at the header. Dragon signature. He downloaded it.

"He's kind of working out, isn't he?" Yvonne's voice murmured over the noise of the screen.

"Mm?" Kevin asked absently.

"Aidan. He's kind of working out, isn't he?" Yvonne added. "He's been really good on the mission planning. We're getting shit done right again. Sector's finally off our asses. Laz is kind of okay with him as commander now, too. I mean, he's stopped pulling shit and getting write-ups from Liza and Damian all the time."

"So have you, for that matter," Kevin added, squinting at the screen. He heard Yvonne snort.

"You know I was only doing shit to keep Laz company."

"Tell that to the last poor bastard you kneed in the crotch," Kevin demurred wryly.

Yvonne gave a little 'humph.' "Guy asked for it, picking on Sarah. If I didn't do it, she would've."

Kevin didn't bother to respond to that comment beyond a murmur of commiseration. Silence.

"You kissed him yet?" Yvonne asked, cocking her head. "Aidan, I mean, not Laz. That'd just be weird."

Kevin finally raised his eyes, giving his friend a long, level look. "Yve, I'd like to live into my forties at least. Don't get sloppy about on-Grid conversations."

Yvonne snorted down her long, delicate nose. "Oh, don't even. We just planned and executed a deep-cover intel drop out of here. If it's secure enough for that, it's secure enough for this. Chickenshit," she added, elbowing him gently.

Kevin sighed, resetting his screen so that it projected at eye level and sitting up a little. "People can have hobbies and platonic relationships. Not everything is about sex, Yve." He stored a copy of the next code snippet, and dug up a new one.

Yvonne flopped back again. He could feel her watching him. "Kev, honey, if you're crushing and you want to get your mind off it, I know this guy, Dustin, on Base 870. He's a nice guy. He's gay. He'd be good for you. I know it's been tough since Peter took off on you, but—"

"No, Yvonne," Kevin replied with the weariness of the world in his voice, deliberately misconstruing her words. "Being gay is a negligible little issue that may get me shot one day. What's 'tough' is the fact that certain people assume you'd like to sleep with every other gay man on the planet. I can make my own arrangements, thank you. I'm all grown up these days."

"Sorry I asked," Yvonne muttered. Kevin wished he'd kept his mouth shut.

Twenty minutes passed in silence. Kevin shut down his tab and stood. "I'm going to run and check in with Dilya. If you want to check up on Rivera, we can head home tomorrow morning."

"Sure," Yvonne murmured absently.

In the doorway, Kevin stopped, glancing back at the woman on the bed. "Sorry," he murmured. Then he was out the door.

Outside, he fell into his easy stride, tucking his 'buds into either ear.

The contact Kevin labeled as Dilya in their base files had a very nice office in the Wash Park area, housed in one of the few renovated nineteenth-century houses that still stood. Kevin climbed the stairs and held his hand out to the discrete thumbprint reader. "I'm expected," he added, and the voice recognition in the security system beeped through the panel. The door at the top of the stairs clicked into its unlocked position.

Dilya's home was what Kevin thought he might have opted for himself, had things gone differently. He let himself relax a little into the warm dark wood, the white walls and the tasteful antiques as he walked through the small loft where the man lived above his offices. At the study door, he knocked softly on the frame and cleared his throat.

"Afternoon."

At the desk, the grizzle-haired man glanced up and smiled. "John!" Standing, he gave Kevin a quick hug, then a handshake. The warm light gleamed on the blue Wellness Chip set in the skin of his wrist.

Kevin shook the older man's hand with a grin. "How is everything? How's the family?"

"We're doing well, very well. Marta's just turned seven, and she passed her ArgusCo Aptitude with flying colors. She's headed to the ArgusCo Primary Education next week." The thickset financial planner beamed. "I had to pull a few strings, but my Corporation has agreed to allow her to move into their workforce and trade outa young man who's more suited to their needs. She'll make a wonderful city planner when she's finished."

Discreetly, Dilya tapped his pen on the desk, and Kevin felt the tingle in his ears as a sound box began to work somewhere in the room.

"And you? How are things? Did the information I got you do any good?" Dilya asked.

"A shocking amount," Kevin agreed with a grim smile. "We very carefully leaked the information on your superior's bad habits in all the right places. You should see it on your news feed any time now. We've already been seeing the turmoil. It's left us a wonderful loophole to empty a few illicit bank accounts while everyone was distracted."

Neither of them said aloud that anyone who could do what the men high in the Denver branch of National Banking had been doing to children at their private club needed to go down in the most public and messy way that could be arranged.

"I think I may have seen it already," the other man replied, his smile cold. "Portam has been given a month's 'sick leave'. I have the feeling he won't be back. As much as I hate the cause, at least this scandal will do some good now that it's out. We think every Denver CES-level member of National Banking's management will be taken down by this." The older man raked fingers through his hair. "Honestly, John, sometimes I wonder if they've edited the empathy out of CES people all together. Children."

Kevin nodded. "And how are the kids?"

"Recovering," the older man replied. "We've got them in a program. They'll heal in time. We're getting them positions in another city when they're old enough."

Kevin nodded, reaching over to clasp the other man's shoulder for a beat. Dilya returned the gesture.

They lived in a strange world. He would never call this man by his real name, yet Kevin had more respect for this man than some base commanders he knew. Anyone brave enough to stay on Grid and fight the system quietly from within was high on his list.

The older man studied his face. "You look tired, son." Stepping around his desk, he pulled out a crystal decanter and a glass, poured a measure. "Do you have time to relax?"

"A little, but I can't take your—"

"Psh." The older man waved a hand. "Grain production was good last year, almost a forty percent survival rate. The price is down. They're practically giving the drink away. Enjoy."

Tentatively, Kevin took a sip. "Thanks."

"Good?"

"Better than I've had in some time." Kevin tipped the glass in acknowledgement. "To a good day's work."

"Skol," the older man agreed, pouring himself a measure.

Kevin had just begun to relax when his tab pinged in his pocket. Pulling it out, he checked the physical screen rather than activating the hologram.

Message Handle: NineOfHearts

Message: FOUND YOUR CODER. Meet me.

Below a GPS coordinate blinked, waiting to be clicked.

Kevin shook his head as he read, suppressing the urge to grin. Leave it to Yvonne.

"Sorry, Dilya, I'm back on duty. We'll finish this drink next time, shall we?"

Yvonne was down an alley when Kevin finally found her, and she was practically vibrating with excitement.

"I checked in with Rivera," she murmured, grabbing Kevin's elbow and leading him further down. "Then I figured I'd say hi to Jazz while I was up this way. Well, that girl, you know, her new assistant?

She was heading out the back and she was looking around all nervous, right? So, I got interested. I followed her down here, and, Kev, there's a whole coding rig down in one of the apartments. A shitty one, but it's a rig all right, in the basement. Saw it through the window."

"Through the window?" Kevin asked in surprise.

Yvonne grinned. "Okay, through a scope shoved under the window. They had it blocked with cardboard was all. And there's no security system. She's too good to have no security."

"Especially with you around, apparently," Kevin agreed dryly. "Curiosity kill the standards as well as the cat, did it?"

Yvonne rolled her eyes. "Cut it out, Kev. I gave you solid intel. You're the officer. Do we follow up?"

Kevin considered the idea, studying the door that led down to the basement level of the building. His mind ran through possibilities, but there were no warning signs here. This kind of Citizen Poor Standing area was too downtrodden to be watched particularly closely.

Eventually, he shrugged. "We can knock on the door while we're here, I suppose. But we're playing this close to the vest, agreed?"

Yvonne bobbed her head in agreement. "I know the drill, boss. You talk, I stand here and look pretty."

Kevin gave her a dry look. "Haha." Straightening his shoulders, he headed down the stairs, Yvonne at his back.

The door squeaked as it opened, and one wide brown eye peeped through the gap between chain and door frame. "What?"

"Afternoon," Kevin began with a gentle smile, hands spread to show them empty. "A mutual friend suggested that we come by for a chat. We hear there's a very good coder in the area, and we've got a project that needs her skills."

The gap closed a fraction as the girl behind the door jerked. "Dunno anybody coding. Who says?"

"A few friends," Kevin deflected easily. "But the sort of contract we can offer could be lucrative if there was a coder around. We offer good money for good work. On the other hand, it's hard to discuss details standing in a hallway..."

Silence behind the door. The eye watched them, panicky. "Get lost."

The door started to close. Adrenaline shot through Kevin. Quickly, he stepped forward and put the toe of his boot in the doorjamb. "Please, just—"

There was an odd scuffle behind the wood, and then the door and the world seemed to explode. A breath later, he was flat on his back, bells were ringing in his head, and a very nasty set of electric brass knuckles were sparking inches from his face.

Event File 20
File Tag: Valuable Skills
Timestamp: 15:00-7-4-2155

"The fuck are you?"

Kevin stared up at the girl straddling him, trying to piece together a coherent sentence through the pain in his head. It was like having an angry starling perched on his chest. She was tiny. She would have been interesting, possibly even pretty, if her face hadn't been a mask of rage. The black leather jacket she wore couldn't be hers. It was at least three sizes too big. Bandaged hands the size of a child's stuck out of sleeves the same color as the shining, straight hair. The eyes were black too in this light. An angry starling. Yes, that was a good description.

He was going to die, and he was spending his last moments deciding on descriptors for his murderer. Funny what the brain did under stress.

"What the fuck? Tweak! Get off him!"

The girl looked up like a feral dog, snarling. "You s-sold us out! Bitch! F-f-fuck you!"

"Oh for godssakes, Tweak, give it a rest." Jazz sighed, coming down the alley. "And get off him, he's harmless."

"Harmless?" Kevin muttered dazedly. "Jazz, you'll ruin a reputation that way."

Jazz's irritated face stared down at him, beaded dreadlocks clacking together. "Yeah, keep talking smart and you'll get a taze in the throat. What the ever loving fuck are you guys doing?" She glanced at the tiny woman still sitting on Kevin's chest. "Tweak. Seriously, you're okay. Get up and put that thing away. These guys are okay. I know them."

As if she'd been electrocuted herself, the little woman leaped off Kevin's chest. Warily, Jazz knelt, offering him a hand.

"Thanks," Kevin managed, slowly levering himself to his feet and waiting for the world to stop spinning. He smiled weakly at Jazz, who didn't smile in return.

"Don't try to play nice, I'm still pissed. The hell are you guys doing here? Don't make me ask again."

"Maybe we can talk inside?" Yvonne suggested quietly. Kevin was glad someone had.

Jazz sighed. "Okay, fine. Tweak? Billie? I swear they won't stay long. I'll get rid of them myself when they get to be a pain. Is it okay?"

Kevin watched dazedly as the tiny Asian girl held her taller friend's eyes. Billie bit her lip. Finally, the taller girl nodded. "I guess?"

Soon enough, Kevin was sitting in a three legged chair with a wet washcloth held to the back of his head, watching the two girls and Jazz. Yvonne leaned against the wall behind him, her hand on his shoulder.

"Okay. Give," Jazz snapped.

Yvonne shrugged. "I saw Billie coming out of your place and I figured I'd give her a job offer, 'cause you weren't doing it. Or give... Tweak the offer I guess. Who codes so good?"

Kevin resisted the instinct to cringe. If the situation hadn't been so delicate, he would have corrected his foster sister's abominable sentence structure.

"Tweak," the black girl murmured, talking down to her hands.

The tiny Asian beside her glared, eyes still slitted. "So?" the girl spat.

"So," Kevin stated, "we always need a good coder. We were wondering if you'd be interested in freelancing. Or in coming on with us, for that matter."

"I warned you, Kevin," Jazz growled. "Don't go there." "Go where?" Tweak demanded, and Kevin was struck by the way she spoke. Every word was said as if she was rationing the air it took, staccato bursts with distinct pauses between them. He wondered where she was from as she continued, "What gives? Who're they?"

Jazz gave a long sigh. "Dusters, Tweak. These two are Dusters."

Tweak's eyes widened. Kevin studied her as she stared at him. He would have liked to ask how old she was. She looked no more than fifteen.

"Dust?" the girl asked, her voice rising. "Off-g-g-Grid?" She stumbled over the word, stuttering it out.

Ah. Not an accent, Kevin thought. An attempt to say things in a way that accommodated a bad stutter. Poor thing.

Moving slowly in case he startled the girl, he nodded. "Logistical division of the Wildcards base. Pleasure to make your acquaintance."

Tweak stared at him blankly. Then she turned to Jazz. "The fuck?"

"Don't worry about Kevin. He collects old words for fun. Problem is he uses them, too. He means hi," Yvonne explained behind him.

Tweak glanced up at her. "He yours?"

Yvonne barked a laugh. "My baby brother, sure. My officer. Nothing else."

Tweak glanced at Billie. Then she turned those black eyes back on Kevin. "How you get off-g-Grid?"

Jazz drew a breath. "Tweak, that's—"

"Gotta," the girl interrupted shortly. "Gotta. Gotta g-go. We g-g-get out. S-s-safe off-g-Grid."

"Depending on your definition of safe," Kevin stated carefully. "I won't mislead you, Tweak, but if you would like off the Grid there are options. With your skills, we'd be overjoyed to count you in our ranks. Or we could arrange to get you out of the country in exchange for some consultation and code work."

"Some?" Tweak demanded, and Kevin smiled. "You'd have to work it out with my commander."

The tiny girl cocked her head. "Who?"

"The commander of my base," Kevin explained. "He's the one who makes decisions. My job is to supply expertise."

"What?"

"The commander tells us what to do and we figure out how to do it," Yvonne explained gently. "So, if you wanted to be a Duster, our commander would have to approve it. And if we made a deal for getting you off Grid, he'd decide how much work that's worth in trade."

Tweak stared at them, hands clenched on the edge of the table. "Where he?"

"At home," Kevin replied, watching both girls carefully. Tweak was practically shaking, and Billie had hunched even lower in her chair. He met Jazz's smoldering eyes. No wonder she'd been so protective. These two were like a pair of street puppies that someone had beaten. One wrong word would set either of them off. But the right words could get the Force that amazing coding skill. How had a CPS level girl as young as this gotten the resources to become such a coding prodigy?

He set that question aside for later analysis. "Our commanders don't come on Grid very often. The danger's too great."

Tweak gave a short, sharp bark of a laugh. "D-danger. No shit."

She cocked her head from one side to the other. "He makes the rules?"

"For our base," Kevin agreed quietly, realizing that he was smiling. "Yes."

"You guys fight the f-fuckers? The Corps?"

Kevin's smile grew cold as he nodded. "Oh, yes. That's what we're here for."

The girl stared at him as if she could read his thoughts off the back of his skull. "You winning?"

Kevin gave a shrug. He'd shoot himself in the foot before he'd admit how close they were to losing, but he wouldn't lie to the girl. "We're trying. We think we do some good."

Tweak's fingers began to tap on the table. She swallowed hard. Then she turned. "Billie? Talk."

Billie slowly raised her head. Then she glanced at the rest of the table apologetically. "We're gonna go into the bedroom for a couple minutes," she whispered. "Be out in a bit."

She stood and followed her friend into the tiny bedroom, leaving the three staring at each other. The sound of the door closing seemed loud in the tight space.

If he strained, Kevin could just make out the murmur of voices. He glanced at Jazz. "This building is clean, isn't it?"

Jazz gave him a dry look. "Too piss poor to be worth a bug. I checked. If I hadn't, I wouldn't be chilling. Cool it."

Kevin nodded, and regretted the movement. Tweak really had fetched a good crack to his head. He should have seen that coming. But she'd been so unbelievably fast. Finally, the two young women stepped out. Standing side by side, they stared at the three people sitting around the table.

"Wanna fight. Wanna k-kick ass," Tweak stated, every word sharp

"Wonderful, we'll make the—" Kevin began, but the girl cut him off

"I wanna talk to your boss first. Deal," Tweak rattled out. "Not m-m-middle m-m… Not you. Your boss. I make deals with the boss. Not the help. "

Kevin tried not to take the girl's bluntness as an insult. Since when had he been the help? "We can arrange a vid call over—"

"No!" The girl slashed a bandaged hand through the air as she spoke.

Bandaged palms. Bandaged arms under that leather jacket, perhaps? Kevin set that aside to consider later as well.

"Vids easy t-to fake. F-face to f-f-face. Or nothing. T-t-t-take it or leave."

"She means we meet who's in charge in person or we don't go, take it or leave it," Billie added quietly.

Tweak stared at him with the fierce, frightened eyes of a street kid. She was breathing so fast that the jacket's zipper jangled a quiet metallic percussion.

Kevin considered his options. Finally, he nodded. "I'm not authorized to make you a promise, but I'll discuss it with my commander. I'm almost certain he'd see the trip to meet you as worth the risk. We'd really value you as part of the team."

No response. His charming smile was going nowhere. He turned to Jazz. "Can we use you as a liaison in setting this up?"

Jazz gave him a glare of disgust. But she glanced at the girls, sighed, and nodded. "Don't guess I got much of a choice. Bastard," she growled.

Kevin repressed a wince as he nodded. "Thanks. You're a great help."

That got him another incendiary glare.

Kevin knew when his welcome was worn out. Carefully, he stood, glad the dizziness had receded into a dull headache. "We'll be in touch within two weeks. Thanks for having us in." He held out his hand to shake. Tweak leaned back in her seat. "Nobody touch me."

Kevin lowered his hand. "My apologies." No response.

Jazz closed the door behind them, following them down the alley. But she stepped in front of the Dusters before they'd reached the street. "You two just tried to recruit a pair of fucking babies who already got it hard into a war. You ever fuck me and mine over like that again and you people can find yourselves another mech'n'tech. Capiche?"

Kevin stared down at the woman, the ache in his head and the sting of truth in her words combining to leave him drained. He said the only thing he could. "I'm sorry Jazz, but they're in a war already. We all are."

Gently, he stepped past her and into the heat of the day.

Event File 21
File Tag: Due Consideration
Timestamp: 10:45-7-5-2155

"She wants what?" Aidan's voice sounded wrong in his own ears.

"An in-person meeting with you, on the Grid, before she decides if she'll come on with us," Kevin repeated carefully, watching his commander with wary eyes across the desk. "That is, if you approve my presentation of recruitment purpose to Sector and they approve us taking her on. It's got its risks but given the edge her work could give us…"

Aidan didn't hear the rest of what Kevin was saying. An on-Grid meeting. On Grid, where you needed to have a Citizen Card coded to your genome to access anything. If security personnel from any of the Corps got nervy and decided to run a DNA sampler over his hand to check his genome against the card, if a store employee didn't like his attitude and decided to log the Citizen Card he was carrying and a sample of his DNA from something he touched? If they saw the mismatch between his appearance and his goddamn chromosomes?

He'd be detained. He'd be dead.

Worse than dead, depending on which Corporation caught him. If it was EagleCorp or AgCo with their Morality Laws, if it was

Cavanaugh and their Perfection Mandate, he wouldn't just be dead. He'd be made an example of. Because he wasn't just a Duster. A Duster was simply the enemy. But him?

He was an aberration in their eyes. A perversion to frighten their people with. Something to destroy as publicly as possible.

He'd seen too many vids of what the Corps did with morality executions in his life. Anything was better than dying like that, as some sick moral-lesson sideshow broadcast on the news feeds for days.

"Is something the matter?"

Aidan snapped his attention back, realizing how fast he was breathing. Kevin was staring at him, brow creased.

"Sir-sorry, Aidan? Are you—"

"Fine," Aidan managed. "Fine, sorry, it's just... Sorry, I was just trying to work it out in my head, I..." He swallowed hard. "So, she won't-she won't do a vid call?"

"She says vid calls are too easy to fake, and I'll admit she does have a point," Kevin replied cautiously, watching him with knit brows.

Could the guy see how frightened he was? God, he hoped not, but the answer was probably yes. Aidan nodded, swallowing to try to get some moisture into his burning throat. "Maybe we could schedule an off-Grid meeting, somewhere on one of the back roads? I'm-I'm really not liking the idea of going on-Grid, with the Command-level information in my head. I kind of don't like the idea of what they could get out of me if the Corps made us."

Yes. He had the perfect defense as commander. After all, what any Corporation would do to any base commander wouldn't be pretty. Maybe not as ugly as what they'd do to someone like him, but worth being afraid of, right?

Across the desk, Kevin nodded slowly, eyes distant. Methodically, he took off his glasses and polished them as he spoke. "Not that I'm disagreeing with you, sir, but I'm not sure if... Well, why don't we speak to Jazz about it? I can schedule a vid-call with her for us this afternoon?"

Aidan jerked his head in a nod. "Yeah. Thank you. That sounds good."

Kevin nodded, but he rose from his seat slowly, standing behind the chair.

"Sir—Sorry, Aidan. I want you to know that I've executed maneuvers of this level in the past with Commander Taylor and other base commanders. If you have any specific concerns just let me know and I can plan for them. But as much as I can assure anything, I'll assure your safety if you do decide to proceed. I know my work."

Specific concerns? Aidan had to tamp down the urge to burst out laughing. If Kevin only knew. But if he did know—No. Not an option. "Thanks, Kevin," Aidan managed finally. "This isn't about my doubting your skills, it's just..." He ran a hand over his hair, sighed, drew a breath. "Let's see what your contact says, okay? If she turns other options down we'll worry about plan B then."

Carefully, Kevin nodded. "Of course."

When he was gone, Aidan closed the door of his office, and let himself have a minute alone with his eyes squeezed shut, working on his breathing.

"Fuck that noise." On the other side of their connection, Jazz shook her head hard enough to make her beaded dreadlocks clack. "Jazz, come on. It's—" Kevin began, but their contact cut him off.

"Don't you ever listen, genius? Do I gotta spell it out?"

"That would probably help, yes," Kevin retorted tartly.

"Because, as of now, I have no idea why you're being insufferably cagey about something as pedestrian as—"

"Jesus, shut up, man," Jazz growled, shooting a glance at Aidan. "Commander Headly, um. Yeah, sorry. But this isn't going to fly."

Aidan was glad he'd stuffed his hands in his pockets. No one could see them shaking there. "Can we—" He cleared his throat and tried again. "Can we get a reason?"

Jazz blew out a long breath. "Well, yeah, the reason is, before I brought them in I found these two girls down under a bridge wearing blue jumpsuits that read 'Property of TechoCo, Proprietary Information Contained.' And if I start parading them all over the CO-WY, what do you think's gonna happen?"

Beside him, Kevin stiffened. "Jazz," he stated very quietly. "You didn't tell me these girls were detainees."

"No shit, CSI," the mech'n'tech retorted sourly. "I'm good at not telling people things that get other people shot. But, yeah. They were detainees. And now they think you guys are Jesus an' the fucking Saints coming to get them off the Grid, 'cause they don't know they'd be going out of the shitter and into the sewer with you people."

"Lovely analogy," Kevin replied dryly. His contact eyed him coldly.

"Don't start with me, man. You're on my last nerve."

Kevin held up his hands in surrender. "Sorry, Jazz. Really. It's only… This does complicate things."

"Yeah, Captain Obvious, it does." Jazz let out another long, hard sigh, turning to stare at Aidan through the screen. Slowly, her shoulders slumped. "Look. Commander. These are babies. The Corps already fucked them over once. I don't want to fuck them over again. They're safe with me. They're doing good work. They're making good cred and so am I. But Tweak wants on with you guys if you're legit. And Billie does what Tweak says, and I'm not their owner. I won't make them stay. So, do you want these kids?"

Aidan's throat felt like it had a cord tied around it. The contact and his officer were staring at him. Waiting for him. These girls were waiting too. This girl. This amazing asset that could do better code than anyone in the Region. Waiting.

On-Grid.

Slowly, he nodded. "Yeah. We want them." He cleared his throat. "We'll get approval from Sector and be in touch about the plan for extraction. Thank you for working with us on this, Jazz. We'll make sure you get a decent pay package."

"You'll make sure these babies are safe," the tech replied coldly. "I'm tired of seeing little kids get fucked over. By the Corps and you people." With a last glare, she slapped her hand against the screen on her end, and the image went blank. Silence.

Kevin cleared his throat. "I'll get the information packet ready, shall I? If it meets your approval you can send it out to Sector tonight."

Aidan nodded, feeling like a man in a dream. "Yeah, thanks, Kevin."

"No trouble," the logistics officer agreed, standing. At the doorway, he paused. "Er, I've got my workload under control. If yours isn't too bad, are we on for tomorrow night?"

"Hunh?" Aidan glanced up. Kevin was smiling that funny little smile that Aidan was starting to think of as his off-duty expression.

"Vids?" the redhead clarified.

Aidan blinked. "Oh. Right. Um, yeah. Yeah, let's plan on it."

"I'll do that," Kevin agreed. With a nod, he stepped out of the office.

Aidan received Kevin's packet on his screen half an hour later. He forced himself to read. Kevin had good points. For a moment, his eyes flicked to the Delete tab. It'd be so easy to toss this and say it was rejected. But if this girl was really this good…

Drawing a slow breath, he hit Encrypt, then Send, forwarding the file to Sector Commander Magnum. An hour later, a window opened on his work screen.

Message Handle: Sector40COM

Message: This recruitment approved. Sector Approval Number 545436gdf

A ping made Aidan lift his tab, where a second message window glowed.

Message Handle: Sector40COM

Message: Good work, Headly. Make sure your team takes your personal risk factors into account.

You promised me a month. It's been three, and I haven't heard you beg for transfer. Improvements noted on your base. I'm impressed.

Carry on.

Aidan let out a long sigh as his gut tightened, forcing the air out of his chest. "Personal risk factors," he whispered. "Fuck. Oh, fuck."

For another hour, he tried to work. It was useless. While the rest of the base headed to dinner, he slunk back to his room. His hands shook as he entered his pass code and biometrics. The hologram resolved into his sister's face.

"Good evening, Aidan," the psychological coach program smiled. "Is something bothering you this evening?"

"Something. Yeah. There's something bothering me," Aidan agreed, curling himself into the corner where his bed touched the wall. The fingers of both hands dug into his scalp

"Shit, Omi." His voice cracked in the syllables, and that was the last straw. Groaning, he buried his head in his hands, holding back a sob with all the energy he had left. It got loose. Omi was quiet for a beat. When she spoke, her digital voice was soft. "Aidan. Talk to me about what has been disturbing you. I'm listening."

Aidan sucked in a shuddering breath. "I have... I have to... have to go... on-Grid. It has to be... me. And I'm... Omi, I'm scared shitless..." His voice squeaked over the last words and he cringed. "Dammit! I don't even sound... I can't... I... They'll know what I— they'll know that I'm trans, and then..."

He gasped for air. It felt as if his binder was cinching tighter, crushing his chest. Omi's voice rose a little.

"Aidan? Can you look at me? Let's run through some breathing exercises. Look at my hands."

Between Omi's hands, a simple flower shape appeared, adding several layers of petals and removing them slowly. Watching it, Aidan did his best to breathe in and out with the mandala's changes.

Slowly, his chest relaxed, and his hitched breathing easing into something closer to normal. "Just…give me a second." Hands fumbling, he yanked off his cooling jacket and shirt. Carefully, wincing, he folded the binder up until he could wriggle free.

Avoiding the mirror, he dug his favorite floppy sweatshirt from a drawer and pulled it on, feeling his body's aches as it came down off the adrenaline overload and adjusted to being loose from the binder. He took his seat in the corner again, knees drawn up to his chest, chin resting on his crossed arms.

Omi watched him with a patient smile. "How do you feel now?"

Aidan sighed. "Like an idiot."

"You shouldn't feel guilty," Omi demurred softly. "You have an extremely valid reason for concern. But you do need to find a way to consider the problem more constructively, because panic is both toxic and potentially life threatening."

Aidan snorted. "Tell me something I don't know."

"Sarcasm is not useful in this situation, Aidan."

Aidan resisted the urge to snap at the program. Much as it looked like his sister, it wasn't her, and yelling at his shrink app really was stupid. He glanced at Omi's hands, and the mandala reappeared. For a while he just focused on breathing.

Finally, he closed his eyes and leaned his head back. "I've got to figure out where all the biometric readers are in the area so I can avoid them. That's the first thing."

"Your logistical officer would be a great deal of help in that endeavor," Omi's voice murmured.

Aidan winced. "Omi, I'm not telling Kevin."

"You believe he will react adversely?" the program asked. When Aidan didn't answer, the hologram began a slow blink in and out of view.

Aidan gave it a death row smile. Jackson had done a hell of a job on this thing. Omi knew just when to push.

"He's Cavanaugh trained," Aidan murmured eventually. "I mean, he's a great Duster, but... Training like that sticks. Attitudes and... stuff."

Omi cocked her head. "I believe you informed me that he self-identifies as gay. Is that not a sign that he has decided to reject much of the Cavanaugh Perfection Mandate?"

"Gay's one thing," Aidan muttered. "But me. . . I mean, trans, that's..."

"A specific physical and psychological condition you have," Omi cut in. "Which those planning missions involving your person and your safety should be made aware of."

Aidan closed his eyes, swallowing hard. "Omi."

"Aidan. You're attracted to him. You enjoy his companionship."

Aidan nodded reluctantly. He'd started to really love the Tuesday nights he spent with Kevin in the vid room. They'd talked. They'd debated ideas. They'd stopped old movies in the middle to look up stuff Aidan had never heard of on their tabs, and they'd just been happy. It was so easy to be around Kevin, to laugh and banter with him. Even getting called "sir" all the time was okay with him at this point, partly because of the quick half-smile Kevin always gave when he realized he'd done it again.

When Kevin talked, Aidan forgot about everything there was to worry about for a while. When Kevin laughed, he felt warm.

"You are feeling guilt and fear concerning whether he will still be friendly towards you once he fully understands your condition?" Omi asked.

Aidan's face scrunched. "Blunt, Omi, really blunt."

"But accurate?"

Aidan sighed. "Yeah. Accurate."

"Then please consider this, Aidan. Avoiding full disclosure with Kevin puts his life in danger as well as your own. He will be on the mission with you, and could be killed as well. That is not something you would want to cause."

Stung by the brutality of the point, Aidan surged up. "God damit Omi, I'm not—"

"Trying to hurt him. I understand that," the psychological coach program agreed. "But intent has very little relation to outcome in battlefield situations, Aidan. To ensure Kevin's safety, you must be honest with him."

Aidan's stomach lurched. He rested his head on his hands, fingernails digging into his arm. When he realized he was drawing blood, he forced his hands to relax.

"I don't know a good way to tell him," he managed, his voice tiny.

Omi's image of a hand made a show of resting on his leg. "May I make a suggestion?"

Aidan nodded wearily.

"You have informed me that Kevin enjoys pre-dissolution film and rock music a great deal? Is this correct?"

Aidan chuckled bleakly. "More than you'd believe. We watched this thing about a town where kids weren't allowed to dance twice in a row just so he could explain stuff in it."

Omi smiled. "Based on this, I have been running several incognito searches in the Greynet, and have found a film that will make approaching the topic much more palatable."

"Yeah?" Aidan asked, feeling a tinge of curiosity. "Um, can I see?"

The cover art for the vid appeared between Omi's hands. The four couples in their four letter-marked slots of primary color made Aidan blink. "Wait. Are those people…"

"This film concerns several couples of many sexual and gender orientations. And it contains music that was famous in the century after its release," Omi stated quietly. "Shall I download a copy?"

Aidan stared at the artwork for a heartbeat. Then, slowly, he smiled. "Yeah. Yeah, Omi. Um, thanks."

The AI smiled.

Event File 22
File Tag: Mission Pertinent Information
Timestamp: 18:30-7-6-2155

Aidan was almost pacing by the time Kevin got to the vid room the next night. The only thing that had stopped him was a half-speed game on the Osmos app that Kevin had put on his tab. He glanced up at the sound of humming coming down the hall, and smiled crookedly as Kevin sauntered in.

"Um, hi."

"Evening," Kevin replied, dropping onto the couch beside him with easy grace and an easy smile. "Sorry I'm running late, been rather swamped with the exchanges we're making for Base 1489."

Aidan shrugged, holding his smile despite the pounding of his heart. "No worries. Found something you might like for the vid, though."

"Oh?" Kevin's lips quirked in a smile. "Has the pupil become the master then? I'm intrigued."

"I mean, it's just one vid, but when I saw the cover art I thought—Anyway." Using his tab, Aidan brought up his vid collection on the screen and selected the new one. Kevin leaned forward, adjusting his glasses on his long, thin nose.

"Huh. That looks pretty old. What sort of movie?"

"Musical," Aidan replied. "Looks better than your farming one, but there's only one way to find out."

Kevin rolled his eyes with a chagrined smile. "Dear God in Heaven, you're never going to let me live down 'Oklahoma', are you? Look, I didn't know it was *that* bad."

"Believe me, it was. It seriously was," Aidan replied with a smile he couldn't hold back.

Kevin sighed and did one of those old-vid moves of his, pressing the back of his wrist to his forehead. "Shall I ever atone for my sin?"

Aidan found himself laughing, amazed by the sound and the tension unraveling in his belly. "Hey, you think it's bad if I give you crap, be glad nobody else saw it! If Laz or Sarah had seen the thing—"

Kevin did another one of those moves that Aidan was pretty sure was for show, touching his brow, breastbone and both shoulders in a quick criss-cross move. "Dear Lord, preserve me from such a fate." Smiling, the redhead relaxed back into the sagging cushions.

Aidan watched him out of the corner of his eye as he pushed Play.

"Gorgeous chorals, and—wait a minute. Seasons of love?" Kevin remarked a few minutes in, "This isn't a bad romance, is it?" One copper brow quirked skeptically.

Aidan shrugged. "Honestly, I have absolutely no idea."

Kevin glanced at him over the rims of his glasses, thin face outlined by the light from the screen. "Mm. Be aware, sir. If this is terrible, I'll get my own back for all that 'Oklahoma' teasing you've been dishing out."

Aidan shot him a sidelong smile. "Yeah, yeah. Watch the vid."

At first, Kevin watched skeptically. But his quirked brows began to rise higher and higher as they watched, and a slow grin pulled at his lips. "They're…We're not going to pay—Wait. They're actually refusing to pay for housing? They actually defied the Corps that blatantly in the street and didn't get…Wow."

"Wow. Oh, wow!" he muttered a few minutes later, leaning forward as the character called Angel finished her dance routine. He laughed as the characters kissed. "This is...I can't believe I never heard of this. This *rocks!*"

"Told you," Aidan remarked, watching Kevin's thin face light up with animation. Damn he was gorgeous when he was happy. And Omi had been right about this thing. Watching the vid, he felt something in him soften and expand. He'd never seen somebody like him portrayed on screen before as a hero. Somebody who had friends and a good life. Seeing Angel die in the middle wasn't exactly fun, but the life the film gave her before that was...

Amazing. That was the word. Amazing. For once, people like him and Kevin got to be the good guys.

Aidan stared at the screen a long time as the end credits rolled to the theme song. Beside him on the couch, Kevin had caught the tune and was singing the lyrics softly, a grin on his lips. Aidan watched his face. Okay. Now or never. Kevin had liked the vid. He hadn't said anything about Angel. Maybe this was going to work.

Maybe.

Eventually, he cleared his throat. "So, better than *Oklahoma?*"

Kevin laughed. "Where in the world did you find this?" he asked, putting an arm companionably around Aidan's shoulders. "I'm surprised it ever got out of Zoncom's networks! This is..." Then he blinked, realizing what he'd done. "I mean—"

He'd already started to pull away when Aidan leaned in. "A lot of searching on the Greynet snagged me a copy," he muttered. His heart was thundering in his ears, but here he was. Kevin had reached out and touched him. He'd wanted to touch him.

Kevin's cheeks flushed red, and he dropped his eyes. "Er. Sorry, sir—Damn. Aidan. Sorry. I-I didn't think."

"No," Aidan murmured, relishing this one moment of warmth. "I kind of... It's okay."

Slowly, Kevin raised his head. Aidan was used to most of Kevin's expressions after three months on-base, but this was the first time Kevin had looked shy. His grey eyes were wary, but his smile was hopeful.

Aidan returned the smile softly, feeling a lump forming in his throat. "But Kevin, one thing. Seriously. Don't call me 'Sir.'"

Kevin smiled thinly at his own gaffe, an expression Aidan had seen a lot more of. "Ah, yes. I'm afraid I generally tend towards manners and deference. Blame my parents."

"That's parents. Fucking up their kids for generations," Aidan agreed, shifting into a more comfortable position on the battered couch. He swallowed hard, drew a breath. Please, please let this work, he thought.

"The thing is, my name's actually kind of important to me. Really important to me. Because…it's mine. I mean, I chose it. I—" He met Kevin's gaze for a long moment before looking away, chewing on the inside of his cheek. This was dangerous. Was saying this going to change this easy companionship they had? Would it get out to the rest of the base? Could he risk it?

Did he have a choice?

Aidan swallowed hard. "Kevin, what I'm going to tell you, I— Promise me it stays between us."

"Sure," Kevin agreed, sitting back, brow furrowed. Aidan's shoulders felt cold with the loss of his touch. "What is it?" the other man asked, head canting to one side.

Aidan opened his mouth twice before he forced the words out, his voice strangled. "I'm not what you think I am. I mean, I am, but I'm not." He ran a hand anxiously over his hair. "God, that doesn't even make sense. I'm sorry, I've just—I'm…" Feeling his heart race, he closed his eyes rather than watch Kevin's face. "I used to be…Amanda. I was born as an Amanda. There. I said it. I understand if you don't want to… or, hell, if you don't even want to talk to me any more off duty but there it is. I said it."

Kevin's face went blank. "You're…Um, wow." Swallowing, he fiddled with his glasses, then pulled them off. He pulled that square of fabric he always kept in his jacket pocket out, scrubbing at an imagined spot on the lens. "I see…" Slipping them back on, he glanced at the screen. "And that was the reason for *Rent*? You were testing me out?"

"Kind of." Aidan admitted quietly. "It's not something that's… I mean, talking about it…" The silence deepened until it seemed as if it might suffocate them both.

"I can sympathize," Kevin interjected gently. "Some things don't exactly trip off the tongue, do they?"

Aidan glanced up gratefully. "Guess not," he managed. "But you asked about specific concerns I had about going on-Grid. Yeah. I'm trans. And I've never been on the Grid before. That's it."

Kevin nodded, looking a little stunned. "That's… Those are quite the specific concerns."

"No shit," Aidan agreed quietly.

Kevin fiddled with his little cleaning cloth, folding and unfolding it. Finally, he raised his eyes. "Well, I can plan around that. We can work out a route that avoids checkpoints with full biometric readers. We'll bring along a vial of phage nanoids to clean up skin cells and the like after us. I don't believe your appearance will…I mean, you're—" He froze as Aidan watched him, the usual easy competence he wore seeming to slip off him and leave him looking skinny, sweet and gawky as he tried and failed to start several sentences. "I… Well, if I'm being blunt, you don't look… I mean. You're… handsome, I mean. Very handsome." Kevin paused, then scrambled to explain, his cheeks flaming. "I mean that's just my observation. Speaking platonically, as a connoisseur of the masculine form," he added, words coming out too fast. "I didn't see anything wrong with… I mean—Oh damn, that came out badly." Glancing away, the pale man bit his lip.

Aidan drew a slow breath. "I take 150 milligrams of testosterone every other week," he muttered, barely audible in the quiet room. "That's why it's on the req list. After all the work to get a hold of that and... some other stuff, I'd be pretty disappointed if I didn't look like what I am."

Silence deepened around them.

"So..." Kevin's voice trailed off, picked up the thread again awkwardly. "Do you want me to—I mean..."

He cleared his throat. When he spoke again, it was as a logistics officer. "On the subject of the req list, I assume Damian's in the loop. Secrets have a snowball's chance in Hell around him. If you'd prefer not to inform anyone else on base, that's a non-issue. As for other difficulties, should we be requisitioning anything you need through our own sources rather than putting in request forms to Sector?"

Aidan blinked, bewildered for a moment. Why was Kevin talking about request forms now? Was he trying to drop the subject? Then he got it. "You're trying to ask if Sector knows what's up with me without straight-out asking, yeah?"

Kevin's lips twitched in the ghost of a smile. "And I failed miserably, apparently. Yes. I wanted to know if I needed to play any games with Sector, if they haven't been informed."

"Magnum knows," Aidan admitted quietly. "And the Sector Medical, Petree, he knows. Gave me a once over before I went into Command training. So, yeah," he finished on a long breath. "Them. Nobody else."

Kevin nodded. "I'll bear it in mind for logistical purposes, and..." He paused, and Aidan could almost see his brain working. What was he trying to figure out how to say politely this time?

Then Kevin gave him a small, crooked smile. "Don't worry about it staying between us. After all," he added, "dissimulation and information retention rather comes with the lifestyle, and the logistics vocation for that matter."

Aidan smiled weakly. "Um, Kevin? I don't know what 'dissimulation' means. Or retention. Shit. Sorry."

Kevin gave him one of his quick damn-I-did-it-again smiles. "Apologies. The lexicon strikes again. I mean I'm good at keeping things to myself. I've practiced quite a lot."

The rush of relief felt as if it might melt the inside of Aidan's chest. This guy had actually gone out of his way to ask how many people he needed to keep Aidan's secret from. He'd been willing to "play games" with Sector. He grinned, sticking out his hand for Kevin to shake. "This means a lot. A whole lot. Thanks."

Kevin took his hand. He didn't pause. "Think nothing of it."

It might have been all in Aidan's head, but he could have sworn that Kevin held his hand a few beats beyond what a handshake required.

Event File 23
File Tag: Job Offer
Timestamp: 11:00-7-15-2155

The printer spat as it finished putting down the last layer on the flat white square. Topher watched it like a cat.

"Okay. Think that worked. The cells are alive. Nutrient base's steady. The melanin's bleached out. Looks like the genome code went in good. I had to mess with the algorithm we use on the bio-inks for normal Synth, so the cell shapes are a little weird, but we're not transplanting these things onto anybody, we're just covering your guys' hands with them. If I'm right they'll shed at the same rate as natskin."

"I still can't believe you got this to work," Kevin replied, watching as the boy handled his experiment. He didn't have to try to sound sincere. What Damian and Topher had come up with between them after Kevin had explained that their commander was a red-hot property on the Grid left him in awe.

Topher gave a noncommittal, critical noise in the back of his throat, studying his work. "Yeah, after four tries I got it. First time, the stuff was fucking Jello, I had to clean the rig out. So, what'd the commander do that he's so high up on the shit list?" Slowly, he lifted the sheet of synthetic human skin tissue out of the 3D rig, blowing on it.

"I mean, I never heard of anybody who the Corps were watching for so close that he had to hide all his gene signatures."

"I didn't think it was my place to ask," Kevin remarked casually. "You might want to take a leaf out of my book."

"Kay," the younger man agreed with a shrug, lost in his own thoughts as he tested the sheet's flexibility.

Kevin watched the translucent layer shiver slightly. The stuff looked more like packing tape than the usual Synth-skin printed and transplanted over wounds. It didn't look promising, but, if this experiment of Topher's worked, it'd mean a new level of protection for every Duster. If they could not only falsify the genome sequences encoded in Citizen cards to match their own but print human skin with genomes they chose, that opened up whole new avenues of evasion and undercover work.

Topher shot him a quick, wide grin. "I think it worked."

"You feeling ready to take it to the Great and All Knowing Damian and have him look over the stuff?" Kevin asked, unable to resist a smile in return for the boy.

The young transport specialist glanced down at the sheet in his hands. "I guess?"

Kevin chuckled, gently ruffling the boy's fedora on his head "Come on, I'll go with you."

Damian's eyes whirred as he focused in on the sheet, studying it with an accuracy neither of the naturally-sighted men could pull off.

"Hmm. Cell shapes are off, but it could be worse."

"So, is it gonna work?" Topher asked.

The lanky doctor gave a shrug. "One way to tell. You got the card you printed to match this?"

Topher held out the card. Taking it, Damian pulled a flat plastic genome reader from one of the drawers set into the white wall. Carefully peeling Topher's experiment off its sheet, he held the tissue-thin stuff between thumb and forefinger.

"Toph, let's see a hand."

Topher held out his left hand. Damian carefully draped the synthetic skin over it, smoothing the edges until they melted into one another.

Lifting his genome reader, he set it to 'recognition' and ran it over the card he and Topher had coded together, giving it the code, it was searching for. Then he ran it over Topher's left hand. The light in the upper corner blipped a reassuring green. Damian ran the flat square over the card again, then over Topher's right hand. The light in the corner glowed red. Damian raised his head, one of his rare grins showing white in his dark face.

"Toph, you may have something here." They tested the process four times with four different genome codes.

"It's gonna work!" Topher announced, and Damian agreed with a slow nod of the head. "Want to help me write the report on your new idea for Sector?"

Topher laughed, holding up both hands in defense. "Man, if I gotta write reports, tell 'em it was your idea!"

Kevin shook his head, chuckling. "All right, you did the heavy lifting. I suppose we'll serve as your secretaries. I'll bring back a report of how it does on its field test. What's the lifespan?"

Damian tapped his fingers on the pristine white ceramic of his work station as he thought. "Five hours in moderate temperatures. But don't push it. These cells are running on nothing but a nutrient solution."

"Roger that," Kevin agreed, glancing at Topher. "Think you can have a set coded up for Aidan and me with cards attached in the morning? We'll leave after breakfast."

"Sure," Topher agreed with a nod, but his eyes held Damian's, wide and wary.

Kevin tipped his head. "Toph, what is it?"

Topher shrugged awkwardly. "I just—You sure you wanna put your ass on the line with something I just started playing around with? Maybe we oughta test it some more?"

So that was it, Kevin thought as he watched the younger man stuff his hands in his pockets. Smiling, he put out a hand and clasped Topher's shoulder. "You worry about getting the machinery to do things no one's tried yet, I'll worry about putting it through its paces. In my experience, your work's eminently trustworthy."

Topher glanced up at him with a small smile. "Thanks, man."

"Honor where it's due," Kevin replied with a teasing smirk for his benefit.

Damian clapped the boy on the back. "Listen to the guy, Toph, even if you only get half of what he says. You did good."

Topher glanced down, grinning. "Yeah, well. I gotta do a prayer real quick, then Dozer's gonna need me. We're redoing one of the bikes. See you guys."

Kevin was halfway to his own office, thinking through plans for the next day, when the sound of jogging feet coming down the hall whipped him around. He was getting far too high strung these days, he told himself with chagrin as Lazarus joined him in the walk down the hall. The narrow space caused them to brush shoulders as they paced.

Lazarus gave him a small smile. "Hey, dude."

"Afternoon," Kevin agreed, smiling carefully. Laz seemed to have himself straightened out, but better safe than sorry.

Lazarus ran a hand through his sun bleached hair. "I hear you're going out on a run with Aidan tomorrow to get that recruit. Hear you're trying new tech to make it work."

Kevin nodded. "Yes, after breakfast. Topher and Damian just finished their tests. It's going to be a really useful—"

"Dude, write me in on this one," Lazarus interjected. Kevin stopped, blinking. "What?"

"Write me in on this run," Lazarus repeated, turning so they faced each other. "You're gonna try something new while you're babysitting a commander and a grid-kid. You need backup. I got some stealth stuff together, guns that'll get through checks."

Kevin winced. "Laz, we're trying to pass unnoticed. This isn't a guns type of mission. A gun is the very last thing we need to get caught with."

"Yeah, but you're going to have a commander with you, a wanted one," Lazarus replied, his expression shockingly earnest after these months of sullenness.

This was the man Kevin knew, he realized. Passionate, annoying as hell sometimes, but bright eyed and full of life. And he was going to have to put that spark of life in Lazarus's eyes out again. He hated to do it, but he knew his work. If they took Lazarus and one of his guns with them into this situation, they might as well shoot themselves with it.

He tried to break it gently. "Laz, I'll watch the commander's back."

"So, who's watching your back?" Lazarus demanded hotly, eyes holding Kevin's. "You need somebody who can shoot if everything goes to shit on this!"

"The last time we were in a mission, you weren't the one shooting, Laz. You were the one who got shot," Kevin replied quietly. He braced himself for the explosion. It came as he expected.

Lazarus took a step back, his expression hardening. "Fuck you, dude! Just because I fucked up one time—*one time*—you think I'm no good anymore?"

Kevin stepped in, putting his hand on Lazarus's shoulder. "Laz, I think you're the best. You know that. That's why I was planning to ask you to do escort out to our extraction point and cover till we're back. We're using the tunnel into the train maintenance system. We could use you on the way out and back."

He raised his voice when Lazarus opened his mouth. "I also think bringing a gun to a meeting with an unstable contact situation when we're already a hot property trying to avoid undue attention is about as smart as playing tag with ViperDrones." Squeezing the other man's shoulder, he smiled crookedly. "I wish you were going in with me. I miss running with you. But today I need to run alone and know you're there at our extraction point to watch my back."

For a moment, Lazarus's lips twitched with words he didn't say. Then he reached out and grabbed Kevin's shoulder hard enough to send pain down his arm. "You come home, you get me?" the other man demanded. His voice was rough over the words.

"I'll come home. I always come home," Kevin agreed quietly, holding Lazarus's eyes.

Finally, the older man glanced away, down the hall. "Yeah, well." He patted Kevin's shoulder awkwardly. "And don't get Aidan killed either. I kinda like this guy."

Kevin quirked a brow. "Considering you hacked his personnel file to add 'assuming the worst will happen' and 'looking confused' to his list of interests, you have a funny way of showing it," he remarked in his usual dry tone.

Lazarus gave him something like one of his signature cock-sure grins. "Dude, I'm in munitions. My job's to take pot-shots at everything." He shrugged, his old goofy self for a moment.

Kevin rolled his eyes. "Ass."

"Dude!" Lazarus yelped in mock horror. "Quit thinking about ass while you're on duty! Go get ass on your own time!"

Kevin felt the blush kindle in his cheeks as he leveled a glare on his old friend. "I hate you sometimes."

Grinning, Lazarus reached over and tousled his hair. "Yeah, yeah, you hate me."

For a moment, the munitions officer studied his younger base mate. Then he pulled him into a quick, one armed hug. "Seriously, Kev. Be safe out there."

"I'll do my best," Kevin murmured into his old friend's shoulder.

♠

Early in the afternoon, Kevin and Aidan climbed through the maintenance room cover and into a disused locker room. Carefully, Kevin unrolled the pack of flat white squares from the duffel bag he'd brought along. Moving with deliberation, he peeled the first Synth off its white nutrient sheet, careful not to rip it.

"We'll have some great notes to send to Sector if this stuff does the trick," he remarked briskly as he folded the thin film over Aidan's hands and wrists, watching it smooth into place. The synthetic human epithelial cell sheet made it look as if Aidan had somewhat calloused hands, but that look wouldn't set off alarm bells. They were travelling as Citizen Acceptable Standing, after all. Any of the jobs CAS folks could get might give you calluses.

Kevin glanced up with a smile. "Last check before we hit the street."

He looked Aidan up and down. It was odd seeing the man in Grid clothing. He looked somehow smaller out of uniform. Vulnerable. Or perhaps that was the anxious hunch to his shoulders. The man. Man. A man now, yes. But what he'd said that night, a week ago…

Kevin forced himself to refocus. Now was not the time to dig through any of that. "Er, your hat… May I?"

"Sure?" Aidan replied, eyes a little bewildered under the hat brim.

Kevin reached up and adjusted the flex-screen in the baseball cap until it clearly showed the gif of a stylized bird flying.

"Screen was fritzing," he added by way of explanation and apology.

Aidan held his gaze with frightened eyes. Kevin's nerves twitched. Looking this nervous in public was tantamount to putting on a shirt with a bull's-eye that read "please stop me for questioning."

"Aidan?" he asked quietly, "May I speak freely?"

The other man blinked. "Uh, yeah?"

Kevin chose his words with care, holding Aidan's eyes. "We're taking CAS level train transport and then a CPS bus. Our meeting is in a little CPS café by the bus stop on Alameda. That's ZonCom land. We're not leaving our own genetic markers anywhere. That's what the Synth is for. They have thousands of people a day on the cheap transport, more than even EagleCorp can track with any accuracy. All they can track and log are the fake fingerprints and cards we've got, and those are attached to nothing. No one is going to pay us any attention unless we give them a reason to. But a furtive attitude draws attention."

Aidan blinked. "Furtive?" he asked helplessly.

Kevin let himself roll his eyes and smirk for Aidan's benefit. "Freaked out. If you look like you're freaked, someone's going to wonder why. Being a face in the crowd is our salvation. Okay?"

Aidan drew a slow breath, eyes closed. Then he nodded. "Okay. Got it." He drew another long breath, opened his eyes. "I got this. Thanks."

Kevin nodded. "No trouble." Turning, he opened the maintenance hall door.

"Oh, don't react to the ad holos when they pop up," he added, working to make the reminder sound like an afterthought. "It's not the done thing on Grid."

The noise of the train station hit like a fist to the ear. The noise of human crowds and the chatter of every ad, vid and jingle projected from walls and floor echoed off the architecture, underpinned by the station's base Muzak. Kevin let the noise wash over him, glancing at his commanding officer.

"Those 'buds would probably be a good idea," he remarked under the sound of thousands of people and thousands of ads. He watched his superior officer slip the 'buds in and pull out his tab for a second, queuing up his own music once the two devices connected.

Kevin smiled, glad he'd gone the extra mile to get the noise cancelling variety for everybody on base and scrub the ZonCom subroutine that made 'buds reject unregistered tabs. The 'buds helped deal with the Gridbuzz so many Dusters got coming in.

He watched Aidan flinch slightly as a popup of a dancing monkey appeared at his shoulder with the words "Job Monkey: Climb Up! Register With Us Today!" flashing around it. The operative word, Kevin reflected sourly, was 'helped', not 'stopped'. So many Dusters suffered from sensory overload on the Grid. They were used to a quieter life.

They passed outside the pop-up's sensor in two steps and the holo's source refocused on the person behind them, leaving the two of them alone. The next one appeared directly in front of them, a waterfall with elegant type reading "Crystal: Pure Water." Beside him Aidan missed a beat and almost stumbled. Kevin worked at keeping from glancing at his companion as he walked through the thing.

This was not good.

The pop-ups stopped in the central concourse, only the wall ads and holos shining cheerfully around the EagleCorp security check in front of the train platform.

Kevin pushed his shoes and cooling coat through the check slot, waiting patiently in the heat as they were scanned and spat out on the other side of the turnstile.

"Card," the bored security man asked, and Kevin pushed his Citizen Card with its chip and its meticulously-falsified information into one side of the turnstile.

"Hand." The guard jerked a thumb at the pad beside Kevin, and he obligingly pressed his hand to it, allowing the machine to read the false fingerprints and genome information of the Synth layered over his hand. The screen turned green, and Kevin took his hand away in time to avoid the little automatic swage armature that wiped it with disinfectant.

"Have a nice day," the man threw out without looking at him. Kevin resisted the urge to roll his eyes, but it took effort. His card popped back out of the other side of the turnstile. Information recorded, fee deducted.

At least, that was what the system thought. Kevin pocketed the card and kept himself cool with that little thought as he waited for Aidan to finish his turn.

His.

It really was going to be hard to stop mulling that over. It shouldn't matter and Kevin knew it. But the sheer fact took some adjusting to. He knew so little about, well, anything the condition entailed. He knew so little. He knew gender nonconformity and gender changes went on. ZonCom had legalized any gender affiliation for its employees almost a century ago. Of course, that had gotten ZonCom employees banned from a lot of franchises owned by one of the conservative Corporations. But all he knew was that people outside the norm were allowed, not what it meant. They didn't teach good Cavanaugh kids things like that. They trained good Cavanaugh kids to shy away from the imperfect and the aberration. Damn them.

Kevin only knew of one other transgender person, and he didn't dare ask her questions. Maybe ZonCom domain sites would have something. He'd get in for a look around.

ZonCom had kept their laissez-faire attitude as a recruitment point on the stipulation that they advertised it with all information deemed "unsuitable" by other Corporations behind domain firewalls and signed their extradition treaties with the other six Corporations, but they didn't exactly put energy into enforcement. People still ran to hide in ZonCom's offices. If they had value and hadn't pissed off anyone too high, they stayed hidden.

It was a good setup for ZonCom. A great way to poach talent from the other Corporations and call it protecting diversity. Of course, if they cared about protecting anything but their talent pool, they'd put pressure on the conservative Corporations to stop holding public Morality Law executions, Kevin thought bitterly.

It wasn't like the other Corporations could hurt them.

The other Corps needed ZonCom's shipping, marketing and merchandising skills, and it needed each of the other six for one thing or another. The seven biggest fish in the American pond had eaten the rest a long time ago. They didn't need to go after one another over anything but petty details any longer. Maybe he'd use his day off to get into an international medical paper forum and start doing some reading. Then he wouldn't spend so much time wondering if the next word he said to Aidan would be wrong.

That was another can of worms. That word. *Wrong.* It had a bad habit of bringing its synonymic friends with it—unnatural, pathological, defective, aberrant. His first instinct had been to recoil from what Aidan had said.

That damn Cavanaugh schooling trying to kick in again. He was glad he'd stopped himself. What would he be recoiling from? A basemate. A friend. The only man he'd really been able to be himself around since Peter went Fringe. And Aidan didn't look wrong. And he didn't act wrong. In fact, he acted-

The screen turned green below Aidan's hand, and the turnstile dinged.

And you're daydreaming on a mission, Kevin told himself with a quick mental refocus. *What a lovely way to get yourself killed.* He smiled as Aidan joined him. "Let's grab seats. Train leaves in five."

The CAS train smelled of cheap disinfectant that tried to resemble lemons. It failed. At least it wasn't fake pine. Kevin popped in his own 'buds, choosing the playlist that he used like armor. The words of the first song made him smile, as they always could.

No, his mind is not for rent
To any god or government
Always hopeful, yet discontent

Focusing on the words, he waited out the ride.

Tweak glanced up sharply as they opened the door to the small back booth, half-standing as if to hide Billie from them before she subsided.

Jazz gave them a long, slow look, waved a hand. "Took long enough. Sit."

"Thanks very much," Kevin replied politely, sliding into the seat nearest the two young women.

Tweak eyed him. "Touch me, lose your balls. Got it, Citizen Excellent?"

Kevin held up his hands in surrender. "I'm just here for the discussion. And I don't have a Citizen Standing rating, by the way. I'm not CES."

Tweak snorted. "Yeah. Right."

Kevin forced himself not to retort to that. No sense protesting too much. If anyone asked, he could remark on the girl's paranoia. She had absolutely no proof of his former Standing. Warily, he brought up the menu holo.

Aidan took his seat, clearing his throat. "Everything's on us."

"Better be." Jazz remarked cooly. Then she seemed to reconsider and held a hand out.

"Jalanda Sims. Jazz. What'd you screw up to get stuck with the Wildcards?"

Aidan breathed a laugh as he took her hand. "A lot of stuff I guess, but some of it other people screwed up first."

"You know, you might actually do better if you didn't begin your conversational gambits with threats," Kevin remarked mildly to Tweak. "Just a suggestion."

"Jack yourself," Tweak shot back, putting in her order.

Over her head, Kevin caught Aidan's eyes, raising his brows. Maybe this recruitment wasn't such a great idea. That kind of attitude wouldn't mesh well with anyone on base.

Holding his eyes, Aidan shrugged and put in his order as well. Kevin relaxed fractionally. The girl was a fugitive running from God-knew-what, and he had just patronized her. Perhaps he'd deserved what he'd gotten.

THE HANDS WERE GIVEN | 211

"Are the boxes on?" Aidan asked quietly. "I don't want to spend a lot more time here than we have to."

"Course you don't," Jazz agreed, deadpan. Kevin noted that she ordered the most expensive thing she could find. Order finished, she sat back. "You paid for the time, Commander. Talk."

Aidan opened his mouth, but Tweak beat him to it.

"What's the job?" the girl asked shortly.

Aidan watched her the way a raccoon watched an oncomingcar. "It's not a simple explanation," he began tentatively. "The overall goal is to. . . well, overthrow the Corporations."

Aidan glanced at Kevin, and Kevin caught the pleading in his eyes. Leaning forward, Kevin steepled his fingers. "What do you know about pre-Dissolution history?" he asked quietly.

Tweak blinked, glancing at Jazz warily.

Jazz scowled and leaned back in her chair to fold her arms over her chest. "It happened. That's about it. This better not be a history lesson."

"It's going somewhere," Aidan promised, though Kevin knew his eyes were watching, too.

That was fine. Kevin kept his eyes on Tweak. "What made the system work was group participation," he murmured. "One man. One vote. Of course, it grew a great deal more sophisticated and ultimately far from its base, but that was the core of the system. The right of a man to have a say in his own life. We've lost that, and it's time it was brought back. What we're proposing is a multi-layered endeavor: the de-indoctrination of all levels of society, neutralizing certain parties, and, most importantly, the reigniting of the Flame of Athens, as it was rather charmingly called. The recreation of a form of Parliament or Congress in America. The return of democracy."

For a moment, there was silence. Then Tweak cocked her head. "You eat a d-dictionary?"

Kevin sighed. So much for inspiring words. Beside him, he heard Aidan give a false cough as he fought down a laugh before speaking.

"What he's trying to say is that people like us had a say back then. We're trying to have the chance to bring back a system that lets people be people."

"How?" Tweak asked, the word sharp.

"It's complicated," Aidan muttered. "But, basically, we use the talents we have and can find in others to bring the Corps down from the bottom up and expose all the bullshit they try to hide. Get people to think for themselves again. It's slow. Really slow. But it's worth—"

And that was when Jazz cut him off with a groan, her lips twisted in a sneer. "Oh, will you cut the bullshit? You people are a bunch of dumbasses. Don't feed these babies that garbage!"

Kevin froze in his seat.

"Yeah, we probably are dumbasses," Aidan agreed after a long moment of silence. "But probably not for the reasons you're thinking. And we're trying—"

"By blowing shit up? Stealing Corps cash? Getting their dirty laundry out in the indie news sites? Knocking over supply depots? You know what that shit does?" Jazz snapped. She held up a hand, ticking off fingers angrily as she made her points. "It pisses off the Corps, it makes them crack down on all the poor fucks just trying to do a day's work and makes our lives evenharder, and every time you asshats go nuts they get one more excuse. When they crack down, you're their excuse," she hissed. "Every time you go nuts, they crack down a little harder and pass it off as internal security. And you know what, shit heads? *People agree.* You're the fucking bogeymen. You *scare* people. You think you fix the whole world? That's your sell point? Bullshit. You've been at it sixty years. I've been hearing all of you say that since I was a baby. I used to believe you, but we're still in this fucking mess. Tell yourself that shit if you need to sleep at night, but don't lie to these kids and tell them they're gonna save the world," she declared, opening her arms to encompass the situation. "Way I see it, you're part of the system, too."

Kevin stared at Jazz in shock. He was familiar with her dubious smile when he spoke idealistically himself, her scorn and backhand comments about "if you guys ever win." But how had he missed this depth of anger boiling inside her? He glanced apprehensively at Aidan, who frowned at Jazz for a long moment before shaking his head slowly.

"Okay, Jazz. Maybe some of that's true." He said the words softly, but there was the note in his voice that Kevin had heard last when Aidan had stared down a border-runner with a gun. "But, you got a better idea? Because from where I'm standing, no one else is doing anything to bring the Corps down." His voice didn't rise, but it took on an intensity that Kevin had never heard.

Slowly, he mirrored her open-arm gesture, holding Jazz's eyes. "Living under the Corps? It screws with you. They get in your head and fuck you over and you don't even notice it. You just know that you hate yourself. You're fucking terrified and you can't get out, and while you're here you might as well buy more shit. They farm people for cash, and people are *dying*. The people who break their Corporation's fucking rules and end up dead. The chop shops. The work days. The shit in the water and the food. And the shit they put people through. There's that. You seen the suicide rates that the indie reporters put out? The real ones? You seen the real death rates from bad air, bad water, bad food? No food?"

"Yeah, well." Jazz shrugged.

Aidan shook his head, blue eyes like chips of ice. "Well nothing. I've heard this stuff since I was a baby, too, Jazz. I was born in the Dust. Difference is, I can't just say 'yeah, well' and let it go. I want… something better than that."

Silence.

Kevin couldn't help but stare at Aidan where he sat, breathing hard, looking as if he might pull out a shining sword at any moment. He had thought of his new commander as good with people and self-

214 | T E A R M A N N

effacing, but he'd been badly mistaken twice today. How much courage did it take to be as honest as Aidan was about his leadership? How much more did it take to be honest about his gender and sexuality? Now that righteous courage was laid bare, and it blazed in Aidan's eyes.

In the silence, the sound of a chair scraping was like a gunshot. Walking around the table, Tweak stood in front of the man and raked Aidan with her eyes.

"So. We work for you?"

Aidan looked her up and down in return, perplexed. "Yeah, technically."

Tweak tipped her head. Then she held up one hand. "Rules. Rule one. Nobody touches me." She tucked a finger down, and repeated the gesture. "Two. Nobody fucks with me. Nobody fucks with Billie. Three. We eat good. Four. We get paid. Five. I code. Don't scrub toilets, don't do laundry. I code. Not a maid. Fuck that." She held up her other hand, "Six. Coffee. Real. Got it?"

Kevin watched as Aidan considered the girl for a long moment before shrugging one shoulder. "I can agree to some of those. Nobody will fuck with you. The rest... We all eat the same thing and rotate base chores. I'll see what my requisitions team can do about real coffee, but no promises. Stuff's hard to get."

"Quite," Kevin agreed distantly, watching Tweak.

She shot a look over her shoulder at Billie. Then she turned curious eyes on Aidan. "Hunh. Okay. Eat good, means..." She shrugged, shoulders thin as a bird's. "Eat twice a day? Deal?"

Aidan smiled and nodded. "Three times a day. As long as we've got the rations."

Tweak studied him, eyes narrowed into black slits. She glanced over her shoulder. "Billie?"

Slowly, Billie nodded. Tweak mirrored the gesture. Then she turned back to glare at Aidan. "Okay. Pay. On time. No three month back pay shit. Imp-por-por-ack." she grimaced, swallowing hard. "Need it," she croaked out.

Aidan studied her for another long moment, then glanced at Kevin. He nodded and held up two fingers. They had the funds for base pay at least. Aidan smiled. "How's two months upfront?"

The woman's black eyes narrowed. "You lie, I fuck you over."

Aidan held Tweak's gaze as he nodded. "I understand. But you have to understand that a lot of your requests depend on the success of our base, a success that you'll need to help us with. The better we work, the better we eat, the more we can pay you. Got it?"

Tweak stood stiff a long moment, taunt. Then she glanced at Kevin, made a moue of distaste, and turned her eyes back to Aidan. "So. When do we go?"

Event File 24
File Tag: Induction
Timestamp: 7-24-2155/ 7-25-2155

"I only wish it hadn't taken three days to get a hold of the fellow with the false-bottomed truck," Kevin remarked, sitting forward until the chair beneath him creaked to point at the main screen, "but now that he's onboard this should go off without a hitch. As long as I've got your approval."

"Yeah. This looks good." Aidan glanced up from the procedural plan Kevin had laid out for the extraction of their new coder, and smiled. "This looks really good."

Kevin smiled a small, professional smile.

"I know sending Sarah along for the pickup as well might be overkill, but I thought someone with her facility for munitions at the drop point might be a good idea, just in case. I only hope the girls take better to Jim and Sarah than they do to myself. I'd love to know what I did to offend Tweak."

Aidan raised a brow, a crooked smile creasing his face. "Um, Kevin, you don't exactly have to do anything. I mean, you're kinda…" He gestured at Kevin in a vague, all encompassing way.

"Kind of what?" Kevin asked, not quite sure if he was being teased.

Aidan shrugged. "Kinda... high class? You know. You look nice, you talk nice. She probably thought you were a Corps plant."

Elation curled in the pit of Kevin's belly. He looked nice, did he? *Enough of that*, he warned himself, sitting up straight. "I'll get the codes together for their cards and Synth then. Jim can leave in the morning."

Aidan blinked in surprise. "Wait. Tomorrow? Isn't this a couple day's worth of work?"

Kevin crossed his arms, allowing himself a cavalier smile. "Only if you're inefficient. And I'm very good at what I do."

Aidan glanced away, smiling, one hand rubbing the back of his neck. "Um, okay, great. While you're here, let's run through the requisitions list for next month and I can approve it now."

"Sounds good," Kevin agreed, watching as Aidan brought up a new holographic window and detached it from his other screens.

His console's whir kicked up a notch, and Kevin sighed. Leaning in, he pulled over the keyboard and typed in "replacement cooling module, Model ZTZX."

"We can't print one?" Aidan asked, and Kevin shook his head absently.

"Mm, not effectively. Topher's tried eight times and—Oh, damn it all, Lazarus."

"What?" Aidan asked, sitting forward.

Kevin let out a sigh of frustration and underlined a line of text under the 'medical requirements' section. Aidan squinted.

"Sterile—Wait."

"No, you read it right," Kevin agreed wearily. "Sterile fallopian tubes. Ha-ha, very funny." He deleted the line. "He probably put in a few more Easter eggs too. Yes, here's another, under 'morale-related.'"

"Inflatable donkey," Aidan read. He re-read them, sounding as if he couldn't believe the words. "Inflatable…" Slowly, he started to grin. "I need to give that guy more work to do."

"Please," Kevin agreed with feeling. "He's been doing this since we were kids. Taylor used to burst out laughing every time, I think it just encouraged him. The only time Taylor ever yelled at him for it was…" Glancing up at Aidan, he shut his mouth as the pit opened in his gut.

Taylor had encouraged him and Lazarus both. He'd encouraged them all. Taylor had trusted Kevin, even after Sector had given him a rundown of exactly what was in his genome, how much he had been genetically improved and what that meant. Taylor had trusted him even after the debacle Kevin had nearly committed in his first week on base. Taylor had trusted Kevin enough to make him an officer.

And Kevin had repaid that trust by letting him die. "Sorry," he remarked, eyes on the screen. "You must be getting rather tired of the reminders concerning your predecessor." The room was very quiet.

"He meant a lot to you guys." Aidan's voice was soft. "I'm okay hearing about that."

Kevin stood so quickly that his chair squeaked against the pre-fab floor. "If you'll look through the rest of that, I should probably get started on the extraction work. Like you said. Lots to do. Thank you for your time, sir."

He was out the door and down the hall before a voice could catch up with him. As he walked, he scolded himself. Idiot. He didn't have the mental resources to waste on this. He had a job to do. And when he made mistakes, people died. That was the lesson he'd learned. He got things right or people died.

He worked until dinner and ate with the crew to reassure everyone. If he didn't, Damian or Blake would only come and scold him. He headed in the direction of his quarters with the general flow, but only to wait for half an hour and open the black-topped bottle.

By the time three in the morning came around, Kevin was well along in his prep work, and stood watching the 3D rig print out sheets of the new Synth. Music pumped in his ears.

He'd done a new card for Jim for this run to protect the man's favorite Grid personae, but that had been easy once Topher taught him. He had Jim's genome and very little had to be falsified. Since he had nothing on the two new recruits he'd had to do a little creative genome fabrication based on their appearances, code it into two cards and sets of Synth, and hope to God above that nobody looked too closely at them on their way from their squat in Commerce City to the Go Depot and the smuggling rig that would move them out to meet Sarah and come on base.

Don't rattle the cage if you wanna come out

Don't rattle the cage if you wanna come out

His 'buds filled his ears with late pre-Dissolution music. His dad wouldn't have liked it. He had preferred music that said something good about humanity. But it fit Kevin's mood. The drumbeat of it kept him focused, the words keeping the fire in him stoked. It was inattention that killed.

If he'd been more attentive to his work five months ago he wouldn't have botched the run that should have gotten them the medicines Commander Taylor had needed.

If he'd been more attentive he would have noticed Commander Taylor's increasing illness before it had advanced so far. If he'd been more attentive, Commander Taylor would be alive.

Flobots' music pounded in his ears as he worked and thought, the words about fire in the sky and masses at the border beating in time with his blood. If he hadn't been such a daydreamer, maybe he would have seen the signs of trouble as a boy. Maybe his parents wouldn't be dead, either.

These were the thoughts of three in the morning, and he knew it. They were only the scraps and old ghosts come to haunt him. He didn't have time for regret either, but he'd learned well from those failures. He had to get this right.

He jumped reflexively at the sound behind him, whipping around. Janice raised her hand in a casual wave where she leaned against the doorjamb. Heart thundering in his ears, Kevin forced his shoulders to relax and pulled out his 'buds.

"Just get in?" he asked, forcing cheer into his voice. "I thought you were still mentoring the new hydraulics trainees out at Regional for a day yet."

"If that's what you call teachin' 'em to tell their ass from an Abramson's lever, sure." Janice yawned hugely as she sauntered into the room, leaning against the rig. The light from its screens outlined the wrinkles around her eyes.

"Saw Suzanna down there. Pissy as ever, even on a base she asked to be assigned to. Said she wasn't surprised Taylor was dead. Asked if you was dead yet."

"And what did you tell her?" Kevin asked with mild interest. Considering how little Janice liked their former basemate, whatever scurrility she had come up with should be amusing.

"Told her to go fuck a frag grenade without lube an' pull the pin while she was at it. How come you're still up?"

"We've a rather important extraction coming up. I wanted to make sure we were prepared as thoroughly as possible," Kevin replied lightly, watching the liquid nutrient as it sprayed from the nozzles.

He yelped when strong fingers grabbed his chin and forced his head to turn. Janice studied his eyes and sighed. "Aw for fuck's sake Kev, you're high again. Where the good goat fuckin' god did you get the stuff?"

"I've got a lot to get done, Janice," he retorted, rubbing his jaw as he took a step back.

The engineer snorted. "Yeah, well, join the fuckin' club. You don't see me hopped up. I thought you were done with that shit." Kevin crossed his arms. "I've seen you take a dose in your time."

"Yeah, when we only have one day of water left and I gotta drill and run algorithms for thirty hours straight. The shit is for bein' on top of the game in emergencies, boy, not for whenever you're not feelin' like thinkin' 'bout anything," Janice drawled scathingly.

"Yes, well, I know when I need to be on top of my game, and that's when someone's life is on the line." The words were brittle on Kevin's tongue. "I already let one person die this year. I'd rather not repeat that performance. Now if you'll excuse me, I'm working."

Turning on his heel, he checked the printing rig. The floor creaked. A calloused hand rested on Kevin's shoulder.

"Kev, quit doin' this."

Kevin stood stiffly, refusing to look at the older woman. "Go to bed, Janice."

"You try tellin' me what to do again an' I'll stick my boot so far up your ass you'll go deaf," the older woman replied with quiet affection. "I mean it. You an' Laz an' Yve gotta stop this. Wasn't my fault or yours he didn't tell us for so long, wasn't your fault he died, an' you three ain't doin' no good actin' like it was."

"Janice." When Kevin's voice came out, it was a whisper. "That's my responsibility. To supply what's needed. I failed. If I'd been on top of things, he would have lived. If I'd found this girl six months ago, or someone like her, or… something, he'd be alive." He swallowed hard. "I can't fail again."

Janice let out a long, slow sigh. "You lil' dumbass." Her fist punched his shoulder gently. "You ain't failin' nobody, but you ain't helpin' by hoppin' up on that shit. I catch you on it again an' I swear I'll stick a pipe scrubber up your ass to get your head out, you got me?"

"I'll make sure you don't catch me then," Kevin replied quietly. He made a point of keeping an eye on the tracker in Jim's tab across the Grid that morning, sucking down cups of the synthetic trash they passed off as coffee so that he could pretend that was the reason for the shaking in his hands. But it was worth it to be standing at the door of the motor pool beside his commander and his personnel officer to welcome the newcomers.

"This's it?" Tweak asked as they climbed from the truck Sarah had been driving. She gave the dusty garage a jaundiced look. "Lame."

"Tweak." Billie murmured, and Tweak rolled her eyes.

"It is lame. Looks like a dump."

Kevin felt a twinge of irritation. As if they'd been living much better on Grid. He'd seen good. They hadn't had it.

But Aidan chuckled and shrugged as Sarah shut the truck door. "It's home. I don't think we're doing too bad. How was it coming in?"

"Easy," Sarah replied as she shoved black spikes of hair back from her eyes. "I didn't even have to use my gun."

"That's a relief," Aidan remarked, glancing at where the transport specialist was checking the truck over now that it was parked. "Hey, Dozer. Meet the new recruits: Tweak and Billie."

The big man glanced up from plugging the truck in and held out his hand. "Dozer. Nice to meetcha."

Tweak looked at the hand, then at Aidan. Her leather-clad arms crossed over her chest. "Rule. One."

Aidan just smiled, though Kevin noted that the expression had taken on a forced quality. "Um, sorry, Dozer, no touching. Not even handshakes, apparently. I'm going to say she means 'nice to meet you.'"

Dozer blinked, lowering his hand. "Yeah, right."

Behind Aidan's back, Liza caught Kevin's eye and made a writing-on-pad gesture. He winced internally. Yes, he did need to fill her in, didn't he?

"How about we show you your rooms?" Aidan asked. "After that Liza will give you the tour, okay?"

"Yeah," Tweak replied distractedly, her eyes taking in every detail. Tweak dropped her bag in her new room with a thunk and began prowling the perimeter like a cat.

"And your room is over here, Billie—" Liza began, but Tweak cut her off. "Nope. This. Ours. No split." She tapped the walls.

"She means we'd like to have the same room." Billie explained in a whisper, staring at the floor.

"Okay. Uh, what're you doing?" Liza asked, watching Tweak stand on the bed to tap the ceiling. "Bugs," Tweak stated shortly.

"Sorry," Billie murmured behind Aidan. "We always checked when we were in the…" She cleared her throat. "Before. Sorry."

Aidan nodded. "I understand. Can't trust folks you don't know."

Kevin was amazed he had the patience. He was getting sick of the girl's disrespect himself, which was saying something considering his standards for disrespect.

Tweak glanced over her shoulder. "We look stupid? Not. Lock on door? Who has the key?"

"Me and Liza have masters. You'll get a key soon as we're sure this is going to work," Aidan replied calmly.

Tweak turned to eye him up and down. "People come in here, fuck with us, they're dead. Nobody's fuck toy."

Kevin felt his body stiffen in anger. What kind of people did this girl think they were?!

"Tweak…" Billie began, but trailed off when Aidan glanced her way, hanging her head.

Kevin felt a little knot of sympathy as he watched her. Something had made a real mess of that poor waif. Detention? CPS life? Impossible to tell, but she was a mouse. The other one, however…

Aidan nodded. "I understand. We only have masters in case of emergency. We're not in the habit of getting into other people's quarters when they haven't invited us."

Kevin drew in a breath. Best foot forward, at least try to be a gentleman. "Can I get you two anything before I head back to my duties for the day?"

"The door," Tweak retorted, flopping on the bed and kicking off her heavy boots. "Shut it. Call us for dinner. "

Billie gave the strangers an apologetic smile. "Thank you?"

"Sure," Liza managed with a careful smile. "I'll get you on the work rosters tomorrow. If there's anything you need, come to me or Aidan."

Neither girl responded.

Quietly, the three officers shut the door. Liza glanced from her old friend to her commander. "Briefing real quick?"

They sat in the canteen with more cups of the bitter stuff they called coffee. Liza swirled hers gently. "I read the file. I get she's got baggage, but... Wow."

"No arguments," Kevin agreed, polishing his glasses. "She was quite the little spitfire on-Grid, but that's rather to be expected. I thought she'd relax once she arrived in friendlier surroundings. If anything, she's... worse."

Slowly, Liza glanced at Aidan. "Don't take this the wrong way, but I'm kind of wondering what the hell you just brought home."

"Yeah," Aidan agreed quietly, "you're not the only one."

Event File 25
File Tag: Field Test
Timestamp:11:00-7-29-2155

"So. This coder. "

Aidan rocked back and forth on his feet, waiting, his hands clasped behind his back. He hated waiting.

At his desk, Sector Commander Magnum sat with ten holographic windows splayed out around him and slowly, slowly scanned Aidan's report. His fingers fumbled over the analog pages. The more he read, the higher his eyebrows rose. "Tell me again why you gave me an analog copy. "

"She's hacked our files three times in four days, sir," Aidan explained. "She got in to delete the medical file we started for her, she did that twice. And then she didn't like the fonts we used, so she changed them in the system. "

He desperately wished he wasn't saying this out loud. He couldn't believe he'd brought home a girl who hacked apart their system because she got bored. He felt like the guy who brought home a kitten and found it eating the couch.

The heavy man stared at him, black brows raised.

"You're telling me this girl hacked the best encryptions we've got. To change fonts. "

Aidan cleared his throat. "Um, according to her, our encryptions have some holes. "

She'd actually said the whole system was a piece of shit and they were a bunch of asshats for using it, and she'd gotten into it with nothing but a personal tab. She could see anything she wanted at this point, and that was fucking terrifying. But Aidan wasn't going to tell the man that.

The man who was still staring at him. "Apparently," Magnum stated, the word hanging in the air. Sighing, the sector commander set down the papers. "Well. Sit down already, Headly. I'm tired of watching you stand there."

Aidan took a seat, watching his sector commander's face. The older man watched him right back, impassive. Aidan worked to keep his breathing even.

"I guess you found the perfect hacker for the Wildcards. She's going to fit right in." Magnum had a way of stating things so gravely that they seemed to hang there after he'd fallen silent.

"Yes, sir." Aidan wasn't sure whether that comment was supposed to be good or not, really, but he didn't want to find out right now. If Magnum was going to ball him out, he'd do it when he wanted. All Aidan had to do was wait.

Magnum studied the slick paperwork, holding it inches from his fleshy nose. "According to this she's seventeen? And her friend is eighteen?"

"That's what they tell us, sir. But Tweak changed her age in one hack. Originally, she said sixteen. She made it seventeen."

The heavy-set man leaned back, crossing his arms. He stared at Aidan long enough to make his throat go dry.

"Do you know why I encouraged Paul Taylor to put a base like the Wildcards together, Headly?"

Aidan really hated open ended questions like that. What the hell was he supposed to say? "Um, no, sir" sounded stupid and "why don't you tell me?" sounded snarky. He stuck with the good underling answer. "Sir?"

The man across the desk smirked. "You know, if you say 'sir' one more time like you're an idiot, I'm going to start believing you."

Aidan wished he could close his eyes. Was there anything he could say right?

"You don't actually believe a nut-bin like the Wildcards came together accidentally, do you?" The man's dark face creased in a smirk.

Aidan swallowed hard. "I don't know, sir."

Commander Magnum sighed. Flicking his screens away, he stood, studying the pic screens hung on his wall. Aidan watched the man's back and gripped the arms of the chair.

"I had two reasons for letting Paul handpick his crew and run his base his own way," Commander Magnum stated eventually, his voice a quiet rumble. "Every organization needs somewhere where the rules are loose, because that's where innovation happens. And I was right. We've gotten more ideas out of the first generation at the 1407 base than most, and the second generation is exceeding them. Specialist Faiz and Doctor Coson's idea with using Synth for faking biometrics? That's going to save lives. Most bases across America are working with Danvers' water algorithms and equipment designs. And I had a theory to test there, too. There's been two decommissions, one disciplinary transfer, and zero suicides in eight years on Base 1407. You know the average, Headly?"

"No sir?" Aidan asked, wondering where the hell this was going and hoping it wasn't going to be a discussion about his own depression. He'd had it under control so well lately, even without meds. It had only flared up a little here and there. It had been so good that he'd actually stopped thinking about it for a few weeks. Had that ever happened before? Was Magnum going to call him out on all that now? Why?

"Three decommissions and a suicide per base, per year," the man stated slowly. "Your base has lower combat death rates, too, and personnel wait longer to sign up for a slot in a retirement base.

"You've had zero friendly fire incidents." Magnum turned finally, looking at Aidan with weariness in his eyes. "I wanted to prove my point, and so did Paul. The Force is still clinging onto what we remember of military thought from a century ago, but we aren't living like the soldiers back then did, Headly. We don't get standard-issue people out here. We get whoever comes to us, and we need to work with that and stop trying to turn everyone into a traditional soldier. You were born Duster. Your dad was a base commander, right? You've seen how it is."

Aidan jerked his head in one brief nod. Oh, he'd seen how it was. His father, the bastard who'd almost driven him to suicide, was one reason he'd hated this idea of being a commander himself. He was never going to be like that.

"We raise our kids as soldiers," Magnum continued. "We tell people that they can't depend on anything and are going to die tomorrow, and we lose them regularly because they buy it. We can't treat our people the way the old government treated its soldiers. When we treat each recruit like a unique asset, find the best fit for them, let them connect with and—yes, I'm going to say it—care about the people they serve with, they fight hard. Which is why I wanted the Wildcards formed, and why I stopped letting Sector Personnel dick around and handpicked you to lead them. Your base is my proof of concept now that it's back on track."

"Yes, sir," Aidan agreed, sticking with the easiest answer.

Everything that had just been dumped on him was going to take days to process. Aidan couldn't believe he'd heard half of it.

Magnum trained his dark eyes like scopes across the desk. "You say that like you don't know what the hell I'm talking about."

Aidan drew a breath. "I don't want to be disrespectful, sir, but... Yeah. I don't know what you want me to say here."

Finally, his superior smiled, pointing a meaty finger. "See, that's the guy I recruited. The honest one."

Aidan blinked. "So, I'm doing this right, I guess?"

Magnum quirked a brow. "Once you get this coder with the program, you mean? The Wildcards aren't back on their old numbers yet, you've still got a ways to go. I want to see more missions run successfully. I want to see your intra-base interactions come back with a lot fewer complaint reports, and I want those requisitions numbers up. But since you took them from pranking every other Duster and no missions to this? Yeah, Headly. You're getting back up there." He carefully stacked the papers Aidan had printed for him, giving them a disbelieving smile as he did.

Aidan cleared his throat. "Sir? May I ask a question?"

"You can always ask, Headly," the older man replied, a smile toying with the corners of his lips. "Only question is will you get an answer."

Aidan drew a breath. "What actually happened with Taylor? I know what the reports say, that he got cancer and died. But on base the guys start talking about him and then they'll quit like they did something out of line and shut down on me. Do I need to know anything?"

"That's something you need to ask your people," the sector commander replied on a sigh. "Though I thought you'd get it by now. Here's a hint: when Paul was dying he told me 'my kids are going to be asses for a while, Ben, 'til they figure out this isn't on them. Slap them around for me but don't take it personally.'"

"On… them?" Aidan asked slowly, but the older man adroitly turned the conversation as he stored the paperwork.

"I notice you haven't asked about your commission incentives." Glancing up at the expression Aidan was working so hard to keep neutral, he frowned. "Your surgical procedures, Headly?"

"Sir?"

"I've got you listed. First one is in six months, the second in eight. Still scheduling the third one. the only specialist in the CO-WY has a long list and a lot to watch out for. That going to work for you?"

Aidan started. He couldn't believe what he'd just heard. Scheduled. After all this. After his dad's garbage. All these years. All this fighting. He'd done it.

He was on the list.

"Well, Headly? That work for you?"

Aidan stood so fast that he knocked his chair and had to catch it before it fell. "Yes, yes, sir!" He cleared his throat, saluting. "Yes, sir. Thank you, sir."

That night, he lay in bed and grinned at the ceiling.

This was really happening. He was finally going to get his body fixed. He was finally going to stop looking in other people's eyes and hating the version of himself he saw there. He was going to prove his dad and Sam and all the bastards who said he was crazy wrong.

He was going to be a real—

The klaxxon blare of an alarm brought him awake with a yelp, adrenaline coursing through his system as the night-cycle lights flashed back into brilliant day-cycle.

And that wasn't a proximity alarm. That was a Shelter-In-Place alarm. That was worse.

His stomach tied itself in a knot and crawled up his throat as he fought his binder, stuffed his packer down his pants, yanked on a shirt and ran out the door, still pulling on his gun belt.

The hall was bedlam. Kevin was already in a flat sprint for the code rig, Janice right behind him. Lazarus's favorite gun click-clacked beside Aidan's ear. "Commander, you want us on look out?" the tow-headed man asked, Sarah tense beside him.

"Wait. Two seconds." Aidan stated as calmly as he could. Pulling up his tab, he read the warning on the lock screen, and felt his guts squeeze in on themselves.

Their slick tarps had rejected a new software update, and it had caused a cascade in the system. The things had switched off. They were sitting completely exposed. He forced himself to raise his head, meeting Lazarus's eyes. Sarah nodded behind him.

"I'll get the mortars out. We can get at least a couple drones down before they touch us."

"Okay," Aidan agreed. "Okay, let's check the proximities." Feverishly, he brought up the drone flight patterns on his tab and flicked the holographic screen on. The layout and the numbers hovered in the air.

Aidan's eyes flicked over them. "We've got three hours, starting now, before the next drone is gonna pass over. Okay! Everybody!" he added, raising his voice. "Anybody not on coding duty get insulating stuff and cover up anything warm and any spots where light can leak. If the tarps aren't up by then, we'll get under stuff in the canteen to hide our heat signatures. I—"

"What the f-fuck was t-t-that?" a voice shrieked down the hall, and Tweak came clomping out, oversized boots trailing their laces. She'd forgotten her coat. She stood in baggy pants, a tank top and ace bandages that wrapped her arms from hand to shoulder, shivering and yelling in a voice that hurt the ears. "The f-f-fuck?! The f-f-fuck w-w-was that?"

Aidan nodded curtly to Sarah and Lazarus with a muttered, "Get out there and be safe," before turning to his newest recruits, trying to dredge up a smile that felt like it would crack his face. "Sorry, girls. Our slick tarps went down. We'll get it sor—Wait." He blinked, then smacked his forehead with the heel of his hand. "Shit, I'm a fucking idiot. Tweak. Think you can give us a hand getting the programming fixed up?"

Around them, people ran with handfuls of heat sink bots, blackout tape, blankets to throw over everything that might give them away from above. In the middle of the hall, Tweak glared at him. "I fix it, then I can s-s-sleep? Show me."

"God damn it! I thought we'd synced the software and hardware patches this time," Kevin was snarling as he typed, Janice working grim and silent beside him as Aidan stepped in.

Both of them were a mess. Janice was still in something shapeless she used for pajamas and her boots were unlaced. Kevin's unbrushed hair stood up like flames and he hadn't bothered with a shirt. His gun belt was slung around a bare torso.

"Don't have space for looky-loos," Janice snapped in irritation.

"Then you get out." Tweak retorted sharply, looking over her shoulder, then Kevin's. She snorted. "Shitheads. Move. Lemme sit." Janice glanced up and opened her mouth to protest, but Aidan caught her eye and shook his head, jerking a thumb at the girl.

Grumbling under her breath, she levered herself out of her chair and motioned for Tweak to take it. "Fine. Rather everybody blame you when we fuckin' die anyway."

Tweak dropped into the chair, pulled the keypad closer, and started to type. A moment later, she pulled a second monitor interface closer, spreading a handful of windows out across both. She typed with one hand, touching the screens and dragging windows into new configurations, never looking down. Never blinking either, Aidan noticed. That was creepy.

"Hah!" Tweak laughed, and the sound was loud as a gunshot after the tense silence. "Bastard. Gotcha!"

"Commander!" Jim yelled down the hall. "We gotta have it up by one! Next drone pass in three hours!"

"I know!" Aidan shouted back. "Working on it!"

"Gimme three seconds," Tweak muttered, and put both hands on the keyboard. She hit a last button, leaned back in her chair, and nodded at her audience. "There. Fixed."

Outside, there was a holler and a whoop. Feet clattered on the outer stairs. "Commander!" Sarah laughed, her hair windblown and her eyes alight. "We're all clear! The tarps are up!"

Aidan let out the breath he'd been holding and leaned against the doorframe, grinning at Tweak. "Holy shit. I've never seen anyone get a slick tarp back up that quickly. Damn, glad you're on our team now."

Tweak gave them all a skeptical look. "That? Couldn't handle that? You guys suck or what?"

Aidan chuckled and shrugged. "Corps get most of the good hackers in their pockets. We don't normally get any of them to come work for us. And everyone else here's got other duties, too. Haven't had a dedicated coder on this base since I've been here. Kevin and Janice were handling it."

Tweak eyed him. Turning, she raked the two Dusters with her eyes. "You let these asshats code? You s-suicidal?"

Aidan's laugh was colder than he had anticipated. Well, yeah, sometimes he was. But not tonight. "Not most of us. Just hard to get coders out here."

Tweak tipped her head. Then the teenager lost interest. "Yeah, whatever. Tired. Bed." Slipping out of her seat, she brushed past the crowd in the doorway, leaving them staring at one another. Aidan met his crew's eyes with a weak smile. "I guess we know we've got a coder now."

"Apparently," Kevin agreed, still sounding a little dazed.

Janice let out a long breath. "So, I'm not gonna work on the software anymore? Thank God."

Aidan's chuckle was more honest this time. "Lucky you. All right, everyone. Try and get some rest. Lazarus, you okay to take watch the rest of the night, just in case?"

"Wasn't planning to do much with my night anyway," the tousled man shrugged, giving his friends a wave as he turned and shouldered his mortar-rifle. "Night, guys."

"Night," Kevin murmured, standing as the crew filtered back towards their bedrooms.

"Well," he added once the doors down the hall were shut. "Wasn't that interesting."

"We can dissect it in the morning," Aidan replied quietly, trying and failing not to watch Kevin.

The man nodded, then yawned expansively. "No complaints here. I hadn't been looking forward to burning the candle at both ends." Glancing at Aidan, he gave a slow, sleepy smile. "It looks like we found a few gems in those girls. Nothing a little polishing won't—" Another yawn cut off the rest of his words.

Aidan chuckled. "Yeah. Just hope they won't kill us before we can polish 'em up." He raised his eyes to Kevin's face, smiling crookedly. "You should get some sleep."

"Yes, sir," Kevin agreed quietly, eyes already half-lidded. Giving Aidan another small smile that made his heart lurch, the wiry man slipped by and headed for his room.

Leaning against the door, Aidan focused on breathing as the last twenty minutes dropped on him like lead.

Event File 26
File Tag: Requisitions Foray
Timestamp: 7-30-2155/ 8-1-2155

"All. Your tech. Sucks." Tweak dropped onto the bench hard enough to make the plates rattle, slapping down her cracked tab beside Aidan's hand.

He pulled back reflexively. "Um." He really didn't need this kind of morning after a drone-alarm night.

"I regret to inform you that we aren't at liberty to walk to the nearest Techo Toys store and buy the best," Kevin added dryly down the table. "We make do, you see. Our deepest apologies."

Unfortunately, his tone was anything but apologetic, and Aidan knew he wasn't the only one to notice it.

Tweak's black eyes narrowed. "You guys. Using shitty stuff. It. Get. You. Dead. You got me?"

"What would we need to get the base up to your standards, Tweak?" Aidan asked, trying to stay as calm as he could for everyone else's benefit. He really, really didn't need this.

"Got a list," Tweak stated, flicking on her tab so that the holo of her screen fizzled up, filled with text. "Red, you need now. Last night.

Software. Band aid. New hardware. Soon. Yellow, you need s-soon. Green can w-w-w-wait." She shut her mouth with an audible click.

Aidan stared at the list, slowly swallowing down the porridge he'd just put in his mouth. "Um, okay. That's a long list."

"Lot of broke shit," Tweak agreed sourly. "I do tech here, I do it right. No spit and d-duct tape. No shit work."

"Okay." Aidan drew a slow breath. "So, what happens if we don't get the stuff in red?"

Tweak gave a quick bark of a laugh. "Your slick tarp dies. You all die. Nobody pay me. Your AC stops reading temps r-r-right in a m-month. You all fry. How you work with this garbage so long?"

"Because we have to, honey," Andrea stated quietly, putting a bowl down in front of Tweak. She ignored it.

"Not your honey. So? Where do I put in an order?"

Kevin gave a sigh that Aidan couldn't quite class as theatrics or real irritation. "You come to me after breakfast." He emphasized the last two words. "And I start looking into it."

Tweak turned like a cat. "Not you," she stated flatly.

Kevin met her eyes with an expression that Aidan hadn't seen before: distant, blank and completely disdainful. Damn, Aidan thought to himself, feeling a shiver run down his back. He hadn't known Kevin got that cold. He looked like an exec staring down a CPS worker, all human empathy genetically removed.

Aidan had been afraid to see an expression like that when he told Kevin the truth. But Kevin had looked like a surprised kid then. Nothing like this.

"Yes, me," Kevin stated, just as flat. "Because, for your information, I'm the logistics and requisitions officer here, and you have yet to earn so much as your specialist rank. Therefore, you will be polite and you'll come to my office to discuss this after breakfast."

Tweak stared at him for a heartbeat. Then she pushed her bowl away, stood, and stamped out of the canteen.

"What the—" Dozer began to say, when Aidan's tab dinged.

Glancing at it, he read

Message Handle: TheTweak

Message: Here's your list. The asshole can get it from you and go fuck himself.

Down his screen, text scrolled in multicolored lines. Aidan resisted the urge to groan. "Kevin, Yvonne, Jim," he managed eventually. "I guess we're having a meeting after breakfast."

Four hours later, his logistics team had covered his desk in plans, timetable windows and tabs whose cooling fans felt like they were slowly cooking the room. He glanced at the clock on the nearest tab and repressed a curse. How had they been doing this four hours?

Kevin idly tapped the table as he stared at the list. He'd put an X beside everything he had figured out how to acquire. Only one red line still blazed unmarked.

"That holoboard's the worst. It's out of production and... Well, there's always the TechoCo dump, I suppose," Kevin stated finally.

Yvonne sucked a breath between her teeth. "Kev, last time..."

Kevin nodded slowly, fingers fiddling with one leg of his glasses absently. "Yes, that was a problem. Maybe the team needs to be smaller. And if we take an older model truck, one with fewer trackable parts..."

"Any older and you'll have to get it off a Fringer," Jim muttered.

Kevin nodded. "I imagine Burl would sell us that 'antique' he's always—"

"That gamma piece of garbage can't drive!" Yvonne cut in indignantly, and Kevin gave her one of his looks over the rims of his glasses.

"For your information, it can and does." Yvonne shook her head. "You're nuts." "Pot and kettle, my dear."

Aidan sat back. Great, another one of these conversations. He was still sitting outside looking in.

Then Kevin glanced at him, his sly smile softened, and he reached over to bring up an image. "Sorry, Aidan. This is what we're discussing."

Aidan blinked at the picture of the ancient rust bucket. "So, that thing runs? It looks older than Dissolution."

"See?" Yvonne shot tartly.

Kevin sighed. "It runs on diesel and has only the tiniest electrical parts. Most drones read it as a particularly ferrous rock, and the satellites don't tag it. Unless a human actually takes the time to read the feeds, it'll be completely ignored when it's parked and only noticed by a particularly alert security drone when it's in motion."

Aidan blinked. "Huh, okay. If you think it'll work."

"Now that's settled," Kevin remarked with a pointed glance Yvonne's way, "let's plan out the schedules. This is going to stretch us thin. We really need to pick up food for the base, and there's that medical shipment that we need to handle and hand off. Oh damn, and we promised we'd pick up the Sector shipment of coolant…"

Kevin brought up six windows with a practiced flick of the fingers, pushing time slots here and there around the trajectories of three layers of surveillance that blanketed the Dust. Finally, he sighed. "All right, that works, provided I head to the dump on my own at seven in the evening, arrive at ten and keep to a time window of—"

The rest of his team drowned his words in dismay before he'd finished. "Alone, are you gamma?" Yvonne demanded.

Kevin held up his hands. I said a small team was better for—"

"Small means two people, not alone, you ass!"

"Yvonne, for once, will you remember that I technically outrank you and listen when I tell you I can—"

"Oh, and we go get your body later? No thanks," Jim snapped.

Kevin's voice took on a harried note. "Oh, come now you guys you know I can run worse than this by—"

"Hey. Everybody?" Aidan asked, but the noise continued. "If you think I'm letting Mister History go out spelunking in the dump again, you—"

"We got exactly what we needed last time. It was not—"

"You got your finger dislocated!"

"Yes and it popped right back in. Will you—"

Aidan inflated his lungs. Naomi used to say he could break glass with his voice when he wanted to, and that had been before he'd started on T. "Guys!"

Three heads snapped around. Perfect silence fell. "I'll go," Aidan stated in the quiet he'd made.

Yvonne bit her lip.

Kevin drew back a little. "Um, are you sure that's wise?"

Aidan smiled wryly. No, he wasn't sure. But they needed those parts, and this arguing wasn't getting them. And he didn't want Kevin going alone.

"I grew up helping out with supply runs like any Dust kid does. I still know how to drive and shoot." He shrugged. "It'll be nice to be somebody's backup again."

Kevin watched him warily. "Sir, I can... Really, I—"

"Get the truck." Aidan put as much firmness as he could scrape together into his voice. "And we'll go tomorrow night."

Forty-eight hours later, Aidan shifted in the cracked seat and listened to the desert silence. The stars were incredibly bright overhead. He glanced at the tab Kevin was manning, cradled in a little tripod Kevin had set on the dash. Still twenty miles to go, and they were only able to go around twenty miles an hour. Damn. Glancing over at Kevin, he smiled tightly.

Kevin gave him a quick smile. "We're still in very good time."

"Yeah, if this thing makes it another twenty miles." Kevin chuckled. "Pessimist."

The desert rolled away.

"Er," Kevin began quietly. "Mind if I put something on?"

"Sure," Aidan murmured, watching the terrain.

A beat later, a song began with rhythmic drumsticks clacking and a fierce voice.

"Sort of the base anthem, this," Kevin remarked as the music played. "I really should have played it for you before now."

Aidan smiled crookedly as he listened. "Yeah, this sounds like you guys." He tipped his head, listening.

"We're not gonna take what?"

"General bullshit, I assume," Kevin quipped. "Rock's usually more about emotion than concrete information, I'll own up to that." He shrugged, smiling.

Glancing out of the corner of his eye, he watched Kevin sing along to the entire thing under his breath, then to the next one. "You know the words to all this stuff?" he asked, unable to stop his incredulous grin.

Kevin ducked his head, smiling sheepishly. "Yes, well. My dad used to play it. Billy Joel, The Who, Styx, Rush, all the classic musicians. He used to pile us in the car for the trip up to Vail, and we'd sing all the way up. It drove Mom nuts."

Aidan grinned at the image, until he heard more than the half remembering, half embarrassed tone in Kevin's voice. "Wait. You guys could afford the Vail Complex?"

On the tab, a new song started in a weird wail Aidan hadn't heard before. Kevin cleared his throat. "Not ourselves, no. It was a Corp perk for the kind of work Dad did. He and Mom used to save up their commendations and perks and pool them into vacations and Mom's garden. Mom bred roses to deal with Colorado summers as a hobby. She met her best friends trying to get cactus genes into rose roots. She had this yellow shrub rose that could take a hundred and twenty degrees without water. It was gorgeous, Dad used to call her The Red Queen because of it. He had a lot of jokes like that." Kevin smiled: a lopsided, unconscious expression. "My dad... He was kind of amazing."

Aidan grunted, watching the road. "Lucky you. Mine was a complete asshole." Kevin didn't say anything to that.

The song filled the cab. The singer put notes to words about secrets that he wished he could forget and things he tried to hide from. His voice cut through the air, aching and fierce.

Aidan felt as if the singer had taken everything he was feeling and wrapped it in music. He could almost understand why Kevin liked this stuff as he listened. One line hit so close to home that it hurt. *Code of silence. No kidding*, Aidan thought as the words went on and that weird instrument wailed. Code of silence was right. There was so much he couldn't talk about. Even here.

Even now.

Kevin changed the song.

Aidan glanced at him. "How long since…"

"Nine years," Kevin replied quietly. "Three days before I joined up actually. We're getting close. I'm going to give the suits one last check over before we arrive, make sure that dodgy one doesn't act up."

Carefully, the logistics officer wormed into the backseat and started checking over pieces of slippery fabric. Aidan didn't know what to say, so he focused on driving.

Aidan's boots hit the ground in a cloud of gritty dust as he slid out of the old wreck of a truck. He gingerly closed the door. If he slammed it too hard, the noise might attract security drones. Or the door itself might fall off. The truck had barely made it the fifty miles from base to this junkyard on the edge of the Grid. Hopefully the journey would be worth it.

"Well, this is the place." Kevin rounded the front of the truck, data tab in hand and bag slung over his shoulder. Sticking out from under the holographic hood of his slick suit, Kevin's bright red hair looked almost purple in the starlight. He looked at Aidan and adjusted the ancient spectacles on his nose. "Might want to get the hood up. Heat sensors will be on us the minute we're inside."

Aidan hated wearing the skin-tight suit instead of a slick poncho. The tech-laden fabric didn't breathe, and once it activated the entire suit needed to be shut down to get a single piece off. But Kevin had traded specifically for them, and it was their best chance at sneaking into the TechCo junkyard, grabbing what they needed, and slipping out again without getting shot.

He reluctantly pulled the hood up over his head and cinched it down around his face. "Security's still running on circuit forty-two, right?"

Kevin tapped at his tablet a moment, gloved fingers nearly silent, then nodded. "Best shot is alpha setting."

Aidan flipped down the face screen of the slick suit and waited for the sensor feeds and settings to pop up on the HUD. It felt like it took hours for the blue text to flicker into life against the backdrop of the junkyard fence. Once it did, Aidan took a moment to double-check the suit's functionality and settings. Alpha setting was the default, so he was good to go.

As long as the suit didn't malfunction. Base 1430 had said it sometimes did. But it was the best they could get in time.

"Ready?" Kevin looked fuzzy with his own slick suit activated, but Aidan could still make out where he stood.

Aidan nodded. "Let's go."

They slipped from the truck to the fence, and Aidan frowned at the fine black net stretched between the electrified struts. They'd been prepared for the nanomesh, but he always hated it. If they didn't get the EMP and the virus right combination right, the nanobots making up the fence would recover from the power surge, heal whatever hole they made in seconds and send up an alert.

Aidan crouched down beside the nearest strut. He held his hand out to Kevin. Kevin dropped the palm-sized EMP into Aidan's hand. Aidan carefully set the black plastic unit against the strut.

A soft thunk reverberated through his hand as it latched onto the metal. When Aidan pulled away, Kevin ducked his head and hit a few buttons on his tab. The small-voltage EMP shuddered and whined. The hairs on Aidan's arms stood up. He hoped like hell Kevin's team had calibrated it to avoid shorting out the slick suits, too. A ripple flowed along the nanomesh fence, as if a breeze had blown through. The suits remained active.

Aidan pulled his knife from his boot. He hesitated as the knife touched the mesh rather than pressing the blade through and beginning to cut their way into the junkyard. They needed to get in there and find all of the equipment on their list before the Corps noticed their presence. If they failed this run, their base might not survive the month and a half it would take to legally reroute new parts. But, if he was too reckless with cutting the fence, failure was certain.

"Precision rather cedes to haste in this circumstance," Kevin muttered.

Aidan took a deep breath and let it out slowly. Kevin was right. They didn't have time to worry about every little thing if they were going to get in, get what they needed, and get out before they got caught. He jammed his knife into the fence and began sawing away at the mesh.

Every second he spent cutting through the fence felt like an eternity. He knew Kevin was watching for guards or drones, but if they were spotted they were dead.

Finally, he completed the upside-down L-shape in the mesh. He pulled the knife away and carefully pinned the material back. The hole was just large enough for them to squeeze through, but making a larger opening would waste too much time.

Aidan waited a heartbeat to make sure the virus would prevent the nanobots from repairing the fence. When it showed no signs of fixing itself and no alarms went off, he took a breath and squeezed through the opening.

The junkyard was only a quarter of a mile square, but inside its shadowed ranks of junk the space felt larger. Aidan and Kevin were dwarfed by piles of scrap metal, broken tech and anything TechCo had labeled as general salvage grade. Nothing in here was any more valuable than its weight in metal and plastic. Of course, a lot of the broken pieces were perfect for filling Tweak's list. The trick would be finding them. Before they got caught, hopefully.

They sifted through the nearest pile as quietly as they could manage. This was going to take forever, but there was no alternative: nobody bothered to keep a catalog on salvage grade parts that could be hacked. Not when it was all going into the smelter. They'd just have to depend on their suits' scanning and image recognition tech.

Kevin compared pieces to the list on his data tab. Most of what looked promising turned out to be the wrong make or model for the equipment they had. The data chips could be overwritten and the slick fabric could be patched into the base defenses for a few weeks, but they needed to find that holoboard to repair the base's camouflage long-term.

They moved onto another pile. Aidan's suit showed a green arrow on his left glove, pointing up. He climbed the mountain of metal, sharp pieces poking his palms through the gloves. He tossed down more data chips and a twisted grav-lift that looked like it could still be salvaged. Then he glanced up, and grinned. What looked to be the model of holoboard they needed sat half-buried in debris just out of his reach. He shifted his footing and stretched upward. The suit's HUD backed up his guess, outlining the piece in green.

Something gave way beneath him. He yelped as he fell, rolling down the metallic slope. Smaller pieces of scrap followed in a jingling imitation of an avalanche. He landed hard on his back, feeling the slick suit's battery compartment crunch beneath him and his knee shoot fire up his leg as it slammed into something. Red text flashed on his HUD:

—Battery compromised. Suit operation at 50%—

Aidan cursed as he gingerly pushed himself up to sitting position.

"Are you all right?" Kevin rested a hand on Aidan's back, helping support him.

He nodded and wincingly bent his aching knee. It flexed. He let out a breath of relief. "I'll be fine. Suit's crapping out, though. Pick up the pace."

Kevin's tab beeped in his other hand and he froze. He cursed under his breath and shoved the tab in the pouch at his waist. "Drones incoming."

Heart constricting, Aidan jumped to his feet, grabbed Kevin's arm and yanked him around another massive pile of junk. There. The rusting hulk of a Go car. He shoved Kevin toward it without a word and scrambled after him. They lay under the chassis, shoulders pressed together. Their breath was loud in Aidan's ears. His heartbeat thumped in his gut. Had the drones been alerted to the hole in the fence? Had they made too much noise in their search? Or was this just a routine sweep?

The whir of rotor blades broke the night. Only one drone by the sound of it. Aidan held his breath. Blue text flickered over the inside of his face screen, almost too fast to read. But one string of characters made him hiss a curse. "Kev, they're scanning on all security circuits. They'll find us."

Before Kevin could respond, something exploded not far away. Metal rained down on the shell of the dead car. Something hit with enough force to bend the floorboard dangerously close to Aidan's head. "Move!" Kevin hissed. He squirmed out of their shelter.

Aidan whispered commands into his suit as he followed, desperately trying to start it cycling through all of its settings. A bright red warning flashed across his vision.

—Suit operation at 40%—

Shit.

The sound of the drone's rotors grew closer.

He stumbled. Kevin steadied him and kept running. Bullets peppered the pile of junk right beside Aidan. A sharp edge cut through the side of his slick suit. The red text flashed across his screen again. The suit briefly tightened around his torso and let loose a soft warning beep, as if the text wasn't enough.

"Get back to the truck," Kevin hissed, shoving the collections bag into Aidan's hands.

Aidan opened his mouth. "Kevin, what—"

But it was already too late. Kevin had turned off his slick suit's camouflage and sprinted into the metal wasteland. The drone would be on him in seconds.

Aidan slung the bag over his shoulder, but he didn't even consider running for the truck. Screw whatever Kevin thought he was doing, Aidan wasn't losing his logistics officer. He wasn't losing Kevin.

His boots crunched into the gritty soil, and he gasped command queries as he ran. Instead of struggling to get his suit to cycle through the security circuits, he ordered it to look for anything that looked like a ranged weapon with enough juice to work.

The drone fired again. Metal fell like killing rain. Kevin yelped somewhere in the dark.

Aidan's suit pinged, a directional arrow appearing on his left glove. He snatched up the welder's bolt gun before he'd realized what it was. The barrel looked slightly warped, but his suit's sensors assured him the inner workings were sound, though this model only had enough charge for ten bolts if he was lucky. He thumbed the on switch and found himself pleasantly surprised when the gun actually started to hum in his hand as it warmed up.

The drone buzzed. Kevin screamed. The pleasure fizzled.

Aidan's footing was unsure on the shifting landscape, but he kept running. The drone flashed between the stars, a black disc three feet wide, barely visible in the night. Aidan aimed the bolt gun at it and hoped like hell it had warmed up enough. He pulled the trigger.

The flash of light nearly blinded him. He hadn't honestly expected to hit the drone on the first try, but his aim was apparently better than he thought. The drone's rotor whined. It dipped toward the ground.

"Kevin, heads up!" Aidan shouted. He couldn't see where Kevin was, or exactly where the drone would hit. All he could do was hope.

The drone crashed into one of the mountains of junk, scattering scrap everywhere. A coil of frayed wire bounced down to land at Aidan's feet. He kicked it away and scrambled in the direction Kevin had gone.

"Kev! Kevin! Talk to me!" The groan was so quiet that Aidan almost didn't hear it. He scrambled towards it. "Kevin?"

Another soft groan, followed by a weak, "I'm okay."

Aidan scrambled toward the sound. He nearly tripped over Kevin, who was lying half-buried under an avalanche of bits and pieces. Ignoring another warning on the inside of his face screen,

—Suit operation at 20%—

Aidan knelt down beside him and started brushing scrap off him. "You dumbass!" he snarled. "What were you thinking, turning your suit off? Get it back on. Now."

Kevin gingerly sat up and shook his head, trying to clear it. "Just a Killdeer gambit. Draw them off your position," he whispered, wincing when Aidan touched his shoulder. He rubbed his cheek where a purple bruise was already spreading. "Damn that hurt."

"Get your suit activated," Aidan snapped. He glanced up at the stars, half-expecting another drone. "That's an order Kevin!"

Kevin shook his head again, but he blurred as he reactivated his slick suit. "You've got to get out of here," the logistics officer whispered, "there'll be another drone soon. Your suit's broken—"

"Then we're leaving together," Aidan hissed back. "Like hell am I leaving you behind."

Aidan shoved aside the last of the debris that had landed on
Kevin. Nothing had so much as torn his suit. Lucky. "Think you can
walk?"

"I'll manage," Kevin murmured. "We need to get the gear back
to base."

Aidan snorted and moved to sling Kevin's arm over his
shoulder. "Then you better get your ass moving." He switched shoulders
when Kevin yelped.

"Did you take the drone down?" Kevin's voice sounded weak as
he levered himself up to his feet, leaning heavily on Aidan.

Aidan nodded and turned back toward the hole they'd cut in the
fence. "Yeah. But they're probably sending another one right now. So
move."

Kevin glanced at the sky, but he walked. His boots crunched
along the metal-strewn ground.

Red flashed across Aidan's vision again:

—Suit functionality shutting down—

"Crap," Aidan whispered despite himself. As if the suit failing to
hide his body heat wasn't bad enough. Now, he might have to cut it off
instead of using the normal electrical release. Great. That took their base
down to a single slick suit, assuming Kevin's didn't take damage before
they got out.

Assuming they made it out.

They made their way across the shifting landscape back toward
the fence. Aidan kept looking at the sky, expecting to see another drone
against the stars. Once or twice, he thought he heard the whine of rotors
spinning toward them.

Aidan skidded to a stop when they reached the fence. The clips
he'd used to hold the mesh back from the hole were still in place, but
there was no hole in sight. The nanobots must have overcome the virus.

"Shit!"

He yanked the knife from his boot again and desperately began sawing at the mesh.

This time, the sound of rotors was real and growing closer.

Definitely more than one drone headed their way. The nanobots shimmered and shifted in the wake of the knife, until Kevin jammed his hands into the cut to keep it open. Bullets pinged off metal behind them. The fence split, and Aidan reached back to shove Kevin through. As he ducked down to follow, the bag they'd filled with supplies caught on the rapidly re-sealing fence. He cursed under his breath and tugged.

Aidan pulled harder on the bag. He tried to push it backward and move it off the snag, but couldn't get the leverage. The fence mesh seemed to cling to it like a high-powered magnet.

Kevin crouched down in front of him. Without a word, he reached over and grabbed the top of the bag, shoved it backward and down, then pulled both it and Aidan out of the junkyard in one smooth motion. He snatched a pistol out of his belt and turned to face the fence. "Get the truck going. Motor has to turn over a few times. I'll watch our backs."

Aidan scrambled out of his crouch. "Kevin!" he hissed, "Don't play hero again!"

"Not the intent," the logistics officer replied coolly, but he didn't move.

Gritting his teeth, Aidan bolted for the truck. It sounded like the drones were right on top of them, but they hadn't started shooting yet. They must still be just out of range. He dove into the driver's seat and turned the keys.

The engine spluttered. Bullets sprayed the ground, kicking up a cloud of dust so thick Aidan could barely see the junkyard fence. He tried again. The engine whined.

The dark shapes of three drones flitted over the junkyard, blotting out the stars. Aidan desperately turned the keys, slamming his foot on the accelerator. The truck's engine finally revved.

Kevin flung open the passenger side door and leapt inside. "Go, go, go!"

Aidan slammed it into reverse and hit the gas. They jumped backward. Once the truck was far enough away from the fence, he changed gears and wrenched the wheel around. They bumped and rattled into the night as fast as Aidan dared without the headlights on.

The heat of the engine would make them easy to follow for the drones' thermal cameras, but the short-range guard drones couldn't go too far from their base of operation before their programming called them back. Aidan just hoped they could outrun them.

He gripped the steering wheel so hard it hurt. He could feel the suit tightening down against his skin. His heart pounded in his chest. Kevin's breathing was ragged beside him.

Another burst of bullets sprayed the ground right in front of them. Aidan yelped and yanked the wheel to avoid getting hit. The truck jittered to the side. Aidan slammed on the gas. The desert night sped past in a blur of blue and red under the starlight.

Slowly, the whir of rotors faded into the distance. Aidan's grip on the steering wheel began to relax. Kevin pulled his tab out of the bag and set it on the dashboard, watching as the screen flipped through the security channels they'd hacked into, keeping track of the location of dozens of drones.

Finally, Aidan pulled up under an overhang of red rock and cut the engine. The wide-range security drones were due to make their fly-over soon. Better to stop for a while and recover, get back on the road when it was safer.

They sat in silence for a long time, listening for rotors over the quiet buzz of the night insects. Aidan rested his arms on the steering wheel and propped his chin on his wrist, watching the star-studded sky.

"You all right?" Kevin breathed. At some point during the drive, he had deactivated his slick suit.

Aidan sighed and leaned back so he could manually flip his face screen up. "Yeah. Think so. Banged my knee pretty bad. Your shoulder?"

"Bruised. Doesn't feel severe." Kevin shrugged.

"Um, good," Aidan whispered eventually.

So. They were alive. They'd gotten out with most of what they'd gone in for.

At the expense of a bad bruise across Kevin's cheek, that or worse to his shoulder, and an action that could have caused so much more.

Slowly, some of his anger seeped back. He took a breath. "You scared the hell out of me back there and acted like a complete gamma, Kev. Don't do that again."

Kevin ducked his head in a slow nod. "I'm sorry, Aidan. I— When I saw you like that, I guess I panicked."

Aidan sighed. Kevin was normally so level-headed. He'd been utterly cool on-Grid, when Aidan had been scared shitless. So why had he acted like this out here?

On the tab screen, the red dot of a drone approached their location. They waited in breathless silence as the long-range drone passed, not even the sound of whirring to announce its presence. The red dot moved out of range.

Aidan breathed out. Kevin looked up with a smile. So close. They were so close.

"That's the last of them. A very fine night's work if I do say so."

Aidan tried to smile, but it faltered. "I didn't get the holoboard. That was the part we needed most."

Kevin smirked as he pulled the bag up from the floorboard and into his lap. He rifled quickly through the materials they had managed to grab, yanked, and pulled out the board with a wink. "Oh, I don't know about that."

"What? How…?" Aidan breathed, feeling the wave of defeat that had been threatening lift.

"Fell down the pile when you did," Kevin whispered, grinning.
"I simply grabbed it up. After all, I am the requisitions officer.
Snatching things is my forte."

A rush of joy shot through Aidan. They'd done it. They'd gotten
everything. Nose to nose with Kevin, he grinned. "Holy shit, we—Holy
shit! You... wow. Kevin, holy shit! This is like one of your vids!"

Kevin's eyes glittered like silver in the low light. "You know, if
this is a vid, I know how the scene ends."

"Yeah?" Aidan asked, still giddy with relief.

Kevin was still smiling, his teeth white outlines in his grin. And
he was leaning closer. Aidan could feel the heat of his skin, his breath.
"Heroes always get a kiss at the end of the adventure. That's the
convention." Kevin tipped his head, eyes holding Aidan's. "Would the
hero like a kiss?"

Aidan froze. Was Kevin actually... Was he...? He wet his lips.
His voice escaped as a whisper. "Am I supposed to be a hero?"

Kevin's smile was soft now, and he was so very close. "I don't
see anyone else in the driver's seat. So you must be." Then he pressed
his lips against Aidan's.

Kevin's lips were hot. Aidan's brain turned inside out. Kevin
was kissing him. Kevin had started kissing him. This was real. He
leaned into the warmth with a pleasure that was almost pain. This was
only going to be a second, but if only this second would last.

Softly, Kevin drew back. "Was that okay?" Kevin's whisper
barely made it through the buzzing in Aidan's brain.

He gasped in a breath. "Um, okay. Yeah." He swallowed hard
and forced himself to sit up. "We-we should get going home..."

Kevin nodded, eyes still holding his as he drew away. "I suppose
we should."

Event File 27
File Tag: Situational Awareness
Timestamp: 11:00-8-7-2155

Kevin woke in darkness. Rolling over, he suppressed a groan and cataloged his condition.

Shoulder, hurt a week ago and still aching. Damian had given him a topical muscle-relaxant for it, and that had helped, but some things had to heal naturally. Deep tissue bruising among them, unfortunately.

Head. Dully pounding. Too long in an intensely loud environment. Throat. Parched. He coughed. The inside of his larynx felt like it had been sandblasted.

That was what a three-day Grid mission did for you when it went wrong, he reflected, and you spent five days hiding with a family in a tiny maintenance apartment above a six-lane highway breathing fumes, with the billboard outside blaring day and night.

Pride. In fairly good shape. That family had been grinning so widely when they boarded their plane to England. The eighteen-year-old daughter had kissed his cheek. He smiled at the memory. Sweet kid. It had been the perfect way out of country for the family too.

In fact, it had been exactly what his own parents had chartered for him when they realized the work they were doing was going to get them killed. They'd made sure he had a way out.

A way out he'd turned down.

Ears. Ringing and aching. No surprise. Stomach. Roiling. What time was it? Rolling over carefully, he got out his glasses, then checked his tab "Damn." he whispered under his breath.

Eleven in the morning. He'd missed breakfast. Granted, the day was his for recuperation, but he still needed to eat and report to Aidan. Aidan. Kevin flopped back onto the bed.

Aidan.

He hadn't seen the man properly since that night in the junkyard. Since he'd leaned in and kissed him, like the idiot romantic he was.

Priorities, he told himself, shaking his head. Focus. Get up, get something to eat, get caffeine, come back and get cleaned up properly. Then go talk to Aidan.

He wasn't at the height of fashion when he stepped into the hall, but he was presentable. Pulling up his messages, he checked what had gone on in his absence, keeping close to the hallway wall in order to leave others room to pass in the cramped space.

The shrill yelp beside him made his heart kick into overdrive. "I said don't touch me!"

Kevin's tab dropped from his hand. He caught it before it hit the floor, turned and glared at Tweak where she had plastered herself across the hall, back against the wall. She glared right back.

Yes, he had officially had enough. He'd had a long week, he was tired, he hadn't eaten, and this girl had just stepped on his last nerve. She might be new, but he was done holding back with her.

"Tweak, believe it or not I have absolutely no inclination whatsoever towards touching you," Kevin snapped, walking faster to get past the girl laminating herself to the wall. "I brushed by you. The hallway is narrow verging on the claustrophobic. It pains me to break your delusional little heart, but I have it on good authority that the world actually does *not* revolve around you. Shocking, I know."

"Fuck off, CES," she called after him.

Kevin grit his teeth and focused on his tab, working at controlling his temper. The girls had been on base two weeks now and he'd never wanted to decommission someone and throw them out to live on the Fringe so badly before. If only Tweak wasn't so bloody good at her work. She was such an asset in a coding chair. Shame she was such an ass everywhere else.

Smiling sourly at his word play, Kevin crossed the canteen and stepped into the kitchen where Andrea stood with flour dust coating her to the elbows. She gave him a grin, the kids at play around her laughing. In the corner, Billie gave him a tiny smile as she poured more bowls of flour into bags. Kevin gave her a smile in return, then gave an exaggerated look around the room.

"What happened here?"

"The food processor spit flour everywhere the first time!" Tommy crowed, still too young to realize what a mistake in his mother's kitchen cost them.

Andrea nodded with a chagrined smile. "Yeah, the processor got grit in its works. But Topher fixed it up, and this second batch worked. With this golden rice flour, we can finally quit with the nutrition powder."

"Glad to hear it, because that stuff has all the appeal of chalk dust," Kevin quipped with a smile. He stooped down to scoop Henrietta from her play crib in the corner of the kitchen and made the little girl giggle with a quick spin and a boop on the nose.

"Yep, I'm gonna try to make pancakes out of it," Andrea remarked as she sifted her new flour.

Kevin shot her a grin. "Fancy making me your test subject? I'm in the mood for a decent breakfast after the week I've had."

"Sure, I can fix something," Andrea agreed, adding. "And while he's watching Hen, Tommy, tell the list to Kevin and me, okay? Kevin hasn't heard you yet."

"Okay!" the little boy agreed brightly, and took a long breath. "NatBank buys us and ZonCom sells—"

"No hon, the list. Not the poem."

"Yeah okay," the boy agreed with a little less enthusiasm. He sucked in another deep breath. Kevin almost expected his cheeks to puff as he began to recite, "The United Corporations Of America. ZonCom owns all companies that do the shipping, trade, and marketing and making all the roads. They react bad to people doing barter, to selling Corporate information and to alternative currency. They react good to nonconformity and to creativity. They're okay even with Gammas whose brains are okay," he began, pronouncing the longer words with careful determination,

"Eaglecorp sells security to all the other Corporations and owns all security stuff, only they lease it out to other Corps. They run the Safety Net with all the patrolling drones and satellites and stuff, and they run the emergency services and the Civilian and the Military Peacekeepers. They react bad to non-conformity, to weapons not registered with them and slick tech. And people who act scared. They react good to people who act chill and don't argue."

As he spoke, the little boy watched his elder's faces for signs that he was succeeding with his recitation. On the griddle, the pancakes began to sizzle.

"TechoCo owns all tech, all the Social Feeds and trains all the reporting services for all the Corps. They own all the bandwidth except the Greynet 'cause it's got ISP's out of other countries.

"Cavanaugh runs all the medical stuff and trains all the doctors and people who make meds, and they make all the meds and implants and stuff.

"ArgusCo builds all the cities and makes all the electricity for them and runs all the Go systems and leases people all the cars and trucks and houses and stuff.

"And American AgCo plants all the crops and owns all the farms and does the stuff that turns plants and animals into food and can I have some pancakes?" he finished in a rush.

Andrea gave him a fishy look. "You skipped over a whole lot there at the end, hon."

"Pleeease, can I have pancakes?" Tommy appealed. "I'll do it again later! Pleeease?"

Andrea smirked and poured batter on for her son as Kevin took his plate and dug in.

"Glad Hen could cheer you up. I heard Tweak yelling at you in the hall," Andrea remarked as he ate.

Kevin rolled his eyes as he dropped to sit cross-legged where the little girl could play with him, pitching his voice into a friendly singsong as Henrietta crawled into his lap and holding his plate out of her reach. "Yes, I may have to throttle that rapacious little starling at some point." He glanced up with a smile at Andrea's snort. "What? It's apt, you have to admit it's apt."

"Just the way you say it," Andrea chuckled. "Rapacious starling. What's a starling anyway? Watch it, she's going for your glasses."

"Well spotted," Kevin remarked wryly as the little girl tried to climb him, reaching for his shiny glasses. He tipped his head back out of reach and gently yanked the back of the little girl's shirt to flop her back onto her bottom. "And to answer your question, the obnoxious black birds that nest in abandoned buildings are starlings."

Andrea tipped her head, considering, then returned her attention to getting her experiment into storage canisters. "Yeah, I guess it does fit. But you could cut her a little slack."

"She's a little beast," Kevin stated, biting off the words as he distracted Henrietta with a toy.

"Beast!" Henrietta repeated, giggling.

At her work station, Billie bowed her head.

"She's a little kid," Andrea corrected gently as she wiped down surfaces and herself. "And she's scared, Kev. I mean we don't know how long she was in holding or what happened. Give her some time, and quit letting her get to you."

"Quit letting her get to me?" Kevin repeated in annoyed tones. "Andrea, everything she says is a barb or a rebuff. She's loud, utterly disrespectful, she doesn't give a damn--excuse me, I mean she doesn't give a curse about why we're doing this work, and God help me, it's like having Suzanna back. I'm sorry Billie, I know she's your friend, but still—"

"It's not that bad," Andrea disagreed.

Kevin sighed. "Well, no. Tweak is vexatious rather than actively malignant, but still. On top of it she would insist on calling me CES at every opportunity."

"Kev, hon, you're doing the words thing again. That's why she's calling you CES. She thinks you're showing off." Turning, Andrea smiled at the teenager slumped in the corner. "Billie? Can you run and get the floors swept?"

"Yeah," Billie whispered, turning away.

Kevin sighed. "Billie? Sorry."

The girl gave him a slow, wide-eyed look. Then she bobbed her head. "Yeah." She slipped from the room like a shadow.

"C'mere, baby." Andrea murmured, kneeling to pull Henrietta into her arms. Andrea studied her friend as she gently joggled the little girl. "You're really getting pissed." Andrea remarked eventually.

"Yes," Kevin agreed wearily. Then he glanced up and chuckled as Tommy gave him a hug.

"Kev," the little boy observed solemnly. "You look tired. You need a nap."

"He's got a point," Andrea agreed, watching him.

"Yes, well," Kevin agreed quietly. "I'm all right Tommy. This shoulder I gamma'd last week is still playing up, and that five-day extraction run on the Grid for the folks we sent on their merry way to Europe wasn't exactly a picnic. But I'm home and fresh as a daisy today," he finished with an attempt at putting some pep in his voice.

Andrea's soft brown eyes didn't waver. "You aren't on StayWake, are you?"

Kevin rolled his eyes. "Why does everyone around here assume I'm high when I say I'm fine?" he asked in the general direction of the ceiling.

"'Cause you did kind of overdo it for a while there, hon," Andrea replied with gentle candor.

Kevin gave her a sheepish smile. "I did, didn't I? Touché." Sighing, he stroked Henrietta's fuzzy hair gently. "I'm not on anything, Scout's honor. I'm just—"

The shrill of the proximity alarm cut him off mid-sentence. Tommy whimpered as Kevin grabbed Henrietta up. "I've got her. In here," he murmured, squeezing into the pantry carefully so as to leave room for Andrea and Tommy to squeeze in beside him. Henrietta started to fuss.

"Sssh, honey, sssh," Andrea whispered, but the little girl started a thin wailing as the lights clunked into blackness and the canteen outside filled with the sound of rustling as everyone else took cover.

Henrietta began to cry in earnest.

"Kev," Andrea whispered, "you know that song you did for her a while back? Do it again okay?"

"Worth a try." Kevin agreed, fumbling for and finding Andrea's hand in a dark so deep it felt like black velvet pressed to his eyes. Kevin cuddled Henrietta close, rocking her as she bawled. He drew a slow breath.

"Hush-a-bye, don't you cry,
Go to sleep my little baby."

He crooned the words in a breathy tenor as the rotors buzzed overhead.

"Way down yonder

In the meadow

Poor little baby is crying

Birds and butterflies

Flutter 'round her eyes

Poor little baby is crying..."

He sang to the little girl as death hovered over them, buzzing like flies. Slowly, Henrietta's wail eased into sniffles, and Kevin eased from one whispered lullaby into another.

"When I find myself in times of trouble

Mother Mary comes to me

Speaking words of wisdom

Let it be..."

The sound of rotors overhead eased as Kevin whispered the song in the dark.

"And when the broken-hearted people

Living in the world agree

There will be an answer

Let it be..."

Slowly, the rotor buzz began to fade. Kevin felt his gut unclench. That hadn't been so-

BANG

The sound was loud enough for a bomb, but the rolling metallic noises, the yowl of someone in pain and the torrent of hissed curse words and scuffles didn't match the initial impression. And, of course, there was the fact that he was still in one piece and breathing.

Breathing extremely fast. Damn, his heart was racing. Had someone run into something in the dark?

"YOU DON'T FUCKING TOUCH ME!" Tweak's voice screeched, the sound bouncing off walls and ricocheting from metal. "NEVER! NEVER T-TOUCH ME! YOU DON'T T-t-t-t..."

There was a weird, whooping noise that Kevin could only compare to the remembered sound of a little Fringer girl he'd met with a breathing problem he couldn't remember the name of.

He squeezed his eyes closed. God Almighty damn the little bitch to the ninth circle of Hell! If he'd had it in his power, he would have stood up and gagged her, but stumbling around in the dark would only make more noise. Noise that the drone could use to pinpoint them as targets. And fucking Tweak had already made plenty of that. Overhead, the noise of rotors returned in full. *Oh wonderful,* Kevin thought to himself, stewing in his anger. Just great. At least someone must have gotten a hold of the little harridan. She'd gone quiet. Kevin's tab buzzed in his pocket, but he had his hands full of frightened little girl. Cuddling Henrietta close, he stroked her curling hair, closed his eyes and waited. Ten minutes. Twenty.

Thirty.

Kevin rocked Henrietta and prayed in silence.

Event File 28
File Tag: Corrective Measures
Timestamp: 12:30-8-7-2155

After an hour, the sound of drone rotors receded. Faded. The lights flickered on. Kevin put Henrietta down beside Andrea and was out into the canteen in two economical movements, eyes narrowed. When he got a hold of Tweak this time, he wasn't going to stop at snark. He was going to…

He froze.

There was the prep table on its side, pots and everything else that had been stored in it spilled out across the floor. There was Topher in the middle of it, blood crusted down his face and blackening the front of his shirt. He gave a tiny grunt as Damian and Dozer knelt over him.

And there was Tweak curled into the furthest corner she'd been able to find, hiding in a cupboard with her head hidden in her bandaged arms. Liza stood in the middle of the mess.

Beside the cupboard, Billie huddled in place, arms wrapped around herself.

"She didn't mean it," the gawky girl whispered frantically as Kevin drew even with the little tableau. "She didn't mean it. She didn't mean… She just gets freaked. We didn't know what was going on. She didn't—She's… Is he okay? We're sorry. I'm sorry. We're so—"

"Enough." Liza rapped out. When she spoke again, her voice shook. "You two are done here. I'm writing the decommission paperwork. Pack." Then she spun on her heel. "Commander? Where's the Commander?"

"Over here," Aidan's voice called across the room.

Kevin let them deal with that part of the problem, and knelt beside Topher instead.

"How is he?" he asked Damian quietly.

"My effing nows is bwoken," Topher groaned, sounding like a man with the head cold from hell. Damian glanced up at Kevin with a patient expression.

"Let's get him into the med bay," Dozer muttered, reaching out to lift his junior specialist like a child.

Topher groaned. "Aw, fuck. But me dawn, man, I can walk!"

"What exactly did you say to her?" Kevin asked as Dozer set the young man on his feet, steadying Topher when he swayed.

The boy's eyes were already beginning to close with incipient swelling. "I towd her it'd be owkay abd twied to put by arm around her shoulders. I was twying to help her chill. That's it, man. Shit. Ow."

"White Knight Complex getting to you, too?" Kevin joked gently, focusing on the friend who needed help instead of the enemy he would have liked to go after. Fucking Tweak. He never should have brought the little monster's talents to anyone's attention. He never should have encouraged them to bring this little viper home. But she was the command division's problem. Let Liza and Aidan deal with her. She'd be gone soon enough. In the meantime, his friend was hurting.

"Come on, Sir Bedevere. Just hang on to us."

"Man, dawn't get weird on be right bow. I can't take it," Topher groaned in reply as Kevin and Dozer steered him down the hall and into the medical bay, Damian walking ahead like the drum marshal of a macabre parade.

"What the hell happened?" Alice asked, glancing from the logistics officer to her superior.

"Tweak," Dozer explained tightly as they settled the boy on the bed.

"Alice, swab and Eze while I prep," Damian called to his assistant medic as he pulled a few things out of drawers.

"Can I help?" Kevin asked, hands still on Topher's shoulders.

"You okay swabbing him down while Alice and I get prepped for procedure?" Damian asked as casually as he would ask for Kevin to grab him a plate at dinner, and Kevin agreed with the same calm for Topher's benefit.

"No problem."

Grabbing swabs from the wall dispenser, he helped Topher out of his cooling jacket and meticulously began to sponge away blood and snot. Dozer hovered beside the bed, wide brow creased.

"Get this on him," Alice added, passing over a bottle of Eze.

"Thanks," Kevin agreed, cracking the bottle at its midpoint, giving it a good shake and taking off the lid. He used the roll-on applicator to apply the inflammatory suppressant under Topher's eyes. Topher sat still for it, but he did switch into Arabic to curse a few times, especially when the applicator was run along either side of the bridge of his nose.

"Hey, easy," Dozer muttered.

Kevin nodded. "I'm being as careful as I can. This is what you get for going after pretty girls in the dark, Toph," he added gently.

Topher groaned. "Seriously man, go fuck yowself."

"Afraid it's not allowed while I'm on duty. Later I'll think about it."

Topher cracked a tiny smirk as his bruises, slowly, started to recede.

Damian stepped in with gloved hands, his imaging screen and his efficiency. "Right. Kevin, out of the way. Alice, hold the screen." He moved with perfect rhythm, spraying the area with a fast-acting anesthetic. "Close your eyes, Topher."

The boy did as he was told, and Alice held the imaging screen at the right angle over Topher's face, letting it show Damian the interior of Topher's nose. The tool projected the hologram of a straight line onto the boy's skin.

Damian nodded. "Looks like it's your lucky day. All we need to do is a closed reduction."

"What's a closed—"

"Hold still."

The cartilage in Topher's nose made a wet, squelching noise as it was slid back into place. He spit something long in Arabic this time, interspersed with a few rude words in French. Dozer and Kevin both winced.

"Shit, Doc," Dozer grumbled.

"He's fine," the doctor informed him as he worked, grabbing a thin sheet and peeling the medicated panel away from its plastic backing. Kevin's stomach gave its usual small lurch at the logo of two cupped hands and the words on the plastic: 'Cavanaugh, The Caring Company'.

The thin filaments melted into Topher's skin. Slowly, he blinked.

"How's the pain now?" Alice asked.

Topher glanced at her, smiled, and nodded. "I'm good. Can I work today?" he asked, glancing from Damian to Dozer.

The doctor gave a scarecrow shrug. "Take another half an hour and let the rest of the swelling go down. After that, as long as nothing touches that nose, yeah, you can work. Come back if you need a second numb patch."

"Got it." the junior transport specialist slid off his seat on the medical table, wobbled, but kept his feet.

"Um, Damian?"

Kevin turned at the sound of Aidan's voice. The commander stood awkwardly in the doorway.

"How's Topher?" Aidan asked with a small smile. "I'm good!" Topher waved a hand, trying for a grin.

Dozer cleared his throat. "You throw the bitch out already, Com—"

Tweak stepped into the room. For a moment, nobody moved. Then Tweak shuffled a boot. "S-s-s-sorry," the girl muttered, staring at the floor. "Got s-s-s-..." She swallowed hard. "Got s-scared. Freaked. S-s-s-sorry."

"Tweak needs to start carrying anti-anxiety meds, Damian," Aidan added after a moment. "Something fast-acting for times like this. Can you get a prescription workup for her?"

"Sure," the tall man agreed slowly. "And maybe a psych interview for—"

"Not. Crazy. Just. Freaked," Tweak snapped out, rapid-fire. Turning her head, she glanced up at Aidan, who was watching her. "Not crazy," she repeated more softly.

"But, if you're staying, you're going to fix this," Aidan said, and a note in his voice told Kevin he was repeating himself too.

Slowly, Tweak nodded. "Yeah. Fix." She glanced at Topher, glanced away. "S-sorry."

"And Tweak is going to put in ten hours of work on any project you got outside her duties, Topher," Aidan added. "To prove it and pay you back."

Tweak nodded in agreement.

Kevin watched the girl in utter astonishment. How had Aidan talked this evil little snipe into a contrite girl willing to work and asking for forgiveness?

Then her black eyes flicked to his. For a moment, they narrowed. "You. You ever shoot down—" She pointed upwards.

"The drones?" Kevin asked, adjusting his glasses on the bridge of his nose, "Not personally, no, but it's been known to happen."

"Want a dead one," Tweak snapped. "You get stuff. Get one."

"You didn't say the magic—" Kevin began sourly, but Aidan caught his eye and shook his head. Mastering himself with some effort, Kevin rephrased. "I can look around. Do you need an intact specimen?"

"Huh?"

"Do you need a whole one?" Kevin rephrased wearily.

"Yeah," Tweak agreed, coldly. "If I see how it works, I can take it down. Maybe take them all down. We'll see. Figure something out. That sucked balls. Fix it."

For a moment, Kevin couldn't figure out what to say. Fix it? Did she actually mean she thought she could put an end to drone pass-overs? Take down the drones? Unbelievable. Impossible.

"Let me get breakfast," he managed eventually. "Then I'll get on it."

Event File 29
File Tag: Private Discussion
Timestamp: 19:15-8-8-2155

Aidan checked his tab again outside the rec-room. Seven-fifteen.
Tuesday night. Just take a deep breath, he told himself. Deep breath.
Check his clothes. Binder was down flat, packer was straight,
everything else was as good as it got.

Deep breath.

He stepped into the rec room. On the couch, Kevin was lounging
at ease, long legs loosely crossed. Aidan couldn't help but smile at the
sight.

The smile twisted awkwardly as his eyes caught on the yellow-
green bruise on Kevin's cheekbone, a reminder of the night when they'd
kissed. They'd both been so busy since then that they hadn't really
talked about it, never mind kissed again. He hadn't even said hello to
Kevin before things went insane with Tweak.

He licked his lips. His mouth had gone dry. "Hey."

Kevin glanced up, the vid screen reflecting blue from his
glasses. He smiled as he snapped out of his thoughts. "Hey, yourself.
Um, glad you made it."

Moving over, he waved his hand in an elegant gesture, offering
Aidan his seat with a bit of ceremony.

Aidan rubbed the back of his neck as he flopped onto the couch. He wished Kevin wasn't acting so formal. They'd been so comfortable with each other until that run. That kiss. The first kiss Aidan had had since... Well, since Sam, a decade ago.

More like a lifetime ago.

He shifted, letting his shoulder brush against Kevin's. He wasn't really sure what else to do. But Kevin didn't move away. "Busy week, huh?" he murmured finally.

Kevin smiled thinly at the screen. "That's putting it mildly. Damian refused me StayWake again, the great autocratic tyrant. Staying awake yesterday and getting any reasonable work done was sheer torment."

"You know you were authorized for a recuperation day, if you needed it," Aidan suggested quietly.

The wiry man beside him sighed, relaxing against the couch, then wincing for a moment before he nodded in a disinterested manner. Aidan wondered if the injury was new or old. Kevin hadn't told him about the run yet.

"I know. I caught a few winks at lunch," Kevin remarked offhandedly. "I vote for something unbearably cheerful as the film of the night. Animation or music. You?"

"Works for me," Aidan agreed with a shrug, watching Kevin out of the corner of his eye for a moment before flicking his gaze away. Kevin wasn't looking at him. Did the man regret what they'd done in the junkyard?

They'd been dancing around this for months. So why was he so sure Kevin had changed his mind? And why couldn't he force the question out of his mouth? He cleared his throat uncomfortably. "Um, Kev? I... How's the shoulder? Your cheek looks better."

Kevin glanced at Aidan this time, and his smile was genuine now, a little ashy. "It's about as sore as I deserve. I, ah—" He pulled off his glasses, checking the lenses for imagined spots against the light. "I suppose a small reminder not to be an ass on runs isn't a bad idea, really." Carefully, he pulled out his cleaning cloth and polished the lenses. "It'll remind me to be more attentive in future. I shouldn't let myself get distracted."

"'Not to be an ass'?" Aidan asked, turning to blink at him. Was that what Kevin thought? That the kiss had been out of line? "Kev, it's not... It was just a bad run. That's all. Turned out okay in the end, right?" He started to reach for Kevin's shoulder, caught himself and pulled back. Shit. Why was he afraid to touch him now? They'd kissed, for godssakes.

"Yes," Kevin swallowed. "But I meant to apologize. You're perfectly capable. I never meant to disrespect your abilities. It's only... When I saw you out there, vulnerable, I..." He glanced down, giving a small snort of a laugh. "I have a bit of a White Knight complex, I'm afraid. Yvonne absolutely hates it." Slowly, he raised his eyes, smiling hopefully. "Apologies?"

That hopeful, worried expression made Aidan's chest tighten as Kevin continued. "And I know I may have stepped over the line. Later," he finished quietly. "So maybe I should apologize for that, too?"

Aidan felt his brow crease as Kevin apologized. Was he really apologizing for being on top of a mission and pulling off an amazing stunt? Crazy and scary as hell, yeah, but amazing. Then an apology for the kiss to top it off, like he hadn't said yes. Twice.

He couldn't help the incredulous smile that stole across his lips. "No, um. Don't apologize. I just..." He paused, trying to put his words in order, trying to figure out what he meant to say. Ducking his head and running a hand over his hair, he sighed. "I just... I was afraid you'd... You know, just... Heat of the moment..."

"That I'd get shot?" What Aidan thought of as Kevin's professional smirk flashed into place for a moment, sharp and dry. "I pride myself in my field abilities. Don't worry about me."

Aidan could feel a blush starting to heat his cheeks as he fumbled for words. He should have thought over how to talk about this beforehand. "No, I meant, I thought you'd—After, you'd regret it. Or didn't mean it. You know. That whole battlefield romance thing."

Kevin gave a tiny chuff of a laugh. "To use 'romance' in its broadest terms. I believe the salient term is 'survival screw'." He said the words with distaste. Aidan watched his face go hard and distant. He shouldn't have said that. Was Kevin pissed?

Then Kevin seemed to come back to the moment. Tentatively, he glanced up. "I—It wasn't that. Well, that may have lowered a few inhibitions, but..." After a moment's pause he sighed, smoothing his flaming hair with one hand.

"Aidan? Can I be frank with you?"

Aidan smiled weakly, his cheeks burning. "Yeah, of course."

Kevin held his eyes for a long moment. "Well, to be frank, I'd rather like to... I believe I took advantage of the situation. I've been looking for an excuse to kiss you for a month, if I could ever work up the courage. Adrenaline did that for me, I suppose. So, I guess what I'm trying to articulate is this:" He drew a breath. "I'd like to give that kiss another go 'round. Interested?"

Aidan felt the odd, thrilled, embarrassed smile curve his lips before he could stop it. Kevin wanted to kiss him. Still wanted to kiss him. The thought made his heart jump and his stomach knot. "Um. Please?"

Kevin smiled softly. Leaning in, he traced the line of Aidan's jaw with two fingers, holding his eyes. Then, so carefully, he laid his lips over Aidan's. Aidan's eyes fluttered closed as Kevin's lips brushed his. It was the opposite of the kiss in the truck. This time, Kevin was hesitant, and the whisper-warm softness of the kiss made Aidan's stomach jump. He shifted closer on the tattered couch, springs groaning beneath him.

"Is this okay?" Kevin asked softly against Aidan's skin, his fingers finding and twining with Aidan's.

"Mmmm," Aidan agreed quietly without opening his eyes. His heart pounded in his throat, heat running through his body. It had been years since he'd been kissed, and never by someone who saw him as he was. Or at least seemed to. He didn't want it to end.

Kevin's free hand trailed up to stroke Aidan's hair as he tipped his head, gently testing a deeper kiss. Holy shit. This was actually happening. "We probably shouldn't do this in the rec room," Kevin whispered when they came up for air. "Terribly bad form, and it tends to render one fodder for the gossip mill the next day. My room's open?" Drawing back, he gave Aidan a quick, sly grin. "If you like," he added with studied teasing in his voice, "Your orders, sir."

Aidan's heart thundered in his chest. It took a long moment for the words to filter into his brain. Kevin's room. His breath caught. Kevin couldn't seriously be asking that. Could he? What if he wanted more than these awkward little kisses? Oh hell, what if Aidan himself wanted more? Would Kevin take his asking for anything as an order from a commander or a request from a partner?

His chest started to tighten. He wanted to say yes, to continue letting Kevin kiss him and just see where things went. But should he? This was why they warned inexperienced commanders about dating subordinates, wasn't it? Things got complicated so damn fast. He licked his lips, feeling like his brain was on standby. "Don't—Don't call me 'sir.' Please. I'm not... If we're going to... I can't be your commander. Not like this."

Gently, Kevin pulled back, studying Aidan's face. For a moment, Aidan saw something flicker in his eyes. Then the man hid whatever he'd been thinking behind a teasing smirk. "And here I thought I was being deliciously scandalous." He laid another soft kiss on Aidan's lips, almost chaste. "So, Aidan? My room or yours?"

"Yours," Aidan breathed, his voice cracking a little. He'd said it. He'd agreed to let Kevin take him to a more private room. Good thing he'd offered his quarters. Kevin knew about him, but there was a difference between knowing and seeing the vials of testosterone, or the binder needing mending, or...No. Don't think about any of that now. That could come if things fell apart. For now, just focus.

Kevin nodded, a quick motion. Then he stood, taking Aidan's hands in his as he did. "Shall we?" he asked, his thumb running over Aidan's knuckles.

Aidan smiled sheepishly and nodded. Of course, when he tried to stand, his knee gave out and sent him tumbling back to the couch. He pulled his hand away with an embarrassed groan. "Shit. Uh, just give me a sec."

Kevin bit back a laugh and knelt, holding out a helping hand. "You really did slam that knee in the junkyard. What did Damian have to say?"

Aidan chuckled in embarrassment and forewent Kevin's offer of help as he carefully pulled himself back up. He couldn't believe he'd just gotten himself worked up enough to fall over. What was wrong with him? At least Kevin had given him a useful excuse. He wondered if Kevin knew that. "Said it's healing fine. Just shouldn't get up so fast."

"I can sympathize. This shoulder's been an absolute bastard," Kevin remarked in reply. And then they were both standing, almost touching. Before the moment could stretch too far, Kevin reached for Aidan's hand. "Right then. My room."

"Can you, uh…" Aidan swallowed. "Can you check the hall first? If people know we're… We don't need drama."

Kevin glanced at him with another one of those studying looks. Then he moved to the doorway and glanced out. "Clear."

"Sorry it's a bit of a jumble," Kevin remarked as he pushed his door open. The room was actually ridiculously neat. The only things out of place were a personal tab and two actual analog books on the bed, one spread wide to show the drawings inside.

Kevin stepped to the bed and closed the books, setting them inside an upended plastic packing crate beside the bed that he'd rigged with slats into a sort of shelving unit. On the wall, his holo showed a vibrant watercolor of a city. People bustled, laughed, walked under tall trees set into the sidewalks. Glancing over his shoulder, Kevin caught Aidan looking at it.

"That's what Denver looked like in 2014," he murmured, leaving his book collection to stand beside Aidan. In private, his smile was wider and more wistful. "Michael Hewitt. That was the artist's name."

"It's beautiful," Aidan replied quietly, keeping his eyes on the flickering painting instead of looking at Kevin. It was a distraction from what they'd been doing, what they were possibly about to do. He was going to try something he hadn't dared since Sam, since the days before he'd accepted how uncomfortable he was in his own body.

And if this didn't work…What would Kevin do if he undressed?

Kevin had mentioned he'd only slept with men before. Was he going to freak out if he saw Aidan's breasts, or his too-wide hips, his miniscule dick? Could Aidan deal with it when he did?

He wasn't sure. And now that he was in Kevin's immaculate room, standing so close, he could barely breathe. This had been a bad decision and he knew it. He should just turn around and leave, get used to being alone again.

The painting changed to another watercolor, a vibrant painting of an outdoor mall in summer. Kevin glanced down, carefully touching Aidan's hand. "Can I show you something?" Glancing up, he gave a half-grin, shy again. "It's rather embarrassing."

Aidan reluctantly tore his gaze away from the digital paintings and hoped he didn't look like a frightened rabbit. He cleared his throat a little. What was Kevin up to? "Um. Sure?"

Kevin's smile gentled. Taking his hand again, he led Aidan to the bed and lifted out one of his analog books, holding it as if it were precious. It probably was. Those things were antiques. "Take a seat," he added, flopping on his belly down on the bed and opening the cover with delicate fingers. Inside, a man was singing against a backdrop of an exuberantly painted American flag. The words 'The Open Road' were blazoned across the image.

Aidan sat on the edge of the bed, not quite touching Kevin. He sandwiched his hands between his knees as he looked at the image, a little taken aback by the fact that Kevin actually had analog books. He knew he shouldn't be surprised, given Kevin's personality and the fact that he was the requisitions officer, but it was still odd. Fancy antiques weren't exactly cheap. But he leaned in to study the pictures as Kevin flipped the pages.

"Wow."

"My dad got this for me when I was thirteen," Kevin's words were quiet. "It's the artistic record of a painter who traveled across the whole continent in 1987. There weren't any Sector checks at all back then. You could drive from one side of America to the other in under four days if you wanted. Just get in your car—back then they were all manuals—and go." He flipped the page to a scene of a city shining at the end of a long roadway, open and absolutely unfettered. The expression on his face softened into a fond yearning. "Imagine that."

Aidan shook his head in amazing. It seemed impossible, a country without Corps Sector checks, with all-manual cars, with... hope.

"Wish we could have seen that."

"That's why I keep this. In here we can," Kevin murmured, flipping to another page. People were dancing, the woman up on stage was throwing her long hair around, and in the foreground a couple in ripped jeans were kissing. Kevin grinned, turning his head so that he and Aidan were nose to nose. "See? Historical proof that people besides myself like my music of choice. I've been vindicated."

"Of all the things to hang onto, I still don't get keeping the music," Aidan muttered, allowing himself a teasing smirk. Music. Safe topic. Teasing. Don't think about how close they were to kissing again, or Kevin's hot breath on his skin, or the fact they were sitting on his bed.

"You and everyone else," Kevin grumbled good naturedly, rolling his eyes. "But look at how happy it made them!"

His eyes flicked to the couple in the painting, back up, grey and wide. "Happy and...adventurous?"

Moving as if he might startle a frightened animal, he leaned in, brushing his lips over Aidan's cheek, then his lips. "What do you think?" he whispered, barely a hair's breadth of space between them.

"About the painting?" Aidan asked breathlessly, his heart thudding again at the gentle touch of Kevin's lips. Damn it. This was a bad idea. He should have left already. He shouldn't let this go on. But he'd been craving this for months, he might as well admit that. How could he just run away from it, no matter how scared he was?

"About being happy?" Kevin answered, parrying the question with another question. "Maybe tonight?" Softly, he raised a hand to trace Aidan's jaw line.

Aidan swallowed hard, even as his face carefully tipped into Kevin's soft, warm touch. Kevin wanted him, despite everything? Did he really? Was this all going to go wrong? It had been so long since he'd had sex. He'd never done it as a man before.

Could he really do it now?

His body thrilled with the idea but his brain balked, making his stomach twist into uncomfortable knots. He caught a breath. "I…You-you know I'm… not really, um, your type."

"Funny, I'd always thought I had a bent towards the sweet, scruffy boys. You seem to fit the bill." Gently, Kevin smoothed Aidan's hair out of his eyes, stroking it. "Especially when you forget to sit down and let Liza cut your hair," he added, chuckling.

Aidan couldn't move. He wanted to, damn he wanted to. But he felt locked in place.

When he didn't get a response, Kevin drew back a little. "Unless you think there'll be problems?" he added delicately. "If it helps, I've worked around issues before. Not this in particular, but I'm fairly resourceful. If you know what I mean."

Aidan flushed and looked down, unable to meet Kevin's gaze. Kevin wanted him. Kevin liked him. So why the hell was he still so nervous? He tried to swallow the lump in his throat and shook his head.

"No, I... Shouldn't be problems," he whispered to his hands. "Just... Haven't really... It's been a long time."

Kevin drew back slightly, though his long fingers remained in Aidan's hair. "We don't have to jump right in, you know. We could take things one step at a time?" Gently, he traced his hand down Aidan's face, down his throat, stroking the skin. "If that's what you want, I'd be happy to just...?"

Aidan sucked in a sharp breath and closed his eyes. The warm fingers set his skin on fire. He wanted more kisses, more touches, but he didn't know how to ask for them. Hell, he was still working on how to overcome the terror of taking his clothes off and risk rejection when Kevin saw his body.

Heart pounding in his throat, he nodded weakly.

Very carefully, Kevin set his book against the side of the bed with one hand. "Not to be crass, but..." Rolling up his sleeve, the redhead pressed the implant hidden under the skin of his bicep. The light gleamed a reassuring blue through his pale skin, the light of the safely distant replacement date on his STD protection implant glowing.

Aidan returned the favor awkwardly, giving Kevin a chagrined smile. "Almost forgot about that. Glad you remembered."

"Caution's my middle name," Kevin agreed. He caught Aidan's hand as he leaned back, pulling gently until they were both lying on their sides. He traced the line of Aidan's body with his own, gently nudging Aidan's legs until he could slip one of his between them and scissor the two of them together. Then his movements stilled.

"Aidan? You're shaking." Quietly he drew back, eyes soft behind his glasses. "If this is too much, just say something. Okay?"

"I'm okay," Aidan whispered. He hesitantly lifted his free hand to run his fingers through Kevin's soft hair. No. He wasn't okay. Not really. He was panicking and he knew it. The last man who'd had him in a bed had held him down and screamed out his hate and disgust in Aidan's face. But he wasn't going to let that get in the way, damn it. Not again. "Um. Kiss me?"

"He's asking for my kisses. Be still my heart." Kevin chuckled, and leaned in for another kiss.

Aidan threw himself into it, trying to focus on the sensation. Kevin kissed him gently, tenderly. It was nothing like the slobbering demands years ago. His hand tightened on Kevin's, using it as an anchor, trying to remind himself that he wanted this and Kevin wasn't Sam. Kevin knew about him and still respected him as a man, still wanted him.

Would that change once their clothes were off?

He tried to shove the fear away. Kevin carded his fingers through Aidan's, his other hand pulling Aidan's head gently down for a proper, deeper kiss. Under Aidan's thigh, he felt Kevin getting hard. Kevin tried to roll them so that the redhead was on top, legs moving to straddle. Aidan felt his muscles going rigid.

"Not your style?" Kevin asked, relaxing and sliding back to lie beside Aidan.

Embarrassed, he shook his head and tried to pull away. "Sorry, it's just... Before I... When I still thought I was... Bad memories, sorry."

"No apologies necessary," Kevin breathed with a smile. "Everyone's got preferences. And memories. Speaking of preferences." Reaching down between them, Kevin unzipped his jeans, and gently guided Aidan's hand to rest over his fly. The heat made his blood burn.

His fingers brushed over the growing hardness under the boxers. A flash of envy ran through him and he shoved it aside. Just because he didn't have what he wanted in his own body didn't mean he had to be jealous of the man sharing his body with him. Was this really what Kevin wanted, or was he just settling because Aidan had freaked out?

Weren't they supposed to take their clothes off or something? He so wanted to see Kevin naked. But words stuck in his throat. Gently, a little awkward, he added pressure to his touch and stroked. Kevin closed his eyes. God, he was gorgeous. He had a face like a statue.

"Works a bit better without the intervening fabric, if you're interested," Kevin remarked, his words soft.

Aidan chuckled self-consciously and shifted just enough to give him access to the waistband of Kevin's boxers. Carefully, awkwardly, he slipped his hand down between hot skin and fabric, his fingers trailing over the piece of anatomy he was so jealous of.

Kevin caught his breath, his lips quirking up at the corners. "Mm. I do like that, but I was thinking about you getting me out of my pants rather than getting in them? Bit of a tight fit and all that."

Aidan winced and mumbled an apology as he drew his hand back. He'd never had to undress someone else before. Sam just used to strip and jump in bed. Jump on him, too.

Where the hell did he start? He cleared his throat anxiously and grabbed for Kevin's waistband.

After a few minutes' fumbling Kevin sat up with a chuckle, helping Aidan get him out of his pants and grabbing another quick kiss in the process. He shucked his shirt before he moved in for another kiss. His glasses scraped up his nose, and he gave a quiet grunt of irritation.

"Aidan, reach over onto the bedside table. There's a black case I keep my glasses in."

Aidan obliged, moving as if he was in a dream. Kevin was sitting beside him, mostly undressed. Aidan's hand fumbled and dropped the case on the floor despite his best effort. He groaned another half-strangled apology. This was so not going the way he'd hoped it would. He was screwing everything up. "Shit. I didn't mean to—"

"It's bulletproof plastic with such events in mind," Kevin remarked quietly, "Don't worry about it." Leaning down, he squinted, fumbled, finally found his case, set his glasses in it, then reached out and put his arms carefully around Aidan.

"The thing with your eyes?" Aidan asked, glad of something to focus on. "It's kind of a risk, isn't it? I mean, if we get a drone blast or something and you can't find them. . ."

"I've done it before, no need to worry." Kevin shrugged, smiling softly as he brushed his fingers over Aidan's hair. "I'm fairly blind without them, but I believe I can see what matters. Let's not talk field procedure in bed."

Aidan nodded, trying to relax his stiff shoulders. Deep breaths. He needed to take deep breaths. He was breathing too fast.

"Aidan?" Kevin asked softly, his high class accent making every word sparkle like a gem. "Those memories you mentioned? If that's the issue, I'm not going to hurt you."

"I'm sorry," Aidan mumbled, squeezing his eyes shut. He wanted to relax into Kevin's arms, keep himself in the moment, stop the sick feeling crawling up his throat. But how? This wasn't how this was supposed to go, damn it! "I know. I'm sorry. I just... I'm sorry."

Kevin's arms tightened around him. Leaning in, he kissed the top of Aidan's head. "What do you say to a change of plans? Vids in bed? We'll use my wall screen, and I'll bring up something I'm not allowed to watch in public. What do you think?" he asked softly, stroking Aidan's cheek.

Aidan didn't dare look up. He didn't want to see Kevin's face. It'd be full of pity or worry. Either one was bad. No, pity was worse. God he was pathetic.

Two fingers slid under his chin, and Kevin gently tipped his head back until he was looking into grey eyes. "I'm asking because it's up to you," Kevin murmured. "Nude vid night? What do you think?"

Aidan searched Kevin's face, his chest tight, the binder feeling like it was cutting into his skin, choking off his breath. His breathing started to rasp. Oh, no. Not now. Not a panic attack. Not now. He hadn't had one in months, and not in front of another base mate on 1407. Let alone Kevin. What the hell was Kevin going to think of him now? Freaking the fuck out because they'd tried to have sex? God, he was pathetic. He squeezed his eyes shut and tried to suck in a deep breath. It didn't work.

Kevin let his hand drop and gently rubbed Aidan's back. Softly, he stroked Aidan's hair. "Aidan, hey. Ssh. I'm not going to ask for anything." Gently, Kevin's arms went around him.

Aidan gasped instinctively.

Kevin slackened his hold. "Do you want me to let go?" he asked softly.

Aidan hesitated. Yes. No. He wanted Kevin to let go and hold him forever, both at once. He'd never had someone hold him through a panic attack before. The closest he had ever got was Naomi wrapping him in a blanket and handing him a mug of hot lemon water, back before their base got hit. Finally, he managed to suck in enough air to whisper, "Need my binder off."

"Binder?" Kevin asked carefully as Aidan moved in his arms.

Aidan couldn't get enough breath to answer. His vision was starting to go black around the edges, the world closing in. As quickly as he could, he fumbled his shirt off and started trying to pull up the heavy binding mesh. He couldn't breathe. He couldn't leave it on.

He'd have to just find a way to deal with Kevin seeing him shirtless.

He had to get air.

Kevin watched in bafflement for a moment as Aidan scrabbled at his undershirt. Then he sat forward with an exclamation of "Oh! Right!"

Gently, he worked his fingers under it. "I guess we should all wear bullet proof, really, but the stuff's so..." then Kevin trailed off.

Aidan closed his eyes as the fabric in his fingers rolled, tightened, rolled with more difficulty. Kevin had seen his fucking breasts. That was why he'd gone silent. Of course he had. Finally, the damn thing was off. He sat back, gasping, feeling the heat of Kevin's hand lying still on his back. His gut sinking, he bowed his head. The hand would be taken away now. The yelling would start in a second.

Soft hands rested on his shoulders. "Better now?" Kevin wasn't shouting. His voice was soft.

Aidan flinched away from Kevin's touch, sitting on the edge of the bed with his elbows on his knees, head hanging as he struggled to calm down. There was no reason to panic, he told himself over and over.

He was okay. He was safe. He was okay. Slowly, the tightness in his chest began to ease, giving way to the deepest embarrassment he'd ever felt. Not only was he sitting here shirtless and awkward, but he'd just had a full-on panic attack. Damn it. He groaned and dropped his head into his hands. "I'm so sorry, Kevin."

Kevin sat stiffly a moment. Of course he was stiff. Aidan knew he'd just freaked the hell out of the guy.

Then he heard Kevin let out a long breath, and a hand rested on his shoulder. "It's just clothing. No need to apologize. Let's get your pants off, and then I've got the perfect movie." The hand massaged his back gently. "Assuming you want to stay?"

"Do you want me to?" Aidan asked, the words coming out in a tight whisper. He hesitated, then glanced up at Kevin's gently smiling face. He blinked away tears and looked away again. "I didn't mean to freak out."

"I did tell you I'm blind without my glasses right?" Kevin murmured, a breath of laughter in his voice. "I didn't see you freak out." He shrugged. "And as for your question, what fun's a vid without an audience?" Reaching around Aidan, he slid his glasses out of their case and slipped them back on. Aidan kept forgetting Kevin actually needed those things.

"Besides, you'll get to see me swoon over an old actor. I'm sure you'll enjoy it."

Aidan wasn't sure how to respond to that. Kevin was just ignoring the fact that he'd had a panic attack? Why? How? He swallowed hard and looked up again, searching Kevin's face and wiping away tears with the back of his wrist. The whole thing was so unbelievable that he chuckled. "Shit. You didn't even... I can't believe you're for real."

Kevin's foxy face grew still. "Aidan, I've seen people fall apart before. Bedmates included. And I've seen people who were—who were hurt deal with it before. America is fucked, and it fucks with our heads if we let it." The curses sounded odd in his perfect pronunciation, but his raincloud eyes held Aidan's as he spoke.

"The least we can do for one another is do our best to embrace one another's quirks, because if we don't we're as bad as the bastards in their offices. That's my thinking on the issue." He smiled ruefully, tipping his head. "A little panic attack I can deal with. Liza has them all the time, but she screams at me when she does. So far, I prefer your approach."

Aidan's smile crept across his face as hesitantly as a frightened cat. Finally, he dared to lean in and rest his head on Kevin's shoulder. Kevin really believed that. Nobody came up with a speech like that on the fly. It was something Kevin must have thought out how to say a few times. And it was so true. If people like them didn't take care of each other, nobody else would.

"Thanks." The word came out barely a breath.

"Any time," Kevin agreed, not much more loudly. He reached over and, haltingly, stroked Aidan's hair. Eventually his fingers found the rhythm, moving slow.

Aidan let his eyes slip closed as Kevin's touch grew comforting. He sighed a long time later. "Kevin? I-I do want to, you know."

"Of course you do," Kevin murmured, the teasing note back in his voice. "After all, you know for a fact that my taste in vids is beyond sublime, right?"

Aidan chuckled weakly. "Sure, we'll go with that. But I meant... I didn't... The attack wasn't because I didn't... I was just afraid you'd... Well, like I said, I'm not really your type."

"Why don't you let me decide what my type is, hm?" Kevin rejoined softly, pushing Aidan's hair back from his face.

Aidan sighed again and closed his eyes, wiping his face once more. Why was Kevin being so damn sweet to him? He didn't deserve this. This gentle touch, this acceptance. He swallowed hard and whispered, "You should know, I've been on testosterone for six years, but I couldn't afford the surgeries."

Kevin nodded, closing his eyes, his face quiet. He grew very still for a moment, and a chill raced down Aidan's spine. Then Kevin drew a long breath. "I don't think that interferes with our plans tonight."

Aidan pulled back just enough to look up at Kevin's face, unable to hide the surprise. He swallowed hard and gave him aweak little smile. "Um. I—I haven't really undressed in front of someone in a long time. You're the first besides Damian in years, and he doesn't exactly count."

That comment earned Aidan a snort of unanticipated laughter. "I should hope not!" Kevin chuckled. "You think this is strange? The idea of Damian being in the dating market makes the brain boggle." Sitting on the edge of the bed, he kicked his boxers off casually, then turned with a smile. "Right, your turn." Leaning in, he kissed Aidan. "Let's get you out of these pants."

"You sure?" Aidan whispered when the kiss broke.

Again, Kevin went oddly still. For a moment, a strange flash of anger crossed Kevin's face, sending a new shiver down his spine. Was Kevin angry at him for not having the body he'd imagined? Or something else?

"Absolutely," Kevin answered quietly, holding Aidan's eyes. Aidan inhaled sharply and gave him a shaky little smile. Then, hesitantly, he leaned forward and kissed Kevin again.

Kevin took this kiss a little less easily, pressing into it this time, making his enthusiasm felt. "You want help?" he asked, catching his breath a moment later.

Aidan's heart hammered in his chest, but the reason had changed. That kiss had been... Well, it had made him feel wanted, really wanted, for the first time in a long time. He smiled stupidly and shook his head, letting the kiss overcome the lingering fear of taking his pants off. "I got it."

He awkwardly wriggled out of jeans and boxers at once, not letting himself hesitate. Kevin had accepted his breasts without blinking. Maybe he could do the same for the oversized hips, the vulva, the tiny penis. Maybe. But it still made it hard to meet Kevin's gaze once he sat completely bared on the bed, and he folded his arms protectively over his chest before he'd realized he'd done it.

Kevin glanced from the packer to the binder, tipping his head. Finally, he gave Aidan a cute, awkward smile that was at least half nervousness.

"Um, I know this is hellaciously impertinent and I don't mean to offend but... Doesn't all that get a touch uncomfortable?"

Aidan laughed weakly despite himself and shrugged with one shoulder. "I've gotten used to it."

Still watching Aidan's face, Kevin smiled nervously and nodded. "I guess you would."

He gave himself a little shake and sat beside Aidan, his shoulder pressed against the other man's, then made a show of flopping down on the bed and stretching luxuriously. "First time I've been cool all day."

Aidan made a soft noise of agreement in the back of his throat and, for the first time, actually let his eyes trail over Kevin's body. Gorgeous. Kevin was like some beautifully sculpted statue left out on the street where people could scuff him up. Aidan took note of every angle, every scar, every freckle, and couldn't help wondering how the hell this had happened. By all rights, it shouldn't have. "Kevin? Um. Thank you."

Kevin opened one eye like an orange and white house cat.

His crooked smile only intensified the similarity. "Don't thank me yet, I haven't put on the vid."

Sitting up, he gently pulled Aidan down to lie beside him. "Actually, I should probably thank you. You easily could have had me in front of Magnum for kissing you in the middle of a mission. I've had a lot of disciplinary notes on my record, but I'd really hate to get 'made advances to an officer like an idiot' on there to top it off. People would start to talk."

Aidan chuckled softly and curled into Kevin's warmth, though it was still a little too hot from the day. "Self-preservation. Writing you up would mean admitting I kissed back, see. Then we'd both get shouted at."

Kevin chuckled. "Well then, since we're already being outrageous, I know just the vid."

With one hand, he reached over and keyed up the syncing program to his wall screen on his tab. The movie began in violin and the sound of church bells.

"Once upon a time, there was a quiet little village..."

Aidan did his best to pay attention to the vid, but the gentle thump of Kevin's heartbeat in his ear, Kevin's fingers running through his hair and the exhaustion that always set in after a panic attack finally hit. Halfway through the film he was asleep, head pillowed on Kevin's chest.

Event File 30
File Tag: Mutual Benefit
Timestamp: 007:30-8-9-2155

"Shit!"

Kevin sat up sharply as his bedmate yelped, heart kicking into overdrive, squinting at the fuzzy outline that stood beside his bed. "Sir? God, sorry. Aidan? Is there a situation? Do we need to move?"

"No, we're fine," Aidan assured him in a voice that was still full of tension. "Just... We're late for duty. I'm getting dressed." After a moment of hesitation, he leaned over to kiss Kevin softly.

Kevin's shoulders relaxed and he leaned up, deepening the kiss. "You know, I've got one day of recuperative downtime I didn't take and you did skip an off-day last week. Do you have anything urgent on your desk?"

Aidan paused. "Not exactly? I mean, I figure I'll just get dressed anyway. You know, be normal again."

For a moment Kevin considered his options. Aidan sounded so uncomfortable. What could he do to help with that?

Then his lips quirked. "Well, you know you're not in normal company. I'm legally blind without my glasses for your information. So, if that's what's worrying you, relax." He stretched, shoving the sheet back. It was already too warm for coverings, and he was going to put this pose to good use.

"I vote we lie about in freakish glory for the morning. You can always say you worked late," he added, smiling up at Aidan where he stood, an indistinct shape in the half-light.

This man was his commander. A kind of person Kevin had only read about. The complications were going to be enormous on every level. Insurmountable, perhaps. And yet...

And yet it was Aidan. Gentle Aidan, who'd laughed with him, who'd almost ended the constant squabbling around the base, who'd picked up a hell of a lot of broken pieces and brought the Wildcards back to something like themselves. Four months ago, they'd been on the verge of disbanding. A week ago they'd gotten a small commendation mark for Damian's Synth idea. Because of Aidan.

This was Aidan, who put up with his own dry humor, his bookishness and oddities, his unattractively acerbic wit. Aidan, who had taken the first real steps towards saving Kevin's family from themselves. Last night, Aidan had said 'I'm not your type.' His type. What was his type?

Someone he didn't have to pretend in front of for once. Someone he could talk to. Someone who listened. Aidan.

He did his best to analyze emotions as he lay, waiting for Aidan to make up his mind. His chest was tight. His mouth was dry. He'd tried to do this the night before, but all he'd come up with was the fact that he was afraid, and the fact that he hated his own cowardice. Was he still scared this morning? Yes.

Why? Because Aidan was so... different. He knew that wasn't the full answer. Ask the questions that tell you the truth, his parents had taught him. Socratic method.

Analyze. The thought system had helped him fight the indoctrination he'd gotten at school. His parents had gone through asking series of questions on topics for years, taught him the terminology of logical fallacies and drilled him until he could walk

THE HANDS WE'RE GIVEN | 289

through finding loopholes and emotional manipulation for himself. It was one of the best things they'd left him with.

So, he said to himself. *Answer the question. Why are you afraid? I'm afraid because this is aberrant. He's aberrant. I'm aberrant for wanting him. I hate that I still think like this. And if I can want him... If I can want him maybe I could have liked girls. I could have been normal.*

A new flash of anger burned up his gut. If that was the reason he was afraid, then he swore he was going to teach himself to stop. Fuck Cavanaugh. Fuck their narrow concepts of human perfection that labeled anything outside the lines 'aberration'. Fuck the noise about morality and improving humanity they'd tried drilling into his head. He'd be damned if he listened to it. They'd taken enough away from him. He was not letting their bullshit deny him the only person he'd felt right with in two years.

He wanted Aidan. Anything that told him he shouldn't could go fuck itself.

Aidan stood still for a moment longer. Kevin heard him gulp. "You really don't mind?"

Kevin smirked, eyes closed. "Aidan, have you ever heard the phrase 'don't look a gift horse in the mouth'?"

"No," Aidan admitted sheepishly, though he carefully sat on the edge of the bed again.

Kevin sighed theatrically. "All my best metaphors are wasted. Lie down?"

Slowly, the weight of Aidan's body settled back in place. Kevin rolled easily to rest his head on Aidan's shoulder. For once someone had stayed the night. Idly, he played with a few locks of Aidan's hair, teasing them between his fingers.

"You really don't mind," Aidan repeated in a whisper. Kevin was silent for a long time, working out the words. "I'm not saying there won't be a few awkward moments. You... er, know I'm a Cavanaugh kid originally. So if I take a little time to adjust to anything? Blame those bastards. I'm still trying to jettison some of what they lumbered me with in the morality department," he murmured eventually, opening his eyes to watch Aidan's face. "But like I said last night: if you can accept my oddities, I owe it to you to return the favor. Right?"

Aidan lay still for a long, long time, studying him. He gave a crooked smile that looked like it might hide something else. Then he wrapped his arms around Kevin in a rush, kissing him.

Kevin pushed down his surprise and returned the kiss with interest, deepening it, drawing it out. He tipped his head, smiling coquettishly. "I take it that's a yes?"

Aidan chuckled breathlessly as the kiss broke and nodded, endearingly bashful.

"By the way?" Kevin added quietly between kisses, "What I said last night about my type stands as well."

"As long as I'm not too much," Aidan muttered in return, one hand sliding hesitantly up to stroke Kevin's hair.

This time Kevin gave in to his instinct to make a joke. He opened his eyes wide and teasingly batted his lashes. "Oh dear." he whispered in a breathless falsetto. "He's so big and manly. I don't know if little me can manage! He's just so *much!*" He pressed one hand to his mouth like a heroine in a bad vid, hiding his grin.

Aidan stared at him for a long moment. Then he burst out laughing. He shoved at Kevin's shoulder. "Oh, shut up."

"Why don't you try and make me?" Kevin retorted with a wicked grin, delighted with this change of mood.

Aidan laughed again and pulled him back down for another kiss, his hands gliding gently along Kevin's naked shoulders.

"Good start," Kevin whispered against Aidan's lips, tracing his cheek with soft fingers. He traced the back of Aidan's neck and his hands skittered over Aidan's back, fingers learning the topography of muscle and bone.

"What's the next move?" Aidan asked in a breath, one hand trailing lightly over Kevin's shoulder blade. His back pressed just a little into Kevin's touch.

"Depends on how long you want to stay in bed," Kevin quipped with a smile. "If I'm not on a timetable, I prefer a more leisurely approach." He slipped his fingers further down Aidan's back, resting on the seat of his spine.

Aidan tensed just a little, but quickly relaxed again. His hand glided across Kevin's side and dipped between them, tracing hesitantly lower. "How leisurely?"

Kevin's lips quirked up as fingers traced down his chest, across his navel. "That's up to you. How much can you draw things out, do you think?"

"Well, I don't really know how the T might have changed my stamina, so... No idea." Aidan smiled weakly, letting his fingers linger in the hollow of Kevin's navel, circling slowly.

Kevin blinked as his teasing come on line was taken and discussed so seriously. He gave a nervous chuckle and covered the puzzlement with a kiss for Aidan's throat. "Okay. Surprise me."

His hand flattened against Aidan's tailbone, pressing them close, his other hand burying itself in Aidan's hair. Pressed against Aidan, he felt his body start to stir.

"I'll try," Aidan whispered, his voice sounding a little strangled. His hand trailed a little lower, fingers brushing Kevin's cock ever so softly.

Behind his teasing manner, Kevin watched his companion's expression carefully as he touched Aidan, now that they were close enough for him to see without his glasses. He moved carefully, wary of sparking off the panic he'd caused last night. He didn't want to ruin this again. Not with the only—yes, man—the only man he'd really wanted in almost two years. His brain stuttered less over the gender this time. He caught his breath as Aidan touched him, then breathed a chuckle as heat thrilled between his legs.

"Keep that up and I'm going to be embarrassed on the stamina issue."

Aidan chuckled softly and ran one finger around the tip of Kevin's slowly rising erection.

"Guess that means I'm not as rusty as I thought."

Kevin swallowed, controlling his breathing as soft electricity ran through him. "Shall I return the favor?" he murmured, bringing his hand around to trace Aidan's thigh, the angle of his hipbone, his navel.

Aidan tensed. "I-I mean, I guess?"

Slowly, Kevin maneuvered his hand past Aidan's and down. Aidan's breath caught as Kevin's fingers found his small member, already swollen. After a moment, he muttered, "Just, um—Just treat it like a dick."

"Right," Kevin agreed softly, hiding the jolt of panic that went through him. How was he supposed to pull that off exactly? But he did his best, and based on the noise Aidan made, his best wasn't too bad at all. "Like lube?" he inquired in a whisper.

Aidan nodded without a word.

Gently slipping away, Kevin rolled and reached under his bed for the small, unmarked bottle there. Rolling back, he slid back into place against his bedmate and popped the lid. Tipping just a little gel onto his fingers, he smiled at Aidan and slid his hand down again, wrapping his hand as best he could around what Aidan had for a cock and stroking, spreading the lube.

Aidan's head tilted back, and Kevin was pleased to hear a few surprised gasps. Aidan whimpered, and his hands stopped their pleasant explorations.

"A little preoccupied?" Kevin chuckled low in his throat. "How about we take care of one thing at a time?"

He pulled gently away from the fumbling fingers and pushed himself up and over Aidan on his arms, settling behind him so that he rested with his chest against Aidan's back, his hardening cock pressed against Aidan's tailbone. After all, a little delayed gratification would be good for his moral fiber, he told himself with a smirk.

He guided Aidan's upper leg back a little, giving himself better access, then returned his hand to its work. He used his free hand to play with Aidan's hair, pulling gently so that Aidan tipped his head back, which gave Kevin perfect access to the soft skin of his throat. "How's this?" he whispered.

Aidan whimpered happily in reply. One hand awkwardly reached back to try and touch some part of Kevin and wound up brushing the curve of his hip.

Kevin grinned against Aidan's cheek. It looked like his own favorite position was going to be just the thing for getting that frantic look out of Aidan's eyes. It hadn't been what he'd expected. He usually was the one letting someone else take control. He'd taken more than one man to bed simply as a means to get to that state of utter peace and release from responsibility, with mixed results.

But Aidan's body relaxing against his was its own satisfaction.

His heat was making Kevin harder all the time, and Aidan's unguarded expression made his heart turn over. He was so lovely. In some ways, this was going to be difficult. But the benefits of having a partner who didn't get off at the drop of a hat? That was going to be fun.

No, that was going to be amazing.

Tentatively, he trailed his free hand down to one of Aidan's breasts as he stroked. Touching the nipples was supposed to feel good, wasn't it?

Aidan tensed again as Kevin's hand touched his breast, his fingers pressing into Kevin's hip.

"You're tensing up. What's wrong?" Kevin asked, kissing his lover's throat up and down again as the back muscles against him stiffened, relaxed slightly.

"Nothing," Aidan muttered, shifting to press further into Kevin's hand. "I'm fine."

Kevin frowned at that, but decided to leave it for now. Whatever it was, he'd soothe it away with touch. He teased Aidan's cock, his own beginning to throb. Strange as Aidan's body was, the way he moved and the expressions on his face were heart wrenchingly gorgeous. Irresistible. A little more daring now, Kevin sucked at the thin skin over Aidan's beating jugular vein, ran the back of one hand over the nipples and sped the strokes of the other.

Aidan gasped and whimpered under his touch, then gave a beautiful little yelp as his body began to shiver.

Kevin kept with Aidan as he rode out his orgasm, holding him as long as he could in bliss. Once Aidan had relaxed completely, he nuzzled against the other man's throat, kissing his cheek.

"Oh, by the way. Good morning."

Aidan chuckled breathlessly and rolled over in a puppyish flop of limbs. He wrapped his arms around Kevin and kissed him, and Kevin grinned when Aidan laughed.

"Good morning for sure," Aidan managed.

"Enjoyed that I take it?" Kevin chuckled, his grin impossible to hide. Aidan was unexpectedly sweet post-orgasm, and Kevin gladly relaxed into his embrace, so relieved that he hadn't screwed up twice in a row.

He'd made this man happy. He felt as if there was a balloon expanding inside his chest, and marveled at it. When had he felt more than a general satisfaction when he pleased a partner? This was more akin to teenage giddiness.

Aidan nodded and kissed him again, running his fingers through Kevin's hair. "You have no idea. Can, um. Can I return the favor?"

"I don't know, can you?" Kevin parried with an inviting grin for Aidan when he looked up. Gently, he opened a little space between them and took Aidan's hand in his, guiding it down his belly. "I'm looking forward to finding out."

Aidan gave a quiet laugh as he let Kevin guide his hand, following it with his eyes. Kevin watched the delight on his face as he glanced back up.

"Where'd the lube go?" the blonde man asked softly.

"Good question," Kevin murmured, his voice a little rough. "You'll have to find it. I can see about as far as your face right now. I think I set it behind you, originally."

"Right, sorry." Aidan twisted around to look for the bottle.

Kevin relaxed and listened to him search, closing his eyes. After a moment Aidan's heat returned, and slick fingers caressed his shaft.

Kevin drew in his breath slowly, luxuriating in the heat and the electric frisson of those first touches. "Here." Slowly, he rolled so that he was on his back, his shoulder and hip pressed into Aidan's warmth, and laced his fingers behind his head in a studied move that looked casual but gave him the benefit of controlling his hands as the pleasure built. He shifted his legs with easy grace, until he lay fully exposed. "All yours," he quipped.

"You're so damn handsome," Aidan whispered. When he spoke the words were so earnest that Kevin opened his eyes. Aidan's face was oddly, beautifully ecstatic. He reminded Kevin of a painted saint attaining paradise, his golden hair catching sunlight from the window in a halo as he ran his thumb over the head of Kevin's cock.

Kevin's lips quirked slightly. The compliment was nothing he could take credit for. His genome had been tailored for good looks, among other things, by some lab tech somewhere. But the way Aidan said the words, the way Aidan was looking at him now, as if he were something newly discovered and precious, made the words mean something more and dispelled his inclination to joke dryly about good genes.

Well, that and the touch. He focused on his breathing, steadying it. It took some work.

As Aidan's hand faltered into a slow, reverential rhythm, he leaned down and kissed along Kevin's hipbone. Kevin arched his hips into the hands and lips playing over him, letting himself cede his control of the moment with the pleasure of a man laying down his burdens. The chance to leave himself absolutely open was nearly as much a pleasure as Aidan's touches. Nearly.

"You really are out to test my staying power," he managed as the hand on his erection stroked, just fast enough to tighten his muscles, just slow enough to be excruciatingly teasing.

Aidan's head jerked up, eyes wide and frightened. His hand sped up a bit. "Sorry. Better?"

Kevin gasped, his back arching involuntarily at the sudden change. "Um, Aidan? Ah... Wasn't a complaint. But this..." He had to gulp in air at that point, and decided on brevity. "Yes, great." The last word was almost a squeak.

Aidan paused for a moment, hands loosening, then drew a breath and continued his strokes at the new speed, his bright eyes watching Kevin's face.

Kevin gave an unintended groan as the strokes paused, started again relentlessly. Usually he had impressive self control in bed, but this was getting impossible. His body was twanging. His heart was hammering. His pulse felt like a snare drum inside his pelvis, and he was so hard that it physically hurt. But the pleasure was still building. His head tipped back as his body tightened further, impossibly further. God, he'd gone far too long without sex. He wasn't ready for this kind of teasing.

Aidan slipped his other hand over Kevin's thigh and carefully fondled his balls.

Kevin moaned aloud, unable to stop the sound, his fingers digging into his own hair. Scintillating fire burned through him as Aidan handled him, as a thumb stroked the soft skin and sent electricity burning through his nerves, adding to the burn of his shaft. If he didn't come soon, he was going to scream.

"Aidan, faster... I need..."

Aidan sucked in a breath and did as Kevin asked, speeding his hand on Kevin's cock, tightening the hand on Kevin's balls.

Kevin's perception exploded. His body spasmed as he lost control and the electric heat ran through him, a live wire burning away everything but this one moment of existence. *Bliss.*

Heat spattered his belly. Slowly, reality reassembled around him as his senses reconnected. His muscles relaxed, his entire body tingling.

"*Very* good morning," he murmured in a breathless chuckle, eyes still closed, savoring. He felt tissues mop his belly and smiled. Not only a conscientious lover but a pragmatic one, Aidan was. Then Aidan was lying beside him, not quite touching.

Kevin turned his head, opened one eye. Aidan was propped up on one elbow, watching Kevin's face as if he were, indeed, one of the angels at the gates into paradise.

He smirked and rolled to curl against Aidan, nudging Aidan's arms open and pushing contentedly into them. He let himself drift in the warm, safe space there. For this little time, there was perfect peace. *Bliss.*

There were going to be issues, he mused as his brain slowly reassembled its faculties. He was going to need to adjust his thinking quite a lot. Maybe some of his expectations. But for now?

Bliss.

"Kev?" Aidan whispered a long time later, his fingers running feather-light circles on Kevin's back. "Thank you. Seriously."

"You're sweet," Kevin chuckled, kissing his collarbone. "But you don't need to thank me. I did it because I enjoyed it. Don't need to thank me for enjoying myself, or you," he added thoughtfully, watching his bedmate.

Aidan really was grateful. Had things really been that bad for him, that he felt this much gratitude for a nice morning's lay? He was Duster born, Kevin knew that. He thought it wasn't so bad for Duster kids to be outside the norm. What had happened to Aidan? That father of his. And some man had hurt him once. He knew that much.

There was so much he didn't know about this man. So much he needed to find out, before he made a hash of something. Aidan just shook his head and held Kevin closer.

Kevin breathed in the scent of Aidan for a time, basking. Then he stretched. "Right. Breakfast. If we don't get up, we'll be left with the soggy tofu everyone else has refused." He smirked. "Or as Sarah calls it, Breakfast of Nymphos. You can guess why."

"So the breakfast she and Yvonne eat every day?" Aidan asked with a crooked little smile.

"Every day off at least," Kevin agreed with sleepy good humor, smiling as he slipped off the bed and walked carefully around the side, feeling along his bedside table until his fingers found his glasses case. He slipped the glasses on and stretched again, feeling the sweet reminder of afterglow in his hips and smiling with satisfaction. Most definitely worth the wait.

Glasses on, he watched Aidan dress while absently dropping his dirty clothes in the hamper and pulling out fresh things. He couldn't help but smile when Aidan glanced his way. In here, in private, he saw that endearing candor on his face again this morning.

"I should swing by my room," Aidan muttered without meeting Kevin's gaze as he self-consciously adjusted his chest under the mesh of his binder. What a nightmare that thing was going to be to take off on a regular basis, Kevin thought absently. He'd almost gotten his fingers stuck last night.

"Grab some clean clothes so we don't get tortured. Um, can you…"

"Can I…?" Kevin tipped his head when Aidan froze, waiting.

Aidan swallowed. "Can you… Can we keep this kind of under the radar?"

Kevin gave the man an incredulous smirk. "Aidan, you have met our base, I assume? What do you think the chances of secrecy are?"

Aidan looked away, and Kevin's smile faded. He looked so vulnerable.

Softly, he crossed the room to brush Aidan's golden hair from his face, kiss his brow. "I'm very good at keeping things to myself, if that's what you need for now. But, trust me, no one here is going to care. As you know, we're rather unconventional in these areas."

Slowly, Aidan raised his eyes and, ever so slowly, smiled. "Yeah, I know. Save me something at breakfast?"

Kevin nodded, smiling quietly. "I'll see if I can manage a little better than tofu, shall I?"

Aidan returned the smile as best he could, then pulled his shirt on. "Thanks."

"Any time, sir," Kevin replied easily, straightening the lapels of his jacket. He saw the expression Aidan was making and realized what he'd said, giving a quick smile of apology. "I'll work on that."

"Good. Makes me feel like I should be reported for coercing a subordinate," Aidan muttered with a wince, ruffling his own hair.

Kevin gave him a sidelong smirk. "Oh, don't worry. No one coerces me into anything. Ever."

Aidan chuckled weakly in return. "Your record definitely backs that up. But it's still weird when you call me 'sir.' Especially now."

Kevin lowered his eyes slightly, an admission. "Like I said, it's a habit I'll work on." Glancing up, he reached up to gently smooth Aidan's hair. "Think you can be patient with me...Aidan?"

Aidan smiled and, after a moment of hesitation, kissed him gently. "You put up with my oddities," he muttered.

"Reciprocity. Sounds good," Kevin murmured with a smile. He stole a last kiss, then opened his door and carefully glanced out.

"Clear."

"Save some of that for the commander," he remarked easily as people idly grabbed toast from the platter in the middle of the table he'd sat down at. "He didn't sign off the work roster until 3am last night. I imagine he'll be coming in late."

Of course, it was Kevin who'd put in that change to the record, but he had hidden that already. He had the chops to code that at least.

"Damian? After breakfast I've got a few things we should run over, if you've got the time. Won't take long," he added, snagging one of the pre-packaged fruit servings he'd grabbed on a lucky run a month ago. Packaged fruit wasn't a patch on fresh, but it was miles better than micronutrient powder on tofu.

Damian's ocular implants whirred quietly as he quirked an eyebrow. "Finally going to let me fix your sight issue?"

Kevin rolled his eyes. "How many times?" he groaned theatrically.

"As many as it takes," the doctor replied easily, though he kept his mechanical gaze on Kevin for a long moment.

Kevin gave him a dry look. "You know the very idea gives me nightmares. After all, I could end up looking like you," he threw out. When he was a teenager those words had been said in anger, but time and repetition had turned them into one more in-joke.

"You, look like him? Mr. Pasty?" Sarah interjected, grinning from ear to ear. Kevin flipped her off, and she held up two fingers in a V and licked the space between.

The corner of Damian's lips twitched just a little and he turned away to ensure his siblings ate their breakfasts.

Glancing casually up, Kevin watched Aidan wander into the room. The pit of his belly warmed, but he had always been good at schooling his expression. He pulled a book up on his tab and read as he ate.

"Morning," he remarked courteously when Aidan sat, but he didn't look up. His smile easily could have been for the subject matter on the page.

Half an hour later, he joined Damian in his walk down the hall with the twins. "You two do your reading for next Monday yet?" he asked teasingly, knowing for a fact that the kids wouldn't touch the tutoring material he and their brother had been assigning them until the morning before he quizzed them.

"Algebra sucks!" Dilly retorted, then paused. "History's kinda cool. But algebra still sucks."

"We're too easy on these kids," Damian remarked, deadpan.

"Don't I know it. I was doing advanced statistical generation models at your age. All I give you two is algebra," Kevin agreed gravely. "And my education was only CSS," he lied easily. "I've heard the CES curriculums are even more intense."

"Yeah, but CES kids don't even think like humans!" Dilly piped with relish, "I read they're so modified, they just suck up information and repeat it, they're like computers on legs."

"Yeah, they don't learn, they get programmed," Donny chimed in.

Damian smirked. "Go on, guys. You have studies to get to, and we've got work."

"But we're helping Janice today," Donny whined. His elder brother looked at him and he pulled a face, but he grabbed his sister's hand and pulled her away.

"Now," Damian said once he and Kevin were ensconced in his little office off the med bay. "What can I do for you?"

"You've always got the best contacts for medically related information. I've got something I'd like professional-grade accurate material on. Confidentially." Kevin held his eyes steadily, though he did swallow hard. "People transitioning from female to male. Any information on the issues related to the condition would be appreciated."

Damian's eyebrows rose, pulling the skin around his eyes and making his ocular implants whir as they adjusted. "That's a lot of information you're asking about. Anything in particular you're looking for?"

Kevin did his level best to keep his expression utterly urbane.

"Anything related to body issues and, ah..." He paused, took a deep breath. This was Damian, he told himself. Damian was the one who'd disabled the key codes on the repair nanoids that resided in his bones and joints. Damian knew exactly how many improvements were in Kevin's genome and what that meant about his antecedents. The man had kept all that quiet for years. He could be trusted. "To be blunt, how someone with a body like that should be... treated." The words forced themselves out of Kevin's throat with difficulty. "And anything that someone close to them should do to... help."

Damian's lips twitched again. "I see. I've got some papers about the effects of testosterone on an estrogen-dominant body to start with. And a few on understanding what's called body dysphoria. The more sexual issues will be personal, but I'll see if there's anything out there."

Kevin gave a sharp jerk of a nod. "Thanks. I appreciate it." Then he forced himself to relax a little, to be a little more human. "Really. I hate trawling the Greynet for things in your area of study. Three-quarters of it's garbage, and I end up feeling like an ignoramus."

Damian snorted and leaned back in his chair, knitting his fingers together. "Most of this won't even be on the Greynet. And, if I were making suggestions? Don't let him know you're researching. I had a hell of a time getting him to confide in me, and I don't want him slipping backwards."

Kevin glanced down at his hands. "Well, thanks. I just...I..." Glancing up, he smiled hopefully. "You know me. I like to be read up before I deal with anything important. Um, is there anything I should do to make him... Or shouldn't... I-I'll shut up now, shall I?"

Damian's implants whirred again. "I think that's a conversation you should have with him. The only thing I can warn you about is that there is a possibility of pregnancy. Which gets much higher if he goes off his hormones. I'm sure neither of you would enjoy that." Kevin's eyes widened. "Um, thanks for the heads up," he managed, wishing he didn't sound quite so thrown.

Damian almost laughed outright. He covered it by clearing his throat. "The odds of that are incredibly slim. He'd need to be off Testosterone for at least three months before he starts ovulating regularly. And I'd be shocked if he ever let himself go that long."

Kevin nodded slowly. "I'll make sure he doesn't have to," he replied, the words heavy on his tongue. They tasted like a vow. "Thanks." He stood, but his feet didn't want to move.

"Damian? In all confidentiality, am I—Is this a bad idea?"

Damian's eyebrows lifted. "You want an answer to that from a doctor, a psychologist, or a friend?"

"Right. Right. Sorry I asked." Kevin turned away sharply, heading for the door.

"Kevin," Damian sighed just before his base mate reached the door, "Is it making you both happy? Is it putting either of you in danger? Those are really the only questions that need answering right now. In my professional opinion."

Kevin froze in the doorway. Happy. Was he happy? His mind flashed over the last months, the last night. This giddy morning. Happy. He glanced over his shoulder, giving Damian a smile. "I think I can work out those answers. Er, thanks."

Damian nodded curtly, the barest hint of a smile on his lips. "Try not to screw yourself up too much. I don't prescribe StayWakes for late nights getting banged. Ask Sarah."

Kevin's sardonic smirk pulled his lips into familiar lines. "Now, Damian, since when was I the one who needed that treatment? I have much better uses for StayWake."

Damian made a small, disbelieving noise in the back of his throat and waved Kevin off.

Grinning, Kevin gave a half-salute and slipped out.

Event File 31
File Tag: Improvements
Timestamp: 15:50-9-10-2155

"You guys eat this shit? Serious?"

Aidan thought about yelling at Tweak, but he didn't want to waste the energy. After a month with her on the base, he knew what would happen. She'd stare at him and then repeat her two favorite words: "Fuck off."

No, yelling at somebody like Tweak was pointless and he knew it. Naomi was just like her.

Had been just like her, he reminded himself. He'd been out of her life long enough that he couldn't be sure anymore. But, when they'd been kids, Naomi had just shut down if their dad or one of the officers yelled at her, pulling on anger like armor. Tweak was just as bad.

"I kind of hate it, too. It tastes better if you don't wait for it to get cold," he remarked quietly. "But try and eat it anyway. It's what we've got right now."

The little techie glanced down at her plate, shrugged and shoved it away, picking up her tools again. "Fix that too. If this works. Wanna show you. This." Turning to the splayed carcass of the ViperDrone, she started to slide a power pad under it.

Fear spiked through the pit of Aidan's gut. "Tweak, uh—"

"Chill, chickenshit. I took its brains and trackers out. Dumped in Dust. Out truck window. This only got routines left."

To Aidan's relief, the machine didn't rise on its rotors and become a killer as he'd half expected. A couple lights blinked, but that was it.

"You guys kept trying for hacks on EagleCorp to t-t-take d-drones d-d-d-d..." Tweak's face scrunched up, and she swallowed hard twice. "Down. Stupid. It's n-not happening. But watch this." Pulling an object that looked like the guts of something else stuffed into a flashlight barrel, she flicked the switch.

Aidan watched a red light flash into existence. One drone rotor started to spin. One articulated member lifted on the gutted drone. Then the ones in the back did the same thing, and the next set, until the drone had started and stopped each of its six rotors.

He blinked. "Tweak. How--?"

"It looks for IR signals. Right?" Tweak shot Aidan a grin that was half feral cat and half happy kid. "I gave it a signal. Only, when it tries to p-process it, it's code. I encode ins-s-s-s-Tell it what to do. With IR. Laser IR. Don't touch me," she added, taking a quick sidestep away from Aidan.

He glanced away from the amazing thing he was seeing to the girl who'd thought it up. "This is kickass, Tweak. Really. I mean it." He hesitated, but he really needed to say it. "But if you're going to work around here, there's a lot of narrow spaces. Nobody's going to try to touch you without your permission, but in places like the hall we really can't help brushing shoulders and stuff. You know medwork is free for you when you're working with us? Maybe you can talk to Damian about getting some psych help for the touch thing."

Tweak shot him another one of her venomous glares. "Not. Crazy. Not. Head. Fucked. Not. Scared. You think I'm a chickenshit? Boo hoo, guy hurt me, now so scared? I'm. Not. Just don't like touch."

That had been more of a tirade than Aidan had ever expected to get out of Tweak. Had that been what happened to her? "I don't think you're chickenshit," he murmured.

She looked him up and down, snorted, then turned her eyes back to her experiment. "Not scared of you an-n-nyway. I could f-fuck you up easy. No sweat."

You're a little too late to fuck me up, Tweak, he thought wryly. But it brought up another point he'd better get taken care of. "Tweak, can you do me a favor?"

"Yeah?" Tweak asked, preoccupied.

"I know we agreed you're a contractor with us, not a Force member, but can you not talk to me like that if my boss or people from other bases are around? If they see you dissing me, they could decide I'm not a big enough asshole to be in command, and then they'll make you work for a real dickhead. If you can watch it, I can make sure that doesn't happen. Deal?"

Tweak glanced up at him, and this time the look was calculating. Putting her new toy down, she crossed her bandaged arms, staring at him. Didn't she ever blink? "Why d'you act like this?" she snapped out.

Aidan froze. "Like what?"

"Chill," Tweak supplied shortly. "You're C-c-commander. You do whatever. Why d'you put up with the shit I d-dish on you?"

Aidan relaxed. That was a hell of a lot better than the questions she could have been asking. He shrugged.

"Because I've seen a lot worse. It isn't going to kill me. Maybe I can ask you why you're dishing so much shit."

Tweak looked away. She moved around the table like a bird looking for crumbs. And back to not talking. Great.

"Can you implement this on a wider range?" Aidan asked, hoping to get her to relax again a little.

"With the right stuff," Tweak agreed quietly. "Still need to get the c-c-code r-r-right. Got some ideas. But, yeah. Get something.

Probably em-m-m—" She paused a beat. "Emitters for people to c-carry, big ones for b-bases. We see. Gonna need stuff."

Aidan nodded. "Talk to Kevin about anything you need, either he'll get it or he'll talk to the Sector Quartermaster and work something out."

Tweak gave another one of her snorts. "That guy. Sucks balls."

Aidan choked down a laugh. Tweak didn't know how right she was. If he had balls, Kevin might have done that for him that morning two weeks ago. What would that be like?

Focus. "He doesn't handle taking shit like I do, is all. No offense, Tweak, but if you were nicer to him, he would probably return the favor. That goes for a lot of people around here." Aidan smiled crookedly in the face of Tweak's sullen glare. "The guys take really badly to anybody who tries to get in their faces, is all. They got rid of two commanders before me because of it. But, if you try working with them, they're actually kind of awesome."

Tweak cocked her head. "You're an asshat."

"A lot of the time, yeah. Probably," Aidan agreed with another shrug. "But I'm still trying."

Tweak shifted her shoulders in a shrug. "Whatevs. I get the stuff, wanna test this. That okay?"

"What kind of test?" Aidan asked carefully.

Tweak tapped a tab in the middle of the jumble, and a map was projected. "Bunch of delivery drones. Go through here. Wanna try… here." She pointed, and a red dot appeared on the map. "Wanna tell them, you've gone blind, go home, get repairs. See if it works."

Aidan studied the map. "Okay, It's fifty miles from our base and not too close to anybody. Yeah. It should be safe. I have to get it approved, but, if you can build it and I get the OK, let's go for it. Let me know when I should start thinking about planning this."

"Yeah." Tweak agreed with another, dismissive shrug. "We'll see."

Aidan glanced at his tab. "I gotta go Tweak. Don't forget it's a day off tomorrow. You don't need to get any work done."

"Doing Topher's thing," Tweak muttered into the works she was poking through.

"Good to hear." Aidan replied, for want of anything better to say. He turned.

"Hey. Boss."

Aidan glanced over his shoulder. "Yeah?"

Tweak was staring at him. "That req guy. You trust him?"

"Kevin?"

"Yeah."

Something warm and gold curled in Aidan's belly. He had to stop himself smiling. "Yeah, I trust him. He's great at logistics and requisitions."

"He's Corps." Tweak stated baldly.

Aidan nodded. "Yeah, he was born Cavanaugh, but he's not the only Duster who was born Corps by a long—"

"No, asshat." Tweak waved a hand, cutting him off, "I mean he's up there. High standing. Got the looks, got the talk. I know Standings. What the f-fuck is he doing out here?"

Aidan studied her standing there, tiny, taunt and angry. What could he tell this girl? Tellher that, according to everything in Kevin's service record, he'd been an amazing logistics and requisitions guy for almost a decade, except for the disciplinary thing? Tellher taking her anger at the Corps out on somebody who was working beside her now because they'd been born above her was bull? That distrusting her basemates and lashing out at them would only hurt them all in the end?

Was he picking sides because this was about Kevin? He rubbed the back of his neck. Finally, he sighed. "Somebody told me that none of us get to decide where we come from. We only get to decide where we're going. Message me if you need me, Tweak."

Tweak's response was to turn away with a grunt.

"I tried your line on Tweak today." Aidan remarked that evening as he fought his way out of his one good binder.

"From your tone, I believe the result was good?" Omi asked as he pulled on his sweatshirt and flopped onto his bed.

Closing his eyes, he nodded. "Yeah, I guess. I still don't know what to do with her some days."

"Simply continue as you are. Based on my understanding, I believe she is progressing."

"Hope so," Aidan muttered.

"Your relationship also seems to be progressing with Kevin," the psychological health coach program said quietly.

Aidan smiled softly. "Yeah."

"Will you be spending your day off with him?" Omi asked.

Aidan opened his eyes, sighed, closed them again. "Omi, I can't exactly do that. I'm trying not to be real obvious about this… thing."

The hologram tipped her head, the hair failing to fall as it would have in reality. "Hiding this relationship will not be healthy for you, Aidan. It will raise your stress to dangerous levels over time."

Aidan snorted. "Yeah, and the crew finding out won't?"

"You have material proof that this base has no issues with homosexuality, Aidan," Omi reproved. "There is no reason to remain secretive."

"Except for the whole thing that I'm a commander who's been dating a subordinate officer?" Aidan retorted acerbically.

Omi's face didn't change. "Do you believe the personnel on this base would react badly?"

Aidan sighed out his frustration. "I don't know. If I knew, would I be this worried?"

Omi was silent for a few beats. Eventually, Aidan stood. Digging in his top drawer, he pulled out his engraving tools and a neat piece of wood he'd picked up. Plugging in his engraver, he set in a bit and started a design, following the contours of the wood with the jittering tip. The machine juddered in his fingers.

He didn't envy Citizen Excellent Standing people their stuff, not really. He didn't even envy their money, though his life would be a whole hell of a lot easier if he had the money for his surgeries. But sometimes he desperately wished he could have gotten the gene therapies and in-vitro brain chemistry adjusting their kids had done.

Rumor said it made them into pre-programmed Corporation drones with no conscience and no empathy, but, just once, it'd be nice to feel like the inside of his head was working right.

His psych-coach program gave a digital imitation of clearing her throat. "I believe it would be very healthy for you to take personal time with him."

Aidan grunted, keeping his eyes on his work. Sometimes he wished Omi wouldn't push so much. But that was what she was there for, after all. To push him when he needed it. "I—Yeah," he muttered eventually, blocking in new strokes. "I know. But sex. . . Omi, I don't really know what I'm doing. And my body's so fucked up, I—I want him to…I…"

"Am I right in thinking that you very much want to please him and are concerned that you aren't able to do so long term?" the coach program offered gently.

Aidan nodded, watching as the engraver carved new lines into the wood. Slowly, the design was coming clear.

"Is your dysphoria causing additional issues between you?"

Aidan nodded wordlessly, focusing minutely on the tiny hairs around the mane.

"Tell me about that."

Aidan bit his lip. "I don't know what he sees when he looks at me naked. I mean, he's so sweet, but if he's just… I don't know. Not pretending, but maybe dealing with it because he has to. I-I just don't know."

"Have you tried discussing it with him?"

Aidan turned off the engraver, staring at what he'd made. "Omi, we've had sex all of four times. If I keep coming up with shit to freak out about, why the hell would he want to keep coming back for more?"

On the wood a horse raced, long and lean and graceful. Kevin had legs just like that.

"Maybe because you will stop 'freaking out' once you have discussed it and are confident?" the program rejoined.

Aidan sighed. He hated it when she made sense sometimes.

"Yeah, I guess," he agreed finally. "I just hope I'm not going to screw any of this up."

Omi smiled at him. "Based on the behavioral projections I have run, I believe that all personnel are improving and the situation has stabilized. Barring information I am not aware of, I do not foresee issues."

Aidan's lips twisted. "Information you're not aware of. That's called life, Omi. Shit happens."

"It does. And until it occurs, the projections are valid."

Aidan let out a long breath, setting the new design on the dresser and putting his tools away. "Yeah. That'll be all tonight. Thanks Omi."

"Good night, Aidan." The program flicked off.

Aidan sighed, crossed to his bed and flopped onto it, staring at the ceiling until his eyes drifted closed.

Event File 32
File Tag: Leisure Time
Timestamp: 9-11-2155/ 9-13-2155

Harry Truman, Doris Day, Red China, Johnnie Ray South Pacific, Walter Winchell, Joe DiMaggio. Kevin's foot tapped against the locker at the foot of his bed as he hummed under his breath, flopped on his belly. "It was always burning since the world's been turning." He hummed in time with the tune, text scrolling down his tab.

Aidan stood awkwardly by the door for what felt like a year, watching Kevin with the music blaring. Kevin was so engrossed in the song that he hadn't heard his door open. He wasn't sure if he should interrupt or not. Did he have the right? Finally, he cleared his throat. "Uh, Kev?"

Kevin jumped, his eyes wide and distant for a moment. Then he smiled. Tapping his tab, he turned down the music.

"Hi. Um, business or pleasure? If it's pleasure, there's room on the bed. Grab a seat?" He rolled onto his side to afford the man in the doorway more room, the song still underpinning the moment with mentions of the past.

"Pleasure," Aidan replied with a shy smile. He crossed the space to the bed and sat uncertainly. "Thought maybe we could... I don't know, just, if you're not busy, hang out maybe?"

Kevin smiled and put out his arm, gently urging Aidan to lie down beside him. Aidan let the strength in the other man's arm pull him down.

"Let me just get this music and the research site closed down, and we can find a vid or something," Kevin replied beside him, "I just need to copy and download a few things. Otherwise, I have a nasty premonition that I'll lose them when I log out. This researcher seems to hedge their bets by never leaving anything interesting up for more than a week or so, and it's giving me hell."

"What're you researching?" Aidan asked, watching images and blocks of text flick by.

"The song that's playing, actually," Kevin replied. "Billy Joel's 'We Didn't Start The Fire'. I've heard it a few times and I love it, but I don't know what more than a quarter of the lyrics refer to and it's driving me nuts. Today, I was planning on giving myself a mental break by diving down a research rabbit hole and not coming out 'til I'd wrung all the in-jokes and period references out of the piece. Anyway, I'll be out of the tor in a second."

"Take your time." Aidan shifted on the bed, propping his head on the crook of his elbow. He could wait for Kevin to finish with his tab. He just liked being in the same room, being able to watch his new partner. Which, as he thought it, sounded creepy as hell. But Kevin was so cute when he relaxed. It was impossible not to watch him.

Kevin tapped at the tab for a few minutes, humming along to the end of the song. Then he caught Aidan watching him and gave a small, nervous smile, eyes darting from the screen to the man's face. "Sorry. I said I'd turn the music off, didn't I? I know this stuff is a little immature."

"It's not bad when it's not at an ear-bleeding volume," Aidan chuckled. He hesitated a moment, then carefully reached over to brush bright red hair out of Kevin's face.

Kevin glanced up, and his nervous smile grew a little wider. Tapping his screen to keep the music playing and keep him logged into his tab, he switched off the screen projection, set it to one side and leaned against Aidan, resting his head on Aidan's shoulder.

"Not bad. That's practically a compliment."

After a heartbeat, he tentatively kissed Aidan's throat. The next song began loose, breezy, and full of adventure; something about driving with the radio on under the sun.

Aidan gasped in surprise as Kevin kissed him. Kevin nuzzled his throat. Finally getting the clue Kevin was trying to hand him, Aidan hesitantly slid one hand down Kevin's cheek and throat, traced his shoulder, then brought it back up to gently tip Kevin's chin. After a long moment of searching Kevin's face, he leaned in and kissed him ever so gently on the lips.

Kevin smiled into the kiss, returning it as gently. For a few minutes they lay like that, exchanging soft kisses, until Kevin drew back with a smile.

"Shall I... Should I get my glasses off?" he asked quietly.

"Um. If you want to?" Aidan agreed uncertainly. They'd had sex four times now, but he was still never quite sure how to... well, start. And after that, he was never sure what Kevin wanted, since there was the little problem of anatomy to get around. He took a breath. Time to stop being such a chicken.

"Maybe, um. Help me out of the binder first?"

"I suppose I would need to see for that, true," Kevin propped himself up on an elbow, starting to ease Aidan's shirt up, but he paused when his eyes met Aidan's.

"Aidan? It..." He swallowed. "It isn't always about what I want, you know. I actually don't prefer it to be me running the show a lot of the time. I like to be... Sometimes I..." As he spoke his high cheekbones reddened, and he glanced down. "That didn't come out quite right."

Aidan swallowed and carefully sat up, tugging his shirt back down over his binder in embarrassment. "Kev, I—You know I..." He bit his lip, trying to figure out what he wanted to say, trying to apologize for his damn body again, trying to do anything to keep from losing this. Not yet. "If you don't want me in here I can go. I'm sorry..."

Kevin sat up as if he'd been electrocuted. "No! Oh God, no. I'm not saying that I don't want you, I'm—God you'd think I could articulate a concept..." He drew a breath, "I don't want less. I'd really like... Well, more of you. More... I mean, I like—"

"Like what?" Aidan asked, watching Kevin with his heart in his throat.

Kevin ran a hand through his hair, eyes on the bed. "I...like being...topped," he managed, the words sounding like something he'd read and was trying to pronounce properly. "And when I can let my partner take control, it's—it's a chance for me to let go. Does that make any sense?" he asked, raising his head and searching Aidan's face. "Not always, but sometimes, if you could take the initiative?" He finished the question on a quavering note.

Aidan sat staring into his partner's pleading eyes. Kevin was scared, too, wasn't he? And the guy wanted him to take initiative. How the hell was he supposed to do that? He wasn't comfortable with his own body, let alone letting someone else touch it. Not yet. He wasn't entirely certain what he liked yet, let alone how that lined up with what Kevin wanted. How was he supposed to take charge in bed? How was he supposed to top, when he had always been relegated to the passive role regardless of what he had wanted?

He had to force the words he did find out of his mouth. "Kev, I—I d-don't know how."

Kevin watched his face for a moment before he leaned in, hugging the other man gently. He brushed his lips over Aidan's. "I'll put it another way. Please touch me like you want me. Not like you're afraid of me."

Aidan squeezed his eyes closed as Kevin kissed him. Touch Kevin like he wanted him? He did. So badly. Kevin was the first man he'd been with who was still interested once he knew exactly how fucked up Aidan was. Kevin was sweet, and hot as hell, and...

And Aidan was terrified. Still. What the hell was he so afraid of? The base knowing? No, that wasn't it. Losing this? Hurting Kevin? Getting hurt? He swallowed hard, took a breath and forced his eyes open again. His hand trembled when he lifted it to try and cup Kevin's face. He dropped it again.

"Shit, I'm a hot mess. Crap, I'm sorry. I'm trying. I want you. I do. I want this. Whatever we are. I'm just—I don't want to... do something you don't like. I mean. I know I'm not exactly your usual type—"

Kevin caught his hand, held his eyes, then dipped his head to kiss Aidan's knuckles gently. "Neither of us is all that usual, and you may have noticed that I'm not exactly good at this either," he added with a grim twist of the lips. "But we can make it work, can't we?"

In the nervous breaths of silence between question and answer, the song seemed loud.

Workin' on a mystery, goin' wherever it leads. . .

Aidan swallowed hard again and looked down at Kevin's hand holding his. Kevin wanted to make this work. They could make this work. It had only been two weeks. "Yeah, I think so. I-I hope so. I like you, Kev. I do. A lot."

"Feeling's mutual," Kevin murmured, glancing up with eyes like spring storm clouds. "I guess, I didn't want to say anything because I didn't want to... Well, you know." He shrugged. "Scare you off, I guess. So, if I ask for what I'd like, I don't want you to think... I mean, is it all right if I..." He swallowed, shaking his head. "Dear Lord, I sound like a high schooler don't I?"

Aidan smiled weakly despite himself. After a heartbeat of hesitation, he leaned in and kissed Kevin again. "We both do. But I-I'll try. If you ask. I just can't promise I'll be any good at it." He glanced up, watching Kevin work hard on a smile before he spoke.

"No one's good at sex, Aidan. I'm fairly sure it's God's way of making sure that, on a regular basis, every human being looks like an egregious dumbass."

"Because I need another way to do that," Aidan chuckled weakly. He took a breath and hesitantly moved Kevin's hand back to the hem of his shirt. "I guess, let's start with that?"

Kevin's smile softened. "Good place to start." He murmured, working Aidan's shirt up with one hand and gently stroking his back with the other.

Aidan lifted his arms up to let Kevin pull his shirt up, leaving him in the old black mesh chest binder like a faded undershirt, ragged around the bottom hem. Aidan winced. Damn this thing was ugly. If he thought about it, he would have worn his nice one or patched that hole in the hem before this. Or really tried to get a new one. But they were hard to get a hold of nowadays, even on the black market.

With his shirt off, he took another breath and leaned forward, carefully sliding his hands under Kevin's shirt. Kevin let his bedmate push his shirt up his body, over his head, then leaned in to press their bodies together. His fingers picked at the binder as they kissed.

"Want this off?" he murmured against the soft flesh of Aidan's throat.

"Don't get me stuck like Monday," Aidan muttered in agreement with a small smile. His hands gently ran over Kevin's shoulders, down his back, caressing the hot, soft skin.

"I'll try, but this thing has a mind of its own," Kevin remarked dryly, beginning the careful process of folding the compressing binder up as Aidan stroked his skin. Aidan's hands ran down his chest, down the planes of his torso. Aidan smiled as he heard Kevin's breathing pick up speed. With an impatient grunt, Kevin gave the binder a hard tug. The folds tightened on each other in the area of Aidan's armpits. Kevin gave a strangled little groan. "Um, Aidan, give me a second." Aidan winced as the binder rolled up and pinched under his arms. Maybe he shouldn't have been so distracting. Now he was caught half-in the damn mesh, his stupid breasts exposed, and Kevin was getting flustered. Why did this always happen? He pulled his hands away and sighed, trying not to squirm or roll his shoulders as he held his arms up over his head to make it a little easier to get the binder off.

For a moment Kevin bit his lip, frozen. His eyes were frightened when he looked at Aidan's face. Aidan hated that look. This sucked, but frightening Kevin was worse.

"Maybe this stuff is smart-weave," Aidan managed with a crooked, broken grin. "It's smarter than both of us anyway."

Kevin began to chuckle, then to laugh, shaking his head. The laughter seemed to relax him enough to work his fingers under the compression fabric, slowly work it free, and finally throw it into the corner before hugging Aidan to him. "Sorry. I was afraid of making it worse. I'm really awful with that damn thing, aren't I?"

Despite the soreness of the mesh scraping against his skin, Aidan hugged him in return as he chuckled. "Yeah. If it makes you feel better though, it took me months to figure it out on my own and I'm the one wearing it."

"I'll get better," Kevin murmured, tracing the line of Aidan's back with his fingers. "And I'll find you a few that are easier to get out of." Pulling away gently, he got around to the comparatively easy task of unbuttoning his own pants.

"Hey," Aidan muttered, catching Kevin's hands. Goosebumps skittered along his skin. He smiled weakly when Kevin looked up. "I thought you wanted me to take initiative?"

Kevin grinned, his hands and body relaxing. He let his hands fall away, open and undemanding. "Be my guest."

Aidan smiled and leaned forward to kiss Kevin gently, his hand running down Kevin's chest until his fingers stopped on a nipple. Gently, hesitantly, he rolled said nipple between his fingertips.

Kevin drew in a sharp breath, his lips quirking up at the corners. "Glasses?" he murmured, eyes closed.

"Glasses," Aidan agreed. He reluctantly pulled his hand away to gently remove Kevin's glasses and set them aside on the upturned box Kevin used for a nightstand.

Kevin kept his eyes closed, giving a surprised gasp when Aidan's fingers returned to their teasing. Aidan watched as all the usual stiff tension easing away. Kevin ran his hands along Aidan's thighs.

Aidan smiled softly as Kevin relaxed under his hands, Kevin's face growing peaceful. So damn handsome. He kissed Kevin again as his hands hesitantly trailed lower, ghosting over Kevin's pants buttons.

"Aidan?" The word came out a whisper. Kevin swallowed hard. "When you get to it… When you're touching me, could you put your fingers inside me? I—Please?"

Aidan paused when Kevin breathed his name. He swallowed at the request. How wonderful would it be to be able to put more than his fingers inside Kevin? No. He couldn't think like that. That'd kill the mood. He took a breath and forced his hands to move again, gliding back up. "Um. I—Is the lube where you put it last time?"

"Head of the bed, between the mattress and the wall," Kevin murmured in agreement.

Aidan tried not to worry, not to let himself think too much. Get the pants off first. He worked the long, slender legs loose of tan fabric. This was what Kevin wanted. He'd asked for it. Aidan had read all about this in the stuff he had scrounged on the GreyNet and ZonCom's only-closed-to-idiots sites. He knew what to do, didn't he? And it didn't matter that he couldn't actually take Kevin like he wanted to. Did it?

He shoved the thought aside and tentatively pulled Kevin's boxers down. His sore breasts pressed against Kevin's back and he winced.

Kevin twisted to make extricating him from his boxers easier, squinting to see Aidan's face. "You all right?" he asked, but Aidan stopped that conversation in the best possible way by running his hand over Kevin's hardening dick. The way Kevin sucked in a breath was a thrill.

"Fine," Aidan murmured, stroking Kevin reverentially with one hand as the other groped for the lube. Finding it, he pressed his body against Kevin's back, holding him.

Eyes closed, Kevin leaned back into him, bare skin rubbing across the fabric of Aidan's pants. Kevin turned his head to catch Aidan's lips. He traced his hand up Aidan's throat as they kissed, along his jaw and into his hair.

Aidan stroked him for a long time as he ran through all the underground articles he'd read about gay sex. Okay. He knew what to do. He could do this. He stroked Kevin's balls and Kevin whimpered. Aidan smiled.

Yeah. He could do this. Aidan's breath came fast as he pulled his hand away from Kevin's erection to carefully dab lube into his palms. God, he wished he could spread the lube on his own dick and press forward. But even after the years on testosterone he was still too small, positioned too low. So he just rolled the lube around his fingers and returned one hand to gently stroking Kevin's erection. The other he slid down his boyfriend's back, hesitantly dipping between his buttocks.

Kevin's back arched as Aidan's nervous fingers teased at his opening, exploring. "Oh yes," he whispered. "Aidan. Yes."

Aidan bit his lip as his breath caught. The sound of that whisper. Kevin wanted this. He sounded so deliciously desperate. Aidan didn't know how he could possibly make someone so aroused, but he wouldn't complain. Very gently, he pressed one finger in. Of course, the concentration made his other hand slow on Kevin's erection.

Kevin groaned softly in dismay, pressed himself back against Aidan, turning his head to bury his face in Aidan's neck. He gulped for enough air to speak. "Two, two fingers Aidan. And... stroke upwards. And, please, God, don't stop."

Aidan's breath caught at Kevin's pleading. He closed his eyes and carefully pressed another finger in, crooking them to try to do as Kevin had asked. Hesitantly, awkwardly, he pressed his hips against Kevin's thigh, his own erection craving. He used his other hand to work Kevin's dick, faster now. Kevin was shivering in his arms, his hips bucking a little. Aidan pressed his fingers in a little harder, moved his hand faster.

Kevin cried Aidan's name against his neck as his seed spilled across Aidan's palm. God, the sound of his own name cried like that, like some kind of prayer, and the man in his arms shaking with release. Nothing could ever match this. Aidan stared down in amazement at the gorgeous body in his arms as he gently relaxed his hands. He'd really made this man happy.

Then Kevin turned in his arms and enveloped Aidan in a ferocious hug. "Thank you," he whispered, the words fervent.

Aidan gasped as Kevin ran his hand along his throat, skipped his chest, ran fingers over Aidan's belly and down, fumbling as he undid Aidan's pants and kissed him hard.

Then Kevin was getting to his feet, a little wobbly, and pulling Aidan's pants off. He left Aidan in his underwear as he grabbed a few wipes from his bedside and leaned in for another long kiss and a quick wiping down of Aidan's hands. Then, slowly, he kissed Aidan's navel and began to peel back his boxers.

"Tell me what you want." Kevin whispered.

Aidan blushed at the request and bit his lip, nodding weakly against the pillow. "Just keep going?"

"As ordered, sir," Kevin agreed with a hint of laughter in his ragged whisper, his fingers working faster.

Aidan chuckled breathlessly as his boxers were pulled off, his packer was laid to one side and Kevin's long body traced his again. One of Kevin's hands traced his navel and down to tease his erection, the fingers of the other twined in Aidan's hair.

"Tell me if this is right."

"Mm," Aidan managed, hips pressing into Kevin's hand. His hand gripped Kevin's shoulder as his breath came faster, the pleasure in his gut spiraling up and up and up.

Kevin kissed him hard and stroked him harder as he felt his body start to shudder and twitch. Kevin sucked the skin over Aidan's collar bone and his body tipped over into orgasm. He heard himself whimper, felt his body buck as pleasure sizzled through once, twice, three times.

Kevin kissed his throat gently as Aidan caught his breath.

"How was that?" Aidan breathed shakily as he spiraled back down to reality, curling against Kevin's warmth and trying to catch his breath. "On the taking charge?"

"Better by far. " Kevin murmured, holding him close. He nuzzled his face down into Aidan's hair, kissing the top of his head. His fingers wandered lazily over Aidan's body. Aidan felt the touch run over the scars on his calves left from the days when he'd gotten his relief by cutting himself.

"What happened here?"

"Got caught in some barbed wire when I was a kid," Aidan muttered. "I tried to fight the stuff and it made things worse."

Kevin gave a soft murmur of commiseration, before falling into a contented silence.

"Kev?" Aidan breathed a long time later. He didn't want to ask the question, but it had been bugging him for days. Omi had told him to get it over with, and she was usually right.

"Mm?" Kevin asked inquiringly, raising his head.

Aidan took a deep breath and kept his eyes closed, unable to look at Kevin's face. "I—You—you still, um… see me as a man, right? With the binder off and everything?"

The silence seemed to last forever. Aidan's gut twisted in on itself. Kevin pulled away. "Aidan? Look at me. Please."

Aidan hated himself in that second. Why the fuck had he opened his mouth and ruined this perfect thing? He didn't want to open his eyes and see Kevin's expression. But he did it.

Kevin sat with his head tipped to one side, a tender smile on his lips. "Aidan, I see you." He drew a slow breath. "I-I see the man in my bed. I see a man who cares." He shrugged a little, a sour smile flashing across his face. "And if you're telling yourself you're a freak, join the club. I know there are issues, but..." He shrugged again, smiling. "I enjoy a good logistical challenge, why do you think I'm in my position?"

Aidan searched Kevin's face. Earnest, hopeful grey eyes squinted back. Little by little, the fear that had been building in Aidan's gut loosened and began to melt. Omi had been right. Kevin had done nothing but call him a man, treat him as one. Why had he been so afraid? He took a breath and smiled weakly. "At least I'm entertaining."

"Very amusing indeed." Kevin agreed softly, leaning in for a kiss. Then he cringed as a song came blaring out of his tab speaker.

'Oh Mickey you're so fine!' 'the singer enthusiastically announced at the top of her lungs. Kevin scrabbled with one hand to shut the thing off. "Dear God, I thought I deleted that stupid..." When silence fell, he shook his head, grinning sheepishly. "And you're probably the only fellow who wouldn't break up with me after *that* came out of my player."

"I've come to accept that I'm dating a man with awful music taste," Aidan rejoined with a small chuckle. "Small price to pay." Kevin pressed a hand to his heart, affecting a stage gasp.

"Awful? I'm crushed! He speaks poniards and every word stabs!"

Aidan laughed despite himself at Kevin's ridiculous act. It was a relief after the tension of making himself ask the question. He reached for Kevin's hand and squeezed, smiling. "You brought it on yourself, you know."

Kevin sighed, raising his eyes to the ceiling. "I always do. The bane of my existence."

Reaching into the box he used as a nightstand, he grabbed the wipes and cleaned his own hands, leaning against Aidan as he worked. Aidan blushed a little as he watched Kevin work. He should have done that like Kevin did for him. Damn.

"Kev? Um. Thank you."

Kevin glanced up, smiling slightly. "Any time."

Two days later, Aidan found a battered box leaning against the door of his room. On it, Kevin's neat script spelled out his name and rank, as well as a heavily underlined postscript enclosed in a thick black rectangle

Commander Headly

No box swapping. I mean it. Requisitions will deliver everyone else's clothing requests next week.

Wait your turn. This means you, Lazarus

-Requisitions

Aidan's eyebrows rose as he read, but he carefully manhandled it into his room, pulling out his pocket knife to slit it open. As he pulled out the first of three black mesh shirts, his breath caught. Binders. In perfect condition. How the hell had Kevin found not one, but three new chest binders in perfect condition? After a moment of marveling, he tossed the binder back in the box and shot out of his room, running for Kevin's office.

Kevin was glaring at a line of code when Aidan got to the doorway. He was on his feet and grabbing for his gun belt the minute he saw the other man. "What's up?" he asked sharply, hands automatically strapping on his belt. "Do we need to move?"

Aidan stared at him for a moment before laughing breathlessly and shaking his head. "No, sorry. Didn't mean to freak you. Just... My package. How the hell did you do it?"

Kevin's tense shoulders relaxed, and he smiled quietly, giving a little shrug. "I did a little digging, traded a few favors before last week's run hit the windmill. Was the size all right?"

"No one makes them anymore," Aidan protested, still in shock.

"There are a few makers yet, actually. Mostly in the retro theatrical groups," Kevin demurred, leaning against the wall. Tipping his head, he looked at Aidan over the rims of his glasses, a teasing smile playing about his lips.

"You know, this is a purely selfish move on my part. I simply refuse to be made a fool of by a piece of clothing again."

Aidan gave a small, breathless laugh. "Sorry. Yeah, um. Haven't tried them on yet. You know new ones are even harder to get on and off, right?"

"You didn't look very closely, did you?" Kevin asked with a spark in his grey eyes. "There's a recessed zipper along the side." The smile on Kevin's face was irresistible, and Aidan felt himself grinning in return as Kevin shrugged.

"Like I keep telling you, logistical puzzles are my forte. You'd be surprised at what I can get my hands on."

"I'm so damn lucky," Aidan muttered. Stepping forward, he kissed Kevin hard. He couldn't help it. This man not only accepted him as he was and listened to him when things really mattered, but had gone out of his way to find new binders to help him be more comfortable in his own skin. Lucky didn't even begin to cover it.

Kevin put an arm around him and, gently, kicked his office door closed.

Event File 33
File Tag: Official Reprimand
Timestamp: 06:30-9-12-2155

Aidan jolted awake and scrambled to grab his tab as it buzzed, heart in his throat. Had the slick tarps malfunctioned again?

Beside him in bed, Kevin sat up with a gasp. "What's—"

"Just my tab. Go back to sleep." Aidan whispered, staring at the words on the screen.

Message incoming. Sector Quartermaster

The words scrolled in flashing red and black.

Message incoming. Sector Quartermaster. Message incoming.

Aidan sucked in a breath and jabbed at the message alert, turning the screen so that the viewer couldn't see Kevin. A sector message. God help him.

Instead of text, a face that seemed to consist mostly of bloodshot eyes set in StayWake induced bags glared up at him. "Base Commander Headly? I want a—God damn it, you're still in bed? No wonder that base is going down the drain."

The man sighed in disgust. "What the hell is your base trying to do, bankrupt us? Don't answer that. Get your ass out of bed and call me. I don't have time to wait for you to wake up and pay attention. Wake up, get to duty and call me. Stat." The tab's screen flicked off as the call ended.

Aidan blinked at the tab for a moment. "The hell was that?"

"That, my dear Aidan, was Sector Quartermaster Shultz, affectionately known as Shitbag Shultz," Kevin remarked, stretching languidly. "And I know this because he's my division superior for the Sector, and he and I have had more words than some litigators. He's probably circumventing me to yell at you about all the supplies we've been getting for the new Synth experiments and Tweak's endless requirements. I'd recommend giving him a lesson in patience," he added, flopping an arm around Aidan again. The wall screen cast a soft golden glow that caught in his hair.

Aidan was tempted. It'd be great to lie back down in Kevin's arms. But he gently disentangled himself with a smile. "If you're already on his shit list, I better give him a reason to like our base. What's wrong with him?" He glanced around as he spoke. "And can I borrow your razor?"

"Feel free. As for Shultz, he's an esurient, malapert windbag with a penchant for flogging a dead horse of a lecture far and away beyond the pale."

Aidan glanced over his shoulder, smiling despite himself. What sort of apps did Cavanaugh schools use to train their kids anyway? The words Kevin came out with sounded more like short poems than conversation sometimes. They sounded nice, but damn they were weird. "Can I get that in English?" he asked, and Kevin chuckled as he slid his glasses on.

"He's a rude, up-on-himself bastard who loves to get a subordinate in front of him and shout their ears off. You were warned."

"I guess so. Thanks," Aidan muttered. What a way to start a morning. He washed his face, shaved, dressed as quickly as he could, then stepped to the door, where his partner was already waiting for him. Kevin kissed him softly and cracked the door, glancing out.

"Clear."

"Thanks," Aidan murmured as he slipped out. He hurried down the corridor toward his office, hoping like hell someone had an explanation for him. Liza turned in her chair with wary eyes, already there ahead of him. She usually was.

"Sector's frothing at the mouth, sir. I was about to call you. They won't talk to me. Won't say why, but the Quartermaster's called twice, and he sounds pissed."

"Yeah, he got my tab," Aidan sighed, sliding the offending piece of tech onto his desk. "No clue what he's angry about, though. You got anything more before I put my ass on the line?"

Liza shrugged, her face wearing that blank mask she hid behind when she was scared. That couldn't be good. "He's got a reputation for going off on rants, sir. And he and Taylor used to have kind of an... issue going. They didn't get along. Watch out?"

Aidan sighed. "Yeah, sure. Thanks, Liza."

He sank into his chair and typed Shultz's tab ID into the call app. The wait to connect made his stomach feel like lead.

The man's paunchy face hadn't improved since he saw it last. If anything, it was redder and uglier. "Headly, I want your logistics officer relieved of duty right this fucking minute. Put him on a charge of abuse of duty."

Aidan blinked at the red face on the tab as his brain tried to do a system reboot. Abuse of duty? What the hell kind of thing warranted an abuse of duty charge handed down from the sector quartermaster? "What for, sir?"

Shultz's face turned purple. "What for? What for? What the fuck are you doing on that base anyway? Do you think this is a little girl's camping trip or a frat house or something? Don't play stupid with me, Headly, and if you aren't playing, you're a *fucking idiot!*"

"It's been a long couple of weeks here, sir," Aidan replied as calmly as he could manage. Which was surprisingly even-keeled given the fact that he was facing a sector-level officer who was furious for a reason he couldn't wrap his brain around. "My tab's stuffed with error code from our slick tarps and I haven't had a chance to sort through it to find other reports. So please, sir, just tell me what Kevin's done and I'll fix it up."

"What he's done is gross abuse of duty, not to mention waste of funds! If he were under me, I'd throw him to the Fringe! Look at these orders!" A file flashed up on Aidan's screen. "Look at this fucking bull shit! Reclining couch? I've got a *reclining couch* sitting in my requisitions center! Chocolate, vodka, a games console! People have to make these requisitions! People *risk their lives* every day to get us what we need, and your. Man. Ordered. *This!* I want him relieved of duty! *Permanently!* Waste of money, waste of time, *risking lives,* Headly! *Do you hear me?*"

Liza winced, leaning away from the screaming coming out of the tab.

Aidan stared at the file Shultz had sent over, stunned by the list. Kevin had ordered this? When? Why the hell had Kevin ordered such frivolous things? How much had it cost to get them, in money and in blood? How long had this been going on without him noticing?

Had he really messed up this badly? Had he been so head over heels about the guy that he hadn't seen things he should have? He swallowed hard and forced himself to minimize the file, facing the angry quartermaster again. "Yes, sir. I'll talk with him. Figure out what's going on and ensure it doesn't happen again."

"You fucking *better!* If you don't, I'll see to it that Magnum *does!*"

The call clicked off. Aidan stared at the blank tab for several long minutes, trying to remind himself to breathe. Kevin had put in orders for things that could have gotten people killed. Carrying a reclining couch through the Dust would have attracted way too much attention, and Kevin had to know that. What the hell was going on? Why would someone as careful as Kevin do something so stupid?

But he wasn't always careful, was he? When he got angry, he got reckless. And when he got scared. And hadn't he just ordered something special for Aidan from God knew where? *"You'd be surprised what I can get my hands on."* The memory of the words Kevin had said knotted his gut.

"Sir? Aidan?"

Aidan took a breath, yanked himself out of his thoughts and looked up to his personnel officer. "Liza. Could you get Kevin, please?"

Liza nodded slowly. "Sure, sure, Commander. Should I—I won't say anything." She stood, her body stiff as she walked to the door. One hand on the frame, she looked over her shoulder. "Sir? I've known Kevin nine years. There's got to be a mistake. He doesn't do this."

Aidan nodded tightly, but wasn't sure what to say to that. People change? Obviously, he did? At this point, he was desperately trying to focus on the damage control he was going to need to do for his base, not the fact that he had been sleeping with a man who might have wasted precious resources and put people in so much danger.

Ten minutes later, Kevin poked his head in, a baffled half-frown on his lips. "What've you done to Liza? She looked like someone walked over... her... grave... What's wrong?" His voice was tight on the last words.

"Did you approve this requisitions list?" Aidan asked, his voice quiet. He couldn't quite meet Kevin's gaze as he pulled up the file Shultz had sent and slid the tab across the desk.

Kevin blinked. Pushing his glasses up his nose, he read, his eyes growing wider with every line. "What the hell?" His head shot up, his eyes wide and panicked. "Aidan, cancel all my credentials. Do it now."

The churning heat that had been building in Aidan's chest released. If Kevin had faked that look of shock on his face, Aidan would eat his desk. He grabbed his tab back and typed furiously. When he had suspended all of Kevin's active credentials and put his IDs on leave, he looked back up.

"You want to tell me what the fuck is going on here?"

Kevin shook his head, bewildered. "I got hacked, but this doesn't make sense. If any of the Corps gained access we should have been attacked, not sent the proverbial box of chocolates. It doesn't... make..." He blinked twice. Then, slowly, he pulled off his glasses and covered his face with one hand.

"Oh Jesus, blessed Mary and Joseph. That importunate, intrusive, egoistic, self serving little mercenary plebeian jackdaw! I'm going to wring her little—Aack!" He kicked the leg of the desk, making the rickety structure rattle.

"Kev?" Aidan asked, watching him and waiting for the whole thing to make any sense.

Kevin raised his head. His face was frighteningly blank. "Tweak."

Aidan's brain froze. Tweak. Of course. This was the kind of thing Tweak would do. He'd been caught so far off-guard by the sudden message from Shultz that he hadn't had the time to put the pieces together.

"Shit," Aidan whispered. "Oh, shit."

Kevin held his gaze, eyes opaque. "You really thought I did this. Didn't you?"

Aidan looked down quickly, fidgeting with his tab. If it had been anyone else on base, he would have been able to look the man in the eye and tell him exactly why he had thought he had done it.

But this was Kevin. The man who knew his secret, who had taken him to bed regardless, who whispered such sweet things to him. How could he tell Kevin he had spent ten minutes sitting in his office and believing that he had approved that ridiculous requisitions list? He tried to lay out the points.

"Kevin, I...Yes. I thought you did it. I mean, like you said, the Corps wouldn't be ordering us these things, and you're the only one with high-level requisitions requests like this, except me."

Kevin didn't say a word. A moment later, his chair rolled back. "Fine." His steps sounded loud in the small room. "If you want to do your job and deal with your hacker, sir, I'd like help. I'm going to go find Tweak and you can shake some sense into her." His voice was flat.

Aidan nodded on auto-pilot. Kevin hadn't betrayed the base. Tweak had. Was that good? Bad? He hadn't had the time to process any of that. No, he'd had time. He hadn't *taken* the time. He'd panicked instead. He'd let an officer's yelling and his own fear of showing favor panic him into blind agreement.

And now he'd fucked up with Kevin, too. He stood and raked his fingers through his hair. "Yeah. I think that would be a good idea."

Frigid silence and a blank grey stare were the only answers he got. Then Kevin turned away and walked out of the room.

Tweak was in the canteen, tapping at her pad and gulping down the crap they called coffee with a grimace, when Kevin shoved his tab with its glowing file under her nose. Aidan had been planning on taking her to his office, but Kevin had beaten him down the hall. The expression on his face was a little bit terrifying. It was that same distant, utterly dismissive look he'd worn the first time Tweak had insulted him.

Aidan considered stepping in, but if Tweak had really done this, maybe Kevin had the right to the first crack at her. Standing behind the table, he watched, ready to break it up if things got hairy.

Silence spread from Kevin like ink spilled into water as his basemates nudged one another and nodded in the direction of the trouble.

"Did you do this?" Kevin demanded, his syllables clinking like ice cubes. "Did you actually take the credentials that I'm entrusted with and use them to order toys and *junk food*?"

Tweak looked up at him blankly, shrugged her shoulders. "Yeah. You never get it. You're cheap. This place's a dump. Needs stuff. Easy." Kevin's face went paper white. Aidan shifted his weight, wary. Could somebody look that angry and keep from violence?

"You are an egocentric little gutter rat," Kevin managed as he watched, voice shaking with rage. "And you have no concept of the damage you've done."

Tweak blinked once, slowly. "Fuck. Off. CES."

Aidan stepped in before somebody got killed. He wasn't sure who'd come out in a fight between these two, but he didn't want to find out.

Kevin gave him a look that made him feel as if his gut had frozen solid when he gently put a hand against his chest and pushed him back. God, the man was so angry at him. And maybe he should be.

But he had to deal with one shit-show at a time. "Tweak," Aidan muttered. "You can't just hack into our credentials and use them any way you want. People could have died because they were carrying a couch we don't need."

Tweak blinked. Her laugh was the staccato yelp of a dog, but her words had a hint of worry in them. "It's just stuff. Didn't hurt n-nobody. Chill."

"I can't chill on this, Tweak," Aidan replied quietly. It was easy to sound calm when his insides felt numb. "Folks get killed bringing us food off the Grid. Stuff you can carry in your pockets is enough to get them targeted. Carrying furniture? It's a downright miracle no one got killed on those runs."

Tweak stared into his eyes. Slowly, her blank expression faded, leaving her face looking much younger. "Seriously? Die? Thought you p-p-people n-never got caught."

"Then you're an ignoramus," Kevin growled.

Aidan held up a hand to silence his requisitions officer. Now wasn't the time. Tweak had made a mistake and his base was going to pay for it through the nose, but she was still just a kid, a scared one. She needed people to teach her this lesson. If they yelled, he knew she'd shut down. "Billie? Can you move over?"

The taller girl scooted down, and Aidan took a seat between them, holding Tweak's eyes. "You ever see reports on the Grid of terrorists brought to justice or killed before they could go through with an attack? More often than not, those are Dusters that got caught. We lose more people daily than any of us like to admit. And stunts like yours add to the body count. Understand?"

Tweak looked away, staring at her bandaged hands. She stood in a blink. "I'll pack."

"No. You won't," Aidan stated, allowing the coldness into his voice. "Sit down."

Tweak sat without looking up, her head sinking onto her chest. The room was so quiet that Aidan could hear the girl's breathing, short sharp pants. He studied her profile.

She was the best hacker he'd ever heard of. They needed her talents. Of course, that meant somehow explaining to Sector why he wasn't decommissioning the person responsible for such an epic fuck up. Well, that was something a commander would have to do.

Finally, he drew in a breath. "You're part of this base, Tweak. And that means I'm not letting you off the hook that easy. You don't just run away. You fucked up. Royally. Now you're going to help me fix it. How much did your requisition list cost?"

Tweak shrugged. "Didn't check. Do the code, stuff's free. Never check."

"Then find out," Aidan replied, keeping his voice to a monotone. He slid his tab across the table to her. "I want to know where you ordered everything, how much it cost, and how you requested it be delivered. And I want your report in twenty minutes. Understood?"

Tweak raised her eyes to give him a scowl, but the expression looked to be made more out of habit than any real emotion.

"Twenty? Think I'm that slow? Ten tops. On your tab."

He nodded. "I guess you better get to work."

Aidan turned away without another word. Keeping his eyes straight ahead, he walked out of the room. He didn't dare look at Kevin.

When he reached his office, he quietly closed the door, crossed to his chair, and dropped into it with his head in his hands, trying to force his brain into motion. It had been awhile since he had had to punish someone beyond a reprimand. He'd have to figure out something serious enough to really get through to the kid without turning her off as an asset. He still had to report back to Shultz. And, on top of it all, he'd started a fight with his lover over this bullshit.

It was going to be long, long day.

Event File 34
File Tag: Adjustments
Timestamp:0900-9-18-2155

Kevin didn't join Aidan for lunch that day, and he didn't knock on
Aidan's door that night. He wasn't there on the couch Tuesday night. It
was late the next Monday morning before Kevin knocked on the frame
of his open office door.

"I'll need my credentials reinstated when you've got the time.
I've got rather a lot of work to do." His tone was conversational, but he
didn't look up from the tab in his hand, and the set of his shoulders was
stiff.

"As soon as I can," Aidan promised with an irritated sigh. He
glanced up from his own tab briefly, considered saying something else,
asking if he could make up for his mistake, but thought better of
bringing that up now.

Instead he took a breath and admitted, "I turned in a full incident
report, but I'm still trying to convince Shultz not to kill Tweak. Might
take a while."

"I might save him the trouble," Kevin muttered. For a moment,
he glanced up, meeting Aidan's eyes. He opened his mouth to speak,
but closed it again, smiled weakly and shrugged.

"I can work around some of it." Then he was gone, his footsteps fading down the hall.

Aidan opened his mouth to call him back, to try and mend things, but no sound came out. He groaned and fell back in his chair, raking his fingers through his hair in irritation. This was driving him insane. He hadn't realized not having Kevin as a confidante, as a bedmate, as... as *Kevin* would be so irritating. And dealing with Shultz wasn't helping either. He'd had another three vid calls with the bastard, all of them heinous.

Speaking of which, he still owed one more.

Swallowing another groan, he tapped Shultz's ID pin into his call app. He still had to arrange a pick-up for all the things Tweak had ordered, since sending them back onto the Grid was even more dangerous. Making an in-person try at convincing the bastard wouldn't hurt either.

"So when are you getting here to fix your mess?" Shultz asked acidly, not even bothering with a greeting this time. "I want this shit out of my hub, Headly. Yesterday. And Magnum wants you in here for an in-person briefing before he approves McIllian's reinstatement. An explanation, Headly, for this entire fuck up. You'll get the summons any time now."

Aidan bit his cheek to keep from groaning aloud. Could this mess get any worse? Doing his best to remain polite, he replied, "I've been waiting for your transportation schedule to get my team together, sir. If you approve it, I can get a truck out this afternoon. And if Commander Magnum needs me, I can be on it, sir."

"You damn well better be," Shultz snapped. The tab clicked off. A heartbeat later a transportation schedule shot up on the screen, a note blinking in red beside the entries.

Commander and Logistics Officer Requested For Debrief

Aidan winced as he accepted the order. Last week had been a dumpster fire, and it was looking like this entire week was going to suck, too. Shoving his chair away from his desk, he stalked out of his office to gather people for the trek.

Tweak yelped when Aidan tapped her shoulder, yanking the cord of her headphones right out she jumped so fast. "Fucker! Don't touch me! Never ever, ever touch!" she gasped, her headphone cord dangling pathetically.

"Then maybe you should make sure you can still hear people through those headphones," Aidan replied dryly, already out of sympathy for the day. "Come on. You're coming with us to the sector base to pick up all your...purchases."

Tweak rolled her eyes, turning in her coding chair. "Already said sorry, okay? J-Jesus."

"On your feet, Tweak. Now," Aidan snapped. Over the last few days the girl had seriously begun to strain his patience. He had barely had time for anything beyond cleaning up her mess and trying to sort Kevin's credentials. He was trying his best, but it was wearing. He wasn't entirely certain what he might do if she kept pushing his buttons and mouthing off right now.

Tweak's black eyes went flat. "Fuck. You." She snapped her head back to her console. "Came. Here. To. Work. Not your dog. Not your bitch. I work, you pay me, that's it. The hell I'm going to—"

"Perhaps you'd like to apologize to the man in the infirmary because of you."

Commander and coder glanced up at the lean figure in the doorway.

"The hell?" Tweak demanded, black hair swinging.

"There's a man with a bullet in his leg and one in his back, because you wanted a crate of vodka." Kevin stated quietly, his thin face empty of emotion. "You hear a lot in my line of work. If it were me, I'd feel the need to pay my respects. But, you'll do as you see fit, I'm sure."

Tweak's knuckles went white on the faux leather of the seat. "Got shot?"

"For your treats," Kevin agreed coolly. "Yes."

Tweak's entire body seemed to flinch. Carefully, she disconnected her headphones, turned off her console and stood. "He okay?"

"You'll have to judge that for yourself when you see him," Kevin stated distantly, turning on his heel. "Commander, Dozer's got the truck ready. Topher's going to drive us."

Aidan turned to thank Kevin, but the man was already gone. Damn it. Were they ever going to have a minute to talk and work things out, or had he really shot this relationship in the face? Honestly, he wouldn't be surprised if he'd permanently screwed up.

That was why he hadn't had a relationship since he transitioned. He always fucked it up. And that was an intrusive thought brought on by stress. Okay. No time for that bullshit.

He took a deep breath, tugged the wrinkles out of his shirt and glanced over his shoulder at Tweak. "We're leaving in five minutes. I expect you to be on that truck."

"Yeah." Tweak's word was a whisper. "Okay."

Aidan nodded and headed for the motor pool, his boots thudding on the pre-fab floor. In minutes, he, Kevin and Topher were crammed into their one working truck, Topher in the driver's seat and Aidan sitting beside Kevin, their shoulders pressed together to make room. Tweak squeezed herself into a ball on the other seat, tab in her lap and 'buds in her ears.

It was a long ride. At first, they chatted and joked with Topher.

Kevin tried to plug in his music player and was forced to defend rock music yet again, which made Topher put in his 'buds. When he stopped talking, silence fell. Tweak hadn't moved in her seat or looked up from her tab since they left. Journey's soft playing didn't shut out the silence in the cab.

Aidan breathed in the silence, trying not to let it weigh on him. It was hard. With the others engrossed in their activities, it was just him, Kevin and the cold gap between them. His hands were tight on the arm rests as they bumped through the Dust. Several times he started to try for a conversation, but the words stuck in his throat like pieces of glass. The truck juddered over another rock.

"These people are my family, you know." Kevin's voice was a jolt in the silence, quiet as it was. "Did you really think I'd risk their lives for baubles and treats?"

Aidan stared at the scuffed seat in front of him. When he spoke, the words came out disjointed. "I don't know, Kev. I didn't want to believe it, but... Well, I'd thought Tweak was past her 'hacking our own files for the hell of it' phase and didn't... With Shultz screaming at me right then, I just..." He sighed and shook his head, "I was scared that I would tell myself it couldn't be you, because you're my. . . because it's you."

"I thought you knew me better than that." Kevin's voice was almost a whisper.

"I've known you for less than six months," Aidan replied just as quietly. After a moment he added, "People do stupid things, Kev. I'm sure no exception. And I... Well, I've had shit judgment in relationships my whole life. Part of me just-just figured I'd had my time with you and it was over. Good things don't last."

Kevin let out a long, slow sigh. "Aidan. You're an idiot, you know that?"

Despite himself, Aidan smiled weakly. "Yeah. Been told that before. It's a goddamn miracle I made Commander."

Kevin stared out the window. "I'd die before I hurt the people I love. For future reference."

"Good to know," Aidan muttered. Watching Kevin's profile, he sighed. "Kev, I-I'm sorry. For what it's worth. I just...didn't think clearly."

"Obviously," Kevin rejoined, ice in his voice. Then he sighed. "Maybe I should apologize as well. But damn it all, Aidan, that hurt. Rather a lot. I thought you trusted me."

Aidan's hands ached from gripping the arm rests. He forced his grip to loosen a bit and focused his eyes on movement as Topher flipped the windshield wipers on for the little good it did against the dust. His voice was barely audible over the sound of the truck rumbling on the rough ground.

"I do. I mean, I want to. So much. You're one of a very small group of people who know what my parents named me. I'm so fucking used to people I trust stabbing me in the back, or going batshit, or—or whatever, that I just... I guess I just assumed you'd be like all the others, eventually. And that—that's my fault, not yours. I'm sorry. Really, I am."

A hand rested on his thigh. "Can you learn to trust me in time?" Pebbles rattled and pinged against the passenger side window, nearly drowning Kevin's quiet words. "Do you want to?"

Aidan peeled one hand off the arm rest and wrapped his fingers around Kevin's. Even that small touch was comforting after days of distance. "Can you be patient with me?"

"Yes." The word was just loud enough to hear. Kevin's fingers squeezed his. When he spoke again, his tone had nearly returned to normal. "Trust me, by this point I'm an aficionado of delayed gratification."

Aidan chuckled weakly, trying for one of those word plays Kevin liked so much. "A lot of which comes from my hand. Lucky you."

It sounded stupid, but Kevin's finely cut lips turned up in the tiniest of smiles. "If you'll come to my room tonight, we'll see about whose hand does what."

"That sounds like I'm in for it," Aidan added quietly, though a wry smile curved his lips. He risked a quick glance down the seat at his oblivious charge, glanced at his preoccupied junior transport specialist, and had to fight the urge to lean over and kiss Kevin right then. He had been so damn certain they were over. Now… now there was still hope.

Kevin caught his eyes and smiled, a real smile instead of the brittle thing he'd been substituting for days. He winked. "It gets rocky up ahead. Hang on tight."

Event File 35
File Tag: Course Correction
Timestamp: 11:00-9-18-2155

They arrived at the hub compound without fanfare, piling out under the slick tarp in time for Shultz to come bustling up.

"You took your time. Inside, now, you're expected."

"What an honor," Kevin quipped dryly.

Shultz eyed him. "Don't push it McIllian. You're already in deep."

"Good thing I know how to swim then, isn't it?" Kevin replied tartly. The older man's frown deepened.

Aidan tried not to wince. Well this was getting off to a great start already.

He glanced at Tweak as they stepped out of their transport. "Tweak. Come with us, will you? I think you should be part of this debrief. Topher, you can hang out with their motor pool guys if you want, or come along, but it's going to be a lot of yelling. Heads up."

"Do I got—" Tweak began, but fell silent under three sets of staring eyes. She tugged her heavy leather jacket's collar up around her throat. "Whatever," she muttered, falling into step.

"Good luck!" Topher called behind them.

Aidan repressed a snort. Luck. Yeah right. Aidan stayed beside Kevin, two steps behind Shultz, and focused on his breathing. Magnum knew him. Magnum knew about Tweak. *Look on the bright side,* he told himself. *Nobody's allowed to punch you any longer. They can shout at you, they can make your life hell, they can even demote you. But they can't touch you.*

Stepping into his commander's office, he saluted crisply. "Commander Magnum, sir."

The big man looked up, surveyed the little group and gave a long, slow sigh. "Well, that explains everything. I was wondering. McIllian? I guess you got hacked. Insubordination I expect from you, but not stupidity."

"Thank you, sir." Kevin replied, bland as milk.

Magnum turned to Aidan with tired eyes. "I'll find another base for the girl this week. Or are you turning her over for decommissioning and drop off?"

Tweak's shoulders hunched.

"With all due respect, sir," Aidan replied quickly, "I didn't bring her here to get rid of her."

Magnum's black brows rose. "Really. After a stunt like this?"

Aidan shrugged. "I told her she had a spot with the Wildcards, sir, and I've taken that to heart. She needs a bit more polishing, but I have no doubt she'll make a fine addition to the team. I just brought her out here to remind her of some things. If it's clear with you, I want her to meet the injured and figure out what she can do to repay this sector."

Every eye turned on Tweak, staring down at her boots.

After a breath, Magnum cleared his throat. "Well, Headly. You are sure about this?"

Aidan swallowed a slightly hysterical laugh. Sure about it? Oh hell no. But he knew Tweak wouldn't make it anywhere else, and all of the Dusters were screwed if they lost her talent. He forced himself to nod. "Yes, sir."

He turned as Tweak stepped forward. But she kept her eyes on her boots and her voice, when she spoke, was tiny. "I wanna see him. Guy got shot. Pay dues."

"In a minute, Tweak," Aidan agreed quietly. He looked back to Magnum. "Before that, sir, are my logistics officer and I off the shit list? And is there anything you can think of that Tweak can do to help repay her debt?"

Magnum looked between them for a long, long handful of heartbeats. Then his lips twitched under his brush of a mustache. "I'll have your new credentials in an hour, McIllian. And, Headly? I'm impressed. As for what you can do, Miss Tweak? I want easy-use back doors into the Net for every commander in the Sector by the end of the month. Untraceable."

Tweak shrugged. "Sure. Then I figure out code scrambles for sur-r-r-rv-veilence. QR code. Print on c-clothes. You guys asshats. Walk around like targets. Fix. I go now?"

Magnum held up a finger. "I also want a researched discussion of command etiquette and protocol with reference to what it does for morale and compound cohesion. By next week."

Tweak made a face, opened her mouth, then caught Aidan's eye and sighed. "Yeah. Whatever. Okay."

Aidan nodded and gave Magnum a grateful look and another salute. Thank God for this guy. A few months ago Aidan had hated his guts for putting him in the middle of this. Now he realized how lucky he was.

"Thank you, sir. Will that be all, sir?"

"Dismissed," the older man agreed. "And, Headly?" he added just before Aidan filed out behind his men.

Aidan turned. "Sir?"

Magnum tipped his head slowly." Nice job."

Aidan smiled tightly and nodded. "Thank you, sir. Let's hope it pays off."

His Sector Commander's lips twitched. He waved a heavy hand. "Go catch up to your people. I don't want that girl loose in here."

Aidan caught up just as Tweak warily stepped into the hub compound's med bay. "Um, gonna sit with Winston?" she eked out in the direction of the medic on duty.

The medic gave her a startled look, then caught Aidan's eye over her shoulder. Aidan gave the man a nod and a thumbs up. The medic smiled and pointed to a bed in one corner. "Over here folks."

"We'll wait back here," Aidan added, leaning on the wall and pulling out his tab. Beneath his lashes, he watched Tweak walk forward.

Winston was a small, dark man. Sitting in the medical bed swathed in white sheets and a flimsy medical gown, he looked even smaller. He glanced up from his tab as the stranger approached and blinked at her. "Uh. Hi. Commander says I'm on med leave for another week, so I really can't help out on anything."

"No, I…" Tweak stared at her boots. Then she gasped in a breath and jerked her head up. "I'm off the base with the d-dumb fuck who g-got y-y-you shot. We c-came to say sorry. See how you w-w-were. Felt b-bad."

Winston shrugged against his pillows. "Nah. I'm the one got myself shot. Should've dropped the goods and ran when I had the chance, 'stead of trying to drag it out. But, thanks."

Tweak shrugged. "Um, you w-want a c-couple b-b-b-bottles? H-help y-you feel g-g-good."

Winston blinked at her, then laughed. "Yeah? Never had vodka before. You from somewhere all high-up? You had stuff that expensive before? Hundred and fifty bucks a bottle, can you believe it?"

"That? That's nothing." Tweak waved a hand. "W-wine? Four thousand fifty a b-bottle. Stole one once."

Aidan filled out paperwork and listened as Winston whistled in appreciation. "Seriously? Was it good, or just over-priced?"

Glancing up, he caught Tweak making a face. "Eeugh. Tasted, put water in, sealed lid, sold it. That tells you."

"Think you can get me some one of these days?" Winston asked with a grin. "Love to taste it, just once. My folks used to swear by it. Always said they wanted to find a way to make real wine out here in the Dust someday."

Tweak raised her eyes to his, giving him a small smile. "Get you a b-b-bottle two w-weeks."

"Seriously? Hot damn. Wish we could work that fast up here!" His grin grew wider and he laughed, until the wound in his back pulled and he winced instead.

Aidan gave up pretending to do paperwork and watched as Tweak's smile faded. She licked her lips. "W-W-Winston? S-seriously. S-sorry."

"S'okay," the man in the bed replied, shifting in an effort to relieve some of the pressure on his back. "I made it home. Did the job, got home in basically one piece. Good run. But thanks."

"Yeah," Tweak agreed quietly. "S-sure. I g-gotta g-go. Leave your b-bottles with someb-b-body? Who?"

"Uh, Jack. My brother. Looks just like me, can't miss him." Winston smiled weakly. "Thanks."

Tweak shrugged. "Yeah. I owe you."

She was quiet on the drive home, and her tab stayed in its bag. She was still quiet when they pulled the truck in and started unloading her goods.

She started to lift a box. Then she set it down, straightening. "Boss?"

"Yeah?" Aidan asked, heaving a crate onto one shoulder. He watched as patiently as he could while Tweak glanced everywhere but at him.

Finally, she gasped in a breath." Not l-like b-b-before. C-can't just c-c-code and g-get stuff l-like b-b-b-before." She gave a tiny laugh. "G-gonna suck."

Aidan dredged up a small smile. Jerking his head, he sidestepped into a quieter part of the garage. The girl followed him. "I guess it will suck for a while," he agreed quietly. "And you're going to have to learn to hide your shipments better if you want special stuff. You're a great coder. Now you just need to learn how to be a decent Duster."

Slowly, Tweak nodded. "Guess. You mean that shit?"

"Which shit now?" Aidan asked, wishing like hell the girl had a clearer way of speaking.

"Said it to your boss," Tweak explained haltingly. "Fine ad-d-ddition to team. Said you was keeping us. Said you w-wanted us."

"Yeah," Aidan agreed, holding her eyes as he nodded, "I meant it."

She cracked a tiny grin, tossing her head in a little 'I wasn't worried anyway' gesture. "You guys need me anyway. Need to get over y-yourselves. I help."

Aidan shook his head, but he couldn't help a tiny smile in reply. "Yeah. Maybe. Just start doing that like Lazarus and the girls do, not by ordering half a ZonCom warehouse. Deal?"

Tweak jerked her head in a nod. "Deal."

<u>Event File 36</u>
<u>File Tag: Reciprocity</u>
<u>Timestamp: 22:00-9-18-2155</u>

Long after lights out, Aidan knocked hesitantly on Kevin's door. The bottle of Tweak's vodka was slippery in his hand. He hoped his body heat hadn't melted the chocolate bar in his jacket pocket. He did his best to breathe normally. Kevin had invited him. He shouldn't be this nervous. They'd done this a dozen times by now.

But not yet after a fight.

The door opened, and Kevin leaned against the doorframe, studying his lover. "Good to see you," he remarked, but his smile didn't quite reach his wary grey eyes.

Aidan's smiled felt weak and crooked. He hoped it looked honest. He lifted the bottle and chocolate bar. "Can I come in?"

Kevin's lips quirked, and he opened the door fully. "Who am I to deny the requests of a superior officer?"

"Are you letting me in because I'm your commander or because I'm your boyfriend?" Aidan asked as lightly as he could as he stepped into the familiar room. It should have been comforting to be allowed in here again, to smell Kevin's aftershave and watch the light from the screen showing old paintings wash everything in soft colors. Instead, he felt like a mouse creeping into a cat's lair.

Kevin closed the door, his back still turned. "Boyfriend? Is that what I am to you?"

"Yeah?" Aidan managed, his heart hammering in his throat, "At least, that was what I thought. Did you think... something else?"

Kevin was silent for too many heartbeats, standing rigid against the door. "You know where I grew up, they used to tell all the girls 'never date the boss'." His laugh sounded brittle. "I suppose now I know why. Things become rather complicated, don't they?"

Aidan bit his lip and shifted, unsure whether he ought to sit on the edge of the bed or stay standing, if he was going to stay or be told to leave. He swallowed, licked his lips and forced the words out. "They don't have to be. I never meant to complicate things."

Kevin's sigh seemed loud. He leaned his forehead against the door. Silence thickened in the small room.

When Kevin spoke, his words were strangled. "You really think that little of me? You really believed I'd be that reckless? That selfish?"

Aidan closed his eyes instead of watching Kevin's back, tracing the tight shoulders with his eyes again and again. His hand tightened on the bottle of vodka. "I didn't know what to think, Kev. I wanted to talk it over with you before I made any judgments, but Schultz kept screaming at me and I just got overwhelmed and let the bastard talk me into it. I was—Like I said. I was scared I'd be acting biased if I didn't consider it."

Kevin's eyes, when he turned, were a little too bright behind his glasses. "I put my life on the line every day for my base. For nearly a decade. And tomorrow, I'll get up and do it again. Did you think I do it for fun? Because it's a job? What? I'm not—" He opened his mouth to say more, but looked away. "Sorry. I thought I'd let this mess go, but..." He shrugged helplessly. "I know you're stressed. But damn it, Aidan. If you can believe that of me, what am I to you?"

A lump grew in Aidan's throat. He set the vodka and chocolate on the floor and closed the distance between them, hesitantly taking both of Kevin's hands in his. "You're the man who's doing a damn fine job keeping me from going batshit." He watched his thumb tracing circles on Kevin's skin instead of meeting his lover's gaze. "You're the only person on this base who... who sees the real me. You're the man I desperately want to talk with when I'm off duty, and laugh with, and kiss, and take to bed. You're the man I'm so fucking afraid of—of being with, because you're too damn good for me, and I'm going to screw it up. I know I screwed up, Kev, and I'm so, so sorry. If I can fix this, I will, but... Can you forgive me?"

There was a heartbeat's silence. "If you—if you feel like that about me, can you try to believe in me?" Kevin's voice was almost a whisper.

Aidan nodded and forced his eyes up to Kevin's face. "Of course. I just might need a kick in the ass for a bit." He tried to smile.

Kevin's lips turned up, tremulous. Taking a shaky breath, he leaned in and brushed his lips over Aidan's. "I'm sure something to put in your ass will make itself available as required."

"I was hoping so," Aidan replied quietly, squeezing Kevin's hands. His smile strengthened just a little. "I brought booze and chocolate. Figured we might need a wind-down, and we dragged the stuff all back here."

"That'd be nice," Kevin agreed, pulling off his glasses and polishing them. This time, Aidan used the chance to step in and put his arms around Kevin's waist, resting his head on Kevin's shoulder instead of letting Kevin use that thing with his glasses to distance himself.

"Sorry about that." Kevin murmured, leaning his warmth into Aidan's. "I'm afraid I'm rather too attached to the concept of my own moral virtue. It's a bit of a tender spot. I guess you noticed."

Aidan smiled into the crook of Kevin's neck, wrapping his arms around the other man. "Yeah. Come on. We might as well enjoy this stuff while we have it."

"True," Kevin agreed, kissing the top of Aidan's head. "And you know, I've never had decent vodka before."

"Me, either," Aidan agreed. He forced himself to step back as the other man replaced his glasses and meet Kevin's gaze. After a long moment, he swallowed. "Kev, I... Can you really forgive me? I don't— I don't want to lose you."

Kevin smiled, the low light catching in his eyes. "I'm standing right here. If you... When you want me, I'll be standing right here."

Aidan smiled in relief and leaned in to kiss him. When Kevin returned the kiss, the smile widened into more of a smirk. "Maybe you'd rather lie down over there, huh?"

Kevin cocked a brow, his smile turning sly. "Hm, propositions already. And the man hasn't gotten me a single drink yet. Well." He leaned in, kissing Aidan long and slow this time. "I suppose the man's rather intoxicating himself."

Aidan chuckled and pulled Kevin closer. "They say sex is better when you're making up. I figured we could give it a shot when we crack open the vodka."

"You do make a convincing argument." Kevin brushed his fingers through Aidan's hair. "By the way, 'boyfriend's' a pretty intoxicating word by itself. You sure you meant to use it?"

Aidan's breath caught. Was he sure? "I guess we'll have to find out."

Kevin's lips traced his throat, fingers twined in Aidan's hair gently tipping his head back. Kevin's other hand pressed against the small of Aidan's back, holding their bodies against one another.

"I'll be looking forward to aiding you in reaching your conclusions," Kevin whispered against his skin. "Now, what was that about lying down?"

"What was that about something up my ass?" Aidan parried.

Kevin blinked. "Really? You want to?"

"Yeah," Aidan agreed with a smile. "I want to."

He didn't, not really. He remembered how it felt being entered. It felt like hell. It felt like being turned into somebody else's toy. But he remembered how much Sam had loved it. If Kevin liked this, it was worth doing to pay him back for doubting him.

"But I want to do it our way, okay? Like men," he added, wishing so much that he didn't have to say that.

Kevin swallowed, his cheekbones flushed pink. Then he nodded, his smile soft. "Well, you do happen to be a man, Aidan. I hadn't considered anything else."

Aidan's chest expanded. Kevin would never know how adorable he was when he lost that suave act he put on and got sweet. And Aidan was never going to be able to do something big enough to repay him for what he'd just said.

Tentatively, Kevin stepped forward and wrapped his arms around Aidan, kissing him. Their bodies leaned into one another. Kevin gently walked them until Aidan's shins were pushed against his bed. Setting his glasses aside, he shucked his jacket, then his shirt.

"Shall we have that drink?"

Aidan knelt and lifted the bottle. Kevin cracked the seal and took a sip.

"Well, at least the little monster has taste."

Aidan accepted it and tasted. The silky smooth liquor washed down his throat. It didn't taste good—it didn't taste like anything really—but it felt good. Kevin's warm lips sealed his.

"Where'd that chocolate bar get to?" Kevin asked against his skin.

"I can get it." Aidan murmured.

Kevin's lips lifted in a smile. "Mm. I think we can put it to rather good use."

Anticipation thrilled through Aidan. Whatever Kevin was thinking, the way he said the words made him willing to give it a try. He set the chocolate bar on the bed, and Kevin's hands were pulling off his shirt. Aidan only stopped him when Kevin reached for the zipper of his binder.

"Not tonight," he breathed. For what he wanted to do tonight, he wanted Kevin looking at him. And if Kevin was looking at him, he wanted Kevin to see him as he wanted to be.

"Mm?" Kevin murmured into another kiss. "Going to be uncomfortable, isn't it?"

"These new ones you got me I could sleep in," Aidan deflected, only half lying. "I want it on for the next bit."

"Sounds like we both have plans," Kevin whispered against his skin, chuckling. "Let's see how they interrelate, shall we?"

Aidan didn't bother answering with words. His fingers undid Kevin's jeans. Leaning over, Kevin grabbed another sip of vodka and kissed Aidan again, sliding his tongue skillfully into Aidan's mouth so the feel of the drink filled him again.

Aidan's belly tensed. He slid Kevin's pants down as Kevin did the same for him.

"Lie down," Kevin whispered when they were both mostly naked. "Just here on the edge of the bed. Let your legs hang off."

Aidan agreed with a murmur, lying back and feeling Kevin follow him down, still kissing him, stroking his hair, fingers running along his throat and down his body. Then Kevin pulled away a little. There was a sound of tearing paper, and Aidan opened his eyes to watch Kevin carefully break off four tiny pieces of chocolate.

Leaning down, he slid one between Aidan's lips, sealing it there with a soft kiss. The taste of chocolate filled Aidan's mouth, and this was the real stuff. He could have gotten lost in that alone, but Kevin was laying the second piece on his collar bone, and the third in his navel. The last he rested just above Aidan's dick. The touch made his body twang.

Kevin gave him one last wicked smile before he lowered his head. He nibbled at Aidan's collar bone. His tongue dipped into Aidan's navel, and Aidan gasped. Then the trail of soft kisses reached his dick.

Kevin raised his head where he knelt between Aidan's legs. His eyes were the color of rain-soaked pavement. "Ever done it like this?"

Aidan snorted. "Haven't done much of anything before you."

Kevin smiled. "Well, then. You put your feet on the edge of the bed, and I do the rest."

Aidan rested his feet where Kevin placed them. For once, his breathing was ragged for a good reason. Good? Screw that. A great reason.

Kevin reached out one arm and pulled the lube bottle from its usual place. With another one of his quick, wicked grins, he lowered his head and started to lick.

Aidan could barely breathe. Before, when somebody had told him what to do in bed he'd felt dirty. This time, he felt so alive. Every muscle in his body felt like the vodka had gotten into it, making him bright and crystal clear inside.

The lid of the lube bottle popped. Warm, wet fingers slid between his cheeks to tease him. Kevin's lips teased him. Then one finger slid inside.

Aidan sucked in a breath and squeezed his eyes shut. Everything he'd thought about how it would feel to be penetrated went out the window. He'd thought he was going to hate it. He had hated it before. But this wasn't someone ramming into him for their fun and ignoring him as a person. Kevin was all about paying attention. He kept everything so slow, so slow, and he made it feel so good. He teased until Aidan was shaking before he slid a second finger inside.

Aidan tried and failed to stop a whimper. He could feel his body stretching, new sensations zinging through him to mix into the familiar ones of a building orgasm.

Kevin added a third wet finger, and his mouth worked Aidan's dick harder.

Aidan tensed and squeaked as pleasure rocketed through him, turning his vision to black and making him curl his fingers desperately in the sheets.

But Kevin didn't stop, not until Aidan cried out and thrust against his hold twice, not until he shuddered and fell back on the bed. Kevin stood, nestling his length to Aidan's. His dick twitched and pulsed against Aidan's hip. "Now I understand you have a plan for the rest of the night?" Kevin's voice had taken on that low tone he only got in bed.

Aidan grinned. "Can you hand me the lube?" he asked in a breathless whisper. His vision was starting to come back, but all he could think about was how good it would feel to have Kevin inside him the second time around.

"Here," Kevin murmured, pressing the bottle against his fingers, "No rush." His shaft made a liar out of him by twitching against Aidan's leg.

Aidan rolled over and dabbed the slick gel onto his palm. Then he rolled back and stroked his hand up Kevin's erection, slathering the lube as he went. Kevin groaned, and he loved it.

He took a long moment to tease with his wet fingers, then swung one leg over Kevin's hips so he lay on top of his boyfriend. He gently guided Kevin's erection inside him, avoiding the goddamned vulva. The entrance ached a little as his body stretched, but it also sent him into pleasant shuddering again.

"Not-not so fast," Kevin gulped out. "You'll hurt your— mmmm—self."

"M'okay," Aidan muttered back, shifting his hips to a different angle. Very carefully, he slid further down Kevin's shaft, wincing just a little and hoping Kevin didn't see it. It felt good once the stretching pain subsided.

Kevin closed his eyes a moment, then opened them, desperately taking in every line of Aidan's face with his eyes as Aidan moved over him. Aidan loved that look so much. This was why he'd kept his binder on. He'd wanted Kevin to stare at him like this as he let Aidan ride him, to look up with that complete, honest abandon Aidan only saw on his face just before he lost it and see Aidan above him.

Kevin's eyes widened, nearly black in the room's low light. "Aidan." The word was a hitched moan.

"Yeah?" Aidan whispered as he began to slide himself back and forth a little faster. He'd never get over hearing his own name said like that. He lowered his head to kiss Kevin deeply, not giving him a chance to respond to his breathy question. He knew that once he had come, it would be easy as shit to make him come again—one of the very few benefits to still having a bit of female in him—and he was certain that Kevin getting off would probably send him over the edge again, too.

Perfect.

Below him Kevin was panting, his hips rocking. His hands gripped Aidan's arms. "Aidan, please, please!" he gasped out.

Aidan laughed without breath and shifted, until Kevin sank even deeper into him. He clenched around Kevin as his own body gave out again, shuddering and rocking uncontrollably.

Kevin cried out beneath him, body bowing up into Aidan's, heat and pressure and pleasure all slamming into him in a rush. They rode the skyrocketing orgasm out together.

Slowly, Kevin's body relaxed under him, until he lay panting for air. "Oh, my God."

Aidan let himself drape over Kevin's chest, gasping for air as the last of his shuddering pleasure dissipated. He hummed happily and shifted to let Kevin slip free from his body while pressing himself closer. Quietly, he murmured, "Thank you."

"I'm... the one who just got... taken for the best ride of my life. Who's... thanking who... now?" Kevin managed, just barely coherent as he flopped limp arms around Aidan's body.

"You forgave me," Aidan whispered.

Kevin's chest moved with a soft laugh. "Yes, well. I was trying to figure out how to express that. That's why I didn't say anything for a while. Couldn't find the right words."

Aidan snorted. "You're the guy with all the words, if you can't figure out the right ones we're screwed."

Kevin sighed. "Let's get cleaned up?"

When they were clean again and lying in each other's arms, Aidan listened to Kevin's heart beating. His binder was starting to bug him, but he could ignore it a little longer.

"About words..." Kevin murmured, and Aidan snuggled against him.

"Yeah?"

"The words people use. For each other." He heard Kevin draw in a breath before he spoke. "Everything people use is so lewd. Date, lay, partner, fuck, toy, 'friend', screw. The connotations are either vile or imprecise. Even lover, which should be beautiful, it's gotten a tarnish. It's the word people use to describe sexual indiscretion, not love."

Aidan's brow furrowed. "Kev, is this going somewhere?"

When Kevin spoke again, his whisper was soft. "Boyfriend was the only word I wanted to use. But I didn't think I had the right."

Aidan's heart ached at the sound of that whisper. Leaning up, he brushed his lips over Kevin's. "Use it."

Kevin let out a breath. "Okay."

"You really thought about which word to use that much?" Aidan asked, tracing Kevin's jaw with his lips. Kevin gave a quiet laugh. "You think this is bad, when I was eighteen and the crew had got me out of my shell a bit, I had a date tell me 'man, you're a pretty good fuck.' He meant it as a compliment. I didn't touch another man for the rest of the year. Those words made me feel so. . . *polluted*. So dirty."

"How do you feel now?" Aidan asked softly.

Kevin's arms tightened around him. "Like somebody's boyfriend," Kevin whispered.

Aidan grinned. "My boyfriend." He kissed Kevin's temple. "My boyfriend needs to go to sleep."

"Mm." Kevin agreed, already halfway there.

Holding his boyfriend close, Aidan unzipped his binder with one hand and closed his eyes.

Event File 37
File Tag: Weather Warning
Timestamp: 14:00-10-14-2155

"Come on, come on. We're gonna miss the ch-ch-chance!" Tweak yapped, standing beside the bikes across the garage.

Yvonne gave Kevin a look, brows raised. "Y'know I can take Sarah and get her out there, let you get back to routine runs."

"Yes, but routine isn't what they pay me for," Kevin replied quietly. "If a month's work for two divisions is going to go down the drain, it really ought to be on the officer's head."

"You don't trust her," Yvonne observed.

"However much she may have sworn her allegiance and her reformation after that mess she caused a month ago, no. I don't trust her," Kevin agreed. "But apparently she's staying. and Aidan keeps telling me to give her a chance, and I'll admit her work is good. The possibilities for this tech she's been working on are fairly stellar. Therefore, I'll coordinate the route and keep an eye on her, personally, for the sake of my own sanity. Call it my gesture of goodwill."

"Come on!" Tweak whined, and Kevin tried not to grimace.

Yvonne sighed. Reaching over, she patted his shoulder. "Just don't lose it with her. She's kind of a good kid under the street junk and the Corps junk."

Kevin rolled his eyes. "Oh, lovely. You, too?"

Yvonne gave him a smirk. "Kev, you know you acted kind of like her when you first got here, right?"

Kevin gave her a dry look. "I highly doubt that."

Yvonne opened her mouth to retort, but Kevin stepped away and crossed the garage. "Right, Tweak. I'll drive."

Grabbing her a poncho off the peg and disconnecting it from its charger, he tossed it to her and pulled his own off. "Get that and your helmet on, store your gear in the back box, and you can hang on behind me."

Tweak caught the poncho in midair and stood staring at it for a moment before snapping her head up. "I'll take that one," she stated sharply, pointing at another bike.

"Tweak, look at the controls. These aren't Go equipped," Kevin replied cooly as he pulled on his poncho. "If you can drive manual and I haven't been informed, feel free to correct me."

Tweak froze. "I'll walk," she muttered after a moment, tugging the poncho on.

Kevin resisted the urge to roll his eyes. Maybe Yvonne had been right. Maybe she ought to be the one to go out with Tweak. He didn't have the patience to deal with this.

"Tweak, it's forty-five miles. You can't walk."

The tiny girl glared at him. If looks could kill, he'd be dead, but Aidan had asked him to try to give the little beast a reason to act like part of their family. And he had said he'd try. Damn it.

Attempting a new tack, Kevin held up the edge of his slick poncho and the heat gloves. They were coming into the cooler part of the year, but better to wear them than not. "I understand that you don't want to be touched, but take a look at what we'll be wearing out there. This stuff is quite thick. Nobody feels anything through it."

Warily, Tweak reached out and felt the corner of the poncho. She gave a quiet grunt. "I guess." Turning, she lifted her helmet, the poncho nearly down to her ankles and barely held up by her small shoulders.

An hour later they were lying in the yellow grass, watching a tiny black box and the mercifully grey sky above it. "Come on, come on, come on, come on."

Kevin heard Tweak whispering in a staccato mantra through his helmet's mic. Kevin was almost whispering it beside her as they lay watching the delivery drone they'd picked out buzz along its trajectory, a box in its articulated grip. All the special runs and barter deals he'd done in addition to his usual duties to get to this point would be wasted if this didn't work. All the care he'd put into getting the little coder out here to run her test safely would be wasted.

He glanced at the readout in the corner of his HUD. "Tweak, we've got twenty minutes before we've got to head to the next test site. There's a ViperDrone pass-over and a satellite twenty minutes after that."

"I know, I know. C-come on, you f-fucker. Move y-your ass," Tweak whispered, her controller gripped in her hand. Under the drone's trajectory, her infrared emitter lay like a crouched predator.

The drone passed over it. Tweak sucked in a breath and hit the controller's button. Kevin hit 'record' on the control panel inlaid in his glove, and a flashing green light steadied into record mode in the corner of his helmet's HUD.

For a split second, Kevin was sure that it had failed. The drone flew on. Then it stumbled in the air. It wobbled. It flew in a circle. It lumbered around and headed back the way it had come.

"Did it...?" Kevin began, but Tweak was up and running to her device, grabbing it up and hugging it like a pet. Standing carefully, Kevin watched her as she bounced up and down in delight, looking like a little kid who'd just won the spelling bee.

"Yes, yes, yes! Yes! Yes! It w-worked!" she yelled as she scrambled back to him, her slick poncho flapping around her tiny body. "It w-worked! It w-w-w-worked!"

"I saw," Kevin agreed, unable to keep from smiling himself, half in amazement. This crazy idea had actually worked. Unbelievable.

"It worked!" Tweak crowed again, grinning up at him as she bounced on her toes, cradling her creation. Then she broke and dashed for their bike. "Let's go let's go next test site I wanna see! Wanna d-double check!"

Grinning, Kevin pulled the bike's slick tarp off. "All right, hang on, it gets rocky ahead."

He barely felt the pressure of her arms around his waist through the layers of two slick ponchos. As a bonus, his assurance had proven correct. She didn't panic about touch with this much fabric between them.

This time it was a small red and white drone with a bag. It spun in a dizzy circle when it caught Tweak's infrared encoded signal before flying back the way it had come.

Tweak whooped, punching the air joyfully. "Yes! Yes! Hell y-yes!" She shouted so loud that the mic in Kevin's helmet crackled. He'd never seen her smile for more than a second. She was usually ready to take your head off at a moment's notice. And yet here she was yelling for joy. He could barely believe it.

Had this happy little girl been hiding behind Tweak's viciousness all the time? Was that how she'd survived? Maybe everyone else had been right.

Tweak was still laughing when she got back into her seat. "I g-gotta tell Billie! She's g-g-gonna freak!"

"You can tell her all about it when we get back, and—" Kevin started to say when his HUD flashed bright red.

Behind him, Tweak yelped. "The fuck was *that*?"

"Weather warning." Kevin replied tightly, blinking twice to bring up the readout.

WARNING. WARNING. HAILSTORM IMMINENT. WARNING. WARNING.

"Bloody hell. Hang on tight," Kevin spat, and gunned the engine.

"Hey! Wrong way!" Tweak's voice crackled in his ear.

"I'll explain when we're safe," Kevin snapped in reply. "Just shut up and hold on." He pushed the engine to eighty, swerving around rocks and running the bike for all he was worthwhile he hunted for some protection, any protection.

There, an up-thrust of red rock like a dead giant's spine. It'd do.

"Hang on!" he snapped into his mic, and gunned the bike up and in.

Tweak screamed like a crow in his ear. And then they were into a crevasse and safe. Breathing hard, Kevin cut the engine and glanced over his shoulder. The cloud front was already racing across the sky, darkening the land.

"The fuck was that?" Tweak demanded, yanking off her helmet, "You fucking nuts or—"

CRACK

Overhead, thunder split the sky as the first of the hailstones came down. Gravel and rock sprayed up as balls of ice that would fill both Kevin's hands if he held one pummeled the ground. Tweak's jaw dropped.

"Never seen a hailstorm before, I take it?" Kevin asked, taking a seat.

Tweak shook her head, standing frozen near the entrance as she watched fury from the heavens. "N-no. "

Watching her, Kevin wondered if he had looked that way the first time he saw the destruction rain down. Bloody hailstorms.

Something this bad could do so much damage to their base. It could play hell with their slick tarps, their solar panels, or the delicate wiring that held all their systems together.

But he couldn't do anything about that now. They'd pick up the mess when they could tell how bad it was. All he could do now was wait.

"This is my third," he remarked from his seat on the gritty rock. "They aren't common, but they do make an impression. Take a seat. This is going to go on for a while."

Pulling out his tab, he saw that a message already blipped on the screen.

Message Handle: QueenOfClubs

Message: You guys safe?

"Liza's checking up on us," he remarked in Tweak's general direction, bringing up his screen and typing a reply.

Message Handle: KingOfHearts

Message: Undercover and doing nicely. You?

The reply came a moment later.

Message Handle: QueenOfClubs

Message: We'll find out when it's over. Keep your heads down. Tell Tweak it's going to be okay.

Over his shoulder, Tweak gave a yap of laughter. "L-liza think's I'm a k-kid."

"Liza thinks we're all about seven," Kevin remarked with a distracted smile as he typed. "She's got a bit of a Big Sister Complex going. Of course, most of us are like siblings to her. We've been together long enough. She and Dozer practically raised Topher."

Message Handle: KingOfHearts

Message: Roger that.

Tweak was silent for a beat. "Where's his folks?"

"Dead," Kevin replied with a shrug, "EagleCorp got them. Don't ask him about it."

"Yeah," Tweak agreed quietly.

Kevin glanced at her as he brought up a game, but she wasn't looking at him. Solitaire began in a flutter of cards.

Tweak's voice was quiet. "How about your folks?"

"Also dead," Kevin replied shortly. "Cavanaugh took them out. It's not something I enjoy discussing."

Silence.

"So that guy, Taylor. He raised you guys."

"Some of us," Kevin agreed, wishing she'd stop talking. "And some of us he helped finish growing up. Why the interest?"

"Way you guys talk about him. All you guys," Tweak stated baldly, shrugging. "It's weird. Weird's bad. People're hiding stuff. H-hidden stuff gets people d-d-dead. So what gives?"

Kevin sighed. "It's not a complex story. He had bone cancer and we couldn't get the therapy he needed. He died."

Silence. "Huh."

"Huh, what?" Kevin asked coldly, his eyes on his digital cards.

"Just, huh," Tweak's high voice replied. "You guys're good at getting shit. All the stuff you got for this test. Food. Clothes. Stuff. You're good."

"Apparently not good enough." Kevin heard the acid in his own voice. He switched the game to Metroid. He needed a real challenge to get his mind off Tweak's words.

The next thing she said almost made him throw the tab at her. "You the one who fucked up, huh?"

Kevin, very quietly, snapped. "Yes, Tweak," he stated, knowing and not caring that his voice was too sharp. "Yes. You win. I was the one who fucked up. I was the one who went eight days without sleep to code every credential we needed. I was the one who stole the proper uniforms and bribed people to take a day off work. I was the one who got my team within a dozen feet of the storage room and the cure we needed, and I was the one who made three coding errors that cost me the commander's treatment package, a bullet in my back, a bullet in my shoulder, a bullet in my best friend's leg and three days in the medbay. I fucked up and it killed the man who took me in, loved me like a son and taught me how to be someone worthwhile. You're right. The clever CES boy is a failure of the most abject kind. I was incompetent and arrogant and, because of it, I killed Commander Taylor. I killed him. "I'm sure you're just thrilled. You were absolutely right all along, and you can tell everyone you meet that Kevin McIllian fucks up so badly that the people who matter most around him die." He ran out of words then, his breath catching in his throat.

Tweak was staring at him like a startled bird.

"Sorry," he managed, dropping his eyes. "That wasn't your fault, or your issue."

A long time later, Tweak cleared her throat. "Asked b-bec-c-cause I sorta get it. My-my issue, too. R-reason s-somebody's d-d-d-dead, too."

Kevin blinked, clearing his eyes of tears that had threatened to escape. "What?"

Tweak gave another one of her signature shrugs. "B-baby brother. My mom. Got s-s-sick. We were broke. S-started s-s-s-sneaking into Techo dump. Found stuff. Fixed it. T-to sell. G-g-g-got me c-c-c-c-c…" She swallowed. "Caught. I w-went to j-j-jail. They d-d-d-died."

Outside the hail rattled down, pounding against the rock. Shards flicked inside to glitter like diamonds before melting. Kevin swallowed down the lump in his throat. "How old were you?"

Tweak's fingers plucked at the hem of her poncho. "'Lleven."

"Eleven?"

"Yeah."

The hail banged down. Kevin's neglected tab went into sleep mode, leaving the crevasse even darker than it had been. Now all Kevin could make out was Tweak's silhouette.

He wondered what he'd act like if he'd been in a detention center since the age of eleven. What he'd be like if he'd gone there knowing his failure had killed his family.

He wondered if he'd be sane at all. After all, look what failing so badly as adults had done to him and his base mates. To go through that as a child…

"Tweak?"

"Yeah?"

"I'm sorry. I didn't know."

Tweak's slender shoulders twitched in a shrug. "I d-didn't say. You d-didn't either."

Kevin smiled weakly. "Touché, Tweak."

The silence between them was brittle. Looking to fill it, Kevin picked up his tab.

"Ever played checkers?"

Tweak shook her head.

Kevin brought up the game. "This is pretty simple."

She was incredibly fast once she understood the rules. Halfway into the game, Kevin glanced up at her face. "Tweak?

"Yeah?"

"From the sound of it, what happened to your family wasn't your fault. I hope you know that."

She stared at him for what felt like ages, then she cocked her head and smirked. "Y-*you* telling *me* don't be g-guilty? Y-you?"

"I'm trying to," Kevin agreed.

Tweak rolled her eyes. "Asshat. Shut up. Play game."

Around the third time Tweak won, the hail let up. They rode slowly back to base, wary of spinning the bike out on the shattered balls of ice and the small potholes they'd begun to melt into. The garage under the slick tarp was unlit. That was Kevin's first warning of disaster. His second was Liza's white face.

"You got to go get us photoelectric cell cradles or the stuff to print them," she rapped out. "We're down to ten percent capacity.

Fucking hail smashed most of the cradles and all the wiring. The power storage unit's only got a five day charge stored for the base. I've got a specialist call out to help Janice once we get the parts, but we need them now."

"Get Yve," Kevin replied in the same tones. "I'll get packed."

Event File 38
File Tag: Fully Functional
Timestamp: 10-18-2155/ 10-19-2155

Kevin didn't remember a lot about the next two days. He had a hundred photoelectric cell attachment cradles and charge controllers to get ahold of. He sent Jim out to the Fringe communities, asked Yvonne to go bartering from base to base, and headed onto the Grid himself.

By day he shopped legitimate home improvement stores and borrowed the credentials of eight different ArgusCo employees to make what appeared to be legitimate deals. By night he cased warehouses, coded and recoded with Tweak's remote help and searched for inroads into shipping schedules in corporation databases.

Every morning, precisely at six, Liza and Janice sent him updates. Their slick tarp was holding. It was being supplemented with Tweak's first base-size transmitter prototype. This one told the ViperDrones that what they saw was just another piece of desert.

They'd shut off the lights and anything else that might drain the power storage unit. Everyone knew what would happen if their slick tarp went down.

Around half past seven, Yvonne and Jim reported in each morning. They'd each scratched up a handful of parts—thirteen cradles, twelve photoelectric plates, a few printer instructions and a few silica and plastics gels for their 3D rig.

Not enough.

Tweak wrote him reports each evening. She had bots out scouring the Net for any hint of any shipment that could help them. He followed every possible lead, anything to do with construction, with fabrication, anything to do with power production stations with possibly a shed full of spares left unguarded.

Nothing.

By the fourth sleepless night, his hands had begun to shake as he typed. It was a distraction he didn't need. StayWake would prevent permanent damage to his brain. That was all that mattered.

He nearly jumped out of his skin when he saw it, scrolling past in an ArgusCo list he'd hacked into.

A new suburb going in near the Copperhead Complex. A truck of supplies being shipped. A semi rig full of photoelectric plates. Enough to use and hand out to everyone else in the Sector. Grinning, he pulled up his Greynet messaging app.

Message Handle: KingOfHearts

Message Authentication x2zß

Message: Bingo. Standby for deets and ETA.

He ran his network mapping program and grabbed the rig's IP address. The rest was simple. It was child's play to get into the rig's damage controls and tell the system it had blown tires. It was easy to tell it to go to a repair station that didn't really exist. Scrambling its GPS was nothing.

Kevin got the message he'd been hoping for at 6am.

Message Handle: NineOfHearts

Message: Struck fucking GOLD :D Come Home. Party time!

Kevin laughed quietly and stood to pack his bags. He almost fell
asleep on the train that took him out as far as a station where he could
slip into the Dust, find the bike and gear he'd hidden and go home. He
noted absently that the lights were on as he stumbled into the base and
walked down the hall, grey eyes too wide in his pale face.

Good sign, he thought distantly. He knew his team wanted to see
him. Everyone would want to see him. They'd want to celebrate. But
that wasn't what he wanted. Peace. He needed peace and quiet and to
get his head down.

He was so tired.

There was a clatter, and a black woman with a toolbox came
slamming out into the hall ahead of him. Catching sight of Kevin, she
froze. He stilled. The woman's eyes narrowed. "Thought for sure *you'd*
be dead by now."

Shit, Kevin's exhausted brain whispered to itself. *Suzanna.*
They'd put out a call for specialist aid. They'd gotten *Suzanna.* The last
thing he needed. "I'm afraid you're doomed to disappointment," he
muttered, brushing past her. She didn't follow to argue, for once. Thank
God for small favors.

Out of her line of sight, he let his feet grow still. Where was he
going?

His room would be empty and cold. No. He couldn't stand that
now. But people? He couldn't stand people. Not noise and demands.
Not now.

Warmth and peace. He tried to think the problem through.
Warmth and peace. Yes. He knew where to go now. Nearly stumbling,
he turned his feet towards Aidan's room and pushed open the door.
Aidan was sitting on the bed, an injector pressed against the inside of
his arm. Kevin smiled weakly when he looked up.

"Hi. Can I come in?"

Aidan stared at him for a moment, eyes widening. Kevin
wondered what kind of mess he must appear to garner such an
expression. His boyfriend fumbled to keep hold of his injector and set it

carefully back on his bedside table before standing and crossing to the door.

"When did you get back? Are you alright?"

"Fine. Did the work. Got the delivery. Just got in," Kevin added, leaning against the doorframe. "Gridbuzz is kind of bad this time. Didn't sleep for four days. I hate that."

"Then you should sleep. I've got insomnia pills if you need them." Aidan kept his voice soft as he twined his fingers between Kevin's. "Your bed's more comfortable than mine. Want me to come back with you?"

"No. Want to be with you," Kevin mumbled, leaning heavily against Aidan, relishing his warmth. "Missed you," he murmured absently into Aidan's chest, head sunk against Aidan's collarbone. "I missed you, too," Aidan muttered. He kicked the door shut behind them and wrapped Kevin in his arms. "Kev, let's get you sat down. D'you need food? Water?"

Kevin tried to walk with his boyfriend, but he found himself leaning more than he'd realized. He flopped onto the bed. "No, just a hard trip. Got it done though," Kevin muttered, sentences choppy as he sat, closing fevered eyes. "Just tired. And Suzanna's here too. I don't need that. Going to raise Cain. Tell me she's leaving soon."

Aidan's hand massaged his back. "She's helping to get the new plates up and working. Sorry, Kev. She's going to be here at least until Monday. But, I'll do my best to keep her away from you, if that's what you need."

"Uh-huh. Otherwise fur flies," Kevin mumbled. He heard the distant, sing-song quality of exhaustion in his words. "She hates me," he added by way of explanation. "For years. Never did get past that."

"I'm sure you'll explain that better to me after you've slept some," Aidan whispered softly. He kissed Kevin's forehead. "Lie down and go to sleep. I'll be right here."

"Mmhmm." Kevin murmured, his body sliding limply into Aidan's lap. "M'kay..."

"Not what I meant," Aidan chuckled, though he didn't move. His touch lulled Kevin, finally, into sleep.

It was light when Kevin woke again. Vials glimmered fuzzily on the dresser in his weak eyesight, catching the sun through the tiny slit window. Beside him, Aidan was just beginning to wake.

"How long was I out?" Kevin asked, stretching, though he made no move to push away the blankets.

"Solid day. Twenty-four hours," Aidan mumbled groggily.

"Damn," Kevin sat up, glancing around. "Where's my glasses? I need to get to—"

"On the dresser," Aidan muttered and rolled over, pulling the blankets tighter around them. "And you don't need to get to anything. You're on recuperative leave and it's Saturday. Everything's set. Janice and her help are down to detail work. You're good, Kev."

His blonde hair tickled Kevin's chin as Aidan laid his head in the crook of Kevin's shoulder, chuckling. "More than good. Hell, you realize you got every base in the area spares and repairs? You know how good you guys made us look?"

"Glad to hear it," Kevin murmured, allowing his fingers to twine themselves in Aidan's hair. "But are you sure we shouldn't get up and—"

Aidan leaned up and kissed him, slow and deep. "You're staying in this bed. End of discussion."

"Yes, sir." Kevin agreed dazedly, a smile on his lips.

Aidan snorted and smacked his shoulder gently. "Brat."

"You were aware of that initially, don't act surprised now," Kevin retorted sleepily, eyelids too heavy to keep open. "Stay with me?"

"Yeah," Aidan agreed, his arms gently enfolding.

The next time Kevin woke, the sun was slanting and he was thirsty. "Did I sleep all day?"

"Yeah. It's around three. Dinner's coming up soon," Aidan agreed softly.

Kevin nodded.

"You need anything?" Aidan's voice was soft.

"Water." Kevin ruffled his red hair as he stretched. "Pass me my glasses?"

Aidan's fingers slid them into his hand.

"You should really think about getting the eyes fixed."

"Personally, I appreciate the reminder that I'm not someone else's design fresh off the assembly line." Kevin replied, slipping them on. "Besides, they're part of my charm." Wincing at the stiffness in his body, he stumbled out of bed. He glanced down at his rumpled Grid clothes with a frown.

"Well these are for the wash." He pumped the foot pedal for the tap at Aidan's sanitation station and used his hands to suck down a few handfuls of water.

"Yesterday, you said there was a problem with the specialist?" Aidan asked behind him.

Kevin studied himself in the mirror. He did look dreadful. It'd take some time before the bags under his eyes faded. "Suzanna? I'll say. Someone at Sector must still be in a snit with us if they sent Suzanna when we asked for aid."

"Are you going to tell me why you think she hates you so much?"

"She used to live on this base, back when I joined up. We were both sixteen and angry," Kevin called back over the sound of the water. "Anyway, she took a dislike to me. I'm erudite; she's uneducated. I once had a good Grid Standing; she's a born Duster. That was enough for her. Oh, and I was a little too loquacious for her tastes, and she a little too prone towards spiteful keyhole peeping and tale-telling for mine. Taylor disciplined her eventually and she requested a base transfer. Good riddance to bad rubbish as the saying goes."

He knew his speech tended to become professorial when he found something distasteful, and he could hear it happening now. But bloody Suzanna did get under his skin. She'd always been looking for reasons to attack him. He knew he hadn't helped by sniping at her.

In the mirror, Kevin watched Aidan sigh and drop back into the pillows. "All I can do is try to keep her at arm's length, Kev. I'm sorry, but she's a great engineer and Janice needed her. She's going home Monday."

"Oh, I've got no problems with her," Kevin shrugged. "I'd as soon ignore her. I just wish she'd do the same."

He splashed his face before turning, shaking his head to complete the waking process. Dusty afternoon light caught in Aidan's hair, making it glow. Kevin couldn't resist. Walking back across the room, he slid back into bed. Aidan smiled, wrapping arms around him. "You scared the shit out of me when you came in."

"You can't write me up for it," Kevin retorted with a soft brush of lips across Aidan's. "That was a perfectly legitimate emergency situation to use StayWake in."

"This time," Aidan pointed out quietly.

"This time," Kevin ceded, kissing him again.

"Feel like helping me out of these clothes?" They wrapped around one another sweet and slow in the golden light. Kevin let Aidan's fingers work the stress out of his body and his mind.

"Liked that thing you did the other night," Aidan whispered against his skin. "We don't have chocolate, but you want me to do that for you?"

Kevin grinned. "Oh, most definitely."

With Aidan's mouth around him, Aidan's fingers inside him, he spiraled up into bliss. He cried out in joy as a supernova went off in his head and another exploded between his legs. It was perfection.

"TOUCHDOWN!"

Kevin's moment of nirvana shattered as Aidan shot off him with a yelp. He sighed, feeling his cheeks burning, tipped his head back and raised his voice. "I hate each and every one of you individually and despise you en masse, you vulgar plebeian second-graders!"

"Love you, too, baby!" Sarah's voice laughed, barely muffled by the wall.

Janice's guffaw rang through the space where one wall didn't quite meet the ceiling. "'Bout time, I been waitin' for you two to get it on for motherfuckin' months! Congrats, Aidan!"

"Touchdown!" Lazarus's voice whooped.

"What the hell is going on?" Aidan whispered, his face close enough that Kevin could see the panic in his eyes.

He smiled wryly. "Welcome to a Touchdown Party. When people get bored around here, they take bets on who newcomers are going to pair off with and how long it'll take. When they hear the new couple... er, together, they call everyone in the betting pool into the room next door and wait for the 'touchdown.' Then they do that," he finished, jerking his head in the direction of the wall.

Aidan stared at him for a long, long moment. Then he groaned, dropping his head against Kevin's collarbone. "Oh, fuck."

Kevin smiled in chagrin, stroking Aidan's hair gently. "I did tell you we wouldn't keep us a secret for long, Aidan. This was rather inevitable."

"Yeah, but—Fucking hell. This is just... Oh, fuck," Aidan groaned, sounding utterly mortified.

Kevin wrapped his arms tight around Aidan, chuckling. "This has happened to me three times. They don't mean anything by it. Trust me, I should know," he added, omitting the fact that he'd taken a swing at Lazarus and Yvonne both the first time they'd pulled this on him. After all, they'd all been kids at the time.

"You guys done or you gonna throw the ball again?" Janice shouted through the wall, and Kevin could hear the leer in her voice.

"Bugger off or I'm requisitioning your bras a cup size too small for the rest of your life, you filthy old voyeur!" Kevin yelled back, half laughing. That only got him another teasing cheer from the next room.

In his arms, Aidan tensed, his breathing too fast. Recognizing the warning, Kevin leaned close, tipping Aidan's chin up with two fingers and holding Aidan's eyes. "Aidan. I mean it. Nobody cares. They're cheering because they're teasing us, yes. But they're cheering. To put it bluntly, they've wanted me to find a good boyfriend for quite some time. Please, try not to worry?"

Slowly, Aidan's body relaxed. "You sure?"

Kevin nodded. "Trust me, I'm sure."

Aidan managed a tiny smile. "You think I can write them up for being asshats?"

Kevin burst out laughing. Shaking his head, he rolled out of bed. "Where's your razor?"

"Top drawer by the sink," Aidan sighed.

"Lovely," Kevin replied over his shoulder. "Once we're tidied, dinner. I'm starving."

Event File 39
File Tag: Security Breach
Timestamp: 18:30-10-19-2155

Aidan walked just behind Kevin, trying to get his breathing back under control. Touchdown party. He knew these guys were crazy, but seriously. A touchdown party.

On the other hand, his boyfriend was walking ahead with something that looked an awful lot like a swagger. Was Kevin actually proud that they'd got caught together? Kevin, who was still fighting Cavanaugh training that made him trip over words for anything remotely related to sex and obsess over how much he hated the slang people used for their partners? Kevin who blushed when somebody winked and made a suggestion?

If Kevin was okay with this mess, maybe it really was all right.

Kevin shot him a quick grin and dropped back to take his hand before they stepped into the canteen.

"Once more into the breach then?"

Aidan studied his face. Then he forced a smile and nodded. "Yeah. Guess so."

The cheer that went up when they stepped inside was ridiculous. Topher was the first out of his chair and giving Kevin a hug, Tommy right behind him. Aidan stepped to one side to let them have their fun. He caught his munitions officer, his munitions specialist and his requisitions specialist grinning from ear to ear. Lazarus waggled his eyebrows.

Aidan smirked, feeling the tightness in his gut relax. It looked like half the crew was cheering because of the stunt Kevin had pulled off with the photoelectric shipment, which explained the level of noise. The ones who were cheering for the other 'achievement' were being quiet about it, though they did make faces and a couple gestures, grinning like idiots.

Glancing up from her dinner, Liza caught her commander's eye and rolled her own, giving him a smile. "No worries, Commander. We're all good again. I checked."

"I hope so," Aidan agreed with a smirk. "'Cause, if I thought a couple people were taking time off a job that needed doing to make my life hell, I'd have to write somebody up."

"Don't you look at me, boy," Janice retorted with a grin. "I did my thing. I'm havin' some fun. You had yours already," she finished with a smirk that was probably illegal.

At the end of the table, Suzanna glanced up. "The project's done, sir," she added, but the tone of her voice turned the title into something close to an insult.

That tone made the hair on the back of Aidan's neck prickle. Kevin hadn't been kidding. This woman was looking for a fight. But, if she decided to have a problem with him, he did out-rank her. If she pushed it, he'd pull her aside and say something. For now, he held her eyes and nodded. "And we appreciated your help."

Suzanna gave him a glare that was very nearly insubordination in itself, but she said nothing.

"If this's a party what're we doin' sittin' in here?" Janice demanded a few moments later. "C'mon. Everybody grab plates an' hit the rec room. I'll get the booze." Grinning, she glanced back down the table. "That work for you, Aidan?"

Aidan grinned. "Yeah, that sounds good. Heroes get to choose the vids, so that's you and Tweak, Kev."

Kevin glanced at Tweak, who blinked. "Imma h-hero?"

"I suppose I'll share the laurels after the hacking work you did this week," Kevin agreed. "But, if you choose a torture porn vid, I reserve my right to retract that offer."

Tweak glanced at him, her brow wrinkled. "The fuck you s-saying?"

Kevin rolled his eyes as Aidan watched, his face alight with amusement. "Never you mind. Come on."

Janice broke out rum. Dozer pulled out Potion and happily passed it around. "Get it down. It's good for you. Brew this myself."

"Out of what, machine oil?" Blake asked with a raised brow.

The mechanic snorted good-naturedly. "Bite me, Blake, you chickenshit."

"Hey, somebody turn on the news. I got a drinking game!" Damian called. "Buzzwords!"

A cheer went up.

"Terrorist, it's a shot!" Lazarus threw out.

"Two sips for 'anarchist elements' and one for 'anti-establishment'," Sarah added judiciously.

Kevin winced. "Someone's getting alcohol poisoning then."

"Guys, don't get that drunk," Liza added, half laughing and half horrified. She glanced at Aidan in his corner of the couch. "Back me up here?"

"Please, don't kill yourselves," Aidan agreed with a laugh. "I need you all alive and not too drunk to deal with attacks."

"Yes, SIR, roger that, SIR!" Lazarus added, standing to attention and throwing a textbook salute.

Yvonne reached over and poked him in the back of the knee with one foot, making him lose his balance to general cheering.

And the drinking game was on, with whoops and cheers for reports of 'terrorist elements stealing supplies from an important new subdivision in the Copperhead Complex.'

"We got 'em on the run! All because of this guy!" Sarah chirped, her birdlike arm slapping Kevin on the back as he poured himself another shot.

Kevin cocked a brow, smirking. "Sarah, next time you're picking on the guys for watching sports and hollering, remember how you act about the news. And, aside from that, a few paltry requisitions aren't a patch on picking up the supplies and putting this old wreck of a base back together, so it's me tipping the hat to you," he finished both his shot and his statement with an elegant half bow before he dropped back into his seat.

Aidan smiled as he watched Kevin move, feeling the warmth of the room seeping into him. They had water. They had power. Kevin was home. Everything would be alright tonight.

Kevin glanced up, caught Aidan's eye, and smiled. Gold poured into Aidan's belly. Across the room, there was a low growl and a scuffle.

Suzanna pushed her way between the people lounging across the floor until she stood blocking Kevin's sight of the screen.

"So now the little Corpy's a hero all over again? Aw, sweet. I get my ass busted working on this shit bin you call a power system, come all the way back to this base, and it's the corp kid who's the hero. Always the corp kid. Gets all the credit, gets all the slack, sucks up and sucks off anybody to get what he wants. You've done it since we was kids and you haven't changed, you little pissant."

Aidan's gut went from gold to lead. The room went quiet.

Kevin glanced up, blinking laconically. "I'm sorry if I bothered you. I'll keep it down."

Suzanna bent so that they were nose to nose. "Don't you try that 'let's play nice' bullshit on me. I'm sick of you weaseling your way in and out of every damn place. I seen good men die on missions. Real men, not a little faggot like you, and you still come back alive all the time. And why? Because you suck up and suck off all the right people and get all the easy work, and then you go around looking like a goddamn hero. What'd you do, pay somebody off with your Corp money? Or did you just let somebody screw your ass? Everybody knows that's how you get your way in this compound, and now you're boy-toy for the new commander. Nice work." Grinning the smile of a feral dog, she turned on Aidan.

"Don't suppose your little fuck toy told you why he's got such a nice spot? Logistics? Don't suppose you checked what you fuck? Well, let me tell you. This little bastard's a Cavanaugh Corporation CEO's kid, Corporation born and bred. I finally got the skills to get into the records. I wasn't letting him get away with this oh-I-just-fake-this-accent-cause-I-like-old-movies bullshit anymore. Daddy was some kinda CEO. Mommy was a corporate VP. Baby is a little pissant. Citizen Excellent Standing, all the way. You been sucking the Corp's dick, Commander. How you like that?"

On the couch, Kevin's face blanched to the color of bone. He looked as if someone had just shot him.

Aidan looked up at Suzanna, feeling something cold and hard rise in him. He knew her smile. He knew the look of somebody breaking something just to see if they could. And he was so fucking sick of seeing people like her grin like that.

Carefully, he stood and put a hand on the woman's shoulder, slowly and firmly pushing her back from his boyfriend.

"I think you need to leave this room, Suzanna. I appreciate your help with the power system, and you will be compensated. But right now, walk away."

The dark woman snorted derisively. "Only came out to help this piss poor compound. I'm calling transport and going home. Sick of this bullshit anyway." She was gone in a rattle of boots.

The room was silent, the news turned off. In his seat, Kevin stared at nothing, his body stiff as marble.

"Well," Sarah muttered. "She's still a bitch."

"Yeah," Aidan agreed, staring down at Kevin. Then he drew a breath and forced his head up. He had a duty to everybody in this room. He had to do it. "Who turned off the show? We've got every right to celebrate."

The crew murmured and glanced at each other, but Dilly reached over and cautiously flicked the screen back on. Its noise filled the room. Tweak pulled out her tab and put on something loud and full of music.

Aidan sat next to his boyfriend. "Kev? Let's go somewhere and talk for a minute."

Kevin didn't look at him. Aidan could barely see him breathing. The look on his face was so empty.

Carefully, he touched Kevin's shoulder. He felt like stone. "Kevin? Come with me okay? Please."

Kevin rose without a word. Aidan led him into the empty canteen. Kevin sat like a remote controlled toy, eyes fixed on his hands.

For a moment panic rose in Aidan's gut. How the hell was he going to get through whatever was going on here? A Cavanaugh Corporation CEO's son. A CES level kid. It clicked so many little things into place. Kevin's looks. The way he talked. The things he let slip about his family vacations. Kevin was from the top of the ladder. Aidan had heard CEOs started training at two years old. They were adjusted in vitro to fit their Corporation's needs. A CES level kid practically was the Corporation in miniature.

Kevin was a CEO's kid.

And Kevin was sitting right here, frozen.

Slowly, Aidan sat. He licked his lips. "You want to tell me what the hell that was about?"

Event File 40
File Tag: Privileged Information
Timestamp: 10-19-2155/ 10-20-2155

Kevin glanced up, opened his mouth and closed it. He glanced back at his twining hands. Then he forced his head up again, the effort it took written in his eyes.

"Please. I'm—I'm not—Please, let me explain. Please, just listen."

Aidan wanted to reach out and hug him. He wanted to turn and run. "I am listening," he stated quietly. "But you have to tell me what's going on."

Kevin nodded slowly. Closing his eyes, he took a few long, slow breaths. "Look, I told you that Cavanaugh killed my parents. That was true. That's why I'm here. But..." He trailed off. His eyes reminded Aidan of a cat he'd seen once in an animal control cage.

Kevin's shoulders shrugged helplessly.

It was the helplessness that did it. Aidan reached over to wrap his fingers around Kevin's and squeeze. "You know my secret," he murmured. "Don't you think it's fair that I know yours?"

Kevin bit his lip and turned his face away, staring at the tabletop as he spoke. "My dad—My parents—Look, he was...was...You told me you changed your name."

"Yeah?" Aidan prompted softly.

Kevin squeezed his eyes closed. Silence came down over them like blown dust, hot and cloying. When Kevin spoke, his voice was choked. "McIllian was my mother's maiden name."

Aidan could feel Kevin's hand shaking beneath his as he sucked in a long breath.

"Craydon. Kevin Craydon. My name on the Grid? It used to be Kevin Craydon."

Aidan jerked, his hand slipping out of Kevin's. "*Craydon*? You—your family used to... You *owned* the Cavanaugh Corporation?"

Kevin shook his head slowly. Pulling his hand away, he wrapped his arms around himself. "No. No, you don't understand. It's more like they owned us. It's—I'm not..." He shook his head, his red hair flopping across his glasses.

Aidan swallowed hard. "Okay. Make me understand. Whatever you need to tell me, tell me. I need to get this."

Kevin stole a glance at him, jerked his eyes away. Seeing him like that was like a knife in the gut.

"When you're up that high," Kevin began in a whisper. "When you're the face of the Corporation and every single thing about you reflects on them. You'll never understand how closely we're scrutinized. How intensively we're groomed. Our training starts when we're two years old and it never stops. It never, ever stops."

He shook his head, his voice a distant monotone. "What people don't understand is the system's rotten all the way up. At the top not only do they tell CES kids that we're a different species, but they lock us into a different *world*. All we have time to think about at the CES level is the responsibilities on us, the duties to the Corporation and the threats from one another. Care about the other Citizen Standings? We're barely allowed to see that they exist. I know how it sounds to somebody who grew up like you did, but… When you're in a school VR with other CES kids, when you're in a boardroom with older CES people, you know that every one of them has a knife behind their back, and they'll cheerfully slit your throat if it'll benefit them or they think it'll benefit Cavanaugh. The Corporation needs the best and most successful leaders at the helm. The unsuccessful… They don't get Childbearing Permits. They have breakdowns. They kill themselves. Or they're discarded. Sometimes physically."

He gave a parody of a laugh. "We're all bred for success. And the CEO position may be hereditary, but dynasties fall. My great-grandfather took the position when the last family who owned it had an… accident. But my dad…"

He swallowed, his long fingers gripping the fabric of his jacket. His knuckles were white. "Do you know the story of Siddhartha?"

"No," Aidan murmured, watching the man across the table wrestle something inside him.

Kevin nodded, still staring at the table. "Siddhartha was a prince thousands of years ago in India. It's part of one of their religions. He lived in a palace that was perfect, because his father wanted him to see nothing but beauty. But, he got loose one day, and wandered all over the city, and he saw people begging and sickness and suffering. And he decided to change the world."

He swallowed. "My dad insisted on traveling before he took his full responsibilities. A year abroad. England. He bribed his minders overseas so he could see life. And he saw it. He saw--he saw us through other people's eyes. He went reading on their unrestricted net. He stayed up all night talking in coffee shops. He met Mom.

"When he came back… He knew the world was bigger than the cage he grew up in. He knew how bad things were." His voice was starting to grow unsteady as he spoke. "He wanted us to be… I suppose you haven't heard of Rockefeller."

Aidan shook his head. What the hell was Kevin trying to tell him?

"Rockefeller was a man who did terrible things to make his fortune in the beginning of American history," Kevin explained softly. "Later, he repented. Or maybe he just felt guilty. I don't know. But he tried to spread his wealth in the best possible ways, help all the people he could. Dad wanted Cavanaugh to be like that. Our ancestors did terrible things. He wanted us to make up for it. He had the greatest ideas, but he had to deal with the board. The Chairman of the Board and the members of the Board, they all watch each other. Each of them is accountable to the rest. They can take down anyone member. Even the Chairman. And they wanted change like a hole in the head. So…"

He drew a shaky breath. "He fought them. Every day. Him and Mom. Cavanaugh let her in on a genetic improvement visa, and they had me. Brain chemistry optimizing's compulsory on the genomes of CES kids in Cavanaugh, along with all the other things they perfect. I don't know if you knew. Mom and Dad, they faked the paperwork and bribed the lab. I didn't get that part of the treatment. It's harder for me to ignore things and assume everything's okay than it is for most CES people. I had trouble processing high-speed VR education. I did better with low-speed and with text based. I don't accept information straight off, I ask questions. And it's harder for me to see other people unhappy."

He drew a shuddering breath. "Mom and Dad had to teach me how to act just like the other kids, but, at home, they taught me everything I didn't learn in school. Mom kept her dual citizenship and I got English history and social studies curriculum apps and vids at home. They got me textbooks to read instead of VR. I learned all about American history via England. Isn't that a laugh."

Aidan wished Kevin would at least look at him.

Instead he paced as he talked, arms tight around himself. "Mom and Dad funded a lot of amnesty work. They did as much as they could publicly. They worked to open up a conversation about the Perfection Mandate and the Morality Law, trying to get those loosened up. They worked on getting rid of the Blacklist that's kept on gammas. But they did plenty under the table. Dad started teaching me about discreet contacts when I was twelve. They funded the work of the Daily Bread Movement, you know, to give workers fair wages? They got money and supplies to the Grapevine to support them and try to help them help the agricultural workers. The people you see in the clinics who come in from American Ag... It's a nightmare. Worse than EagleCorp. The things they do to people..."

He shook his head, pacing the length of the table twice before he managed to speak again. "Mom did most of that. The hidden work. She hid it with her gardening hobby. Our contacts were her friends. A plant geneticist and a botanist. She pretended to be a sweet little philanthropic Corporation wife who gardened and did clinic visits. She took me with her for the look of it. It was a good act.

Dad did a lot of the public work. He was good at dealing with the assholes from the other Corporations, and our own." Kevin shook his head, smiling to himself. "He used to talk about the nineteen eighties and nineties all the time. The Golden Age of America. When he said it, it didn't mean go back to the good old days and get rid of foreigners and freaks. It meant what we fight for."

In the half-light, he looked like a statue carved from brittle white stone.

"He got in plenty of rows—sorry, in fights—with the board, but he had allies, and we had our position, so he got through. But, then this thing came up when I was fifteen, part of a new kidney bionic setup. Dad found out that it was killing people, but worse, the board knew. They'd been trying to hide it from him. And they knew it was cheaper to pay for benefits to families than fix the problem, so they were leaving it in. People were dying.

"So Dad started digging and making noise and really throwing his weight as CEO around. He found other devices with the same sort of problems. He told the board he'd take them all down if he had to and replace them. And then my mom was—" Kevin swallowed hard. "She was beaten to death. Dumped under a bridge. Random mugging, the Peace Officers said." He snorted, kicking the leg of the table.

"Bullshit. They did it to break Dad. But he just fought harder. And then he…" Kevin was still for so long that Aidan's gut clenched. Then he shrugged, his head bowed.

"They killed him. Made it look natural. Heart attack. And they made sure I wouldn't inherit his seat." He finally looked up at Aidan, and his eyes were luminous with tears. "One of the last things Dad told me was that we needed to do something in this world. So, when he— When I read the letter he left me, I decided he was right. He had this plan all set up to get me out of the country, make it look like I'd overdosed in an alley and get me to England, but I couldn't. I *couldn't* run away and leave those sons of bitches to keep on. I made a fuss until the Duster who was my courier agreed to take me off-Grid with him if I'd shut up, and…" He shrugged again, a helpless gesture.

Aidan watched his boyfriend for a long moment, his mind numb. What could he say after that? What could he do? Kevin's family had owned one of the Corporations that destroyed people every day.

The enemy.

But people born on enemy territory weren't born enemies, were they? Were they the enemy if they fought the way Kevin's family had, behind enemy lines? Were they the enemy when they opened their arms and their hearts the way Kevin had? Were they the enemy when they stood there utterly vulnerable, eyes wide, tears streaking their cheeks?

Aidan's gut churned as if he'd swallowed a rattlesnake. His chest ached.

Kevin didn't move.

He had to do something. Slowly, carefully, he stood and walked around the table. Kevin flinched back when he put a hand on his shoulder.

Aidan's heart turned over. "Kev?" he cleared his throat, tried again, "If my parents were like that, I'd be proud." Gently, he brushed his lips over Kevin's brow. "Sounds like they were good people."

Kevin watched him with terrified eyes. "Yes, but I wasn't—You need to know I'm—I mean I don't... I'm not..." He covered his face with one hand, drew a breath. "I was born Citizen Excellent Standing," he ground out, "but I swear to God and the blessed Virgin, I'm not *like* that. I *hate* the Corporations, because I've been inside, and I see what they do to people. Even their own. Either you die in body or you die in spirit. And I swear, I didn't mean to lie to you. I just..." He shook his head.

"Kev, look at me," Aidan gently pulled Kevin's hand down, brushing his lips over the other man's as the words he needed finally came to him. "I know that. I know you. At least I'm pretty sure I do. You're with us here for a reason. If you were really Corps, you'd still be there in some boardroom futzing your life away. But you're here. You're helping us with the work that matters. Until today, I haven't heard a bad word against your work. And the words I did hear today, I'm pretty inclined to ignore. Okay? Sure, you were born Corps. Sure you've got their crap version of 'perfect' written all over you. But you're right, you're not like that. You looked at me and saw me. You look at everybody and try to see them. Even when you have to work hard at it, you try. You're getting rid of all the shit they taught you, day by day, and I know that must be a hell of a lot of work. You worked to really be democratic, didn't you? To see people for who they are, not what they are? Maybe that makes you more Duster than some people born out here ever were. And maybe some Dusters are just Corps kids with no cash."

Kevin's lips twitched, some of the color returning to his high cheekbones. He leaned his shoulder against Aidan's, voice still hesitant. "I didn't mean to lie, but I thought that if everyone here found out that—or if you knew what I was that you'd—" Then he glanced up, his smile rueful. "I can't believe I just said that to you. Or thought it." With a deprecating breath of laughter, he laid his head on Aidan's shoulder. "Let's make our lives easier and agree to refrain from lying to each other, shall we?"

Aidan chuckled softly and kissed the top of Kevin's head. "Deal. You okay?"

Kevin shook his head. "No." He drew a shuddering breath. "But I will be."

"You want to go back in there?" Aidan asked, stroking his back in gentle circles.

Kevin shook his head. "I-I can't tonight. In the morning, but not tonight."

Aidan nodded. "Okay. Not tonight. Let's get you to your room." In bed, Aidan wrapped himself around Kevin, holding him until he'd fallen asleep.

It was late the next morning before Kevin woke, stretched, and rolled to nestle beside Aidan, who was lying awake in bed. After a moment, Kevin opened his eyes, taking in his boyfriend. "Thanks," he whispered.

"For what?" Aidan asked softly, turning to study Kevin's bone china face.

Kevin shrugged. "You know." He closed his eyes for a moment.

"Why do you have the same look on your face as someone contemplating a visit from the Bureau of Internal Affairs, exactly?" he asked sleepily, brushing sandy hair back from Aidan's brow with slow fingers.

"Because we have to deal with the shit Suzanna started last night," Aidan muttered, turning his eyes back to the ceiling.

Kevin gave an irritated grunt in the back of his throat, flopping onto Aidan's chest. "You know, I really hate that bitch. But with the crew and the Corps thing..." He trailed off, body growing tense against Aidan's. Then he shrugged. "It won't interfere with my duties."

"It's not your duties I'm worried about," Aidan sighed. He wrapped one arm around Kevin and squeezed him gently. "Let's talk about it later. Come on. I'm starved."

The canteen fell silent as Kevin and Aidan entered, all eyes swiveling to study their commander and logistics officer. Alice set her knitting down. Yvonne turned off the vid she'd been showing. Glances were shared around the table as Kevin fetched himself powdered milk and cereal. Even Lazarus had a deadpan expression. Aidan watched him warily as he took his seat. Any other day, that would be the expression Lazarus wore just before he pulled a prank, but today…

Kevin added water to his breakfast as Aidan watched the crew. No one was saying a word. That couldn't be good.

"So, now we get the truth," Lazarus intoned, sounding frighteningly like an EagleCorp officer.

Kevin glanced up at the other officer with that cat-in-a-cage expression Aidan had seen the night before, and Aidan felt every muscle in his body tense.

And that was when Lazarus burst out laughing. "God man, you should see the look on your face!"

Around the table, little titters and snorts of laughter unfurled like dandelions after rain.

Kevin gave the table a comprehensive stare of pure shock. "What—?"

"Aw, c'mon. You didn't actually fall for that?" Topher called from his end of the table. "We were just kidding."

"Kidding?" Kevin asked, glancing from one laughing face to another. "Wait. Are you guys…? Wait. Did you guys *know*?"

Aidan blinked at his crew. He probably looked like a confused owl, but he didn't have the brain power to care. Of all the reactions to what had happened last night, he hadn't expected laughter.

"About what? You and Aidan? Kevin, sweetie, we've been waiting sooooo long for our little baby to figure out what your man parts were for, we were *thrilled* when you got to it," Blake replied in an overly sugary tone.

Kevin sighed, raising his eyes to the ceiling. "Bite me, Blake."

"Oh, *honey,* I've wanted to for *years* but that's robbing the cradle."

"God damn it. You know what I—" Kevin snapped out, but Liza laid a hand on his shoulder, trying to quash her laughter. "Okay, guys, let up. Get real."

"But it's too *precious!*" Blake enthused. "Before I retired to Financial, I was logistics officer since—"

"The dawn of time." Damian put in, which got him a haughty look from the pudgy old man, who otherwise ignored him to continue.

"And the same week the only Corporation family worth a damn gets killed off, this poor baby boy arrives with a bleeding hole in his wrist right where a Wellness Chip should be. A poor little boy who can't seem to remember his own last name, and he actually thought that he could hand me—*me!*—over four million dollars the day he arrives, and I wouldn't know exactly who has that kind of money to throw around?"

"And, of course, what Blake knows on base gossip, everybody knows," Yvonne agreed pointedly.

"You handed him four million dollars when you showed up?" Aidan asked with an incredulous glance at Kevin. The taller man shrugged. "I had to get out fast. It was all I could grab."

"Look at Mr. Modest," Liza put in with a grin. "From what I hear, it was four million bucks plus half a dozen access codes for high speed 'net and a nice stack of medical supplies. You were loaded!"

Aidan set his mug down before he dropped it. "So, you guys already knew? Makes me kind of the idiot here, doesn't it?"

"Just the newcomer. He's the idiot," Damian added, pointing a fork at Kevin. "Actually, thought we were stupid enough not to notice?"

"You never said anything," Kevin muttered, his pale skin flushing hotly as he focused on his breakfast.

"Commander Taylor told all us old hands, an' we kept an eye on you," Janice put in. "But you worked out real good, once you settled in an' I took a couple strips offa you. Pretty soon you was workin' Blake there into the ground, an' we knew we got a Duster. We let the kids know it when they got t'be specialists sos' they could watch your back an' watch what they said. It matter any where you come from?"

Kevin glanced up, half grinning and half chagrined. "So why the need for the years of idiotic charade?"

In answer, nearly everyone at the table chorused, "Taylor." Lazarus provided a sheepish grin. "He wanted to see how long it'd take for you to come clean, you know? See if it mattered at all."

Kevin gave the table a comprehensive glare. "I hate you all right now, you know that."

"Dude, you freaked when we figured out you were into dick after you'd been here a whole freaking year," Lazarus remarked as he took a bite of his breakfast. "I mean you literally tried to punch me out. We figured if we said anything about anything else your system would crash."

Kevin raised an exaggerated brow. He was trying for one of his mock-haughty expressions, Aidan could tell, but there was a grin tugging at his lips. "You know Lazarus, we should have you stuffed and mounted as a textbook example of the original horse's ass."

"Yeah, but then we'd be down a munitions officer," Aidan muttered with a glint in his own eye, now that he had wrapped his head around what was going on. "And I kind of like being able to blow shit up when we need to."

Kevin gave one of his showy, theatrical sighs. "I suppose I'll spare him then."

Laughing, the crew got down to breakfast.

<u>Event File 41</u>
<u>File Tag: System Reboot</u>
<u>Timestamp:10-20-2155/ 10-23-2155</u>

"And that's it?" Magnum asked.

"That's it," Aidan agreed, nodding to Tweak. She ducked her head in a nod, avoiding everyone's eyes.

Kevin watched her carefully as she stared at her feet. Now would really not be the time for one of her outbursts. After all, it was her work on show. It had taken ages to get her to agree to go with them to present her new IR emitters and vid clips of their effects to the Sector Commander. Now that they were here and Tweak was standing hunch-shouldered and nervous, Kevin wondered if it had been such a good idea.

The dark man across the desk studied them for far too long once their presentation was done. Kevin forced his face to remain politely blank. He could see Aidan's knuckles whitening on his crossed arms, and forced down the urge to reach over and put a hand on Aidan's shoulder.

"All right," Magnum stated finally. "You're barracking here tonight and giving that speech again Wednesday at six in the evening. Message your base. You're going to need visuals of the schematics and parts lists, not just vids of the results." He nodded at Tweak. "And Miss Tweak? If you're going to speak, figure out how to do it more clearly."

"What audience will we be addressing, sir?" Kevin asked as deferentially as he could, trying to compensate for the way Tweak raised her eyes to glare at the man.

The Sector Commander glanced at him. "The Sector Technical officer and all the people in logistics and technical divisions that I can gather here with a day's notice, McIllian. You did want this anti-drone tech to get into general use, didn't you?"

Oh bloody hell, Kevin's mind whispered to itself. "Yes, sir," his mouth agreed.

Sector Commander Magnum nodded, parceling another one of his looks out between them.

"Mcillian. Tweak. Dismissed. Room 32 C and D are yours for the stay. Headly, with me for a minute," he stated eventually.

"We in trouble?" Tweak asked, dropping onto the cot in her borrowed room.

"Not yet," Kevin replied carefully, leaning against the wall by the door.

Tweak pulled out her tab, the device taking up both her small hands. "I gonna have to talk? To people?"

"Probably," Kevin agreed, watching the door and willing it to open

Tweak sighed. "I'm g-gonna f-f-fuck up."

The words finally kicked Kevin's brain back into gear. Turning his head, he blinked. "Tweak, you did perfectly well in there, even with Magnum staring at us like a dog eyeing a squirrel."

Tweak shrugged. "That was j-just the old d-dude and you g-guys. You g-guys don't scare me."

"That could have been worded better, but I take the point," Kevin rejoined dryly. Crossing his arms, he studied Tweak. "Does it help if you memorize the speech?"

"What's the M thing?" Tweak asked, staring at her tab, though she hadn't turned it on.

"Memorize. Know something well enough to remember it by heart," Kevin explained carefully.

Tweak considered his words, but shook her head. Her foot started to tap against the cot's upright. "P-people l-l-looking at me."

The door opened. Aidan stepped in like a street dog watching for animal control.

"What'd Magnum have to say?" Kevin asked, stepping in to close the door and take Aidan's hand.

Aidan gave him a weak smile. "Basically? He's trusting us, so we better not screw this up."

Tweak drew her knees up to her chest and wrapped her arms around them. Kevin caught Aidan's eye, raised his brow and nodded in her direction. He mimed an explosion with one hand. The line between Aidan's brows deepened.

Carefully, the blonde man took a seat near Tweak on the bed, just out of reach.

"You okay?"

Tweak shook her head.

"How come?" Aidan asked, and Kevin heard the gentleness in his voice that had cut through his own paralyzing terror not so long ago.

"P-p-p-people l-l-l... S-s-shit." Tweak turned on her tab, brought up the screen with a flick and typed, letting both men read.

There will be people looking at me, and I know I'm going to fuck up when people are staring at me. If this speech has to be good, make Kevin do it.

"Gladly, but this isn't my area of expertise, Tweak. I won't be as good at talking about it as you are," Kevin added, rephrasing the statement in his addendum for her sake.

"Maybe if we practice today and tomorrow you won't be scared by Wednesday?" Aidan asked quietly. "Want to try?"

Slowly, warily, Tweak raised her head to meet his eyes. Finally, she nodded.

For the next two days, Kevin helped Tweak and Aidan polish the presentation. Tweak drew up schematics that could be presented. They practiced the speech, and Kevin discovered that Tweak didn't stutter nearly as badly when she was reading her text off her tab. It was when she had to look people in the face that she had problems.

Kevin wasn't sure if it was far too soon or not soon enough when the sun sank on Wednesday and the clock read 16:45. He and Aidan already pulled on dress uniforms borrowed from Sector stores, though Tweak had taken one look at the thing available in her size and sneered. At least she'd brushed her hair and agreed to cover her tank top and bandaged arms with a nice button-down shirt. Thank God for small favors, Kevin told himself wryly.

"We'd best get along," he suggested. Both Tweak and Aidan glanced up, both pulled from their thoughts, both nervy.

Kevin drew in a calming breath. "Shall we?"

The hall buzzed with voices half heard through the briefing room door. Behind the two men, Tweak froze. Kevin glanced over his shoulder and winced.

"Tweak, please don't—"

"Kev?" Aidan cut in quietly. "I got this." Giving his hand a quick squeeze, Aidan stepped back to stand in front of his youngest specialist. Kevin held his breath.

"This is really gonna suck, hunh?" Aidan asked. Staring at her feet, the girl nodded.

Aidan made a noise of commiseration in the back of his throat. "If you think about it, you know nobody in there can touch you for skills, right?"

Tweak's lips quirked. Her head jerked in a tiny nod. "Yeah."

"So really, there's nobody to be scared of in there," Aidan murmured in that quiet, calming voice he was so good at using. "You can kick all their asses. Right?"

Finally, Tweak raised her head and gave him a tiny smile. "Yeah."

"So let's go do it." Aidan murmured. Stepping forward, he opened the door and held it for her. Kevin waited to bring up the rear.

Twenty minutes later, Kevin let out the breath he felt like he'd been holding for two days.

"And that concludes your team's remarks, Commander Headly?" Magnum asked across the room. Aidan nodded.

"Yes sir."

On the other side of the holo-screen set on the floor, Kevin watched Tweak with a fair amount of satisfaction.

She'd done well reading off her tab and keeping her eyes focused on the holo as she brought up specific points on the schematics. The room full of technical officers and logistics officers were nodding to one another, watching the three of them with interest.

She'd really pulled it off. Between them, the holo-screen juddered and flickered. Tweak gently kicked the emitter by her foot. The image of her large and small IR code emitter prototypes settled into place, screens with their schematics and supply lists rotating like satellites.

Magnum turned in his chair to survey his cramped room of technical officers. The heavy, dark face was as inscrutable as it had ever been, but Kevin had a sneaking suspicion that Magnum was repressing a smile.

"Officers. Questions?"

"How many tests have been run to date?"

"Six. Two f-first day, on d-d-delivery d-drones. Two on v-v-v-v…" Tweak shot Kevin a 'help me out here?' look. He gave her a quick nod.

"Two tests were completed on ViperDrones themselves, using the handheld model on an unmanned bike parked with its slick tech disengaged," he began. "We've run three tests on bases, one at our own after the hailstorm two months ago. The others were performed to supplement or replace a slick tarp on base 1401 and base 1320 until they could be repaired. I want to stress at this juncture that the emitters are only effective on low flying surveillance drones. They won't have any effect on satellite reads, so this isn't our Holy Grail.

"I'd recommend treating it as a supplement to slick tech as well as a new tool in our arsenal. At the present time, we can instruct drones to believe they're reading innocuous signals and pass a target by, to believe they're damaged and land for repairs, to believe their sensors are offline or to believe they've been summoned back to their point of origin. Our repertoire will grow as we uncover more command prompts that work. The caveat on this idea is that, if we get slipshod, one of the Corps is going to sort out what we're doing and find ways to counter it, which is why I have to stress that this is a special-use tool and not a Swiss army knife. "

A polite chuckle ran through the room.

"What's the range?" another officer called.

For the next twenty minutes, the three of them fielded questions and debated points. Tweak became surprisingly eloquent on the use of substitute parts for her original list.

And then there were no more questions and no more hands raised.

Slowly, Magnum stood. He studied the holos for what felt like na geologic age. Then he turned to the assembled crowd.

"All right. I want everyone implementing this as soon as the Winter Holiday is over. Go home, have your break and then get to work on this."

"Sir!" the men and women in the room agreed en masse.

Magnum acknowledged them with a nod.

"And while we're all together, one more thing." Turning, the bigger man faced Aidan. Kevin watched as his boyfriend very subtly leaned back on his heels, trying not to wince in sympathy. But Aidan didn't take a step back, and he didn't flinch. "Commander Headly?" Magnum intoned.

"Sir?" Aidan asked, and Kevin had to force down the urge to step across the space between them.

"Your base has been formally commended by Regional Command for sterling work on a technology that will tangibly aid the Force." The screen flickered to an image of an award.

"Furthermore," the big man added. "I'd like to formally congratulate Base 1407 for returning to and exceeding the high standard of work it was known for before its loss of leadership. Well done."

One of the sector commander's wide, dark hands clapped Aidan on the back, the other enfolded Aidan's for shaking. Magnum passed by Tweak with a smile and shook Kevin's hand. He was too poleaxed to do anything but shake hands and smile like an idiot.

Behind them, the officers in the room clapped.

"Did you know he was going to do that?" Kevin asked when the three of them had climbed back into their truck and were rattling home.

"No freaking idea," Aidan replied, wide eyes on the road. "All he said to me beforehand was 'don't screw it up on Wednesday.'"

Kevin grinned, shaking his head. "Quintessential Magnum."

Catching Aidan's eye, he couldn't help but laugh.

"So." Tweak asked from the back seat, "We're okay? We did good?"

Aidan glanced in the rearview mirror for a moment, still grinning. "Yeah Tweak. We did good. We did really, really good. That thing, the commendation? It means everybody's saying in public that we did a great job on something."

"The cash bonus for the base is a nice sign of gratitude as well of course." Kevin added, and Aidan chuckled. "Yeah. Blake'll be happy."

"He quit bitching 'bout costs?" Tweak asked.

Kevin shook his head. "I don't think that's physically possible, unfortunately. Blake was born irritated. I should know, I trained under him long enough."

Leaning back, he crossed his legs and closed his eyes, grinning so widely that his face ached. In eight months, they'd gone from being under threat of disbanding to a regional commendation. How had that happened?

But he knew the answer to that. Aidan.

Opening his eyes, he watched Aidan as he drove. This gorgeous, complicated man who had so much going on inside him had yanked them all back together. He'd brought out the best in every one of them with his quiet manner. Some days, Kevin still couldn't believe it had happened.

Aidan glanced at him then and smiled, and the world was perfect.

"Hey. Guys. G-googly eyes later," Tweak's voice commanded from the back seat. "Watch the d-d-driving."

Kevin turned in his seat to give Tweak a dry stare. "You have no romance in your soul."

"Good." Tweak snapped back, "C-can't make me s-s-s-stupid l-like you." She gave him a ridiculously cheesy grin. He rolled his eyes and dropped back into his seat.

When they rattled into base, it was long after dinner. Only a few night owls were in the rec room, and only Janice was crazy enough to still be working.

"We'll tell the crew about it in the morning," Aidan remarked, repressing a yawn. "Hit the sack, Tweak."

"Roger," Tweak agreed, walking down the hall.

Kevin watched her with a smile. "She's got a spring in her step."

"She did kind of do something amazing," Aidan admitted, yawning now that Kevin was the only one watching him.

Kevin chuckled, putting an arm around Aidan's waist. "Yes, she didn't utterly mortify us in public this time. By the way, she's not the only one who needs to hit the sack. Come on."

He fell asleep listening to Aidan's heartbeat.

It took some time before the entire crew filed in for breakfast, and by the time they'd all sat down, the morning larks had at least five conversations going at once.

"Now, you think?" Aidan asked quietly under the racket.

Kevin glanced around the room. "Mm, well Jim's eyes are open and Janice is up to the caffeine level of speaking with civility, I'd say now's best." Under the table, he gave Aidan's hand a quick squeeze.

Aidan smiled as he stood. Kevin watched him as he walked to the head of the main table. "Hey, guys?"

A few people looked up, but most of the conversations went on unabated.

Janice raised her head lazily, spearing her reconstituted eggs. Looking down the table, she caught Kevin's eye and smirked. Then she opened her mouth. "Hey jackasses! Commander's talking!"

The room went silent.

Aidan cleared his throat. "Um, thanks Janice."

"I think I'm deaf," Lazarus whispered, then yelped as Sarah, Kevin assumed, kicked him under the table.

"So, I've got an announcement," Aidan continued, holding his tab in both hands. Setting it down on the table, he flicked on his screen and enlarged it. "This happened."

The regional commendation floated in the air. Beside it, Aidan brought up a notice Kevin hadn't seen.

Review Conclusions: Base 1407

It is suggested by this Sector that, in the light of Base 1407's exemplary work, they should be regarded as returned to full-function. The conclusion has been reached that the detriments related to close bonding between members of a stable base are outweighed by the impressive level of coordination and dedication presented by a functional base trained in this mode of operation.

This Sector recommends, upon review, encouraging similar strong social bonds and stable working networks on other bases.

The cheer went off like a bomb in the canteen. All around him Kevin's family hugged one another, hugged him and hugged Aidan. Liza started to cry with joy. The kids ran in wild circles, whooping like animals.

Kevin felt as if his heart might burst its bonds in his ribs. Worming his way between all his friends, he found Aidan in the crush and pulled him into his arms, kissing his boyfriend long and deep.

Together. They were going to stay together.

On second thought, he decided as Aidan's arms wrapped around him, screw settling for that. They were the Wildcards. They were back on top of their game.

They were going to kick the world's ass together.

CALL THE BLUFF

O. E. TEARMANN

ACES HIGH **2** JOKERS WILD

Turn the page for a sneak peek at the Wildcard's next adventure

WHUMP!

The explosion sent a geyser of dust into the sky. Base Commander Aidan Headly cursed as pebbles rained down on him. He crawled out of the empty cistern pit he'd leaped into and stood, trying to wave the dust away without much success. The grit settled on him like a second skin.

Adrenaline was treating his guts like its personal skate park and taking some extra turns around his heart. But that wasn't his biggest problem right now. Hell, it didn't make top ten on his list.

He scrambled up the hill and raised his voice.

"What the hell was that? We weren't supposed to be blowing anything up today!"

Two dark faces peered out from under helmets in their own culvert, trepidation in their eyes. Aidan sighed. Dilly and Donny. Again.

The twins had turned thirteen a week ago. Maybe he should be happy that they had started begging to do vocational apprenticeship the minute they'd gotten out of bed on their birthday, but if they kept up this kind of crap they wouldn't live to fourteen.

"Sorry Aidan!" the girl called.

"We're trying out a new setting mechanism!" The boy beside her hollered over. "I think I know what I did wrong!"

"You better know what you did wrong," Aidan growled as he scrambled down the other side of the new site's hill toward his charges, chest still tight with the dregs of his fear. "We can't afford a blast like that again, you hear me? You guys know how dangerous drawing attention is!"

Dilly flinched. Her twin's shoulders stiffened.

"Okay, but we hit water!" Donny countered, "There's water down there, and—"

"The fuck did you two little gamma-gets do?!"

Both twins flinched as Janice Danvers climbed out of the nearest water tank, still on its side and empty so soon after the base's site change. Fire in her black eyes, the hydroelectrics specialist stalked across the dusty red earth and grabbed the collars of both teenagers' ponchos like the scruffs on a pair of puppies, shaking them in what looked like ferocity. Since the kids were barely shifting for all the show Janice put on, Aidan pushed down his instinct to step between an angry adult getting physical and a pair of kids. In the seven months since Aidan had taken his place commanding the Wildcards unit of the Democratic State Force, he'd learned to let Janice have her say with anyone pulling idiot stunts. She was a more effective scolder than him any day.

"The ever-loving frag grenade-fucking hell does 'wait till I get it damped down' mean to you two little sons of sister-fuckers, hunh?! Or how 'bout 'let me check your work 'fore we go to the next bit?!'" Janice demanded. "I said wait! You coulda' killed yourselves, you cluster-fucked CPS dumbasses! What are you, a pair of gammas? This's the middle of a relocation setup, you think I got time for you two playin' around? You wanna help me out you listen to me, you hear?!" She knocked their heads together, and Aidan noted the control the muscled woman used in doing it: just hard enough to sting, nowhere near hard enough to do the damage Janice could have dished out.

"Aw Jan—" Dilly began, but Janice cut her off.

"Ah! Don't start. You two ain't—" She glanced up, caught sight of another dark figure in the blazing sun and raised her voice. "Damian! Come over here an' deal with your family!"

Turning, the scarecrow of a man got a look at the two dust-covered teenagers. He sighed, putting a hand over his cybernetic eyes. "Dilly, Donny, what'd you do now?"

"Nothing!" Dilly defended. Striding over, Damian set a hand on each teenager's shoulder, raising a brow. His ocular implants whirred, punctuating the expression.

"*Nothing*, hunh?" He glanced with pointed attention from the crater, to the boxes of explosive material much too close for comfort, to the teens. "Funny, doesn't look like *nothing* to me."

Dilly rolled her eyes, letting out a dramatic sigh. "Fiiine. We screwed up. Sorry."

The medical officer gave his superior a wry smile. "Sorry about the monsters, Aidan. 'Go help out,' I said. I should've known better. These two are working in the garage for the rest of the week," he added darkly, letting go of Dilly long enough to straighten the wide-brimmed hat on his shaved head. Today everybody in their eighteen-man crew wore the brown ponchos and wide-brimmed hats that had earned their Force the nickname of Dusters. Inlaid with coolant, the gear kept them comfortable and made sure they weren't spotted on infrared by EagleCorp's ViperDrones. The clothes would be some protection until the base that sustained them was set up and secure again.

Aidan found himself reflexively glancing up. The readings had given them a window of a few hours before the next drone pass. Technically, they were safe for now. But blowing holes in the Dust would make them a new point of interest if the blast had been picked up by a satellite.

He forced his eyes down. If a drone was up there, it wouldn't have waited this long to drop a bomb. He knew that.

Out of the corner of his eye, he spotted Janice stealing a glance upwards.

Aidan reminded himself to take a breath, shrugging as he motioned to the crater. "They did find water, Damian. So, I'd say their punishment is hauling it up and storing it for us."

Both kids groaned.

"But water hauling sucks!" Dilly whined.

Janice gave her a deadpan look. "Shoulda' thoughta that 'fore you fucked up. Get the pipes an' the lil' pump an' get over there, I ain't baby-sittin' you two no more today. Git!"

When the teens were out of earshot, Janice turned to her base mates with a sigh. "I swear those two are gonna give me a heart attack. I ain't never lettin' them assist again."

"Funny, I thought I heard that last time." Damian stated, face unreadable. "And when I heard it last time, I had thought for some reason that we made an agreement about my sibs staying away from things that go bang."

Janice gave the man a scathing look. "An' who told 'em to 'go help' an' let 'em off the leash with no more n' that? An' who's their minder around here? Cause I ain't wearin' no frilly hat an' I don't think I look much like the nanny, d'you?"

Aidan knew Janice's drawling agricultural worker's accent only grew that thick when she was rattled. Beside him, Damian opened his mouth, but Aidan spoke first.

"Guys? Relocation days suck for everybody."

Damian had the good grace to nod in acknowledgment, leaving whatever he'd planned to say unspoken.

Aidan watched the teens manhandle the temporary water pump into place, attach it to a primary cistern tank and start spooling the weighted siphon line down into the hole, where it could get to work pulling up water. The groundwater from the aquifer would be decontaminated by the systems inside the cistern, before being hooked into the base's plumbing. It'd make a good stop-gap while the main water drilling rig was being calibrated to supplement the base's water-recycling system.

We really need to get better at water recycling and depend less on ground water sources, Aidan thought with dismay. *This aquifer might be as good as Janice thought, but the aquifers are getting smaller all the time.*

"Keeping them away from explosives is probably good for everybody... they didn't screw up the well though, did they?" He glanced at the three full cistern tanks they had, squatting like deformed pineapples on wheels off to his left. The reflective condensate fins designed to catch any humidity in the air during the cool nights and turn it into supplemental water gleamed dully in the sun. The supply of water in the tanks was all the crew had until Janice, Topher and Dozer finished hooking up the systems. Was it enough? They'd come to this site for the water. If they had to drill a new well, would the water last that long?

Janice waved a hand. "Nah, we hit shale an' I didn't want the fuckin' stuff collapsin' everywhere, was the reason for the new setting mechanism. Kids set it off 'fore I was ready, is all. We'll have a new well by the end of the day."

"I'll get the kids to help me shelve and prep the med bay when they're worn out." Damian added, glancing at the module that housed his workspace, sitting on its wide wheels at an angle to the module that served as their canteen. The separate modular units that connected to make their home looked like a kid's dropped toys, each module sitting where they'd left it when they arrived.

Aidan drew in a long, slow breath, feeling the adrenaline ebb from his system. "Sounds good." He dusted himself off as best he could, picking pebbles from his hair. "Is anyone on sentry yet? My guess is that blast got us on the map for the next drone sweep, and we need to be ready."

"On it." Sarah called, setting down the crate she'd been carrying and whistling loud and sharp. On a rise, Lazarus waved a hand. Aidan blinked, then couldn't help but smile. Lazarus was kitted out in a slick poncho, the fiberoptic mesh weave mirroring the surroundings. On top of that he'd piled a couple tumbleweeds and sprinkled dusty soil over himself. If the munitions officer hadn't moved, Aidan never would have seen the guy.

"Okay great, slick tarps?" Aidan asked, counting seconds in his head. He knew the laborious process of unfolding and tying the slick tarps to their struts would take at least twenty minutes if he got a full division on it. They had an hour before the next drone flyover, but there were always watching satellites. That blast would have drawn attention.

Better be transport division with Tweak checking the connections, considering the tarps' weight and the muscles on Dozer and Topher.

"Yep!" Tweak called down from the roof of the main module. Grabbing a loose guideline meant to tie the tarp to its support struts, the tiny coder slid to the ground like something off an action vid and ran past with the line in hand, talking in bursts as she went. "All connected, software g-good, hardware up in forty. Should w-work. W-worked on l-little p-piece. We see."

"Can we move it, forty minutes is—" Aidan started to ask as Tweak looped the last line to its connecting strut, pulled out her tab and hit something. Every line snapped taut, and the carefully folded fiber-optic mesh tarps unfurled like wings. Sliding smoothly into place, the slick tarp cast dappled shade over the half-assembled base and its watching crew, protecting them from blazing sun and searching enemies. Aidan's sentence never finished.

"Goddamn." Janice murmured. "Ain't never seen it go that fast, how'd she—"

"Seconds," Tweak interrupted, trotting up with a hint of a smile. "Forty. Not minutes. Seconds." Her eyes caught the light, glinting with triumph.

"I noticed." Aidan agreed, staring up with a smile tugging at the corners of his lips.

Join the Wildcards' next adventure wherever books are sold

A Note From the Commander:
If you're struggling, you're not alone. Reach out.

Hi. Aidan here. You guys know I'm dealing with some crap, and I bet I'm not the only one. But in your world, there's a lot of resources if you're dealing with anxiety, depression and/or LGBT issues in the USA.

Crisis Text Line

Text 741-741 anywhere, any time to talk to somebody for free when you're in a crisis. That doesn't just mean suicide: it's any painful emotion for which you need support. The first two responses are automated. They tell you that you're being connected with a Crisis Counselor and invite you to share a bit more. It usually takes less than five minutes to connect you with a Crisis Counselor.

Trevor Lifeline

If you are a young person in crisis, feeling suicidal, or in need of a safe and judgment-free place to talk, call the Trevor Lifeline at 1-866-488-7386. Or text START to678678.

Trevor Space

If you need to hang out, Trevor Space is a social networking site for lesbian, gay, bisexual, transgender, queer & questioning (LGBTQ) youth under 25 and their friends and allies.

Suicide Prevention Lifeline

1-800-273-TALK (8255)

TTY: 1-800-799-4889

Website: www. suicidepreventionlifeline. org

24- hour, toll-free, confidential suicide prevention hotline available to anyone in suicidal crisis or emotional distress. Your call is routed to the nearest crisis center in the national network of more than 150 crisis centers.

Everyone Is Gay

Everyone Is Gay is a collection of voices lending advice and support to Lesbian, Gay, Bisexual, Transgender, Questioning/Queer, Intersex, and Asexual (LGBTQIA) youth, and also offers comprehensive lists of nationwide LGBTQIA resources.

Website: http://everyoneisgay. com

SAMHSA's National Helpline

1-800-662-HELP (4357)

TTY: 1-800-487-4889

Website: www. samhsa. gov/find-help/national-helplineAlso known as the Treatment Referral Routing Service,

this helpline provides 24-hour free and confidential treatment referral and information about mental and/or substance use disorders, prevention, and recovery in English and Spanish.

Veteran's Crisis Line

1-800-273-TALK (8255)

TTY: 1-800-799-4889

Website: www. veteranscrisisline. net

Connects veterans in crisis (and their families and friends) with qualified, caring Department of Veterans Affairs responders through a confidential toll-free hotline, online chat, or text.

S. A. F. E. Alternatives

S. A. F. E. is a nationally recognized treatment approach, professional network, and educational resource base committed to helping you and others achieve an end to self-injurious behavior.

Website: https://selfinjury. com/

ACES HIGH

JOKERS
WILD

A Wildcards Playlist, Part I

Flobots. "There's A War Going On For Your Mind" *Fight With Tools*, 2007.

Flobots. "Sleeping Giant" *NOENEMIES*, 2017.

Flobots. "Rattle The Cage" *NOENEMIES*, 2017. (*Quoted Page 181.*)

Midnight Oil. "Beds Are Burning" *Diesel and Dust1987*.

Twisted Sister. "We're Not Gonna Take It" *Official Singles*, 2008. (*Quoted Page 198.*)

Jonathan Larson. "Rent" *Rent [Original Soundtrack] Disc 1*, 2005.

The Who. "My Generation" *My Generation, 1965*

Kansas. "Carry On Wayward Son" *The Best of Kansas*, 1999. BONJOVI.

"No Apologies" *Greatest Hits (Japan, SHM-CD, UICL-9095), 2010.*

Mischief Brew. "Roll Me Through The Gates Of Hell"

Smash The Windows, 2005.

BON JOVI. "Raise Your Hands" *B-sides & Rarities*, 2005.

Genesis. "Land of Confusion" Turn It On Again: The Hits (The Tour Edition) [Remastered], 2007.

Rush. "Tom Sawyer" *Chronicles (Remastered)*, 1969. *(Quoted Page 172.)*

Don Henley. "The Garden Of Allah" Actual Miles, 1995. Jonathan Larson. "What You Own" *Rent [Original Soundtrack]* Disc 2, 2005.

Men At Work. "Snakes And Ladders" *Contraband -The Best Of Men At Work, 1984.*

BON JOVI. "Bounce" *Bounce*, 2002. *Quoted Page89*

BON JOVI. "Work For The Working Man" *The Circle*, 2009.

Mischief Brew. "Thanks, Bastards!" *Songs From Under The Sink*, 2006.

Don Henley. "I Will Not Go Quietly" *Actual Miles*, 1989.

Flobots. "Stand Up" *Fight With Tools*, 2007.

The Gaslight Anthem. "American Slang" *American Slang*, 2010.

Tom Petty. "Runnin' Down A Dream" *Full Moon Fever*, 1989. (*Quoted Page 260, 262)*

Mischief Brew. "Gratitude And Thanks" *Songs From Under The Sink,* 2006. Bruce Springsteen. "Born In The U. S. A." *Born In The U. S. A.*, 1984.

Billy Joel. "Code Of Silence" *The Bridge*, 1986. *Quoted Pages 198, 199.*

The Goo Goo Dolls "Iris" *Greatest Hits, Vol. 1: The Singles*, 2007.

Barefoot Truth. "Drink To You" *Carry Us On*, 2011.

Flobots. "Pray (Extended)" *NO ENEMIES*, 2017.

BON JOVI. "It's My Life" *Greatest Hits (Japan, SHM-CD, UICL-9095)*, 2010.

BON JOVI. "Unbreakable" *Have A Nice Day (Japan import)*, 2005.

Mischief Brew. "Swing Against The Nazis" *Smash The Windows*, 2005.

Debajo Del Agua. "Doublespeak" *Arte Sano*, 2007.

Great Big Sea. "Chemical Worker's Song" *Up*, 1997.

Flobots. "Blood in the River" *NOENEMIES*, 2017.

John Mellencamp. "Pink Houses" T*he Best That I Could Do*, 1997.

Flobots. "Related" *NOENEMIES*, 2017.

John Mellencamp. "Authority Song" *The Best That I Could Do*, 1997.

Jonathan Larson. "La Vie Boheme A, B" *Rent [Original Soundtrack] Disc 2*, 2005.

The Beatles. "Let It Be", *Let It Be*, 1970. *Quoted Page 215*

Peter Gabriel. "Don't Give Up" *Shaking The Tree*, 1990

(Note: "Hey Mickey" *Word of Mouth*. 1981, by Toni Basil is quoted on page 266. But it shouldn't be included on the play list. Don't listen to it. Seriously. Save your precious ears and your personal pride.)

About The Author

O. E. Tearmann lives in the shadow of the Rocky Mountains, in what may become the CO-WY Grid. They share the house with a brat in fur, a husband and a great many books. Their search engine history may garner them a call from the FBI one day. When they're not living on base 1407 they advocate for a more equitable society and more sustainable agricultural practices, participate in sundry geekdom and do their best to walk their characters' talk.

Read more and download an exclusive free short story at

aceshighjokerswild.com/read-for-free

Made in the USA
Middletown, DE
13 September 2020